## Acknowledgments

I'd like to warmly thank the following people whose work and encouragement helped make this book possible: Giles Anderson, Susan Betz, Tom Bevan, Donna DeRenzis, Valerie Dixon, Susan Hahn, Linda K. Harris, Bill Henderson, and Deborah Leigh Scott. Thanks also to the University of Illinois Press, which published my short story "Song of the Earth," in my collection *Private Fame* (1991), where some of the characters and ideas for this novel first appeared.

# 1

He stopped and looked down through the trees where the noise came from. Muted shrieks, hysterical yelling, and laughter like a kind of singing. Only kids make sounds like that, Ray thought, smiling. Under the full afternoon sun everything was shining. The wooden supports on the playground that were painted red, yellow, or blue were preternaturally bright, while the swings and slides they held up sparkled like silver. The colors were so intense and strangely beautiful that Ray continued to stare. The kids, mostly seven- or eight-year-olds, were running in every direction in their shorts and T-shirts while their parents or babysitters sat on benches against the nearby fence. At the far end of the playground, two five-year-olds were hugging inside a tire that slowly rotated in the shade of a tree. He walked a couple of blocks uptown toward his apartment, wondering if he could approximate the sounds from the kids' playground with violins, flutes, and piccolos. Then he heard a different sound, dim but unmistakable—a basketball bouncing on concrete—and through the spaces between the trees saw boys flashing by in the middle of a game. This was a different playground, inhabited mostly by teenagers. He watched the boys for a minute—who were furiously focused on their task (behind them in the distance were bright blue patches of the river)—then walked another block.

It basically all came down to a handshake, Ray thought, this annoying decision he was trying to make about Arnold's party. Every June, Arnold threw a party for the people in his circle, mostly composers in their thirties and forties, who inevitably spent the night kvetching and consoling one another about their careers. In the frame of mind he was in, he could certainly make up an excuse and skip the party this time (it was so much more enjoyable just to be outside), but he'd heard that Perry Green was going to attend. Assuming this was true, and not a pathetic trick of Arnold's to ensure a decent-sized crowd, what would it matter anyway? He'd gone to other parties that featured a famous guest—though none perhaps quite of the stature and influence of Perry Green—and, of course, nothing had come of it, for him or anyone else. He knew the routine well. The extra time the guests took with their appearance; the extra drink to screw up their courage; their standing, not exactly in a receiving line, but for the same purpose, to get their chance to shake hands and pay tribute to the famous musician, who no doubt thought as soon as it was over, The speck has shaken hands with me and now can go back to his speck world with a smile on his face. No, he wouldn't fall for it this time. He'd be much better off spending the time composing, or doing anything else, for that matter.

He crossed at 104th Street, heading toward West End Avenue. At the corner he saw his building, the red paint around the windows clashing with the once-red bricks. It was not merely shabby but sinister, he thought as he went inside. He looked at the doorman, at his dimly lit table by the elevator, bent over a newspaper (probably the racing forms). Was he reading? Sleeping? It was impossible to tell. The doorman was wearing his thick black sunglasses which could perfectly disguise whatever he was thinking or doing. As a result, Ray never talked to him—any more than he would talk to anyone else who was sleeping or reading. Besides, the doorman was often not there; at least half the time he was absent from the lobby, and Ray sometimes entertained the notion that he wasn't really his doorman at all but some impostor who intermittently used the lobby as his private lounge. There was something else bizarre about the doorman. In addition to a uniform, complete with hat, he always wore a scarf high on his neck, regardless of how hot it was, so that almost none of his flesh was visible.

"My Glenn Gould doorman" Ray had dubbed him when describing him once to Joy. "I still don't know if he's black, white, or Asian. Not that it matters, of course, but it's odd not to know."

Riding up in the elevator, he thought that if he were still with Joy, it wouldn't matter if they went to the party or not; they'd have a good time either way. It was peculiar how difficult it sometimes was to decide things like this without her.

He stepped out on the eleventh floor, and the smell of cabbage cooking rose to greet him. Quickly, he looked at his feet, but there was no imminent danger, and a relatively clear path appeared to lead toward his door. In the last few months, the hallway had increasingly become his neighbor's backyard, littered with the assorted paraphernalia of her two-year-old grandson, Eugene. Ray had tripped once and invariably had to navigate the stroller and the toys to reach his apartment. Apparently, Grandma Love, as he nicknamed her, had done some "gardening" today, as Eugene's stroller, felt balls, gum machine, numbered and lettered building blocks, coloring pad, and over-sized crayons were all neatly arranged against the wall beside her door.

Ray had once intended to complain to her the next time he saw her, in the hallway or lobby, but she had such a smiling, round, innocent face beneath her dyed yellow hair, and she radiated such relentless love for that rambunctious, quasi-hysterical child, that he never could. Then one afternoon, when he was feeling particularly discouraged about his career, she approached him in the lobby, her angelic smile in place, and told him that she thought his piano playing that morning "was especially beautiful." He had been planning to speak to Eugene's ostensible mother, a dark, brooding, obese woman who visited intermittently (he'd never seen the father), but the grandmother's sly compliment touched Ray and made it impossible for him ever to say anything about the toys or Eugene.

The hallway was so dark he had to press his face next to his door to find the keyhole. It's dark enough here to be a restaurant, he thought as his key finally fit. Maybe if I imagined it was a restaurant, it wouldn't get on my nerves. He laughed to himself, opening the door and facing his studio.

A rare burst of direct sunlight accentuated how small and cramped it was, made it appear strange and startling—like a starfish suddenly encountered on the beach. Had he really lived here for two years, since he'd moved out from Joy's? Here with the refrigerator that came up to his knees, with the hot plate on top of it, looking like a monkey wearing a hat when he squinted? Here, with the rust in the tiny bathtub that would never come off, with the bathroom windows painted and nailed shut, and the white trails of boric acid in all the corners to kill the cockroaches—like a New York version of Hansel and Gretel's trail. He sat down at the upright piano that dominated the studio and played a few chords to steady himself.

Bryna would say he'd be a fool to stay in his place tonight, especially in the mood he was in. "Stop being so sensitive and falsely proud and just go. And when you're there, use your assets, network! You say a famous conductor is going to be there—why assume nothing will happen? Get to know him, make him like you, make something happen," et cetera, et cetera.

Ray smiled as he pictured how animated her eyes would

get, how expansive her gestures, while she urged him on. Few people could be funnier than Bryna when she became enthusiastic about something, though she was probably right about making things happen. She was older; she knew about such things, and to judge by her suddenly flourishing career as a performance artist—a success out of all proportion to her talent— she was living her own philosophy very well.

He got up from the piano bench thinking that maybe he should call Bryna. Imagining her advice was not the same as actually hearing it, but then she would probably want to go with him, and that wouldn't work either. He got the feeling from his last conversation with her that she wanted to sleep with him, and he didn't want to hurt her by saying no. He wished they could be platonic friends again (just the reverse of his situation with Joy) and had avoided seeing her lately, until he could figure out how to accomplish this delicate transition.

He lay down on his bed, feeling too tired to unfold it, and let his feet dangle over the edge. He wondered how Joy was doing at Tanglewood. She'd moved into her cottage there a week ago to teach and take classes, and now that he knew she wouldn't be in New York or Philadelphia all summer, he was missing her even more than he thought he would.

He closed his eyes and soon was able to hear the opening of his violin and piano sonata that he'd dedicated to her and that was perhaps the most expressive piece he'd ever composed. It brought him pleasure to hear it in his head (it had only been performed once, at a tiny concert in Arnold's loft), and he was glad he could remember it so well. It was peculiar how compositions were like relationships, or so he sometimes thought of his own. There were beginnings, some more dramatic than others, there were developments based on the introductory material, and, of course, they both eventually ended, some more dramatically than others. Like his deepest relationships, his best pieces persisted most intensely in his memory. He was almost halfway through the first movement of this one when a new wave of fatigue overcame him, and a moment later, he fell asleep with the sonata for Joy still flooding his mind.

HE WOKE up, saw his small TV resting like a plant on his windowsill, saw the unmarked staffs of composition paper on his piano, the same white as the boric acid on his floor. It had gotten darker. He stood up and tried to find the sun. There were only about thirty to forty minutes a day when it was visible over or between the three apartment buildings that took up almost all his view. He sometimes felt as if he were playing dodgeball with the sun. Right now it was dodging him; in fact, when judged by the light outside, it had succeeded in avoiding him for the rest of the day.

Why am I so anxious about going to Arnold's party, he thought as he began to change his clothes. It wasn't as if he'd be the only composer there who had no records or major publications. And at thirty-two, he was still younger than most of them. Ironically, as far as the regulars at the party went, it was probably Arnold himself who'd had the most success as a composer, though Arnold no longer composed. Arnold Weisman was an old-guard serialist whose career, Ray had often thought, could serve as a textbook case of early promise terminally frustrated. He was the first semisuccessful composer Ray had met after moving to New York and had been something of a mentor figure to Ray in those first years, always acting enthusiastic about his scores and always eager to inform him about grants and fellowships. Later, when Ray went to Juilliard, Arnold gave him valuable advice about his juries as well as strategies to deal with the politics in the small but intense composition department.

But as quickly as Arnold's success arrived, it began to evaporate. He stopped getting commissions and winning competitions and eventually stopped writing. Ray remembered urging him to compose again during a number of late-night talks on the phone or in various bars, but Arnold always deflected his advice with self-deprecating jokes and, when he wasn't joking, seemed to mean it when he said he was much happier since he'd stopped composing.

The one ongoing piece of good fortune in Arnold's life was the loft he had acquired in TriBeCa in the late seventies, when such things were still affordable. Since most of his colleagues lived in grim little studios or one-bedroom apartments, he'd become indispensable as a host of occasional parties and musical events. What continued to surprise Ray was that, while Arnold had stopped composing and had also inherited some substantial money from his father, he still clung to his old musician friends, still couldn't bear to leave the scene. Talking to a musical demigod like Perry Green would make Arnold's year, was exactly the kind of moment he now lived for.

Still, he could always enjoy Arnold's company at the party (and a couple of the other regulars now that he thought about it), and he supposed he owed it to their friendship to go. Besides, meeting Perry Green would be exciting—assuming he really would be there—but he wouldn't dress up. He'd wear the pink cotton shirt and black pants that he'd just put on, which looked pretty good with his black leather jacket anyway. And he wouldn't arrive as early as he normally did. He looked at himself quickly in his tiny bathroom mirror. When he didn't use a conditioner, as he hadn't for weeks, his thick dark hair began to curl more than his simple comb could effectively manage. He noticed also that there were dark circles under his hazel eyes. Instinctively, he put some water on his face as if that would wash away the circles, then laughed at himself. He went back to the piano, improvised quite joyfully for a half hour, and then left for the party.

On the train, holding the bottle of Chardonnay he'd just bought for Arnold, he sat leaning forward waiting for something interesting to look at. It was as if, for a while, he thought the random images in his car were a movie he could legitimately expect to make sense of, or in some way find entertaining. But everyone's face was turned away from him; they were either thinking or reading, or reading/sleeping like his doorman. He wished he'd brought a book. At Fifty-ninth Street a lot of people got on, and the seats next to him were suddenly filled. He began to obliquely look at his neighbors when a woman passed through his car, almost ghostlike, with long yellow hair, the approximate color of Joy's. It was really only the hair he saw, as if it were passing disembodied through the train. He got up from his seat for a moment thinking he'd follow it, then sat down again. A moment later, a favorite memory of Joy came back to him. She was on a beach in Martha's Vineyard with him. (He had splurged and taken her there on her birthday.) The sun was shining on her long blond hair and on her face, which was close to his. Her hand was on his arm, too, and she was smiling just before she kissed him.

His life with her had been so rich! They had shared everything: music, families, travel, careers. Even if he never got her back, he felt he had been blessed just to know her.

HIS STOP came and a number of the averted faces and twisted necks snapped back into place and left the train with him, soldierlike into the night. In a couple of blocks he was at Arnold's building on North Moore Street. An elevator led directly to the living room portion of the loft. On the third floor Ray literally stepped out of the elevator into the living room and looked at the scene that resembled every other party of Arnold's he'd ever attended. There were lots of men in the room—twice as many as women—wearing T-shirts, jeans, and glasses, with protruding stomachs and receding hairlines, holding their drinks tightly and gesturing with them expressively, as if they were instruments. The women (several of whom were also composers) favored jeans or black skirts. As usual, no music was being played at the party—an unstated act of deference by Arnold to his guests' fragile egos. Even elevator music could wound them or start an argument. These were the people who formed the closest thing he had to a social circle. Some he had met while at Juilliard, others at concerts of contemporary music he'd attended over the years, since at least half of the thirty or so people at those concerts were composers themselves.

What was different this time was that nearly everyone was clustered at one side of Arnold's loft. On the other side, in magnificent isolation by the punch bowl, with his silver hair and cream-colored suit, though looking slightly shorter and frailer, Ray thought, than he did onstage, was Perry Green, indisputably one of the world's most famous classical musicians, the embodiment of the wildest career fantasies of everyone else in the loft. It was no accident that Perry was alone. In a strange collective gesture of shyness and pride, the other guests pretended not to notice Perry, although as Ray watched more closely, he saw that they couldn't resist looking over at Perry every few seconds.

Ray decided that he wouldn't play their game. If necessary, he'd be the first to have his handshake and thirty seconds of conversation with the great man. Waving to a couple of people who saw him, Ray circled around Perry on "his" side of the loft until he reached the bar table, where he deposited his bottle of Chardonnay and quickly fixed himself a gin and tonic. When he looked up from his drink, he noticed that Arnold was now talking to Perry. Fine, he would be second then, he thought, as he took a large swallow of his drink and watched the other guests still playing their cat-and-mouse game with Perry, while no doubt resenting Arnold's sudden act of successful aggression. There was fat, bespectacled Marty Goldstein dressed all in black—a forty-something composer who wrote simpleminded trance music in the Arvo Pärt mode—talking to Barry Margolis, an avant-garde violinist who'd managed to get a number of composers at the party to write pieces for him in exchange for performing them at the "thirty-people concerts." Ray had also received an offer to write for Margolis and was seriously considering it, if only for the guaranteed performance and the bit of exposure that came with it.

Behind them was Larry Rosen, a Phil Glass wanna-be, who had formed his own ensemble à la Glass, to play Rosen's own compositions. He'd gotten some good press lately in the *Village Voice* that Ray felt was mostly undeserved. Now armed with his good review and membership in the downtown music scene, Rosen could carry off his act of indifference toward Perry's presence more convincingly than most.

The woman Rosen was talking to was an attractive flutist named Janis. Ray had once flirted with her at a different party, but never followed through—typical of his post-Joy dealings with women.

"Waiting for your chance?" a woman suddenly said to him, indicating Perry with a sideways nod. The sarcastic smirk on her thin lips made Ray smile.

"I have traveled long and far for my audience," he said. "And you?"

"My pilgrimage has also been difficult, but I've decided to pass on it. I just came over to have another drink," she said. "That's why I usually come to Arnold's. It's a great place to get drunk."

Ray laughed as she fixed herself a vodka tonic. She had brown hair and eyes and was wearing a short skirt. He thought she was vaguely attractive, but didn't think he'd seen her before.

"I'm Sarah Rogers." She shook his hand.

"Hi, I'm Ray Stoneson."

"I've seen you before."

"Oh? Refresh my memory. Was it Rome? Paris? Madrid? Another pope, a different palace?"

"Actually that night a number of people had pilgrimaged

to see *you,* or hear you, and a number of other composers. It was a concert right here at Arnold's loft about six months ago. I heard your piano trio."

"No kidding? You were one of the twenty-two people in attendance, then. My audiences, like the pope's, are also very exclusive—though for very different reasons."

She laughed. "You were very dashing. It's not every night I get to see the proverbial tall, dark, and handsome man playing such impressive piano."

"Thank you, but your hallucinations are embarrassing me. I'm no pianist, and I don't deserve your other compliments either."

"Yes you do. I liked your playing that night, a lot. I liked your piece too. It was scary and very moving at the end. Quite impressive. Obviously, it made a big impression on me." She looked at him a bit more seriously this time.

"Well thank you, and bless your heart. I don't know what to say," he said, more serious himself now. "I wonder why I didn't speak to you that night or . . . "

"Remember me?" She laughed a little, then took a swallow of her drink. "You seemed to be very involved with a tall blond woman, who I must admit was quite gorgeous. I figured she was your wife or your girlfriend, so . . . "

"We never spoke?"

"Not until now."

"I'm glad we finally did."

"So, was I right about the blond woman?"

"We were friends then. Though you're right; we were once a lot more than that." Ray looked away as she continued talking to him. He noticed that Arnold had just shaken hands with Perry, had, in fact, moved away from him, leaving Perry temporarily alone, which was both atypically rude of Arnold and an indication of how preoccupied he'd been with his conversation. Meanwhile Sarah, who'd looked stricken for a moment after he'd told her about Joy, was beginning to prove more disconcerting than amusing. At her first pause, Ray said, "But I see the moment for my audience has arrived. Maybe we can talk some more later?"

"Sure. I'd like that," she said, with an ambiguous smile, taking her half-empty glass and returning slowly to the other side of the loft. Arnold smiled unabashedly as he moved toward Ray, extending his hand.

"Thanks for coming, man. I haven't seen you for a while."

"It's good to see you. Thanks for inviting me."

They stood facing each other, without speaking, for a few seconds.

"So . . . ," Ray said, more softly now, "as we used to say about each other's girlfriends, how was he?"

"Very, very nice. My head is in a whirl," Arnold answered in a soft voice as well, for Perry was conceivably within listening distance.

"Good, I'm glad for you. It's a real coup to have him here," Ray said, suddenly wishing he had dressed a bit more formally.

"You'll like him, too," Arnold said. "Why don't you introduce yourself before everyone else finally gets unglued and starts to mob him?"

"Good idea. I'll follow your advice, and catch up with you later. You'll have to explain how you got him here in the first place." He patted Arnold on the back just before walking in a straight line toward Perry, who was half turned away from him now.

"Excuse me, Maestro," he said, extending his hand, "I'm Ray Stoneson and I'm honored to meet you."

Perry turned, adjusted his glasses, and shook hands with him, an oddly serene smile on his face, which was a little older looking than Ray had thought.

"Thank you, Ray. Are you also a musician?"

"I'm a composer."

"Well," Perry said with a laugh, "I'm a composer, too. I hope that makes me a musician."

"You're definitely a musician," Ray said, smiling, immediately wishing he had taken the opportunity to tell him how much he admired him. "May I ask what you're writing now?" he said, hoping that Perry, whose greatest fame was as a conductor, might enjoy talking about his compositions.

"I'm writing words these days instead of music. They've asked me to do a book on Stravinsky, so I've got to turn something in by October. It's kind of silly to write another book about Stravinsky, in a way—you'd think Robert Craft had pretty much covered the terrain—but I'm under contract, so when I'm not conducting I work on the book as much as I can. I'm afraid that doesn't leave me much time for composing."

"You know, Maestro, I have to tell you—"

"Oh, please, call me Perry. 'Maestro' is such a feudalistic word, don't you think?" Perry said with another laugh.

"OK, Perry. I wanted to say that I've learned a lot from everything I've read by you, especially your book on orchestration, which, of course, is just superb."

"Thank you again, Ray. You're being too kind."

"Believe me, it's a pleasure to finally get a chance to tell you a little of what you've meant to me. The truth is I'm thrilled to meet you. For as long as I can remember, I've thought of you as one of our few real national treasures."

"My goodness," Perry said, "I'm beginning to think I should be insured." Then he laughed, and Ray's laugh followed as in a fugue. They talked a few more minutes about a variety of topics: Stravinsky's books with Craft, more briefly about Arnold and his party, and then the weather and what New York was like in the summer. When Ray had imagined talking with Perry, he thought he'd feel vaguely stimulated or faintly nervous. Instead he felt exhilarated in a way that made everything else around him temporarily disappear. This famous man, whom he'd admired his whole musical life, seemed extraordinarily nice and, moreover, was paying a lot of attention to him. When there was a brief silence, Ray worried that their conversation would end and hurriedly asked Perry how he'd happened to come to the party.

"That's a pretty involved story," Perry said, chuckling. "Arnold asked an old friend of mine, a composer named Kenneth Phillips."

"Yes, I know his work."

"And Kenneth asked Arnold if I could come with him. Apparently Arnold didn't object, and wrote me a very kind letter inviting me. Then Kenneth got sick and couldn't come after all, and Arnold asked me if I'd still attend, and I said yes. I'm glad I decided to come, too. I've had a good time, and, of course, I've gotten to meet you."

"Thank you."

"Tell me, do you ever get a chance to go to Tanglewood?"

"Every summer until a few years ago . . . though usually just for a short time."

"Marvelous. Why don't you call me the next time you do. I'm going to Tanglewood on Monday for the rest of the summer. I have a house in Interlaken, and it's turned out to be quite a convenient place to work. I canceled the master classes I usually teach so I can finish my silly book, though I did agree to conduct the BSO for one concert and then one concert with the student orchestra."

"I'll definitely come up for those concerts."

"Thank you, but they aren't till August. There's no need to wait to visit. Besides, that's not such a good time to see me, anyway. When I conduct, there always seem to be so many people around."

"I can imagine," Ray said, but he was thinking that he couldn't imagine Perry's life at all.

"Let me ask you another question," Perry said, moving a step closer toward Ray. "Do you like to swim?"

The serious look on Perry's face confused him, and he hesitated before saying, "Sure. I love to."

"Wonderful," Perry said, releasing his reassuring smile. "I think I've finally got my pool in good enough shape for you. You look like you're very athletic. Are you a good swimmer?"

"I'm OK. Nothing special."

"I think when someone is able to leave New York, one of the best things they can do is go swimming. Don't you agree?"

"Absolutely," Ray said, with a little laugh.

"Now, tell me, do you also play piano?"

"Yes, but not very well."

"Because I have a grand at the house. Nothing spectacular, but quite serviceable. So if I start to bore you or you don't feel like swimming, you can turn to my piano for solace, or maybe we could play some duets."

"That would be a pleasure."

"Well, this all sounds like loads of fun. I have an idea: Why don't you come up next week before the weekend concerts start? That way we'll avoid the start of Tanglewood and all the crowds."

Ray almost said that he had to teach his piano students during the week—his main source of income these days. But the rapport between them was too good to jeopardize. He'd tell his students he was sick and would reschedule.

"Sounds terrific. I'll try to do it."

"Well, let's exchange addresses. I don't have a card. I hope you don't think less of me, but one of my secret ambitions is to sneak through life without ever having a card. I do have a pen though."

"And I have a piece of paper," Ray said. He was surprised that his hand shook a little as he took it out of his back pants pocket and handed it to Perry.

"You see, we're a good team, or at least efficient," Perry said as he wrote his address, then ripped the paper, and asked Ray to write his address on the other half.

Perry looked at his watch and complained that he had to leave Arnold's party soon, where he'd had so much fun, to attend "a boring sit-down dinner at a restaurant to receive some award I don't even know the name of. Isn't that ridiculous?"

They laughed, and Ray thought that he, too, wanted to leave the party as soon as possible. He merely had to thank Arnold and talk briefly to Marty and Margolis, whom he now noticed milling about at the head of a loose line of people that had suddenly materialized, waiting to meet Perry.

They shook hands, and Perry told him again he hoped he'd visit soon. Smiling broadly, in spite of his resolve to look cool, Ray walked away, nodding at Margolis and patting Marty briefly but warmly on the shoulder. He didn't want to be near them, or Perry either, lest anything mar the smooth ending of their conversation, so he walked back to the bar table at the end of the loft. His mind was racing. It would be more convenient to rent a car, but probably cheaper to take a bus to Tanglewood, and every penny counted, especially if he stayed at a hotel for two nights as he would have to do. In either case, he'd need to ask Bryna for a loan—his savings account having dipped below two hundred. What a time to be tapped out again! But he couldn't brood about that now. By staying two days and nights, he'd also have a much better chance to see Joy. In fact, if he hurried home, he could call her tonight and tell her the news.

"Hello, again."

He turned, didn't recognize Sarah for a moment, and hesitated before saying hello.

"I see your audience lasted a long time with His Eminence."

Ray nodded, barely able to pay attention to her, and excused himself for a moment to get a drink. He was thinking that he had gotten along especially well with Joy in their last two phone conversations. Who knew what could happen in the Berkshires, where they'd spent a number of nights when they were lovers? At the very least, she'd be the ideal person to advise him on his visit to Perry. There was also the matter of which scores to show Perry, should he ask to see some. In the final analysis, he trusted Joy's opinion on his music even more than Arnold's.

Yes, remarkable opportunities were suddenly materializing, but he knew that he had to be careful not to act impulsively with either Joy or Perry. With Perry he also needed to consider the undeniably flirtatious element to their meeting, which was slightly disconcerting. Perry was widely assumed to be gay, but that wouldn't have to be an issue, certainly not during his first visit, not if he kept a proper distance but was at the same time sensitive and respectful.

"So was it everything you'd hoped for?" Sarah asked him.

Ray turned toward her, smiling as fully as he could. "More so," he said.

# 2

n his memories of his practice room at Juilliard, he recalled
often feeling he was being spied upon. He would look up from
the piano and see someone watching him through the narrow
windows in the door. The practice rooms were the focal point of
every student's day, yet there weren't enough of them. Students
roamed the halls, waiting and spying, and often knocked on the
door, insisting that the occupants had been there longer than
they had. Sometimes when he'd seen no one and had gotten
through his time uninterrupted, he'd open the door and almost
bump into a student who'd clearly been listening, checking out
the competition while waiting. If anyone listened to him for
more than a few minutes, they'd realize he wasn't a pianist,
merely a composer working at the piano, and so no threat to
most of them. Still, in all the times he found people listening, no
one ever said anything to him about his music, which turned out
to be their ultimate revenge.

He got up from the bed with a start. So much for just
closing his eyes and letting his mind drift where it would for a
minute or two before the call. He looked through the window at
the dark tangle of trees, then back at the photograph on the
desk of the little blond girl who was smiling while she held her

doll, dressed as a baby. It was a photograph of Joy as a child, and he felt himself grow calmer as he continued to stare at it until finally he faced the phone. His finger moved once, twice, but it felt unnaturally soft, like a raindrop against a building. He stopped dialing and sat down on Joy's bed again. He decided that this time he'd do it differently; he'd select his memory. There was one he could rely on, that had worked before. He closed his eyes, seeing nothing at first except a purple and black mass tinged with dull orange. Then the memory emerged (as if he were witnessing its almost instantaneous birth), and he saw himself at the piano in his living room in Somerville—the last chord of "Summer Interludes" shaking the air, cutting through until it staked out its home, then still persisting, still ringing organlike in the startled room. He was fourteen years old and had just finished his first recital of his own compositions.

He turned and a wave of applause filled the living room. There were his parents and beside them balding Mr. Bocchine, his piano teacher from Boston, and there was Billy Patterson and his parents who lived across the street, and Lianne Fisher from his freshman English class, who occasionally provoked a suspicious glance from his mother. She was the first girl he'd ever felt up, and he dreamed of doing much more with her. All of them were smiling now, and when he took his bow, the wave surged again and doubled.

He opened his eyes, flexed his fingers (which were *his* fingers again, no longer those strengthless impostors), stood up, and dialed the full number.

Immediately he was struck by the richness of Perry's voice as he said hello, but, of course, Ray had to be polite and pretend first.

"Could I speak to Perry Green please?"

"This is he."

"Hi, it's Ray Stoneson."

"Ray, where are you? Are you in Tanglewood?"

"Yes, I'm at a friend's house in Mahkeenac Heights."

"Marvelous! When can I see you? I hope you've got a spot for me on your agenda."

"Of course. Whenever it's convenient for you."

"Why don't you have lunch with me tomorrow? We can eat by my pool around twelvish and then go swimming. You brought your bathing suit, I hope."

"Yes." He laughed for a moment. "I remembered."

"Excellent. I think you'll enjoy it. Let me give you directions."

He pressed his ear closer to the phone and wrote down everything Perry said. A minute later, when it was over, he let out a little victory scream and jumped with raised fists, slightly bruising his knuckles against the wooden beams. Then he began turning on every light he could find, for the trees were thick and so near the windows that the cottage was already dark and chilly. He thought of trying to start a fire to surprise Joy when she got back from her run, but doubted there was enough time. Instead, he fixed himself a drink and sat down with it on the Turkish rug in front of the fireplace, reviewing his sudden run of dazzling good fortune while he sipped. He started with his conversation with Perry at Arnold's party, their getting along so well that Perry had actually invited him to visit in Tanglewood, and his calling Joy the next day and her willingness, even eagerness, to let him stay at her home. Now, finally, the phone call which had ended with Perry inviting him to his house tomorrow for lunch and a swim. It was a stunning series of events, not the least of which was the chance to spend a good part of the next two days with Joy. To judge by her enthusiasm when she invited him, as well as the way they'd talked on the phone recently, he thought this visit might be his breakthrough opportunity. Of course, he knew he shouldn't push too hard or too fast with her. In the past year he'd made a few mild physical passes and some unmistakable verbal offers, all of which she'd rejected. After each rejection their friendship became more awkward for a while, and he always feared she might decide to end that, too. He therefore had to allow some time to pass between his attempts and not try again until just the right moment.

Ray finished his drink but remained lying on the rug awhile longer, staring at the empty fireplace, wondering when Joy would return. . . . There was something about Joy, two contradictory traits, he supposed, that both touched and excited him. On the one hand, she was one of the very few genuinely modest people he'd ever known. Though she was a gifted singer, and a handsome, highly intelligent woman, she didn't think of herself as having an important destiny or ever mattering very much to the world. Nor did that seem to bother her. She valued her family and the few people she chose to get close to. With them, she was funny, direct, and guileless. Her only secret was her modesty—almost to the point of vulnerability—which explained a lot about her, now that he thought about it, like her quirky sense of humor that could camouflage her fragility, or her relative lack of ambition. The contradiction occurred when they made love, where she often surprised him with thrillingly out-of-character acts of aggression. Once, while they were swimming, she began seducing him underwater, and they ended up having intercourse half standing in the water. On the day on Martha's Vineyard he was again remembering, she'd pressed him to take a walk with her. After staying close to the shoreline for a few minutes, she suddenly changed direction and walked uphill, without asking him, until she found the kind of sand dune she wanted. Then she led him behind it, pulled down his bathing suit, sat down on top of him, and made love with him on the sand. Having conquered him, she returned almost immediately to her joking, unassuming self, as if nothing unusual had happened.

He sat down on the futon, found the *Berkshire Eagle,* and read an article about the new Tanglewood. He was beginning to worry a little about Joy. When she finally returned, he'd finished the arts page and the editorials and was reading an old Tanglewood program, which he immediately put down beside him. While she toweled off by the fireplace, she told him a long joke about a couple she'd seen at the beach. He pretended to laugh but took advantage of the moment to study her. She looked amazingly good. She was thirty-two, his age, but he thought she looked younger than he did. She'd always had what he considered a classic female figure except for her unusually broad shoulders, which, coupled with her height (she was only a few inches shorter than he was), at times gave her appearance a slightly forbidding quality. Yet he thought her shoulders were also tremendously exciting, perhaps just because they were a bit incongruous in her otherwise gracefully proportioned body.

"So did you speak to Perry yet?" she finally said, stretching her legs as she spoke. She was wearing a navy-blue running suit.

"Just twenty minutes ago. He invited me to his home tomorrow for lunch."

"Wow!" she said, springing forward as her face exploded into a smile. "Congratulations! You're going to have lunch with Perry Green! That's exciting. Now that Bernstein is dead, he's probably the only triple-threat man in music, except for maybe André Previn or Gunther Schuller. He's always championing new music, he's definitely one of the most influential critics, and he must be on eight zillion juries or boards of directors."

"He's also a composer. You forgot that."

"That too."

"No, not 'that too.' As far as he's concerned, *that's* his real identity."

"That's interesting. Did he say that to you?"

"Not in so many words. It's just something I know."

Joy nodded uncertainly. "What did you talk about? Did you tell him you have an old girlfriend who once sang in one of his song cycles at Tanglewood?"

Ray laughed and said he would tell Perry all about her tomorrow. At the time, though, he thought it best to steer clear of shop talk.

"Yes sir," Joy said, "that's a real coup. Maybe he can even help you a little."

"I'm afraid to think about that, though I did bring some scores with me in case he asks. Could I ask you about them tomorrow morning?"

"Of course."

"Anyway, nothing would have happened if you weren't kind enough to let me stay here."

"Stop thanking me. I enjoy having you here, not to mention that it's oodles of fun to see you on the threshold of such a momentous meeting."

Joy smiled again, and he couldn't help staring at her bright, even teeth longer than he should have.

"Guess what! I've got another favor to ask you," he finally said.

"Shoot."

"Do you think you can drop me off there tomorrow, around twelve?"

"I'll do better than that. I'll make you dinner tonight too if you promise to tell me everything you know about Perry Green in slow, delicious detail."

Ray said it was a good deal, but only if she'd let him take her to dinner tomorrow night. They walked into the kitchen laughing, and she prepared chicken crepes, with broccoli and carrots, and tapioca pudding—all his favorites—while he told her about Arnold's party and the highlights of his meeting with Perry.

After he finished the story, she congratulated him again, but he thought he saw something faintly disapproving in her eyes. Was it because Perry was supposed to be gay, or was it something from her own agenda? Quickly he offered to introduce her to Perry, and she said that would be great.

"Of course, I should have made that clear to you when I first called."

"Don't worry about it." She gestured dismissively with her hand. "That's the last thing on my mind. But it would be really neat to meet him, if you think it's OK."

DINNER WAS extraordinarily good. They sat in the kitchen afterward, talking about their jobs, laughing and swapping stories about musicians. When Ray asked about her family, who lived in Ohio, she started telling him a series of amusing anecdotes. He smiled, feeling mesmerized by her voice, and thought that this was a strange peak of happiness in his life, a kind of eternal moment. This was the only woman he had ever really loved, the woman he should have married (which explained why his sexual desire for other women had all but evaporated), and now she was helping him at this potential turning point in his life. And it might not be too late to change things between them, for what was stopping them except the memories of their former selves? Yes, he had been selfish and egotistical too much of the time when they were together and an utter fool the one time he'd been unfaithful. She'd been completely justified in breaking up with him. But he had changed since then, matured—they both had. There was no reason that they couldn't reverse the patterns of their past and do whatever they wanted now. That was the horrible and wonderful meaning of freedom—people could always do what they wanted once they realized they could.

Ray sneaked a look at his watch. It was five of eleven; they'd been in the kitchen telling stories an unusually long time, as if afraid to acknowledge the presence of a room with a bed in it. He again remembered bits of the day at Martha's Vineyard, Joy's leading him by the hand to the sand dune, then shook his head when she wasn't looking to expel the memory and the expression he feared was in his eyes. When they were lovers, he was often amazed at how accurately she could read his feelings just by looking closely at him. Had that ability atrophied because they hadn't slept together in the last two years, or was it just as sharp as ever, except that now she chose not to reveal what she knew he wanted? At any rate, he couldn't try to convince her to sleep with him tonight, couldn't make a pass at her, not even with his eyes. That would be an intrusion which would break her spell, and she was enjoying herself too much, he couldn't bear to threaten that. The only thing he could do was be patient and, in effect, study *her* eyes, hoping that one time soon their expression would change.

"Ray?"

"Yes?"

"You're not listening to me, are you?"

"What do you mean?"

"Don't you know women get paranoid about not being listened to?"

"Sorry. If I knew anything about women, I wouldn't have lost you."

Her face reddened a little. "Anyway, I didn't mean to make a big deal about it, and I *was* definitely rambling. When I talk about my family, I do tend to ramble."

"The truth is I was thinking about you."

"Oh? Were they pleasant thoughts, I hope?"

"More than pleasant."

Joy stood up suddenly and stretched, then yawned with exaggerated emphasis. "God, Ray, I'm really tired. I'm afraid fatigue has pounded this girl into submission. Aren't you tired, too?"

"Not really," he said, head bowed toward the floor so she wouldn't see how disappointed he felt.

"But you've got a hugely exciting day ahead. Don't you think you should get some sleep so you can be fresh for it? I really want you to succeed big time tomorrow."

"What do you mean?" he said uneasily. She smiled at him

quizzically. He could hear the crickets outside and the wind which had picked up in the last hour.

"I just want things to go well with Perry. I feel the fickle hand of fate in all this. I really do. I think it's all pointing your way now, ready to scoop you up and carry you to some unimaginably dazzling future. How's that sound, cowboy?"

"Sounds good to me."

She extended her hand (which he quickly grasped) and half pretended, half pulled him up from his chair.

"Come on, young man."

"I'm coming."

"Come into the living room and Momma'll fix up the futon for you while she still has the energy, OK?"

"OK," he said.

# 3

---

Who are you staying with?" Perry asked. They were
sitting outside in their bathing suits at a white Formica table shaded by a blue-and-white umbrella rising from its center.

"An old friend named Joy Davis," Ray said. "She's a
teacher and singer, actually, who sang in the chorus of your
'American Song Cycle' at Tanglewood a couple of summers ago."

"Really? Did she drive you here?"

Ray nodded. "I wanted to introduce her to you, but she
got shy at the last minute."

Perry chuckled and adjusted his sunglasses. "I have a
friend staying with me, too. His name is Bobby. You'll have to
talk to him later. He's delightful."

A silence followed, until, just as Ray was about to compliment his yard, Perry spoke again. "Tell me what kind of music
you write. I'm sorry I'm not familiar with it."

"There haven't been many performances of it in New
York, or really many scores published by anyone important.
And, of course, no records yet. But I keep plugging away. It's
tonal, mostly. Some might call it neo-Romantic, though I don't
like the label."

"Labels are for librarians. They call me a Romantic too and a conservative. But I think I'm kind of a wild man, wouldn't you say?"

"Sure," Ray said. Then, after Perry began laughing, he laughed too.

"I hope you brought a score for me to read."

Ray felt his heart beat.

"I have some back at Joy's house. A short symphony I've just finished and a violin and piano sonata."

"Splendid! You'll have to bring them to me tomorrow, or tonight if you can come over."

"Really?"

"Of course. Bobby will fix us dinner. He's an excellent cook."

"Thanks so much."

"And bring Joy too. I'd like to meet her."

"She'll certainly be thrilled to meet you," he said, immediately wishing he hadn't been so florid.

"So how do you like it here?" Perry said, gesturing toward his yard and swimming pool.

"What's not to like? It's beautiful."

"It didn't fall too far below your expectations?"

"Not at all. It exceeded them."

"It's a little obscene to have a pool here, I suppose, but I often feel too tired to bother with the lake."

"It's a fabulous pool."

"Well, shall we have a quick swim before lunch? Bobby's running a little late today, so we'll probably have fifteen minutes or so to spend in the water."

"Sounds good."

Perry took off his glasses and his white polo shirt. Ray waited until Perry finished placing his glasses on the table, then removed his T-shirt in one quick motion. He moved at the same pace as Perry as they walked toward the pool, staying a couple of steps behind him.

"It always seems a little cold at first, even though we'll swear it's warm later," Perry said, smiling.

Ray smiled at him as he stood on the step nearest the pool and tried to keep his eyes off the thick gray hair on Perry's surprisingly muscular chest. Considering his age, Perry had an extraordinarily impressive physique.

"I'll tell you the real reason I'm smiling," Perry said. "I was hearing 'La Mer' as we tiptoed into the water. The grand theme in the last section. That shows how silly I am, doesn't it?"

Ray laughed as they walked down another step. The water was now up to their knees.

"Look at our feet!" Perry said, pointing at the water. "They look identical. That must mean we're twins."

Ray looked at their feet under the water and nodded. A sudden chill went through him and he said, "Do you mind if I take a few strokes now?"

"Of course not. Go on ahead."

Ray dove into the water and when he turned to look back was momentarily reassured by Perry's warm expression. It reminded him of the way his father had smiled at him while he was teaching him how to swim at Revere Beach. He did his crawl around the pool (Perry still standing on the last step, smiling and watching him), then flipped onto his back and began to backstroke—closing his eyes against the strong sun that filled the bright blue sky. At the end of his rotation around the pool, he saw Perry signaling to him.

"Ray, you Olympian you, can you stop for a second? There's someone who wants to say hello."

Ray stopped swimming and walked through the water toward the steps by the side of the pool. A young blond man with blue eyes and slightly protruding front teeth was also smiling.

"Ray, this is Bobby."

"Hi," Bobby said as they shook hands. Ray said a couple of words to Bobby, then stopped abruptly when Perry dove into the water.

"Nice dive," he said, looking at Bobby.

"He's amazing," Bobby said with what appeared to be utter admiration.

"I didn't even notice him getting on the diving board."

"Perry can move like a dancer or a burglar when he wants to," Bobby said.

"Do you live near here, Bobby?"

"I wish. I live in New York among the teeming millions."

"Me too. What part?"

"Kind of the fringes of the East Village. And you?"

"Upper West Side, near Columbia."

"I hear a little accent in your voice. Are you from Boston by any chance?"

"Very good. I'm from Somerville, just a few miles from Boston. And you? I can't say I hear New York in your voice either."

"I'm supposed to have a neutral voice, since I'm an actor, or an aspiring actor. So I'm glad you said that."

"Consider yourself accent free."

"I'm from Iowa, believe it or not."

Ray raised his eyebrows in surprise.

"There, you've finally met one," Bobby said, laughing. "I came here about four years ago."

"So how has the New York experience been?" Ray said lightly.

Bobby paused as if considering the question seriously before answering. "The New York experience has really been in two different parts for me," he said with an earnestness Ray hadn't expected. "In the first part, it was pretty awful. I was really lonely and sad and just scared out of my mind. But then I met Perry, and things have been a lot better ever since. He's just one of those life-changing people, I guess. Anyway, he completely turned my life around."

"That's great," Ray said.

"Oh, I know how lucky I am. I know I am blessed."

Perry came out of the pool then and walked toward them.

"Bravo for the dive," Ray said.

"Why thank you. How nice of you to notice. Aren't you youngsters getting hungry yet?"

"I am, I am," Bobby said, playfully raising his hand. "I've already made lunch, Perry; it's waiting for us in the kitchen."

"But it's so beautiful out. Wouldn't it be nice to eat by the pool?"

"I'll go get it," Bobby said, already heading for the path of descending stone stairs cut into the backyard and leading to the house. Ray began to follow him until Perry put a hand on his shoulder. "No, no, you stay here. You're the special guest."

"I'd really like to help him," Ray said, in a tone so firm Ray himself was surprised by it.

"OK then," Perry said, releasing his hand. "You are a restless spirit. I, for one, am going to sit at the table and let the sun and the breeze slowly dry me off."

The three of them ate a simple lunch of tuna fish, white wine, and Tostito chips at the Formica table that shaded them from the sun. The wine made Bobby's spirits even lighter, and he laughed (almost giggled) a number of times. Instinctively Ray looked at Perry each time to see how it "played" with him, but Perry inevitably smiled. He seemed to be thoroughly enjoying himself. It soon became clear that he not only liked the giggling but was trying to make Bobby do it more.

He must really need to be around young people, Ray thought, even childish ones. Who would think it when seeing him onstage, where he was all serious business and, in the tradition of Monteux, was one of the least demonstrative of the great conductors?

After lunch Bobby cleared the table, and Perry began reminiscing about "old friends" like Aaron Copland and Virgil Thomson. Bobby listened glassy eyed without saying a word. It occurred to Ray that Bobby might have no idea whom Perry was talking about beyond the fact that these men, now dead, were once Perry's friends. Bobby seemed to have only a minimal interest in music. He didn't speak about it and had told Ray in the kitchen that he played no instrument and was only planning to go to one concert this summer when Perry conducted the BSO at Tanglewood. His only aesthetic interest was acting, he'd said, though he hadn't earned any real money from it yet—he earned his money as a waiter in a Greenwich Village café. "Perry helped me get the job," he admitted. "It was a real step up from the first place I worked."

Like so many of Perry's compositions, Bobby's lunch had been crisp, civilized, and light. Perry seemed so deeply relaxed that Ray felt some of his own tension dissolve as he looked out at the green hills around and below them, unusually bright under the strong sun. When Bobby asked Ray a couple of questions about his music, Perry said, "I'm going to get a chance to read some of Ray's scores tonight. I must say, I'm more than curious."

"I'll never understand how you can look at a sheet of music and actually hear the sounds of the instruments in your head," Bobby said.

"It's like reading the script of a play," Perry said. "It's not really unlike that at all."

A minute later, Bobby was trying to convince Perry to get a dog—apparently a subject he'd brought up before. "I would have been completely lost as a kid without my collies. You don't realize how much a dog could do for you."

"I do, I do. I'm not oblivious to the charms of dogs. The question is, what could I do for the dog?"

"A dog would love it here. You have a big yard and there are lots of other dogs in the neighborhood, and lots of places for it to run."

"But dear heart, I'm not always here. I live in New York City, and I travel a lot."

"I'll help you take care of it in New York, and I'll keep it when you go away," Bobby continued. Ray couldn't help smiling. When he had first heard of Bobby, he thought he was probably Perry's lover and worried that Bobby might resent or feel threatened by his sudden appearance. But looking at him now, as he spoke eloquently about the joy of dogs, he felt that anxiety dissolve. Bobby didn't appear to have a heart of darkness. Instead, he seemed to be one of those odd, simple souls whom Ray had last seen in a Dostoyevsky novel.

A moment later, Bobby suddenly announced that he was going to Stockbridge to do the shopping for that night's dinner.

"Thank you, dear Bobby," Perry said, taking off his sunglasses and smiling at him. "And don't forget to pick up the dill pickles and the couscous."

"I won't forget," Bobby said, his face a single smile as he stood up in the sun and descended the stone steps. "Trust me to remember, OK?"

"Of course."

"He seems to be in a good mood," Ray said a moment later.

"Oh, Bobby's a wonderful person, a wonderful person. He loves it up here. Usually he visits on Saturdays, but he had a few days off this week and no auditions, so he came up yesterday."

Ray nodded, wanting to ask more about Perry's relationship with Bobby but thinking that he shouldn't. Then Perry began talking about Leonard Bernstein, and Ray forgot about Bobby for a while. It was not that it was so unusual to hear a story about Bernstein. He had heard stories about him much of his adult life and had even met him twice at Tanglewood. But to hear someone of comparable stature discuss "Lenny" (and since Bernstein's death Perry was already being written about as his "successor") was unique in Ray's experience, and he cherished each sentence. It was strange to think of Perry's becoming as potentially popular with the general public as Bernstein, perhaps because he lacked Bernstein's physical presence and dramatic flair. Indeed, Perry Green was most renowned for his restraint, his economy of gesture and classic taste—qualities that would seem to be massive impediments for anyone trying to reach the general public, and yet, slowly, undeniably, it was happening. In the last six months alone there'd been major articles about Perry in *Time, Newsweek,* and the *New York Times* and a special on PBS. Somehow, the time seemed right for his subtle charisma and delicately eccentric personality. Ray was thinking it was almost as if Perry didn't have to orchestrate that at all. He really could just continue being himself, and it would all happen naturally.

Around three o'clock Perry said he needed a nap. Ray offered to call Joy and have her pick him up, but Perry wouldn't hear of it. "I only rest for thirty minutes. Why don't you use the guest room for your own nap or else play the piano? In any case you can't go now; it's much too early."

Ray decided that Perry meant what he said and told him he'd like to stay by the pool and maybe swim again.

"Another swim? It's so exciting to be young," Perry said. "All that wild energy." He laughed a little, then walked down the steps in a careful, almost stately manner (not unlike the way he approached the podium when he conducted) before disappearing into his house.

Ray lay down on the chaise longue by the pool for a moment, then went toward the diving board, where he had a better view of the house. Now that his simple excitement at meeting Perry had settled in, he wondered what exactly Perry wanted from him. Perry was certainly a master of mixed messages and, as a result, had kept him off balance all day. The most perplexing thing was the adoring way he treated Bobby. Surely they were sleeping together. But if Perry were so happy and had no vulnerabilities in his love life, then what was his interest in him? It couldn't be musical, since he'd never seen or heard a note he'd written. But if it were romantic, why invite him when Bobby was so visibly around, and why invite Joy to the dinner as well?

For several minutes Ray had been walking from the diving board to the patio table and then back, turning every few steps to look at the house below. On one such trip he stubbed his toe near the table, swore out loud, and then sat down in a chair, telling himself to calm down. He inhaled deeply a few times and watched a pine needle drift over his head in the light breeze. Above him the cloudless sky was a deep azure. When he was young and came to Tanglewood with his parents, he used to call them "Mahler skies." How inexpressibly beautiful it was to hear Mahler's "Resurrection Symphony" or "The Song of the Earth" under such a sky across from the tree-lined lake. Of course, Tanglewood was much more built up now, infinitely more commercial. With the installation of Ozawa Hall and the other buildings on the land the orchestra had recently acquired and dubbed the Leonard Bernstein Performers Pavilion, Tanglewood was now twice as big with three times as many snack bars and gift shops. He could never feel about Tanglewood (or even about Mahler) the way he had twenty years ago.

Looking down at the pool, he remembered the most stunning moment of his afternoon, when Perry had pointed to their feet below the water and said, "They look identical. That must mean we're twins." That was the closest Perry had come to actually flirting with him, but was it serious flirting? And if it was, and if Perry persisted, he'd better think about the language he'd use in rejecting him, which needed to be definite yet soft enough to keep alive the possibility of their still being friends.

He walked to the table, picked up his watch, and realized that Joy would be leaving to pick him up soon, if she hadn't left already. He began walking down the stone stairs to the house, when he heard someone say, "Hello there." It was Perry, waving in his bathing suit and bathrobe, standing just in front of the back entrance.

"Hi. I was just going to see if I could find a phone to call Joy and invite her for dinner."

"There's one right behind me. I was watching you for a while pacing back and forth like a young Beethoven. You looked terribly romantic. What were you thinking about?"

"A section of a piece I'm writing," Ray said, hoping that he sounded believable as he continued down the steps.

"I thought it had to be either music or love that would make someone look that way and take those Beethoven-like strides around the pool."

"Is it all right if I use this phone?"

"Of course. I'll let you talk alone."

"No, no, that's not necessary," Ray said, making a quick disparaging gesture with his free hand. He was dialing Joy at the cottage, increasingly worried that she might have already left. But Joy answered on the third ring in her characteristically cheerful voice and said she was "thrilled" (the exact word Ray had used to Perry to describe her probable reaction) about the dinner.

"Let me talk to her," Perry suddenly said, and Ray handed him the phone.

"Hi, Joy, this is Perry Green. I understand you're going to be able to come over tonight for our impromptu dinner?"

For the next few minutes Ray stood off to the side and listened to Perry banter with Joy, feeling vaguely jealous, as if Perry were in some bizarre way competing with him, though when the conversation was over, he smiled.

"It's all set," Perry said as he hung up the phone. "The lady will be here at seven."

# 4

They were in the living room laughing and sipping their predinner drinks. Perry had just finished describing his first meeting with Virgil Thomson, a man who played no small role in helping his career, when the bell rang.

"I think our lady guest has arrived," Perry said, springing to his feet while gesturing to Bobby that he would answer the door himself. Ray, who had been consulting his watch whenever he thought Perry wasn't noticing, took a big swallow of his white wine.

He could hear Joy saying she was sorry for being late, then a remark from Perry he didn't catch, followed immediately by the two of them laughing—Perry's low civilized signature laugh, quickly eclipsed by Joy's intense, overarching soprano that tonight seemed to contain elements of hysteria. It was a laugh he'd heard only when she was extremely nervous or overstimulated, and it seemed to last twice as long as it should have, as if it didn't know how to end.

They walked into the living room with arms linked for a moment before Perry detached himself to make introductions.

"Joy, this is Bobby Martin, young actor extraordinaire. Bobby, this is Joy Davis, a singer who is certainly beautiful enough to be an actress."

Joy laughed again, less intensely this time, as she shook hands with Bobby.

"Ray, I gather, you know very well," Perry said.

"Oh yes," she said, her eyes finally fixing on his. She moved toward him, deftly handing him his briefcase that contained his scores.

"We're old friends," Ray said as they lightly embraced, kissing each other on the cheek. He quickly moved the briefcase out of sight behind the sofa, then excused himself to use the bathroom. When he returned, he looked at Joy more closely. He was surprised that she was wearing her most expensive white cocktail dress with long turquoise earrings, a pearl necklace, and gold and turquoise rings, one of which (the turquoise) he had given her three Christmases ago. He noticed that she'd worn more eyeliner than usual and a heavy dose of red lipstick— a color she generally shunned. The cumulative effect was made still more incongruous by the fact that none of the casually dressed men was wearing even a sports jacket. Ray wondered if she'd misunderstood something Perry said and thought he'd intended something more elegant than this semispontaneous meal, and he worried that now she might become still more nervous.

"Come into the living room and make yourself at home," Perry said with a flowing gesture of his right hand. "And by all means sit next to me on the sofa. At my age, it's a rare treat to sit next to a woman as young and as dazzling as you are."

"Thank you," she said. "That's very sweet." She had barely had time to take in the grand piano, the photographs of the renowned musicians, and the paintings by de Kooning and Larry Rivers on the walls, and now she'd already been flattered by perhaps the greatest living musician in America. She was smiling, albeit rigidly, and where Ray might have expected some additional color in her cheeks, they were unnaturally white.

"We've been enjoying some good California wine. Would you like to try some?"

"That sounds perfect."

Bobby moved toward the bottle, but Perry gave him a stop signal and poured a glass for Joy and a new one for Ray.

"I propose a toast," Perry said, and everyone else raised their glasses and waited with smiles. "To friends and lovers, and to beauty," Perry said, nodding toward Joy.

"And to music," added Ray.

"Amen," Perry said, and everyone clinked glasses and laughed.

"Your home is so beautiful," Joy said, after a brief group silence.

"Why thank you," Perry said. Ray looked at Bobby, who was beaming, his eyes fixed on Joy.

"There's something about the combination of things in your living room that's so . . . "

She paused, unable to find the adjective until Perry finally said, "Museumlike."

Then she and Bobby laughed quickly in support.

"An alternative to the Rockwell Museum down the road, perhaps," he said with a whimsical smile. "At any rate, I hope it isn't too pretentious, my little museum." Perry looked closely at Ray for a moment.

"Oh no!" said Joy.

"It isn't meant to be. It's really just a record of my sentimentality. I'm one of those who never throws things out, if they are given to me by friends or people I admire," he said, half pointing to the signed photographs of Bernstein and Copland just behind him on the wall. "I end up putting them on the wall instead of in an attic or a closet where they might get lost or damaged. I don't want to forget the past. I'm one of those who wants to remember. Especially when I was young, because that will never happen again."

"But young people all over the country admire you, Perry," Joy said. "God, you're a national treasure."

Ray winced, wondering if Perry remembered his use of the same phrase at Arnold's. If he did, Perry certainly didn't give any indication. He merely smiled and said, "I can see why your name is Joy. You bring so much of it to people. But your glass is empty, and Ray's is too."

"I'll open a new bottle," Bobby said, getting up from the sofa and walking toward the kitchen.

"Thank you," Perry said. "He's a joy, too. There is no life without friends, is there?"

PERRY'S HOMOSEXUALITY was one of those things people in the music world assumed to be true, although he had never made a statement about it one way or the other. In fact, Perry was one of the very few celebrities Ray knew of who was so distinguished that interviewers would never pose such a question. Or perhaps Perry was careful about whom he let interview him. Yet while never publicly admitting it, Perry used his presumed homosexuality to do the kind of harmless flirting he'd just done with Joy, and women responded in kind, as Joy had. That was certainly one way to look at it, he thought as he sat next to Joy in the dining room and ate the lamb that Bobby had prepared. But precisely because Perry had never come out, one couldn't be absolutely sure about his sexuality, and when Ray thought that way, he couldn't help feeling a little jealous of the flirtation that Perry had initiated and was carrying on with Joy.

Another scenario occurred to Ray. In this one, Perry noticed how nervous Joy was and hoped his barrage of compliments would have a tranquilizing effect. But before he could explore this thesis, Joy began talking about Richard Steiner (a critic whose dislike of Perry's music was well known) and the harm he'd done Eric Shipley, a definitely gay composer who'd incorporated a radical gay text into his latest opera.

"I remember reading about that in the *Voice,*" said Bobby, who'd said hardly anything till then.

"I haven't heard the piece you're talking about," Perry said, lightly, "or seen the score either. I've been so dutifully immersed in my little opus about Stravinsky that half the world has probably passed me by, and I haven't noticed. Terribly unfair of the world, isn't it?" he said, laughing.

"But what do you think of the point Steiner makes about politics being anathema to music as soon as it becomes an overt part of it?" Joy asked.

Ray noted with some concern that she'd nearly finished her new drink.

"I don't know about that. Political passion has certainly inspired a lot of music, from Beethoven to Prokofiev. There's also Schoenberg's 'A Survivor from Warsaw,' Copland's 'Lincoln Portrait,' and there's Penderecki's 'Threnody for the Victims of Hiroshima.' Of course, political orthodoxy hurt Shostakovich to a degree, and some would say Prokofiev too. Now this gets into the question of how you define 'political.' For some people, everything is political, or at least has a political hue. I hate to generalize myself. I'm an Aristotelian—I believe in individual cases."

"But if a composer wants to protest the ways gays are treated, it's not wrong to use music to make his or her point, is it?"

"Not at all. Again, I would have to hear the particular piece."

"So what's your opinion of Steiner as a critic?" Joy said, raising her eyebrows meaningfully. Ray looked at her sharply—would she never get off this subject? Didn't she know that Steiner consistently trashed Perry's music? Why was she putting him on the spot like this, or did she naively think that providing him a publicly sympathetic forum in which to trash Steiner back was doing him a favor?

"He's not my favorite critic," Perry said between bites of lamb. "The truth is the older I get, the less time I find I have to read critics. I guess the more I continue to love music, the less interest I have in reading about it."

"But you've written criticism," Joy protested. "You're one of our most respected critics."

"Have I been caught being a hypocrite again?" he said, pointing an index finger at his chest. "Nasty habit I have, isn't it?"

Bobby laughed, but Ray continued to look sharply at Joy.

"Yes, I have written about music; I'll plead guilty to that. But at least I've never written reviews, which is what Mr. Steiner is chiefly known for, isn't it? To write reviews of performances that will never exist again, where in many cases there won't ever be a repeat performance, strikes me as a bizarre and perversely superfluous activity. But tell me, Joy, what do *you* think about Mr. Steiner?"

"I enjoy some of what he writes. I think he's good on the nineteenth century in particular, and he's generally pretty accurate when he evaluates singers. I just think he has some real blind spots when it comes to the twentieth century."

"Why is that?" Perry asked.

"Because he has his own agenda that he brings with him. You know, the old idea of the German succession: Schoenberg, Berg, Webern. You must be a serialist, or at least atonal. You must have an academic theory behind your music, preferably with German roots, and that makes him blind to a lot of good music. I also think he has a problem with gay people and takes it out on gay composers whenever he can."

The darker look that had been temporarily occupying Perry's face gave way to a smile.

"That shouldn't be an issue in evaluating music," he said.

"That shouldn't be an issue in evaluating anything," Ray added.

He caught Joy's eye and noticed her face looked slightly flushed. She finally let the subject drop, but before Bobby had finished bringing in the dessert, she was asking Perry if he'd read the recent article in *Time* about him.

"I did read it, yes. I sometimes wish I were one of those people who are too high-minded to read things about themselves, but I weaken every time and read them."

"Did you think it was a good article?"

"It was much too flattering to be true, but, of course, I loved every word of it."

Everyone laughed, and Ray thought this line of questioning would finally end. But a moment later Joy asked Perry about another article and then about the biography that had appeared last year—the first one about Perry published by a major house. Perry remained light and unflappable while Ray kept his head down and drank another glass of wine. He thought he understood what Joy was doing. She had ambitions of her own and certainly wasn't above playing up to Perry in the hopes that somewhere down the line, in some nebulous way, he might be able to help her. He felt a tinge of jealousy at how lavishly she complimented Perry, but he certainly could understand it. But why couldn't she say two words about his own music when she knew it was such a crucial time for him? It was because of his contact with Perry, after all, that she was here, and she hadn't said anything (or had only very briefly) about him. Now he worried that the subject of his scores would never come up.

He looked up again when he heard Joy excuse herself to use the bathroom and saw that Perry was staring directly at him. It was an extraordinarily penetrating look that seemed equally composed of passion and tenderness—the kind of look that took place in D. H. Lawrence stories or in a Fitzgerald novel, as when Daisy shows Gatsby she loves him again after all those years. In his own life, Ray had only seen that kind of look in the early part of his relationship with Joy, shortly after they'd started sleeping together. To get that look from Perry now was profoundly disconcerting, and he immediately checked to see if Bobby had noticed. But Bobby was still out of the room, having cleared away the last of the dishes. In fact, Ray could hear him laughing and talking with Joy in the kitchen.

"Did Joy bring your scores here?" Perry finally said.

"Yes, I have them in my briefcase."

"Good. I was hoping you'd remember. I'm very eager to get your music in my hands . . . and to read it, to hear it in my head."

"Thanks so much. I'd value anything you'd say about it. It would really mean a lot to me."

Perry removed his glasses and smiled, and Ray found himself staring for a moment at his wrinkles.

"Are you free to come for a swim tomorrow before you leave?"

"Sure, I'd love to."

"Say twelvish again?"

"Sounds great."

So there would be another day, and he could very well get some kind of verdict on his pieces by then, or if not, he'd certainly have a valid excuse to contact Perry again. Joy returned, smiling radiantly, thanking Perry and Bobby for the dinner. The hurt that Ray had been nursing about her left him as he smiled and thanked them both, too.

THERE WAS another moment alone with Perry, just before he and Joy left. Joy had said she wanted to see the pool. So they all left the house, and Bobby turned on the pool lights and led Joy up the steps.

"God, I wish I could go swimming. This pool looks so infinitely inviting," Joy said.

"Perry might have something you could wear," Bobby said. "He has a little collection of bathing suits he keeps for guests."

In the black night, hearing their giddy enthusiasm, Ray thought they might have been two twelve-year-old kids. Perry had begged off, saying, "Ray tired me out with all his swimming this afternoon. He swims like an Olympian." Ray was uncertain what to do and had taken a few steps uphill when Perry called his name.

"Why don't you give me your scores now?"

"Sure, they're just inside, in my—"

"Could you bring them to me? I'm enjoying the night air so much, and besides," Perry said, pointing toward the pool, "I don't want to miss out on the youngsters' fun."

Ray went inside. He removed the scores from his brief-case by the living room sofa, then handed them to Perry, who was still smiling gently in the half light of the porch.

"Thank you, Ray," he said, pressing the scores for a moment to his heart. "I'm very excited about reading these. I'm very excited in general. It's been such a marvelous day and night. I like Joy so much and Bobby seems to, too. And, of course, it's been delightful to spend this time with you. Even more delightful than I would have imagined. And to think that I'll see you tomorrow—well, that's so exciting, I wonder if I'll be able to sleep tonight."

"I've had a great time too. It was a wonderful dinner," Ray said, a little nervously. Perry's sudden burst of enthusiasm had him slightly nonplussed, and without knowing why, Ray suddenly extended his hand. The two men shook hands warmly but appropriately, Ray felt.

Joy and Bobby returned. More tributes flowed, more laughter followed, then a minute later, Ray and Joy were walking toward her car.

Driving back too fast on the black Berkshire roads, Joy sang bits of various arias, mixing in dirty puns and laughing continuously. Ray kept his eyes fixed on the road, asking her to slow down occasionally. He was thinking that he hadn't been this close to her in the dark in two years and that he wanted very much to touch her and so couldn't even turn his head to look at her for more than a few seconds.

"Isn't Perry amazing?" she said once they were back in the cottage as she again made up the futon for him. "Now I can die and go to heaven. I've dined with a great man. Aren't you happy too?"

"He wants to meet me tomorrow. He took my scores just before I left."

"God, what an opportunity! So you're happy, right?"

"I'm pleased," he said, with a tentative smile.

"I should think so," she said, putting a hand on the hip of her white dress. "Haven't you gotten everything you've wanted?"

Their eyes met, and he felt she was looking at him meaningfully.

"Not exactly," he said, moving toward her and touching her left shoulder with his hand. He kept it there for a few seconds, but when he started to move his hand down her back, Joy stepped away.

"What's this, young man?" she said, raising her eyebrows in mock horror, but still smiling.

"This is me and you alone in your house at the end of a happy night."

"Ah! That does sound nice. Why don't you give me a goodnight kiss on the cheek, and it will be the perfect ending for me."

He kissed her on the cheek, then on the lips, trying to open her mouth with his tongue.

"Ray, what are you doing, dearest?" she said, backing away from him.

"We were lovers once. Have you forgotten?"

"I haven't forgotten that, but have you forgotten what we've been for the last two years? We're friends, Ray; that feels right to me for now. And I take it seriously."

He looked down at the floor for a moment. "I'm sorry.

Sometimes it's easier to forget than others, no matter how much you remind me."

"For me too. It's not always easy for me either. Believe me, there are times when I still get tempted. But this friendship thing feels right. I'm sure of that."

"Why, if you're tempted, if you're really still attracted to me? . . . Are you?"

"Of course I am. You're the most sensitive and expressive person I've ever known, and most of the time you're a total sweetheart."

"So I don't understand. I feel all that about you and it makes me want to do something about it."

"Part of me wants to do something about it, too, but I keep that part at a safe distance."

"Why?"

"Because, my dear, part of me doesn't trust you anymore. Sorry, but you asked. And it isn't just the infidelity thing."

"That was the worst thing I ever did. That would never happen again. Never."

"I believe that you mean that now. I even believe that if we were together again you probably wouldn't do it. But there's another way that I don't completely trust you. Are you sure you want me to go on?"

"Yes, absolutely, go on."

"OK, I'll take you at your word. . . . There was something in our relationship that was missing, something missing in the way you loved me."

"What do you mean, 'missing'?"

"That not enough of you was there, . . . but someplace else. Sometimes I thought it was because your career was what you really loved. Other times I felt it was just a fear of really loving and committing to me or maybe any woman. . . . "

"What do you mean? That I can't love women? What are you saying?"

"God, Ray, I feel like I'm hurting you and—"

"Don't worry about that. That doesn't matter."

"It does to me."

"I need to hear this more than anything."

"All right. OK. What I'm trying to say is if we were making love or playing music together or on a vacation, I'd have the greatest time in the world. But as far as day-in, day-out life goes, as far as counting on you and, God forbid, ever getting married and having children—which was, is, very important to me—I began to feel that it would never happen. That you were like a dream always just out of my grasp. And then when you cheated on me, all my fears were confirmed. The little dam of my trust that I built in my mind every day so we could be together just collapsed."

"But I've changed, I've grown. I'm not as selfish and immature anymore."

"I know that. I've grown, too, by the way. And you've been a wonderful friend—patient, devoted. My opinion of you has gotten much higher, believe me."

"So is this distrust thing permanent? Is it irreversible?"

She smiled at him sadly. "I don't know. But for now and maybe for always being friends feels right."

He saw tears forming in her eyes and said, "I'm sorry. I don't want to lose you as a friend."

"Small chance of that happening, I'm afraid. . . . So I'll see you in the morning. You can have a long sleep dreaming about your triumph with Perry. And tomorrow we'll have a big breakfast, OK?"

"OK," he said, and a moment later she walked away from him toward her room.

WHAT IS the matter with me? he wondered later on the futon, unable to sleep. It had been a big mistake to have forced himself on her earlier just because she had her hand on her hip when she said a slightly ambiguous sentence—ambiguous only because he'd interpreted it that way. And it had been tough to listen to so much criticism, albeit valid criticism. But perhaps not that much damage had been done after all. It was certainly reassuring to see how much feeling she still had for him. As long as that was there, there was hope. Besides, she'd said she was trusting him more now, so perhaps it was a question of just being patient.

He turned on his side and began thinking about Perry, wondering if he would look at his work before they met for their swim. Would there be a way Perry might really offer to help him? Did Perry even think of him as a professional? Sometimes, because he'd had so little success, it was hard for him to think of himself that way. But assuming that Perry did take him seriously, what exactly could Perry do to help? Make a phone call to a conductor, write a recommendation for a fellowship? It wouldn't take much. Perry could breathe on his career and double it. But what would he expect in return? He remembered Perry's long look at him and shuddered, then quickly reminded himself that Perry was over sixty and had even complained once about his heart. Perhaps he merely enjoyed flirting and wouldn't want anything too drastic to happen right away.

But what would he do if something did happen? Of course he would reject him because he had never had sex with a man, and with AIDS around, sex with Perry was unthinkable. But exactly what would he say? He tried focusing on the question of just how he would reject Perry but found it excruciating to think about. Instead he thought about the look in Joy's eyes when he first told her about his call to Perry, her long blond hair and big shoulders. Then he thought about the anger he felt toward her at Perry's house. There was something he needed to settle with her before he could even seriously attempt to sleep. He turned on a dim lamp by the couch, put on his slippers, and walked to her room, the floor creaking with his every step.

"Joy," he said softly as he tapped twice on her door in the near-total darkness.

"What's up?" she said matter-of-factly. "Come in."

"Me, obviously. I'm having trouble sleeping."

"Sounds like the Ray I know."

"Were you having trouble sleeping, too?"

"Me? No, you know I'm too uncomplicated to be an insomniac."

"Sorry. I guess I'm disturbing you, then."

"No problem," she said.

"Can we talk for a few minutes?"

"God, whence cometh all this need for communication? OK, what's on your mind?" she said, turning on a bed lamp before he could ask her not to. Her face looked strained in the light, as if she were fighting against something, and he felt strangely anxious.

"I guess I'm nervous waiting to hear what Perry will say tomorrow."

"Don't worry; it'll work out. Why wouldn't it? Your music's good, he seems to want to help the people he cares about, and he cares about you, don't you think?"

Something in her tone stung him. It was one thing to be sexually rejected by her, but quite another to be put on the defensive like this again.

"I think he cares equally about you. And you certainly showed the whole night long how much you cared about him. I've never seen you so enthusiastic."

"He's an incredible musician and a nice man. Why shouldn't I be enthusiastic? I don't think I get your point, Ray."

"There's no point. It's just that I never knew you could pursue something so relentlessly."

"That's a strange thing to say. God, Ray, I don't know that

I appreciate that. It seems a little hypocritical, too, under the circumstances."

He took a step back toward the doorway.

"How's it hypocritical?"

"I didn't leave my scores with him."

"You're not a composer."

"I didn't leave my business card either."

"So what are you saying? That it's a sin for me to try to help myself? That I shouldn't show him anything I've done and should just be a meek little music teacher in New York City the rest of my life with my humble head bent down, and never get anywhere?"

"I'm saying I think you're maybe accusing me of something you're doing yourself."

"And I'm saying you're maybe a little jealous and maybe a lot more like me than you're admitting."

He shut the door then—he didn't think he slammed it, but it made an inordinately loud noise. By the time he reached the futon, he already regretted it and realized he should apologize. How could he create such an ugly scene after she'd just poured her heart out to him and given him more hope about coming back to him than he'd had in two years? How self-destructive could he be? He should immediately apologize, but how? It suddenly seemed a difficult thing to do. He had always considered himself direct and spontaneous, but he was becoming so ineffectual and Hamlet-like. Was it this Perry business? Or maybe it had really started years ago, when he moved from Somerville to New York. But that was too painful and ridiculous to think about. In Somerville he had been a child with no conception at all about how careers were made. Somerville was about long afternoons at the piano while the other kids were out playing football or baseball. It was about summer trips to Tanglewood and dreaming about being the next Mahler. A movie a few years ago had shown how Mahler had not only gone to New

York but converted to Catholicism to help his career. Was it true? Had Mahler been forced to be a kind of refugee from himself and put in his New York years as well?

Ray walked back across the living room and knocked on her door again, and she told him to come in.

"I want to apologize. You've been exceedingly generous to let me stay here, and I was a pig to say what I said."

"I'm sorry for some of the things I said, too."

"Can I just talk to you for a minute?" Ray said.

"Sure."

"I want to explain something. There was a subtext which might explain why I acted the way I did, not only a few minutes ago, but even back at Perry's house . . . and then, of course, when I sort of attacked you in the living room."

Joy laughed. "I wouldn't say you attacked me."

"OK, I put you on the spot by making an inappropriate pass at you—one I had no reason to expect you to reciprocate. I mean, you've made it clear to me how you feel about that for a long time . . . and then, to top it off, I made you spell it all out to me about your distrust and everything."

"OK, so what's this mysterious subtext? You've more than piqued my curiosity."

"The mysterious subtext is . . . OK, I've already told you that I was a little jealous about how much you and Perry liked each other and all the attention you paid to him."

"But he isn't interested in me; you know that. Nor I in him, as any kind of love interest. How could you think that? I mean he lives with Bobby, doesn't he?"

"They don't live together."

"Well, Bobby's his lover, isn't he?"

"I suppose so."

"I would never act that way in front of you with someone I thought you might perceive as a potential romantic interest of mine. Never."

"OK, well, like I said, I was just a *little* jealous. Nothing like what I, unfortunately, used to be like at times when we were together. But the point is, and here I'm getting back to the subtext, I probably wouldn't have felt jealous at all if you'd said a word or two about me or my music to Perry. I guess I was hurt, given how important this chance is for me, that I didn't hear that."

"But I did say that."

"I don't remember."

"I said it twice. Once right after I came in. I made a remark about seeing the 'two terrific composers.'"

"I didn't catch it. I guess I was freaked out that you were late."

"Then while you were in the bathroom, I asked him if he knew any of your music. And when he said he didn't, I told him how brilliant I think it is, how versatile and innovative your music is, and how lucky I was that you'd written a couple of pieces for me. It was just easier and seemed more appropriate to say that while you were out of the room. But you should know I'd take care of you in a situation like that—and also that I meant what I said to him."

Ray bowed his head. "I owe you another apology, then. What can I say, I'm humbled and grateful and ashamed of myself for doubting you. . . . It just shows how distorted a person's perspective can become when he gets no feedback from the world about what he's doing. That you even doubt the person you love the most. . . . You know, since we broke up, things haven't gotten any easier for me professionally."

"I know that."

"And it isn't as if I haven't tried."

"You've tried very hard, I know that."

"I've sent out my tapes to Lukas Foss and Gunther Schuller and George Crumb and Paul Zukofsky and Charles Rosen and even to the goddamn Kronos Quartet. I've worked the crummy extra jobs at Xerox places and bookstores to get the money to have some of my scores printed. I've applied to Tanglewood and Aspen; I've *gone* to Tanglewood and Aspen. I've pilgrimaged to Marlboro just because of a nice letter I once got from Peter Serkin, but I never got anyone behind me who could really help."

"I know this. You've had some rotten luck, and you deserve much better. That's one of the reasons I offered to try to get you a job in Philadelphia at my school. You could still probably get something there."

"I appreciated that—I did. But I'm not talking about just money here. I'm talking about my so-called composing career. Granted, I made mistakes. I was too idealistic and too angry at Columbia and I alienated the electronic crowd. And I basically did the same thing at Juilliard."

"You're not an electronic composer or a Juilliard groupie. It's just not you."

"But I could have played my cards differently, and I didn't have to be so snobbish and stupid and ultimately alienate the downtown music crowd, too. I could have courted them, at least."

"But you don't like their music. You can't regret that you didn't pretend to be something you're not."

"The point is I'm starting to panic now. The music-world economy sucks, and I'm thirty-two years old, and I can barely afford my crummy apartment. I can barely afford to be alive."

"When we were going out, you were panicking then. You'll make it. You have a lot of will."

"That was different. That was postgraduate school–young–man–in–New York–beginning–his–life panic. It's different to panic at twenty-eight than at thirty-two."

"Granted," she said, with a little laugh.

"So now I get what looks like an opportunity, and I feel that you, who matters so much to me, somehow aren't approving of what I'm doing, even though you did put in a good word for me with Perry. But you won't say exactly why or what it is you're not approving of."

"That's not true, Ray. I was thrilled for you, and I'm rooting hard for you, too."

"But on some level you disapprove."

"I don't judge you. My life is a lot simpler. I don't have your ambitions. I'm content to just teach and sing wherever I can. I have a steady income, modest but steady. I don't care if I ever make a record. I don't care if I ever make it in New York. You know, I still like being alive."

"So you think it's wrong for me to care so much?"

"I don't judge. Just don't lose your perspective, that's all."

"You think I have?"

"No, I'm not saying anything like that. God, I don't even know why I used that word. I hate it. It's my mother's word."

There was a silence, and the floor creaked as he shuffled his feet in her doorway.

"Well, I'm sorry to have gone on like this, like a world-class whiner. And thanks for letting me cry on your shoulder."

"That's OK."

"You've been really kind. But I guess I should finally let you get some sleep."

"Yeah, tomorrow's a big day for you. You're just feeling the jitters. You'll feel a lot better in the morning, and after you see Perry, you'll feel better still. I'm sure he's going to like your stuff."

"Thanks, Joy. And again I'm sorry."

"Forget it," she said, rolling onto her side, away from him. A moment later they said good night, and he turned to walk back to his futon in the dark.

# 5

In the morning, Ray woke up feeling uneasy. He went to the bathroom, put on his pink T-shirt and black bathing suit under his pants, heard Joy walking around in the kitchen, then returned to the living room, and packed his overnight bag before saying good morning to her. While she was fixing him breakfast, he watched her carefully for signs. Clearly she was making some effort to be cheerful after last night, but her voice was still disappointingly neutral. Moreover, she avoided his eyes more often than not, something she used to do whenever he'd disappointed her.

In the car on the way to Perry's, he thanked her profusely, and she smiled spontaneously for a second. But when he proposed taking her out afterward to a farewell dinner, she quickly found a reason that she couldn't do it. He felt she wanted to avoid having an intimate situation with him so soon after all they'd said the night before. He understood that, but he couldn't help feeling so discouraged that he told her Perry had gotten Bobby to give him a ride to the bus stop, and that she needn't call for him. Then there were some awkward words, a tepid kiss on the cheek, an inscrutable smile on Joy's face before she drove off, leaving him at the iron gate to Perry's house.

"This is ridiculous," he said out loud when he discovered that the gate was locked. It took him a confused minute or so to find the buzzer and another few minutes before Bobby emerged in a pair of madras shorts and a white T-shirt to let him in. He had his characteristic smile, which Ray alternately saw as either innocent or empty. After he opened the gate, he shook hands with Ray effusively. "I'm going into town to do some shopping for Perry."

"To Stockbridge on foot?"

Bobby laughed. "I need the exercise. At least, Perry thinks so."

"Which store are you going to?"

"A lot of them, practically all of them. He has very particular tastes. But I guess exercise is a good cause."

"Well, if I'm gone before you come back, good luck to you."

Bobby's smile faded. "I'm sure I'll see you soon. Oh, by the way, Perry's in his room. He asked if he could meet you there."

"Sure," Ray mumbled.

"You can get in the house from the back." Bobby waved and smiled again, then began whistling a show tune Ray couldn't remember (unless it was supposed to be "On the Street Where You Live") as he headed down the road.

Ray walked up the stone steps cut into the front lawn, then circled around the left side of the house, where there were alternating gardens of dahlias and tiger lilies. In the backyard he stood on tiptoe to view the pool but could see just a sliver of water before he was in the house. For a moment he wondered which way to turn until he heard Perry's voice.

"Ray, is that you? Keep turning left and then turn left again."

Perry was sitting at his desk arranging papers. It was a large, airy room filled with photographs on the walls and dominated by an unmade king-size bed against the far wall. Perry rose from his chair and shook Ray's hand warmly, asking him to sit down on a green velvet chair just behind him.

"You can see I didn't make it to the pool yet."

"Did I come too early?"

"Not at all. You're as precise as ever. I just went a little overtime on my book. I'm writing about the opening of 'Orpheus.' It's kind of silly to try to put it into words, don't you think? The whole book may really be an exercise in futility, but I'm supposed to be a champion of Stravinsky. The Stravinsky Society even gave me their medal," he said, pointing to his wall, where it hung between autographed pictures of Munch and Phil Glass.

"Say, you look even more glamorous today than you did yesterday. I love your pink shirt, and your sunglasses make you look so mysterious—like Marcello Mastroianni."

Ray laughed a little, then took them off. "It is silly wearing them indoors, however," he said.

Perry studied his face. "Well, maybe you're right. You do have such expressive hazel eyes, with so much green in them that you should never hide them for long, though right now you look a little anxious. Would you like it better out by the pool?"

Ray shrugged—too boyishly, he thought.

"I think so," Perry said, still pointedly studying him. "I'll change into my suit, then, if you don't mind."

"Of course not," Ray said. He kept his eyes fixed on the photograph of Hindemith, resolving not to look at Perry for a second as he fumbled out of his pants, then took off his own pants so that he was only wearing his T-shirt and bathing suit.

"I looked at your stuff last night. Seems pretty interesting to me. I like the flute against the drums in the waltz section."

Ray waited to hear more, but all he heard was the sound of Perry changing clothes. Finally, he said, "Thank you."

"You look a little sad, but now that I know you're a composer it makes sense, I suppose. That's a good enough reason to be sad."

Ray turned and looked at him. Perry was wearing a baggy navy-blue bathing suit and a white polo shirt. He looked short and a little tired. At least he doesn't try to look young, Ray thought. That was also not the Perry Green style.

"May I keep your pieces a little longer so I can try to understand them better?"

"Of course."

"I get the feeling that I've disappointed you somehow. I hope not, of course. I liked a good bit of what I saw."

"Oh no. I'm very grateful. Anything you say means a lot to me."

"Tell me the truth, Ray. Do you really want to be a famous composer?"

"Only if my work deserves it."

"That's a good answer. The problem is so many people think their work does. It's curious why people chase so hard after public fame when they can make *each other* feel famous so easily."

"How do they do that?" Ray said, feeling as if everything else in the world had receded from him except their conversation.

"Why through love, of course. But people hold back so stupidly. It's a tragedy, really."

"But you're famous. You're famous all over the world. Are you the exception to the rule?"

"I never expected it. I did hope for it at a certain time in my life, and I did do things to help my cause, but I never compromised myself, I don't think. At least not too badly," he said, laughing. "I haven't, at any rate, been as lucky in my pursuit of private fame. I think you have a much better chance of getting public fame than I do of getting my private one."

"Why's that?"

"I think it's very obvious why. You're young and crushingly handsome and you have drive and talent, and I'm getting older, my energy's petering out, and I just feel my chances dwindling all the time," he said, looking deeply, almost incriminatingly, Ray thought, into his eyes.

"Let me ask you one more question, Ray," Perry said as he took another step toward him. Ray had gotten up from his chair as well; they were now standing a few feet from each other in the middle of the room. "Do you think of your life as a challenge or a disappointment?"

He thought of Joy and of his tiny apartment on the Upper West Side.

"Both probably."

"Touché. Well, then, do you consider yourself disappointed with your life so far? That's a better way to put it."

He felt that he had never loved anyone but Joy happily, and that had only lasted two years and might never happen again. He felt that he'd never accomplished even one of his career goals.

"It's fair to say I'm somewhat disappointed so far. So where does that leave us?"

"How rarely are absolutes attained, how valuable are compromises," Perry said, smiling. "You see, I've always believed the way to avoid disappointments is not to expect absolute victories in either love or work. Take solace in small victories whenever you can. You can believe they're real at least. That's why they call the other fantasies or dreams."

Ray stopped himself from making a joke about Perry philosophizing so much. "But you've gotten so much success, you've realized your dreams."

"Ah, you can't be too sure about what I've gotten. You'd have to know what I wanted first. For instance, I'm not going to get you the way I want, am I?"

Perry's lips trembled as he asked his question. Ray

stared at them and at the moisture that had gathered above his upper lip.

"No, I guess not."

"And maybe you had hopes that I could make you famous, but I can't. It's really beyond my power. So much for absolutes. On the other hand, I could lend a hand here and there, help you out a bit every now and then. I think you're very bright and just tremendously attractive."

"And what could I do for you in light of what I just said?"

"The pleasure of your occasional company is the main thing. Small things. No absolutes. Can I, for example, give your back a massage now?"

"Here?"

"Don't look so mistrustful. I mean literally what I said. A back rub; that's all. Just lie down on my bed. You don't even have to take off your shirt if you don't want to."

Ray looked up for a moment at the rows of autographed pictures on the walls. He realized that this weekend was just another illusion, that Joy was really through with him, and that Perry was not going to help his career—unless he cooperated. But how could he?

"Well, Ray, are you going to grant me my request?"

"You just want to rub my back for a few minutes?"

"Yes, Ray, I do."

It didn't feel real, like he was shocking himself without knowing why, but he walked toward Perry's bed and lay down on his stomach, a green velvet pillow propping up his head. He suddenly doubted that Perry would be satisfied with just a back rub, suddenly felt the inevitability of his situation, and wondered why he hadn't thought more about it before. It was his despair about Joy, perhaps, but thinking about that would do no good now. Besides, things still might be saved as long as he thought quickly and carefully. He remembered the stories he'd heard throughout Juilliard about this kind of thing. A couple of times students had even told him about their own experiences in a bragging way. But they had been gay and much younger than he was now, and even if they weren't, what did it matter what happened to other people? This was his life, and this was happening to him or would happen unless he put a clear stop to it.

Perry's touch, under his shirt, was surprisingly strong and skillful, and so far he was sticking to the rules. When he thought about who Perry was—a truly world-famous musician, rubbing his back and trying to please him—it was, even, vaguely pleasurable. The key was being sure he stuck to the agreement, for Perry had said he would help him, hadn't he, and Ray didn't think he was lying.

"These hands have played duets with Heifetz and Hindemith," Perry said softly. "You shouldn't find them so repulsive. On the contrary, you should find them at least somewhat interesting. After all, they can make a hundred men sit down and play beautiful music. How does it feel to have them rub your back?"

Ray said nothing. He certainly wasn't going to say anything that might excite Perry, though he worried that if he stayed silent much longer he might seem too passive. "You're very good at it."

"Ah, and I'll get better yet. You merely have to tell me what you like and I'll adjust."

Ray closed his eyes and tried to focus on the pleasant physical feeling alone. For the next few minutes, the only sound he heard was that of his skin being rubbed. It sounded like the lake lapping up against the sand. Then he started to wonder when he should end it and how. He certainly didn't want to do it in such a way as to destroy what he'd already accomplished, for Perry had definitely said he'd help him, and though they were just words, that still had to count for something.

Suddenly, with no sign except for his slightly heightened

breathing, Perry's hands began moving down Ray's body. For a few seconds he simply felt the warm hands on his buttocks, his thighs, and then his genitals, without saying anything.

"What's happening? What are you doing?" he finally said, turning his head.

"I'm being naughty," Perry said in a husky voice. "If you'll let me." Perry removed his hand from the base of Ray's penis but kept a hand on each of his thighs.

"We didn't agree to this," Ray said, staring at the pale green wall again that looked white now in the strange light. "I can't do this."

"I thought we just agreed to help each other."

"I can't. . . . Aren't you afraid of AIDS?" he blurted. He wanted to sound angry and definitive, but it sounded more like an infant's anger than an adult's.

"I have a condom. I'm a prudent man. I, too, want to live as long as possible."

"No. I can't do this. I never have."

"I can see that. But I find you utterly irresistible. Let me just rub against your back then. No penetration, I promise. I'll do it with the condom on, so your back won't feel a single drop. OK?"

Ray shook his head no but said nothing. Finally he said, "Can't you just jerk off?"

Perry laughed. "You're a tough negotiator. But an exciting one. OK. Let's compromise. I'll rub against you just a little. It will feel just like a cat's tail against your skin."

"I hate cats."

"OK, then, a dog. Think of me as your little dog, OK? My condom is on now and nothing can possibly happen to either of us."

Ray said nothing, kept still. I've already said no, he thought, so in a way he's commiting rape or some kind of crime, something that will inhibit him, keep him from breaking the agreement again. He closed his eyes. He had a fear of seeing either Perry's face or his own, afraid his mind might record either image forever.

He could hear, or thought he could, the slight, persistent sound of Perry touching himself, drowned out periodically by his heavy rush of breathing. Then he felt Perry's weight on him and barely fought back the urge to throw him off with one violent push. He closed his eyes and tried to imagine it was Joy's weight he was feeling—after all, their weight was about the same. For a minute, it seemed to work, and he even felt a slight erection until he saw the look Perry gave him last night by the porch—that love-found look—and he felt a shiver of repulsion and outrage run through him, though the impulse to hurl him against the wall was less powerful this time, like a mild aftershock of an earthquake.

How long would this take, he wondered, given Perry's age? He couldn't stand it much longer—he would scream at him or really hit him no matter how old he was. Perry was panting now, rubbing himself all wrapped in plastic against the bare skin of his lower back and almost crying, it seemed, as he came in a couple of quick, spastic, doglike thrusts.

The weight was removed. There was silence and he opened his eyes. He saw the blank wall in front of him but still didn't turn around. He told himself that if he left in a rage, he'd destroy everything, but if he bartered right away, it could be effective; there would never be a better time for making some of his own demands than right now.

"Thank you, Ray," he heard a softly earnest voice say. "Thank you very much."

Instinctively, he rubbed his hand over his back, but it was dry. He noticed that his other hand was shaking and tried to stop it.

"I'm sorry if I lost control a little, Ray. I am sorry," he

heard Perry say in a thin wavering voice, floating toward him ghostlike from the other side of the room.

"Don't worry about it," he said, his own voice more fluttery than he wanted. To compensate, he forced himself to turn around. He saw Perry looking genuinely sad and vulnerable behind his glasses. He was wearing his underpants and a shirt.

"Are you angry?"

Ray shook his head. "I don't know what I am."

"Are you feeling bad?"

Ray tucked in his shirt and stood up. He was trying to focus on what Perry would do for him. He would not, could not, come out of this with nothing.

"I'm feeling eager."

"Eager?" Perry said, quizzically. For once he seemed off guard.

"To see what happens next."

"A lot of that's up to you, Ray. I don't know how you feel."

"Really? I thought it was up to you." He forced himself to look directly at Perry until he was sure Perry understood.

"Of course I'm going to help you to the extent I can, if that's what you mean. . . . What exactly I can do is another question. You mustn't exaggerate my powers in your mind. Lots of people do. But my powers are limited. I'm an old man, not a god. There's only so much I can do, and I won't do more than I can."

Perry sounded as close to angry as Ray had heard him when he spoke his last line. Was it heartfelt or a mere tactic? Ray gambled it was the latter, said nothing, and aimed his gaze directly at Perry, again.

"Excuse me, Ray. I need to get rid of this," Perry said, indicating the condom he was holding in his left hand. Ray hadn't noticed it before and felt a quiver of rage as Perry left the room. He mustn't think about that, of course; anger, like self-pity, was a useless emotion now except to the extent that it could keep him focused on his agenda. For the first time it was unclear who was actually controlling the situation. It was his first glimpse of Perry on the defensive and so critical now that he concentrate on his situation and not think about what had just happened in bed.

He heard a toilet flush. A few seconds later Perry walked back into the room with his pants on and a concerned look in his eyes.

"Sit down, Ray, will you?"

Ray sat in the blue velvet chair, but Perry remained standing, pacing a little while he spoke, ten feet in front of him.

"I was thinking about your situation and maybe there's something I can do. I can't promise anything, but I could make some calls, although it's very late, absurdly late, but I think I might be able to get you a Tanglewood fellowship, if you're interested."

Ray tried not to show his excitement. Of course, under normal circumstances he would jump at it. He had tried before several times and never gotten one, but now it would place him too near Perry for the whole summer, and who knew what he'd expect then?

"I appreciate that; normally I'd say yes in a second, but I have a part-time teaching job, two actually, and I don't want to lose them."

"But getting a fellowship would look very good on your resume and help you get a better job, I would think."

"I know that but . . ."

"And wouldn't your schools understand?"

"I've committed to a school, and classes for the summer session start in a week. I count on that. There are also my private students, who are counting on me to be there."

"Couldn't you commute from Tanglewood to your school and pupils—work out something along those lines?"

"It would be hard. My life is a delicate coalition of different sources of money, and I think it probably always will be. I don't have a doctorate or a body of performed work, so I'm not really thinking about getting tenured at a university anymore. I've accepted that I'm going to have to have these different part-time jobs, and I'm going to have to hustle pupils and be punctual and always be there for them for the foreseeable future. But thanks for the offer, it is generous of you, but as far as the fellowship goes, the only part of it that really matters to me would be getting my work performed. I mean, at this stage, building an academic resume isn't a top priority. It's getting my work performed and maybe reviewed. That's all that matters. You can understand that, can't you?"

"But if you were a fellow, your work *would* be performed. And if people talked it up, it would get reviewed. There are other people besides me who could help you at Tanglewood, too. And I could help you meet them. I could tell them how special you are."

Ray bristled. Was Perry suggesting that Ray would even consider doing something with any other man?

"Could I think about it? It's hard to think clearly right now."

"I wish you would think about it overnight and let me know. By the way, what are your plans for tonight?"

"I have to go back to New York."

"Are you going with Joy?"

"No. She's here for the summer. I thought I told you that."

"Perhaps you did."

"She lives in Philadelphia, anyway."

"Does that mean more commuting for you?"

"What do you mean?"

"To see her."

"I told you we're just friends, platonic friends."

"But you were lovers once, weren't you?"

Ray smiled thinly. "You're very perceptive. Yes, long ago and far away. What does it matter?"

"You were New York lovers."

"Yes . . . that's true. We were. By the way, what about Bobby—what kind of relationship do you have with him?"

"Do you really care about that?"

"I do now."

"What is it that you want to know?" Perry sat down in the green velvet chair and turned his head at a slight angle toward the magic wall of photographs.

"Are you sleeping with him?"

"I'm not sure that's a legitimate question."

"I think it's very legitimate under the circumstances."

"OK. Fine. We sleep together. There's a sexual part to our friendship, occasionally. But we're friends first. We don't have such hard and fast rules as you do, perhaps, in your relationships."

"What I'm asking you is what kind of understanding do you have with him? How would he feel about what just happened with us?"

"To the extent that you thrilled me, and you did, I hope he'd be happy for me. He might also feel a little concerned for you, as I do, too."

"So does he sleep with other people, too?"

"He says he doesn't, and Bobby always tells me the truth."

"So basically you can do whatever you want, and he's faithful to you."

"He can do whatever he wants to as long as he does it safely—staying alive being the greatest good, as I said before. And by the way I'll be happy to show you both of our negative AIDS tests."

"And how many other lovers do you have?"

"None at all, as I was complaining to you before. Of course, if you became my lover you'd be the only one."

"What about Bobby?"

"I'd be willing to give up that part of my relationship with him while I was with you. . . . But you look so frightened and disturbed when I say that, that I think I'm probably being terribly presumptuous."

Ray looked at the floor. He noticed that his left hand was shaking again.

"I have an idea," Perry announced brightly. "Why don't we go swimming in the pool? Or take a walk to the lake? That might be even more fun."

"I have to get going. I have to go to the bus stop."

"But you've just gotten here. You can't leave now."

"It's been a short stay but a momentous one, wouldn't you say?" Ray said with a smile.

"This is all because of the back rub, I assume."

"I need to think about things, that's all."

"You can think here; we can think together about how to help you."

"I need to think alone."

"You could go to the lake. It's not a long walk, or I could drive you there."

"Look, this was a big thing for me."

"For me too."

"I've never done anything even remotely like this, and I need to think about it, alone in my home."

Perry nodded, and the smile went out of his eyes. "Do you know when the next bus leaves?"

"I have a schedule."

"How are you going to get to the bus stop?"

"Call a cab. Hitch a ride. Walk."

"You silly man. Handsome and dashing, but silly. I'll drive you, of course."

"Thank you. That's kind of you."

"Ray, I am kind. I hope you realize that and also how fond of you I am."

Ray nodded. Perry tied his shoes, looked for and found his sunglasses, absentmindedly pulled a comb across his thin silver-gray hair.

"Do you want to go now, this moment?"

"Yes, if that's OK."

"Follow me then."

They went out the front door, Perry walking over the grass while Ray walked on the stones cut into the lawn. A white jeep and a blue limousine-sized Lincoln were parked in a gravel driveway, and Perry took the Lincoln.

Ray felt the grip of a vague but persistent anxiety as the hills and trees passed by, sometimes parting enough for a glimpse of the lake. They were quiet at first, but then a conversation about contemporary composers developed. Perry said that he thought Pärt was overrated but that he liked John Corigliano, although he thought he was overrated, too. Then Perry asked Ray to tell him about his students and laughed sympathetically as Ray described their various musical deficiencies.

A half block before the stop in Stockbridge, he pulled the car over underneath a maple tree.

"I shall miss you, Ray, and I will hope to see you again soon. Meanwhile I'll be thinking of just what I can do to make your situation better."

Ray said nothing to that, but a few seconds later thanked Perry for looking at his scores.

"I'd like to keep them a few days longer before I return them, if that's all right."

"Sure."

"Well . . . just give me a hug before you get out of the car. I don't expect you to kiss me yet."

Ray obliged and for a moment felt strangely touched to have the old conductor in his arms.

# 6

His thinking didn't begin until he was back in his apartment. Thoughtless, dreamless, he felt the bus ride had been almost abstract, except that he had read a newspaper, one article after another, remembering just a tiny percentage of what he read. It was in bed in his apartment that images from his weekend with Perry began repeating themselves. He saw Perry pointing to their feet at the bottom of the pool, saying, "They look identical. That must mean we're twins." He saw himself pacing from the diving board to the patio table thinking about Mahler as a pine needle drifted by. Then Bobby's innocent, loopy smile as he stood over him at the side of the pool, heard his softly admiring voice say, "He's amazing. . . . Perry can move like a dancer or a burglar when he wants to." Heard Bobby giggle as Perry said, "Don't forget to pick up the dill pickles and the couscous." Saw Bobby wave to him on his way to shop at Stockbridge while he stood before Perry's iron gate, then saw the photographs in Perry's room—of Hindemith, Casals, and Shostakovich; of Heifetz, Copland, Bernstein, and Stravinsky—all shimmering on those ever-enlarging walls. And then the green velvet chair, the blue velvet chair. Perry and he standing in the middle of the room, the drops of perspiration so out of place above Perry's upper lip, so surreally out of place on any part of Perry, as he said, "I'm not going to get you the way I want, am I?"

Of the act itself he had few memories, but they repeated themselves mercilessly—the blank wall he stared at while Perry fondled him, Perry's disembodied voice saying, "I'm being naughty. If you'll let me," the desire to throw him off his body, against the wall, which he was barely able to suppress, Perry's humble thank you afterward, then the vulnerable look in his aging eyes—the half-humorous, half-pathetic line, "I don't expect you to kiss me yet," as they hugged in his limousine-sized car.

How had it all happened? Had he wanted it to in some unconscious way? He tried to remember exactly what he felt emotionally toward Perry before the incident in his room. Mostly he'd felt a mixture of awe, admiration, and anxiety, a desire to please him with every remark or response he made (all elements that Perry took advantage of). But given Perry's stature and how he'd admired him his whole life, that seemed normal enough. It was true that while they talked at Arnold's party and a couple of times at Perry's house, he'd felt an exhilaration, a sense of the rest of the world disappearing, that he'd never felt before—but then he'd never met anyone with a status in the world, *his* world, like Perry's, who also talked with him in such an intimate way. And by the pool when he admired Perry's physique and diving ability? But he'd admired lots of men's physiques and athletic abilities without thinking of having sex with any of them. No man had ever touched his penis since he and a couple of his eleven-year-old friends goosed each other as a joke. Even in the few circle jerks he was part of as a kid, no one dreamed of touching each other: the whole point was to have others witness how effectively you could touch yourself.

He got up, turned on his light, walked to his window and then back into the bathroom where he swallowed an Ativan.

Then he turned the TV on low (the walls were thin and he didn't want to disturb his next-door neighbor, whose name he still didn't know). There were many late nights and especially early mornings when that neighbor disturbed him. At first he thought he was just inconsiderate or drugged out until he realized it was because he was living in a kind of acoustic hell. For instance, he could hear every word on his next-door neighbor's answering machine. When the phone rang in his neighbor's apartment, he often reached for his own. As a result, despite the compliments from Grandma Love, he only played his piano softly and in the middle of the afternoon. He felt that every sound he made must be hideously amplified. The acoustics inhibited him in countless other ways, as well.

Finally he fell asleep for an hour. Just before he woke up he dreamed he was playing Parcheesi with Joy, Bryna, and a third, older woman he didn't recognize. When it was his turn to play, his father suddenly joined the game, shook the dice, and sent his son's pieces back to their starting point. The next thing Ray knew he was in a different room and unable to return to the game, although he could still hear it being played.

After waking from the dream, he couldn't sleep. His goal was only to stop the pictures of Joy that kept repeating themselves as soon as he regained consciousness—languorous, erotic, unreachable images—as if she were the sole representative of a world he had once luxuriated in and now had been banished from. He saw himself standing outside Joy's room, heard the floor creaking in the dark, saw himself shifting feet and the floor creaking again under his weight while she talked to him in bed and he wanted her. He saw her put a hand on the hip of her white dress and say, "Haven't you gotten everything you've wanted?"

Better not to remember those scenes. If he was to think about Joy, better to remember the time when they both lived in New York and spent part of some afternoons in bed having sex, as perfect as he had ever had it, where anything seemed possible as they explored every opening of each other's body over and over, not even talking, not even asking permission. . . . But this was also too painful to remember on the night after he'd let an old man come on his back, the same old man who had possibly doomed his chance of getting Joy back. Because how could he tell her about Perry, yet how could he lie to her? No, it was best not to think of Joy at all right now, though he found himself missing her horribly. Several times he had seriously thought of calling her on one pretext or another, but what could that pretext be at one in the morning, especially with a new tension between them? Wouldn't she correctly see that as another example of his self-indulgence at her expense? Sending her a letter would be better, but knowing what to say was hard. Nevertheless he eventually wrote a first-draft letter of apology and gratitude.

He began putting his clothes on—a green shirt close to the color of his eyes and gray pants—different clothes than he wore in the Berkshires. He had given up on the possibility of falling asleep and knew he didn't have the concentration to compose or even to watch TV. On the way out, he said hello to the Glenn Gould doorman, who didn't answer him, of course. This time Ray was sure he was asleep. Outside, he turned at the first light and walked across Duke Ellington Boulevard, heading up Broadway. For a moment he considered sitting on a bench at the little park on 106th Street, but the men sitting there looked too sad and desperate. Instead, he walked toward Columbia, struck again by how gentrified it had become. The West End, the bar where Ginsberg used to meet with Burroughs, was now an ersatz European-style café. Everywhere were clothing stores and nouvelle cuisine food markets and brightly painted grotesque awnings. A sign in a window proclaimed WE MAKE PARTY PLAT-TERS. The old neighborhood was actually trying to become quaint. A big mistake aesthetically, but times were desperate economically, and businesspeople couldn't screw around with aesthetics, of course, as a composer would; they had to follow the dollars.

The next thing he knew he was approaching the Columbia subway stop and only then realized that he was going to see Bryna. It's another case of my feet knowing what's best for me before I do, he thought with a smile. Then he called her from a pay phone on the street. It rang five times before she answered.

"Bryna, can you forgive me for calling this late?"

"Ray? Yes, of course. So, how are you?"

"Not so good."

"How did it go in the Berkshires?"

"Not completely the way I'd hoped. I was wondering . . ."

"Do you want to come over and tell me about it?"

"Sure, if I could."

"Of course."

"I'm at One Hundred Sixteenth Street. I'll be there in thirty minutes."

On the downtown train to Spring Street, a sickly yellow light filled the car, making the other passengers look like zombies, Ray thought as he turned away from them. He thought about Bryna. He had an odd relationship with her. She was ten years older than he and had been his freshman composition teacher at Columbia. She was a good teacher, too, intense, enthusiastic, and warm, though nothing outside the normal teacher-student relationship had ever happened then. But a few months after Joy broke up with him, he met Bryna at a SoHo loft party. She seemed ecstatic to see him, claimed to have followed his career through the grapevine and the alumni news and to be his biggest fan. "And probably my only one," he'd added. She'd chided him for his "absurd modesty" and told him he was "fantastically talented." She seemed so sincerely enthusiastic to see him that Ray kept talking to her. She'd been through a baffling and extraordinary series of personal transformations. She'd moved to Israel, married an Israeli artist, and lived on a kibbutz. She'd gotten divorced, renounced the kibbutz and Orthodox Judaism (then later embraced her "own style of Judaism"), and moved back to the States. She lived in Berkeley for a while, then traveled cross-country and wound up experimenting with LSD in a commune in Vermont, where she "shed the last vestiges of her constricting self-doubt" and became an artist. Meanwhile, her parents had died within a year of each other, and she'd inherited some money with which she bought her loft. Incredibly, in a short time she'd established a reputation as a performance artist in New York, though Ray secretly felt disdainful of her work. They ended up sleeping together that night of the SoHo party—and several times subsequently. Whenever neither was involved with anyone else and both wanted to was their agreement. He always thought of her much more as a friend than as a lover, and always worried that she didn't think the same of him.

Bryna's enormous loft was at the top of a three-floor building on Wooster Street. He could only get to her loft by riding an elevator that seemed to move in slow motion, making the three floors seem like thirty. When he finally reached her floor, she was waiting for him in a purple bathrobe and Reeboks—her long dark hair mostly uncombed, and wearing little if any makeup except for a slash of purple lipstick. As soon as they disengaged from their typically ambiguous hug, she said, "I want to prepare you for a surprise, you bum."

"Why am I a bum—I mean besides the fact that I'm poor and a failure?"

"You're a bum because you only see me when you feel you have no other alternatives."

"That's not true."

"And you never come to my loft anymore. Never mind, I've got a surprise for you now that I've finally got you here."

"What's that?"

"You know me as a performance artist, right? The surprise is I've been doing nothing but sculpture the last two months. When you were over before, they still weren't ready to show."

She opened the door to her loft and turned on a series of large fluorescent lights. Ray walked in and saw some forty different sculptures of sheep in front of him. Some were on the floor in various positions, some were suspended from the ceiling as if they were floating, others were attached to the wall, and a few, apparently still being worked on, were spread out on a long table. Ray didn't think they had anything to do with art.

"So, what do you think of my flock?"

"They're really something." He saw her disappointment, so he walked up to one of the suspended sheep and examined it closely, running his fingers over the material. The sheep was life-size and expressed a maudlin kind of anguish.

"It's stunning," he said in what he hoped was a convincing voice.

"Believe me, it takes a lot of work to be stunning. I have two part-time assistants who help me tack on the wool and do the spray painting. There are forty-two sheep in my flock already; I've been doing about one a day, and now I'm starting to do black sheep."

She pointed to a sofa he hadn't noticed, and he saw one of her black sheep standing by it like a soldier. When he thought about what this all must have cost, he couldn't help feeling envious.

"It must be pretty expensive to buy all the materials."

"Don't talk to me about expensive. The project's cost over ten thousand so far, but what can I do?" She made a gesture of resignation.

"I thought you were committed to performance pieces."

"I still am. I was at Performing Artists' Space a week ago. You were invited, but you didn't come, you bum."

"Sorry, it's the first performance of yours I've missed in quite a while."

"See, I'm expanding not abandoning. New York knows me as a performance artist now, but soon they'll get to know me as a sculptor, too."

She took him by the arm and led him to a sofa in the center of the large loft, sitting next to him.

"So what do you think, Ray? Do you think Leo Castelli will buy them for his gallery?"

He couldn't tell if she was joking and wound up shrugging.

"Well, somebody better, 'cause I don't want to show in one of the cooperatives again or I'll lose another small fortune."

"It's funny—I'd expect to see a lot of religious imagery in your pieces, but I guess a sheep *is* a religious symbol," Ray said. He was all too familiar with having to pay to have performances of his own work done and wanted to change the subject.

"I have a few paintings and some prints from my days in Israel. I have the Star of David over my bed. That's about it. Jewishness is a state of mind; it doesn't really need images. But tell me about your own state of mind. How did things work out with Perry Green?"

He felt a tightness in his stomach and knew instantly that he couldn't tell her.

"I'm hopeful something nice might come out of it, even though things could have gone better."

Bryna raised her eyebrows and smiled knowingly. "I'm impressed. He's the Godfather of the music biz, am I right?"

"The classical music biz, yes, he's one of them."

"Congratulations. He could do a lot to help you."

Ray nodded and looked away for a moment.

"Perry Green . . . he's gay, isn't he?"

"That's what people say."

"You better be careful."

"What do you mean by that?"

"Be careful he understands that *you're* not gay, that you're as ungay as they come. You don't want any misunderstandings like that to screw up your relationship."

"Don't worry," Ray said, but he was suddenly feeling anxious, as if she'd already sensed what had happened. "Do you think I could have a drink, Bryna? I'm feeling a . . . "

"Of course. I should have offered before."

She walked to a far corner of the loft where there was a stove, a refrigerator, and a table. A miniature white sheep with a clownlike smile stood on top of her refrigerator.

"I can't offer you a great variety. You wouldn't want any sherry or bourbon, you wouldn't want a beer?"

He was about to say yes when she offered him a scotch, and he said that would be fine. While she fixed his drink, he thought about how he wanted to tell her what happened with Perry, but his desire for sex was stronger, and to do the former might well make the latter impossible.

She returned holding his drink.

"Thanks. Aren't you going to drink with me?"

"I thought I'd smoke a little, if that's OK?"

"Sure," he said as she withdrew a joint and lighter from a vase on the table. This signaled that she wanted to have sex with him, since she often smoked pot before they made love. It was going the way he'd hoped, but he felt nervous, as if because of the episode with Perry he was forever altered in a way he couldn't yet understand. He tried to block out such thoughts as he drank, but they came anyway. What if in the middle of it all, he flashed back to Perry and broke down, started yelling at Bryna or just started sobbing uncontrollably? What if he was not able to perform at all? He tried to project himself into a sexual situation with her but felt only an immovable softness between his legs.

"You look like you're having a serious line of thought, but

maybe it's a line you want to keep private? You know I hate being a buttinsky."

"Sorry. They were just career thoughts."

"I know it's an important time for you, and this business with Perry must be very exciting. I just hope in all the excitement you can focus on me a little. It's been a long time, Ray."

"Nobody new for you on the horizon?"

She smiled. "Not even much of a horizon."

"I'm sorry."

"Please," she said, gesturing with her hand and smiling enough to reveal a slightly chipped front tooth. "As you can see," she used both hands to indicate her loft full of sheep, "I haven't exactly been pining away, but on the other hand, I'm more than pleased to see you."

"It's good to see you, too."

"And I hope, even though you've caught me without my face on and I look every one of my forty-two years, I hope you might like to stay the night or at least spend some time with me."

She extended her free hand and he held it. Her eyes were dark, vulnerable, looking right at him.

"Could I have some of that joint?"

"Of course. Why don't you finish it and I'll start another."

When she came back to the sofa with the new joint in her mouth, she'd untied her bathrobe. He saw her dark-nippled breasts, disproportionately large on her five-foot-two-inch body. He'd always told her they excited him, but they only did when he was in certain moods. He inhaled deeply. If he smoked enough, his body would take over, and he might get excited by her breasts again, be able to reclaim his place on the board from which he'd been expelled in his dream.

Soon she was leading him by the hand across the dark loft, which felt soft underfoot, like a meadow. Climbing the stairs to her room, he felt possessed by a longing for Joy. The only way to save the situation was to imagine it was Joy's tongue that was now in his mouth, Joy whose hands were caressing all parts of his body, and who was moaning beneath him as their bodies locked into position, kissing him wildly and speaking to him in her thrilling soprano singer's voice.

# 7

I t was night, and he realized he couldn't remember with any confidence what he'd done the last few days. When he tried to visualize them it was like watching the turning of clothes in a washing machine—nothing seen clearly though he roughly knew the contents. Hour after hour of teaching elementary harmony at the school or of listening to his private students (a divorced woman in her fifties, an accountant whom he sometimes thought was gay, a widow in her sixties, et cetera) butcher the "Contradance" or the "Mikrokosmos." He didn't think at all during the days. He couldn't think while he was teaching and he still wasn't able to compose. A number of times he almost called Joy or Bryna, who had left him a couple of messages, but ultimately decided not to. Instead, he finished and mailed his thank-you/apology letter, and when his parents called he spoke to them for as short a time as possible. He felt he needed all his psychic energy to get through his classes and lessons. He had to pay the rent, after all; he had to eat.

But at night he'd pace his studio or lie in bed trying to comprehend his situation, trying to figure out what to do next. For four nights in a row, for example, he thought about the Tanglewood fellowship that Perry had dangled in front of him.

Of course, there were many reasons to take it. The college could be made to understand—he was only an adjunct and taught there just one afternoon a week—and his private students could understand and reschedule, too. Besides, as Perry had said, the fellowship could lead to jobs at better schools and to much else. Everything Perry had said was clearly, obviously true. He had known that at the time, too, though he'd pretended otherwise. But he also knew what it meant if he lived two miles away during the whole summer. He'd owe him everything then, and there would be no excuse not to see him and eventually be expected to service him again. Geography was his ally, and in New York he was just far enough away.

Even if he changed his mind about the fellowship, it was probably too late, and Perry might not want to go through with it anymore or want to see him again, for all he knew. Perhaps Perry was already fantasizing about someone new he'd spotted at Tanglewood Beach or in Stockbridge, and he was already yesterday's news. There was no way to know what to expect from Perry—there had been nothing but silence from Tanglewood all week long. Still, he hadn't gotten his pieces back, and as long as he hadn't, he could still call him if he wanted. But what could he say and how should he act? He grit his teeth in anger as he realized that the fellowship *was* his chance, that he was going to come out of this with nothing to show for his humiliation.

Well, at least he hadn't made him an enemy, and Perry would remember his name for a while, a voice in his mind said, but it was overruled by the stronger voice that said, No, you've gotten nothing from all of this, absolutely nothing. You're back where you started from, only with a lower opinion of yourself.

He decided that he had to call someone. He thought of Joy but couldn't bear the thought that she might not want to hear from him. Instead, he phoned Bryna, who answered on the first ring, as if she'd been expecting him.

"Where are you? Are you in SoHo?"

"No, I'm at home."

"I was starting to wonder if I was ever going to hear from you again."

"I'm sorry. I should have called you back sooner."

"It's OK. I'd understand under normal circumstances, but after we have sex I get a little paranoid if you don't return my call."

"Again, I'm sorry. It's been a pretty bad time for me."

"So what happened? How are things going with Perry Green?"

"I don't really want to get into it. Let's just say it hasn't gone as I'd hoped."

"Is he going to conduct any of your pieces?"

"Not exactly. I didn't get what I wanted from him, and I probably never will. Can we leave it at that?"

"Of course we can leave it at that. I'm sorry to hear it."

"Thanks, I appreciate that. So what's going on with you? Is it too late for me to see you tonight?"

"It's not too late. It's not too late at all, but I want to talk about something before you come over."

"Go ahead."

"I feel funny saying this, and maybe a little self-destructive, too, but I don't want to have sex with you tonight and maybe not for a while, OK?"

"Why's that?"

"Look, I know you didn't do anything wrong, and I know about our agreement, and I know we're supposed to have this honest, sophisticated relationship, but after the last time when you didn't call me—even though it's only been four or five days—I started to feel really vulnerable, which I know is what we said we were never going to feel, but still I felt lonely and needy and rejected and all that crap, and I started thinking maybe I need to protect myself more, at least for a while, and not set myself up to be hurt this way, which has been happening lately when I sleep with you. So what do you think?"

"Sure, I understand. Though it's a little strange to hear this coming from you."

"I know. I know. I'm supposed to be this tough avant-garde performance artist, unpuritanical as can be, who just looks at sex as one of life's pleasures for the taking. But let's face it. I'm also full of shit and at my age there's not much future in being full of shit."

Ray laughed. "I guess not." He knew it would take a lot of arguing and effort to change her mind and didn't feel up to it, or even that it was right to try.

"So I hope I haven't added to your depression."

"No. Well, I mean yes, I do love making love with you," Ray said, suddenly touched in spite of himself, "but I can't pretend I don't know what you're saying. I mean, it all makes sense."

"So we'll still be friends, you'll still call and see me. We'll still drink beer at Fanelli's and so forth."

"Of course. No doubt about it."

"I hope I haven't added to your troubles."

That's exactly what you've done, Ray thought angrily. But he controlled himself quickly. He knew what Bryna was doing now—speaking from the part of herself that was insecure, giving him the chance to either wound or temporarily assuage her troubled ego. He had to be careful; it was a complicated situation, more difficult than it at first appeared. "I'm going to miss that part of our relationship a lot."

"Thank you."

"I don't have anybody else."

"You will."

"You've always had more confidence in me than I've had in myself, professionally and romantically."

She laughed. "Just trust me. You might have to be a little patient, but you will."

"What about you? Do you have someone in mind?"

"In my mind I have thoughts you wouldn't believe. My mind is relentlessly pornographic. In reality there isn't anyone I could even go out with right now. But remember I didn't say this was for all time. I might feel differently a month from now or even two weeks. I want you to remember that, OK?"

"Sure. Of course I'll remember, and I'll ask again, hopefully without begging too much."

She laughed.

"So there's really no possibility at all with anyone else?"

"There's one guy who works at a gallery who's gone to my performances. And he's sort of asked me out for drinks, you know, a halfhearted New York horny guy's date, but I happened to find out—because he told me—that he used to be bisexual, so I had to rule him out. I mean, I'm sorry, but I can't sleep with someone who used to sleep with men."

"Even if he tested negative?"

"He told me that, too, worked it right into the conversation. But no, I know myself, I'm just too scared of AIDS. But at least I respect him for telling me."

Ray felt himself shudder. Was she speaking in some kind of code because she somehow sensed what had happened at Tanglewood? He covered himself with a couple of jokes but got off the phone quickly, went into the bathroom and took an Ativan, then put on Prokofiev's first violin concerto and lay down.

To lie down was to drift, was to be visited by ghosts that came most often in the form of Joy—emissary from the world of women from which he still felt expelled. Or it was to regret decisions he made at Columbia, and Juilliard, and beyond.

The other choice was to get up, to not think or regret at all, but to move automatically through the world of New York robots. It was to get his food, do his laundry, read the papers, take the train or the bus to his New York or New Jersey pupils. It was to stare straight ahead at anything, at the other robots or the train's graffiti, or a slice of the river as the bus went by. At the lessons he tried to humanize himself. He couldn't tell if the pupils sensed his effort. He was also afraid to hear the music they played, for even though they often littered their Bartók or Debussy with mistakes, a chord sequence or semibutchered arpeggio alone could set him back to his drifting state, to days at the beach with Joy or to pine needles floating in Tanglewood.

The phone rang. He turned off his CD and answered on the second ring, hoping it was Joy.

"Ray, how are you? It's Perry."

"I'm all right," he said, feeling an odd combination of intense concentration and unreality.

"I finished your scores. I like them a good deal. I'm impressed. There's a lot of subtle detail in each of them that I missed the first time, and there's some really nice color. I hope you don't mind, but I negotiated your orchestral work to be included in my concert with the student orchestra."

"You're kidding! Thank you—that means a great deal to me."

"Good. I hoped you'd feel that way." Perry laughed. "Really, I should stop calling them the student orchestra since they're better than ninety percent of the orchestras in the country, and two-thirds of the players are already in professional orchestras. I should call them by their proper name, the Berkshire Music Center Orchestra, shouldn't I? They're unusually strong this year, too. I hope we can do justice to your piece."

"I'm thrilled and flabbergasted. Thank you again."

"I'm glad something I do thrills you. By the way, there's a good chance the *Times* will send up a reviewer for the concert. They usually review when I conduct the BMC, so you'll be getting some exposure."

"Again, Perry, thank you so much. When's the concert?"

"Two weeks from now. The other pieces are all by fellowship composers, BMC people—that's the tradition—so it was a

little tricky getting you in, especially at the last minute, but I explained that you were going to be a fellowship student until extreme hardship prevented you. Don't worry, no one will ask you about it. It's a done deal."

"Literally two weeks, then?"

"Yes. Thursday night, eight o'clock, at Ozawa Hall. You'll be there of course?"

"Of course."

"But I hope I'll see you before then. You could come to rehearsals, for example. I'd like to hear your view on things. Couldn't you call in sick one day from your teaching?"

"I'll try."

"Bobby's driving up tomorrow afternoon from the city, and I'm sure he'd be happy to give you a ride up. In fact, I've already asked him about it, and he said he'd be delighted for the company. That way I could ask you a few questions about your piece over the weekend when you don't have to teach."

"Wouldn't he be staying with you?"

"He will be. But you can stay, too. There's room for all. I have two guest rooms, don't you remember? So what do you think, Ray?"

"Yes, sure. What time is Bobby coming?"

"Why don't I give you his number and you two can work it out?"

He didn't remember any more of the conversation, not even how they said good-bye a minute later. He was off the phone, alone with his news. He jumped and touched the ceiling. A line of Frost's ran through his mind, "For Once Then Something." He didn't remember the rest of the poem, but that line expressed exactly how he felt. Perry Green had paid him back. Big time. And he hadn't mentioned anything about sexual favors either. And wouldn't until after the concert, he was pretty sure of that. As for the weekend, he could use Bobby as an excuse while he was at Perry's. Besides, Perry had taken pains to explain he needn't worry. So he *wouldn't* worry about that for now. If the *Times* reviewed him, he'd be on the map; his whole life could change. His life—his whole life—that's what was suddenly making dramatic, immediate sense to him. That's what Perry had given him, just when it seemed he'd taken it away. He'd given him his life back with huge dividends. "For Once Then Something." He wanted to call Joy but was afraid of what she might think. Maybe he should call his parents. But they'd get flustered and somehow make him doubt it. On the one hand they were supportive; on the other they were eternally skeptical. Making them believe in this would be difficult—they'd gotten so used to his failures, as indeed he had himself. He thought of calling Bryna but felt that would require too much explaining as well. He had to be careful how he explained this to anyone. It was such an outrageous coup that had happened to such an unlikely person that he had to be careful about how he would ultimately tell anyone.

He sat down at his upright and played a series of short études that were among his first compositions. It felt good to play the piano that he hadn't touched since his visit to Tanglewood. After his études he played a couple of Bill Evans tunes, his favorite jazz pianist, then played the opening measure of his own piano sonata, when he got up from the bench with a start. It was getting late and he had to call Bobby about the ride! But he better not tell Bobby about his piece either. Who knew what was going on in Bobby's mind?

# 8

Ray had to force himself not to laugh as he looked out the window at the tree-lined highway. Something in Bobby's tone of voice, its earnestness, perhaps, as he asked him how he liked living on the Upper West Side struck him as funny.

"I've never lived anywhere else in the city, so the truth is I don't know. I did live a year in a dormitory at Juilliard, but that didn't count."

"Was Juilliard fun?"

"'Fun' isn't the first word that leaps to mind, unless you yearn to be in one of the world capitals of neurosis."

Bobby laughed. "I never went to college."

"Really?"

"It was never important to my father. He just wanted me to make money, so I worked for a few years after I graduated high school and, then, I sort of ran away to New York and had to work as soon as I got here, so college was never much of an option."

"Where did you run from?"

"From my parents. In Iowa."

Ray immediately pictured a farm but thought he shouldn't ask.

"Are you in touch with them now?"

"I write them letters, and I call them on the holidays. A couple of Christmases ago I visited them, but it didn't work out too well."

"Do you tell them what you're doing—you know, as an actor?"

"Sort of. They're not too knowledgeable about the arts. I told them about Perry and how much he's helped me, and they'd never even heard of him," Bobby said, laughing a little, while Ray looked out the window at the Berkshire hills he could already see in the distance.

"Perry's really done a lot for you, hasn't he?"

"Oh my God, yes. Just knowing him, of course, is the greatest thing. He's so brilliant and wise and generous. He helped get me a job at a much better restaurant than the first place I worked at. I guess I told you that. He gave me this car, just to give you another example."

Ray suddenly looked at the car as if it were a present just opened in front of a Christmas tree. It was a blue 1987 Oldsmobile. Yes, that was a nice thing to do, and Ray said so, but he couldn't help wondering how many lovers Perry had made Bobby escort to Tanglewood in it.

"Has he been able to help you with your acting any?"

"Oh sure . . . indirectly. Perry knows a lot about the theater. He's written music for it a couple of times. He's critiqued me sometimes when I've asked him to. And then, just watching him onstage, you know, when he conducts or gives a lecture. He has terrific stage presence, don't you think?"

"Yes, he does. But I meant has he been able to help you in getting jobs and that kind of thing?"

Bobby smiled, and Ray thought he saw some additional red in his cheeks.

"Well I can't really be sure how much. But he does know the director of the play I'm in now . . ."

"Off Broadway?"

"Off-Off-Broadway—it's my first speaking part, and Perry put in a word for me before I auditioned or just after. I didn't ask him to. That's just the way he is."

"He's a very powerful man."

"And a very wonderful man," Bobby said, almost dreamily.

"How did you meet him?"

"I was his waiter at this restaurant in the Village. It really wasn't much of a restaurant, more like a coffee shop. It was my first job in New York and I'd been in the city less than a year. I didn't recognize him when he walked in—I didn't even know who he was."

"So you two just started talking?"

"Yeah, we clicked like that, right away. He made me laugh a lot, he's always been able to do that. It really embarrasses me when I think about how I was then—even though it was only three years ago. I was a totally different person."

"How so?"

For the first time Ray saw a look of torment in Bobby's eyes. "I was at a pretty low point in my life and I couldn't see a way out of it, you know . . . but Perry changed that. I guess he's one of those people who has the power to turn someone's life around and get it going in the right direction. He's certainly done that for me, in his own gentle way. See, Perry's really a very modest person, considering how much power he has within him."

Ray mumbled something and looked out the window. So that's the way it would be. There were no chinks in Perry's armor—at least none that Bobby was going to talk about. He was a well-trained seal or else well convinced. But probably it was a blessing in disguise, for what really was the point of his questions to Bobby, anyway? Was he making a character check on Perry at this late date? Was he searching for additional data on Perry's personality defects, trying to find someone else who felt manipulated by the maestro? He'd be better served to put all that analytic-vindictive stuff away and concentrate on his new agenda, which was primarily the need for additional proof that the concert was really going to take place, was, in fact, a done deal. Second, he had to make sure there was no preconcert attempt at sex. The concert was Perry's payback to him; until then he owed Perry nothing, and he shouldn't act as if he did. This was the position he knew he had to adopt with Perry, and he had to present it in a friendly but strong and absolutely unwavering way. They were silent for a while, a silence Ray thought might last the rest of the trip. But twenty miles from Lenox, Bobby said, "Are you going to be staying with Joy again?"

Ray was surprised for a second, then recovered, and said, "No, I don't think so. It was too sudden and I think she has other people staying there. Actually, Perry was kind enough to say I could stay in one of his guest rooms."

Bobby said nothing, and when Ray sneaked a look at him, he was smiling his cryptic, sad clown's smile with his mouth partly open. The smile, preceded by the utterly earnest way he asked the question, made Ray think that he had no idea about what had happened with Perry and him, that he'd no idea even about Perry's desires. The sad smile then was probably because Bobby feared he might have to go through with the charade of staying in a guest room himself, as long as Ray was there.

A new, denser quiet settled over them that lasted until they reached Perry's house in Interlaken, halfway between Lenox and Stockbridge. He hadn't thought much about the possibility of seeing Joy during this visit, or hadn't allowed himself to think about it, but now that Bobby had mentioned her he couldn't resist imagining it. Couldn't they meet for a drink at, say, the Red Lion Inn, where he could tell her about the concert? And possibly, if anything had already been printed about it, a flyer or even an early program, she already *knew,* in which case she might be offended if he didn't call her soon. They might grow even farther apart then, and just as he was becoming convinced that a real opportunity still existed for them.

But this line of thinking could well be utterly misdirected. In all likelihood she knew nothing about Perry's conducting his piece (it was, after all, a last-minute addition), and to call her now might reveal too much. How, for instance, in light of what she knew already and what their argument had been about when he stayed at her place, could he explain staying at Perry's?

No, he'd have to use self-discipline and postpone speaking to her until the program was made public. Maybe then he could invite her to the concert as his guest? That was something worth fantasizing about. . . .

Perry was in the front yard to greet them. He was sitting on a lawn chair, reading the *Times,* in his white cotton pants, a navy-blue shirt, and sunglasses. He hugged Bobby warmly, who almost ran to him like a puppy, Ray thought. Perry's embrace of him was much shorter, but a little too intense for Ray's taste. The three of them finally settled in the backyard at the white Formica table by the pool.

"You boys must have brought the sunshine with you," Perry said, gesturing toward the sky. "This is the first decent day we've had all week."

Ray smiled perfunctorily and, while Bobby answered Perry's question about the trip from New York, made a point of looking at each of them for equal amounts of time. One reason was that he wanted to establish right away that nothing special was going to happen between him and Perry on this visit, that this was strictly a fact-finding trip—though he knew he must stay patient and control his impulse to ask questions about the concert right away. Also, he didn't want to fan any suspicions Bobby might have gotten in the car, suspicions that might have contributed to his sad smile that was still fresh in Ray's mind.

"Did Ray tell you the exciting news about his concert?"

Bobby's eyes opened up wide in response as he turned and stared at Ray. "I don't think so."

"I'm going to be conducting one of his pieces with the Berkshire Music Center Orchestra in two weeks."

"Congratulations," Bobby said as he shook Ray's hand vigorously. "That's great news."

"Imagine Ray not even mentioning it. He's going to need a good press agent, I can see that. That's one of the reasons I wanted to see him this weekend, so I could go over a few things with him in the score. We're going to have to work on building up his ego, Bobby, don't you think, now that he's becoming a musical celebrity."

They laughed and Ray laughed as well.

"So everything's definite then?" he said.

"Of course. I won't conduct without it," Perry said, still smiling. "Have you seen Ozawa Hall yet?"

"I've certainly heard about it, but I haven't seen it yet."

"Well, you're apt to be a bit shocked, then. It's a big three-story brick building—with balconies hanging over the stage—a bit like a fat man who hasn't tucked in his shirt. Yes, it's a genuine eyesore on the green."

" 'The Darkening Green,' " Ray added.

"Bobby, who knows more about these things, says it looks like one of those giant gyms in Indiana. I'd always thought it looked like an oversized silo."

They all laughed.

"How are the acoustics?" Ray said.

"Controversial. But don't worry, we'll be heard. I'll try extra hard to overcome the environmental hazards. Much of the rest of the new Tanglewood is quite lovely, though it's all sort of too big, like a musical Yellowstone Park. It used to be you could hear music from any point in Tanglewood, but not anymore. There's so much land now and, of course, so many more places where you can eat and drink and spend money. But the library they named after Aaron is very nice. So is the Leon Fleisher Carriage House."

Ray thought he detected a note of bitterness in Perry's voice and said, "I can't believe they didn't name anything after you."

Perry tried to look surprised. "I suppose I'll have to die first or give them a half-million dollars. Anyway—what does Borges say?—the most important names on any list are always the ones that are omitted."

Everyone laughed again, and a moment later Ray thought this was one of the happiest days of his life. He wanted desperately to be with Joy, then, to at least talk to her about what was happening to him, but he knew it could be a mistake to call now, that this was just the kind of impulse he had to guard against.

Later in the afternoon, after Bobby had been dispatched to go shopping, Perry went over those parts of his score he'd said he wanted to discuss. As Ray expected, he was not so much consulted as told what Perry wanted to do in terms of tempo and dynamics. But this was a good sign—it meant Perry was giving Ray's work some serious thought and professional commitment. What more could he ask for, since Perry was in fact one of the great conductors in the world, with a lifetime of experience, in addition to being familiar with the particular orchestra that would be playing. Because Perry would be conducting them, they would not merely be committing his piece to memory, but pressing it to their hearts as well.

Perry had finished demonstrating on the piano how he felt the rhythmic, last phrases of the second movement should be accented when he asked Ray to come to the piano.

"This is a nice time, now, isn't it?" he said, looking up at Ray, who stood beside the piano bench.

"Yes. It's a really nice time for me. I'm very happy."

Perry slipped an arm around Ray's waist.

"If you'd like to stay here until the concert, you can; I'd love to have you. You could go to the rehearsals, meet some other conductors, meet some of the press."

"Believe me, it's tempting, but I can't. My job, my students, that's really it. I know you'll be masterful, anyway, Perry. Who better to trust with an orchestra than you?"

"Thank you, Ray."

"I'll come up for the concert, of course."

"Maybe I'll be able to see you then . . . the next day?"

"Sure. I'd love to."

"So this is really a special time now because it's the last time we'll be alone like this, probably until after your concert. That's why I asked Bobby to go shopping. I wanted to be alone with you and I've enjoyed it, Ray; it's been lovely."

"I've enjoyed it too."

"We could go to my bedroom and enjoy it in other ways, if you like."

"No, I can't," Ray said gently, deciding he shouldn't break free of Perry's embrace for the moment.

"Why's that?"

"I just can't think about anything like that, not until after the concert."

"I see," Perry said, removing his arm. "Perhaps I'm being a little impatient then . . . "

"It also bothers me about Bobby."

"I thought we talked about Bobby last time."

"I'm not really sure he has the kind of laissez-faire attitude you attribute to him."

"How so?"

"You make it sound like you have this quasi-platonic yet totally open kind of relationship with him, but I get the feeling, after listening to him talk about you during the drive down, that he's completely in love with you."

Perry's eyes twinkled for a second. "There are many different kinds of love."

"And I think the kind he has would be hurt or damaged if he knew about us."

"I see. And how can I convince you otherwise? Can I tell him, perhaps in your presence? He should be back soon, any minute really."

"No. I don't want him to know, I don't want anyone to know."

"So what do I do? I told you sex is a minor part of my relationship with him and that I'll end it for you. It isn't why he loves me, nor I him. You act like I'm manipulating him in some horrible way, but I've always tried to help him."

"I know that. He told me he was at a real low point when he met you."

"He was dangerously alcoholic."

"Leaving home and his loutish parents, and coming to New York and all that."

"It wasn't the parents so much as his first lover, or the first man he'd allowed himself to love, who jilted him. Bobby is extremely sensitive. He was drinking because of his pain."

"And now you talk about leaving him."

"Not leaving him. Simply no longer sleeping with him if I can have you. Bobby will still love me; I will still love Bobby. It may be more paternalistic, as you put it, but . . . "

"Look," Ray said, "maybe I didn't really have the right to say those things."

"Of course you did."

"I kind of regret saying them already."

"Nonsense."

"The real point is I can't be absolutely certain what can happen and what can't. The only thing I do know is that I can't think about any of it until after the concert," he said, looking away from Perry at the photographs on the wall.

Perry said nothing, waiting, or so it seemed to Ray, until their eyes finally met.

"Fair enough. I can wait. I think you'll find that where you're concerned I can be a very patient man." Then turning toward the piano, he said, "I want to show you how I think the flute solo should go."

He began playing again in his light, precise, vigorous way. Ray watched for a while, but something made him turn his head. For a second he saw Bobby, his head pressed against the outside glass of the living room window, watching them as if simultaneously fascinated and violated, and Ray wondered how long he'd been watching them and how much he knew.

# 9

n the days before the concert, when Ray was done teaching, he often felt too restless to compose or even to watch TV in his apartment and so began walking again by the parks on Riverside Drive.

He sent Joy a second letter, in which he apologized again and told her about his Tanglewood concert. He instructed himself not to expect to hear from her, but she called him right after reading the letter, telling him she'd completely forgotten about the argument and that she was thrilled about his concert.

"One day, I'll be able to say I was there from the beginning," she'd said to him. He got off the phone feeling that his stock had never been higher with her, but reminding himself not to expect anything imminently dramatic. But that was as difficult as not hoping that the concert would have a dramatic effect on his career. Sitting still was getting harder, and he left his apartment, oblivious to the cabbage smell that filled the littered hallway. In the lobby, the invisible doorman was back at his desk. It was odd, but he'd been there for days now, bent over the racing forms like a weeping willow.

Ray went outside. Intermittently, as if they were playing

dodgeball with him, he would see pictures of Perry's face and hear again words Perry had said to him. It seemed to happen whenever he began fantasizing about Joy, as if to warn him not to expect too much. Yet thinking of Joy, after being hit by Perry's image, was paradoxically what helped him avoid further images of Perry, often keeping them, at least temporarily, at bay. The last few walks, that technique had been especially successful. For example, he was walking now on Riverside Drive and wasn't reminded at all of Perry's yard or of the trees that shaded Perry's pool. Instead, he thought of the tall evergreens that lined the walk at Tanglewood where his piece would be performed in a little more than forty-eight hours.

He returned to his apartment, exhilarated, and discovered a message from Joy on his machine. She said some nice things about his music and about how she was sure the concert would be a success, and while she didn't ask him to call her, something in her tone made him think he should. She answered on the second ring with a slight anticipation in her voice.

"Joy? Hi, it's Ray."

"Hi, I just called you. Did you get my message?"

"Yes, I did. It was really kind of you."

"So how are you doing? Are you freaking out or keeping your cool?"

"Somewhere between the two. It's definitely different. What about you, what are you up to?"

"I was about to go out for my run and I started thinking about you."

"Oh. What were your thoughts?"

"Good. They were good thoughts."

"You won't tell me any more than that?" he said, laughing a little.

"I was thinking how much this concert means to you and how proud of you I am that you've accomplished it. And also, how well you've been handling all the pressure, that you've really come a long way, not only professionally but emotionally. Those kind of thoughts."

"Thank you, that means a lot. And it meant a lot to me that you let me stay at your house, too. Thanks again for that."

"Ray, please, you've got to stop thanking me. I've just gotten two letters from you, and they were so kind and so thoughtful of you, that I was thinking I should have thanked you more when I spoke to you before, but don't you see the absurdity potential of this thank-you syndrome? If we don't stop, we're going to become like those Gogol characters who keep insisting that the other should go through the door first, and so neither of them is able to move, 'cause they're frozen in a politeness cycle."

Ray laughed. "What's that in, *The Inspector General?*"

"No, I think it's in *Dead Souls.* Anyway, we don't want to do a Gogol over our thank-yous."

"No, I guess not. I'm just sorry that I went into that little snit after our dinner at Perry's and that there was all that tension between us . . . "

"I'm sorry, too. Look, let's not do a Gogol over our 'sorrys' either. It wasn't that bad. In the past we would have had a fight. When I thought about it, I was actually impressed with the way you handled it. It didn't used to be the easiest thing in the world for you to apologize, at least not until we'd done lots and lots of fighting. So I was surprised and impressed."

"I'll accept that. Thank you."

"I mean, you always had a capacity for tenderness, but I hadn't experienced it, you know, as your primary response in a while, not when that was what I most needed, and that came through too . . . in a very nice way."

Ray was silent for a moment. Does this mean . . . ? he wanted to say, but stopped himself.

"So, do you want to sit together at the concert?" she asked.

"I must be crazy to say this, but probably not. You know how I am at my concerts."

"I remember it well."

"Even though I would rather sit next to you than anyone else, by the way, on a beach or on a subway, or in a movie or restaurant or a lot of other places, I think this time, I'd better be alone. I'm going to be nervous as hell, you know, and I'm going to be tortured by every extraneous noise in the hall. Every time a person sneezes, I'll be furious. If a baby starts crying, I'll be apoplectic."

"I know what it's like to be with you when you're nervous," she said, laughing. "I have lots of experience there. But you can still change your mind."

"And I also make faces when my music is being played. I know I do. You know, absurdly emotional and embarrassing expressions take over my face, and even though you've probably seen that before, once or twice . . . "

"Once or twice."

"It still makes me self-conscious and embarrasses the hell out of me, so . . . "

"*Je comprends.*"

"If the situation were reversed, wouldn't you rather sit alone? I mean if someone made a movie of you giving a recital and that movie was being premiered in front of your peers and bosses and the general public, wouldn't you want to slink into the theater at the last minute and watch it alone in the dark?"

"I think I'd rather sit next to someone who could hold my hand and reassure me. I'd rather not go through it alone. But I do understand how you feel, and no offense is taken whatsoever. Really."

"If you could come backstage and say hello afterward that would mean a great deal."

"That goes without saying, silly."

"I could use the support then."

"Of course, I'll see you there, then. Backstage."

"Great."

"Ray, this is so exciting. I have to keep pinching myself. It feels like a dream, the way it suddenly happened after so long, the way everything is changing for the better for you."

Ray saw an image of the perspiration on Perry's upper lip and shuddered for a moment.

"It's funny the way dreams happen, isn't it?" he said. "Too bad there's always a latent content people don't know about."

"Don't start putting that negative Stoneson spin on this. You just have to accept that your dream's coming true this time, and there doesn't always have to be a terrible price to pay. OK? Can you try thinking that way this time?"

# 10

For almost as long as Ray could remember, he had hoped that someone or something would change his life. At each party he went to in high school and college, he hoped to meet that life-changing person, who at that time he always imagined would be a woman. When his parents spent a summer vacation at Cape Cod or Atlantic City, he sometimes thought he might meet her at the beach or in a restaurant or an amusement park. Later, back in Somerville, he thought he might meet her in Harvard Square at a bookstore, or else walking by the Charles River. It was as if having read Rilke's famous line "You Must Change Your Life," he'd taken it relentlessly to heart.

When he moved to New York, he wouldn't allow himself to believe in this quite so openly, but he still continued his search. Moreover, at Juilliard the nature of his wish changed. Then it began to mean winning a key composing competition, getting an important commission from a string quartet, or winning a major grant or award. The life-changing moment suddenly no longer required flesh. It might come in the mail or during a phone call. Thus the delivery of the mail gradually went from a nonevent to a dramatic one, and the ringing of the telephone assumed a new urgency. Meanwhile, he knew his life *was* changing, but slowly, incrementally, like a piece by Reich or Glass, when what he still hoped for was a sudden, Mahler-type apocalypse.

Now, less than a half hour after the performance of his "Essay for Orchestra," which had been well played and responded to with something more than polite applause, he had the peculiar experience of listening to people telling him that his life would change dramatically for the better.

First, Arnold surprised him by driving up from New York. (Ray had successfully discouraged Bryna from making the same trip because he wanted to be free to pursue Joy.) "Your life is going to change now," he said, smiling behind his glasses as they talked backstage.

"I'm not sure how, but I'm ready for it."

"People are going to start calling you in the city, people are going to start commissioning you, conducting you, and if the *Times* should give you a good review, all that stuff will quadruple."

"I think you're wildly exaggerating, but I appreciate the thought," Ray said, looking around the room, which was rapidly filling up—already ten people were in line to congratulate Perry.

"Don't play the naïf with me, Stoneson. I've known you too long."

"For one thing, who knows what the *Times* will say?"

"Doesn't matter, really. Perry Green has just conducted you. He's the most influential music critic around, at least in the music world. He's the biggest wave, and the ripples will flow out everywhere, you'll see. But I agree, a good review wouldn't hurt."

Ray thanked him and, noticing how the room was continuing to fill up, changed the subject to Arnold's loft, which he'd heard might be up for sale.

"I was thinking about it for a while, but it's a bad time to sell. Real estate's going to hell along with everything else. Besides, I love the place. I'd miss it badly. So I'm trying to scrape by, drum up some more pupils: I couldn't bear to teach full time. Marty's gonna give me a couple of his, says he has to take a break for a while. I think the woman he's with has a lot of money or something, so he hopes he can stop teaching. High hopes, huh?"

Ray laughed, then turned to shake hands with a couple of members of the orchestra who had drifted over from the circle surrounding Perry at the other end of the room. He congratulated the flutist, a tall Japanese man who'd played his solo better than Ray had imagined he could, and the percussionist as well, and introduced them both to Arnold. He thought he should take the initiative and congratulate the other composers, each of whom was holding a mini-court on one side of the room (the whole other side was conceded to Perry). He thought that they might be acting aloof because they resented his not being a Tanglewood fellow and had probably figured out about Perry and him. At any rate, he would gain nothing by being aloof from them. But before he could say more than hello to Rachel Morris, the composer of the neo-Romantic piece (too much in the John Adams's bag for his taste), he saw his mother moving toward him, smiling tearfully, and his tall, slightly stooped father following close behind.

"Darling, congratulations," she said, embracing him. She was wearing a green evening gown he hadn't seen before and her best costume jewelry.

"Congratulations, Ray," his father said, shaking his hand and giving him a little hug. Ray was surprised to see him in a sports jacket and tie. He asked his father if he liked his piece, and he said he did, that his music had come a long way. Then Ray asked him if he was taking off work Friday, and his mother said, "We made reservations at a motel in Lenox and thought we'd drive back early in the morning, but your father thinks he might like to drive back tonight."

"Less traffic, less hassle," he said. Ray smiled and took them each by the hand.

"Come on, I want you to meet Perry Green, who not only conducted my piece but picked it to be performed."

"Will we be able to spend a little time with you later?" his mother asked, her large brown eyes looking faintly agitated.

"Of course."

"We want to take you to Blantyres or the Red Lion Inn for dessert, we thought that might be nice," she said, turning to his father, who shrugged modestly.

"Sounds great. But first I want you to meet Perry Green, the man who made it all possible, and I want him to meet you."

"Ray, you must be so excited by all this," she said, gesturing to indicate the room.

"I am."

"It seemed to happen so suddenly, like a bolt in the dark."

"That's why I want to introduce you to the man who made it all happen."

"Oh, Perry Green is a great musician—everyone knows him."

Ray looked closely at his mother and realized she was nervous about meeting Perry. There were still four or five people ahead of them in line, but Perry and he had made eye contact, and Ray thought that when he was through talking to whomever he was talking to now, he might somehow see them next. He had told Perry that he'd probably stay with Joy as a way of preempting any request to stay at his house, but his parents would make an even more effective excuse, since Perry couldn't possibly be jealous of them.

"Congratulations, Ray," someone said, tapping him on the shoulder. He turned and saw Bobby in jeans, a brown sports jacket, and a red tie. He looked slightly eccentric, but he didn't look bad, Ray thought, as he introduced him to his parents.

"You must be really proud of Ray tonight."

"Oh, we are," his mother said, putting her arm around Ray's shoulders.

His father was looking at Bobby thoughtfully when Perry exclaimed, "Excuse me, I'll return in a minute, but I simply must say hello to these people."

He approached them with open arms in two elegant steps but made certain that he embraced Ray first.

"Hello, darling," he whispered in Ray's ear. Ray turned away and looked at Bobby—his cryptic smile still in place. His parents also had apparently heard nothing unusual. Quickly he introduced Perry to them. His father typically said little but conveyed a proper amount of admiration. His mother was overly effusive but managed to be more charming than embarrassing.

"Your son's life is changing in dramatic ways," Perry said, "and all for the better."

"Thanks to you," his mother said. Perry held up a hand. He often used his hands while he talked, Ray realized, as if they were conducting not only his speech but the response of his listeners as well.

"He's the man who wrote the piece, not me. He's the star of the evening."

"You're not mentioning the four other composers on tonight's program," Ray said.

"We enjoyed them all very much," his mother said.

"They were all good, all promising," Perry said, and then leaning closer to them, he whispered, "but I liked Ray's piece the most."

Everyone laughed and Ray tried to overlook the distinct possibility that Perry was making a secret pun.

"You must be looking forward to spending some time with him," Perry said.

"We are," his father said.

"It's a shame we have to drive back to Boston tonight," his mother said.

"Are you going to Boston, too?" Perry asked him.

"I'm going to be staying at Joy's place," Ray said.

"It's a pity you can't go to Boston! I've always loved Boston," Perry said.

"We've heard you conduct there a number of times," his father said.

"And loved every one of them," his mother added. "You're our favorite conductor."

Perry smiled. "Why, thank you. That's very kind of you. I see where Ray gets his kindness."

A minute later Perry excused himself (though not before getting a promise from Ray to call him the next day at noon) to return to the people waiting for him, and his parents walked away thoroughly charmed. Ray told them he wanted to congratulate the other composers and said that, after that, they could leave for the Red Lion Inn. He was still waiting for Joy to come backstage. He had seen her just before the concert began but had been afraid to look at her during the concert. If she didn't come, he'd have to borrow some money from his parents to stay at a hotel.

The first composer he congratulated was the serialist Paul Kessington, who was gravely polite, speaking as if they'd just been through a funeral instead of a concert. Ray decided it was his natural personality and that he wouldn't take it personally. They shook hands, and then Ray began talking to Frank Trigona, whose eclectic but lively "Serenade" he had actually liked. Frank was still charged up and jumpy. After Ray told him he was from New York, Frank said, "Did you see anyone from the *Times* here?"

"I was going to ask you the same thing. Do you think they sent someone?"

"They must have. With Perry conducting, they had to. The guy makes news when he spits. Of course they covered it, I think, I hope. I was just too fucking nervous to notice, really. I couldn't even look at the orchestra. I just kept my head down and stared at the ground as if I was some kind of worm inspector."

Ray laughed and said he'd been staring at the orchestra the whole time, but without seeing them, which was why he didn't know which critics, if any, had come.

"Composers live a helluva life, don't we?" Frank said. "There're only a few nights a year, tops, we even care about, and then we spend them being too frightened to watch *or* listen. Instead we worry about mistakes, or if anybody'll review us, or if the press will deign to give us a few lines on the bottom of page one hundred eighty-seven. It's almost like we're not part of the world."

Ray told Frank he'd summed it up pretty well, then began telling him in more detail how much he'd enjoyed his piece. Looking up, he suddenly saw Joy in the middle of the room. He tried not to break verbal stride but couldn't keep his eyes away from her for very long. She looked so lovely in her dress, the same white one she'd worn to Perry's that night that now seemed long ago. A minute later, after exchanging phone numbers with Frank, he began walking toward her.

"Joy," he said, extending his hand. He saw her face break into a smile—as she rushed into his arms.

"It was fabulous, Ray. Everything was. You must be so happy."

"I am. It's kind of scary."

"Well, don't be scared. You deserve it. God, Ray, you got performed at Seji Ozawa Hall with Perry Green conducting."

"Pretty amazing, isn't it?"

"Yuh, it's pretty amazing," she said, the same full smile still on her face.

"You look so beautiful."

Joy blushed slightly and thanked him.

"You're wearing the same dress you wore at Perry's."

"But fewer accessories this time. I really overdid it for some reason that night."

"My parents are here."

"I saw them. I was going to say hello to them after I saw you. Are they staying at a hotel?"

"No, they're driving back tonight, actually."

"Are you going with them?"

"I wasn't planning to."

"So do you have a place to stay?"

He blushed slightly himself now and shook his head.

"God, the star of the night has no place to sleep. You know you can stay at my place."

"Really?"

"Of course. You'll help the real estate value of my house if I can say you slept there."

Ray laughed. "Why don't you have some dessert with me and my parents?"

She cupped a hand over her ear. It was an exquisite ear, he thought, shaped like a delicate violin.

"Dessert? Did I hear dessert? Where to, Master?"

Ray took her hand and led her to his parents, whom she hadn't seen since she and Ray were a couple. His mother was predictably warm, and even his father leaned in for a kiss. Ray was eager to celebrate now and began shepherding them out of the room, forgetting to congratulate the last two composers. Just before they left the room, Joy said, "Oh, there's Perry and Bobby. Let me say hello to them. Hi, Bobby!" she nearly sang out to him.

Bobby had that strangely piercing look in his eyes that made Ray uncomfortable, but after seeing Joy he waved and smiled again. Then Joy made a beeline for Perry, and soon they were embracing.

"She looks beautiful tonight," Ray's mother said.

"She usually does."

"Even more beautiful than she did when you went out with her. Why did you ever let her get away?"

"An excellent question. I've been asking myself that for

quite a while, but let's not bring it up when we're out with her, OK?"

"Of course not, darling. I'm not the idiot you think I am. Stan doesn't think I'm an idiot, do you, dear?"

"Oh no," Ray's father said, smiling, as he had the habit of doing, with his eyes alone. "I think you're at least twice as smart as me, and I don't even think I'm that much of an idiot."

Outside, the black sky was lit with stars and a half moon. They walked on a dirt path with his parents in the lead. To their left was a little forest of pine trees and ferns. Soon he could see the moonlight on Lake Mahkeenac, and looking at it on this extraordinarily clear night, he thought he could make out the outline of the hills that surrounded the lake. He heard the sound of distant high heels on the gravel walk leading toward the main gate and the parking lot beyond, now largely empty of cars, then saw the rows of huge evergreens on either side of the sidewalk, heard them moving in the light wind. It seemed he couldn't stop cataloging his favorite images of Tanglewood, as if he were already memorializing this night when the most improbable event of his life had just occurred. That he should have been performed by Perry Green, and not in the Theatre Music Hall where the often spottily attended events of the Contemporary Music Festival were usually held, but in Seji Ozawa Hall with a full house! That he was now walking on the same grounds he'd walked through so many times as a boy, an adolescent, and a college student, where he had had vague dreams about such a night as this but still could only really imagine being a high school or college music teacher. That was essentially what he still was, but now, for the first time, he could also legitimately think of himself as a composer. This was more than he had let himself dream for several years. Actually, for the last few years he doubted it would ever happen—he simply couldn't see the way. And he'd felt old; he was already thirty-two, and he'd been turned down again and again in countless competitions—and now suddenly he was someone, and like any other composer he would wait and worry to see how he was reviewed.

It was strange, too, dreamlike, to be walking with Joy and his parents—so that for a few minutes they were the family they always should have been. He would ride in Joy's car, and they'd meet his parents for dessert in Stockbridge at the Red Lion Inn. Joy was being remarkably nice to him, too. Whatever tension had existed last time was gone. She'd even invited him to stay with her at her house again—this woman he should never have been separated from—and he thought if he were ever going to break through to her, he would have to do something about it tonight.

At the restaurant he didn't feel anxious as he thought he might. They all ordered ice-cream sundaes and ate outside, where the tables were lit by candles. The conversation went fairly smoothly. He enjoyed his father's jokes, his mother's talk about the grammar school where she taught English. He wanted to be alone with Joy but didn't feel rushed. When Joy answered questions about her life, he enjoyed watching her face work, seeing how alert and spirited her eyes were. There was a calming sense of inevitability about everything, yet after his parents left and he was sitting beside her in her car, he suddenly fell silent. For the first couple of miles Joy didn't say anything either. She was driving fast again, as she often did when she was nervous or overstimulated, and he was wondering if he should ask her to slow down.

"It's been quite a night for you," she finally said. "You must be exhausted."

"It's been a great night, but I'm not even a little bit tired. . . . I'm so glad you went out with my parents, really glad."

"Me too."

She began to slow down and he looked at her, but her eyes were focused straight ahead. It was a typical, notoriously black Berkshire night. Without the headlights they couldn't see five feet in front of themselves because the trees blocked out everything except part of the moon, and there were no street lamps on the road.

"There was no way I'd miss them," she said.

He didn't say anything for a while. He thought he might mention how pleased Perry seemed to see her, but then thought better of it and said nothing except to remind her about a couple of turns as they came up and to comment on the absolute black of the night.

In her house they circled each other a few times in the kitchen, or maybe it was he who was circling her as she stood by the table.

"I'm going to fix you a drink so you can calm down a little."

"Good idea," he said, laughing. "Will you have one, too?"

She didn't say anything, but he saw her make a second vodka tonic for herself. He was thinking that in a way everything had begun in this cottage. He was remembering how he leaped after his call to Perry, hurting his hand slightly when it brushed against the ceiling beams. That was the signal that his life might change, and now there was the chance to change it again.

"To your career and its meteoric rise," she said, toasting him while they stood a few feet apart in the middle of her kitchen.

"To us," he said, looking at her seriously. Finally she met his eyes, and he felt that she knew what he was feeling and that she wouldn't pretend otherwise or try to stop him this time. He reached out and put his free hand on her shoulder, that fantastically incongruous shoulder, and looked at her again while he slowly caressed it. He thought he saw something like a blend of fright and sadness in her eyes before she turned her face away and swallowed some more of her drink.

"Well, if you want to sleep with me tonight, I guess I have the right to finish my drink first," she said jokingly.

He put his own drink on the table, tipping it and spilling its last drops. He picked up the glass, then drew her to him so that both his arms were around her. They began swaying together while she slowly maneuvered so she could set down her empty glass. Then they began kissing—first tentative, exploratory kisses before they kissed a long time, the way they did two years ago. She used to sometimes joke and talk dirty with him in bed, but he was glad that so far she wasn't doing either. Instead, they were both being quiet as they walked into her room, and each began undressing as if they were going for a swim together in an unlit pool.

"I guess I'm a little scared," she said, while they were still standing by her bed, and he began touching her again. "Even though I've been trusting you more lately. A lot more. . . . The letters you wrote and the whole way you've been handling things."

"Don't be scared," he said. He kissed her cheek, her neck, and then just above her eyes.

"I hope this is the right thing to do."

"It is. I've cared about you for a long time."

"I know, but . . . "

"I love you, Joy. I'm in love with you, more than ever."

They kissed two or three times in bed before they began throwing off their underclothes in the dark.

"Ray, you have to wear a condom, OK? Please. I'm more paranoid than ever about that. Do you have one with you?"

"Yes, I do."

"I won't ask you what you're using them for."

He felt his heart pound. He had brought them because he'd hoped for something like this.

"For the unexpected, the marvelous, for you. There's no-body else."

She laughed. "Come here, you phrasemaker, you long-lost lover." She kissed him on the lips, then said, "OK, let's do this for tonight, then, but no promises, no strings, as we singers like to put it."

"Sure," he said laughing, although he found himself yearning exactly for such promises.

# 11

In the early morning just before he woke up, he dreamed he was with Joy on a beach somewhere in California. They were in bathing suits walking over a firm sandbar in a kind of syncopation. The sky was a cloudless, deep blue. "Look at the ocean," he said, turning suddenly and pointing to it. It was simultaneously a brilliant blue and a rich emerald green.

He woke up electrified. He was beside her; the first light of the morning filled the room like a bright mist. He saw her long blond hair, her shoulders. He sat up, pulled the covers down softly, and looked at her back. She'd slept naked, probably passing out before she could find any clothes in the dark.

"Hi," she said softly, half awake.

"Hi," he said, as he lay down gently on top of her back, then began massaging her.

"What's up?"

"I am. You make me get up, get excited."

He rubbed her back for a few minutes, progressing downward slowly. He was sitting up, wetting his fingers before he slid them into her—Joy cooperating by arching herself slightly. Soon she began moaning softly; she was wet, it seemed, in a matter of seconds. He wanted to penetrate her, but he loved building her excitement gradually with his mouth and fingers alone while he could also spy on the exquisite sight of her pleasure as she slowly lost control. Then she arched higher and he entered her, moving his hand around her thighs to touch her clitoris. Immediately he felt a tremendous surge of pleasure and was afraid he would come too soon, so he turned her around and went in her again. Her eyes were closed tight, her muscles straining while they moved. A few minutes later they came together, yelling, then laughing.

"I may as well die now," Ray said, "I'll never be happier than this."

They embraced, but a moment later she turned away from him and hid her face in the pillow. She was crying, something she rarely did.

"What is it?"

She sat up and faced him with most of the signs of her tears gone except for a slight narrowing of her eyes.

"Sorry," she said.

"Are you happy or sad?"

"Oh yes, sure. The sex part was great. I wouldn't have expected anything less with you. It's just that . . . what now?"

"What do you mean?"

"What happens next with you and me?"

"Yes, I see your point. Well, you said 'no strings' last night. So if you still feel that way, I guess I make you breakfast and we play it by ear."

"What about you? How do you feel? What do you want?"

"I want you," he said with a little smile.

"You just had me. Again. Come on, Ray, you know what I mean."

"But I do mean it seriously. I want to be with you always. I love you, a lot, like I said last night. I want us to be together, only this time we'll do it right. This time I want it to last, which I guess means we get married at some point, if you'll have me."

119

She looked away from him for a moment. Her expression had changed, but the tightness around her eyes was still there.

"Well, you're certainly saying the right things. God knows I would've killed to hear them a few years ago."

"I was a nervous, narcissistic, self-destructive child then."

"Yeah? The thing is I've grown more skeptical as I've grown older. Or maybe being alone so much lately has made me mistrustful. But I do have more trouble trusting people now than I did then."

"Including me?"

"Well, Ray, I haven't known you—I mean known you intimately—in a long time, though I admit my trust meter has been tilting in your favor lately, along with all the other parts of me," she said, laughing. "So don't get me wrong. There are things I know I love about you that I know are real. Otherwise last night wouldn't have happened. Your talent and your sensitivity and I'd have to say the way you look and so forth, but I guess I've just grown more fearful. I mean, I can't pretend that I've forgotten what happened at the end of our relationship when you cheated on me, even though you've explained and apologized endlessly and feel terrible about it. But I can't pretend it doesn't make it somewhat difficult to totally trust you now. And, of course, AIDS hasn't exactly made me want to have a lot of sex lately either. It's one of the reasons I'd feel conflicted about getting involved with anybody."

"But I'm not anybody. I'm Ray."

"I'm sorry, maybe I didn't say that right. Look, why don't we postpone this heavy dialogue. I already regret it."

"No, you shouldn't. I need to know."

"OK, and I appreciate it, but why don't you let me make you breakfast now?"

"I want to make *you* breakfast."

"No, come on, you have your mind on your reviews. Should I go get a *Berkshire Eagle* first?"

"It won't be out yet."

"Do you want me to wait with you till the reviews come out? What do you want to do today, anyway? I have most of the day free."

Ray turned away from her and after a brief search put on his underpants and socks.

"Perry invited me to his place for lunch."

"Oh."

"Would you like to come with me? I'm sure he'd love to see you."

"No, I don't think that would be apropos. You two should be together after the concert."

"I'm sure he'd enjoy your coming, but . . . as you wish," he said softly. His back was still to her as he put on his pants.

"Have you been seeing Perry a lot lately?"

"Just once since our dinner. I saw him a couple of weeks ago about the piece."

"Oh. I wish you'd called me then."

"Believe me I wanted to. Badly. I was feeling tension from the last time, too. At the time, it made me almost give up thinking you'd ever consider me again . . . you know, in the way I wanted. And I've waited so long for that."

Their eyes met briefly and he saw that he'd provoked a look of pleasure from her that temporarily obliterated any traces of anxiety. Then she stood up bare chested, wearing only her pale pink panties. She stretched and yawned for a moment, and he felt excited again and wondered if he shouldn't try to make love with her one more time, in a half hour or so.

Meanwhile she was on her own clothes search and had already thrown on a man's long nightshirt.

"So who else have you been keeping company with these

days? What about that woman friend in New York who I never met . . . Bryna? Have you been seeing her?"

"Not really. I've been pretty preoccupied with the concert."

"I can imagine."

"And nervous."

"I can imagine that, too."

"It's made me withdraw from people, for the most part."

"I guess what I'm saying is if we're going to give this thing a legitimate chance, I don't know if I can handle you sleeping with anyone else. Let me rephrase that. I can't handle it. That's got to be absolutely out-of-bounds."

"Of course. There is no one else. There's no one else I'd even consider or want to sleep with."

"Thank you, Ray. I hope so." She turned and stood next to him and they hugged. Then he followed her into the kitchen. "So what made you finally try to seduce me last night?" she said with her characteristically impish smile. She'd begun boiling water on the stove.

"I guess the concert gave me the extra confidence."

"Well, your stock certainly has risen in my eyes and everybody else's. I'm really proud of you. You were fantastic, in *both* your performances."

He laughed.

"Now you've got to figure out how to cash in on this."

"I'll have to wait for the reviews before I do that."

"The hell with the reviews. You've been performed by Perry Green at Tanglewood. You've already made it."

"Do you think I've made it enough to get that job you told me about in Philadelphia?"

"At my school?"

"Yes."

"You could get that tomorrow."

"Would you call them for me?"

"Of course. That's not a problem. I always said I could do that, but would you really want to leave New York?"

"It's something to think about, isn't it? But why not? It's much less expensive in Philly, I don't have a full-time job in New York, I've never had a full-time job in New York, and, of course, from my point of view I'd love to be near you."

"We could have lots of fun in the city," Joy said with a sudden burst of energy. "Philadelphia's a lot more fun and interesting than people realize. And it's a nice environment for composers, too. I think they support each other more there. Gee, Ray, you're getting me excited about this. You might really move and get a full-time job and live in the same city as me, and we might really have a real relationship after all?"

And this time they both laughed, longer and harder than they had before.

# 12

I've missed you, even more than I thought I would," Perry said. He turned his head toward his living room window for a few seconds before looking back at Ray, who moved forward in his chair as if Perry were speaking too softly to be heard. "You look concerned. Am I upsetting you by being so direct?"

"I guess I'm just surprised that you're saying things like that here," Ray said, indicating the living room with his hands.

"I thought a man's home was his castle."

"What about Bobby?"

"What about him, darling?"

"Where is he?"

"He isn't here now. I thought you knew that."

"No, I didn't."

"I sent him out to get some things for dinner."

"And if he were here? Would you speak that way to me in front of him?"

"No, I wouldn't, seeing how upset it seems to make you. I'd be much more circumspect."

"You called me 'darling' backstage last night."

"You are a darling to me."

"The point is my parents were just a few feet away."

"And so was Joy," Perry said, raising his eyebrows meaningfully.

"And so was Joy."

"Are you sleeping with her again? Is that what this is all about?"

"I told you she's a friend. I don't want to talk about her."

"Well, it only seems fair if you're going to ask me questions about Bobby."

"Joy isn't going to walk through this door any minute, and Bobby is. What does he know about us?"

"I think he knows. I can't be one hundred percent sure because he doesn't ask. He's a very discreet person."

"How would he feel if he did know?"

"I told you about our policy. Anyway, he's more like a son than a lover to me. We hardly ever have what you'd consider sex these days. It's all terribly sweet and old-fashioned . . . just a lot of hugs and kisses really. And certainly nothing has happened since we were together, and as long as we are together nothing ever will, I told you that."

"You also told me that he became an alcoholic when his first lover left him, so obviously Bobby gets very attached to people, maybe even dangerously attached."

"He does get attached to people and he is attached to me. You simply have trouble perceiving the *nature* of his attachment, which is essentially platonic. We are friends, we may even be a kind of father and son—that's the essence of the attraction—not sex. So your anxiety is misplaced. Let me get you a glass of wine, Ray. I think you're nervous about the reviews. That's what's really troubling you. But soon you won't have to worry anymore. Someone's going to call me as soon as the *Times* review is out. It should come any minute. I think the news is going to be good. And the *Berkshire Eagle* will be out in an hour. I think you'll do well there, too. But let's not argue while we're waiting. How does the Beatles' song go? 'Life is very short and there's no time for fussing and fighting, my friend.'"

Ray smiled. "I didn't know you were a fan."

"I am. I think they did much good for the world. Did you know that I met both John and Paul?"

"No, I didn't know that."

"They were both very nice to me."

Ray smiled. Perhaps that was what Perry meant by their doing much good for the world.

"Why don't we listen to a record now? Not by the Beatles, because I don't have any here, but something that will give us some spiritual sustenance. Something by Bach. Say, the Brandenburg Fifth."

"Did you record that?"

"I did, once as conductor and once as pianist, though I couldn't play it very well these days. But I wasn't going to suggest my recordings. I wanted to hear the one with Lukas Foss playing piano with the Boston Symphony members in the solo parts."

Perry got up from the sofa and opened a sliding glass door underneath the stereo, where his records were housed.

"Don't you have it on CD?"

"No, I don't. I don't have CDs really. I don't even like that term. It sounds like a new venereal disease. Just what the world needs, huh?"

Ray laughed. "So you don't even own a compact-disc player?"

"I finally broke down and got one just to satisfy those people who keep talking about it and the laser disc as if they're the saviors of music. Good music is the only thing that will save music, not gadgets, but Americans always look to science for answers, don't they?"

Ray shrugged, thinking, But you're an American, too, damn it.

"Also, think about all the records that haven't and never will be made into CDs. That's one of the world's truly endangered species. Instead of the indestructibility of the CD that everyone is always writing about, someone should write an article about all the great music consigned to oblivion because it's going out of stock and isn't profitable enough to be made into compact disks."

"Your records have been made into CDs, haven't they?"

"Not all of them, not by a long shot. And some of them probably never will be," Perry said with a bitter expression Ray had never seen before.

"Anyway," Perry said as he put on the record, "shall we enjoy our Bach?"

For the first few minutes, Ray's mind wandered and he barely heard the music. He felt oddly self-conscious, embarrassed to look at Perry's face, as if they were each invading the other's privacy. His eyes drifted from object to object in the large, sunny living room. Everything was expensive but tastefully understated, the Wolford lamp on the long blue sofa, the thick off-white carpet, the silver and gold frames for the photographs, the grand piano, and, of course, the smallish paintings by de Kooning and Larry Rivers that he assumed, without asking, were gifts because Perry was friends with everyone. . . . A visual catalog of Perry's possessions was just another numbing confirmation of his power. He wondered when he would see (when he would have to see) Perry's apartment in New York, and then he suddenly wished he were in Philadelphia at the job interview, at Joy's school, nailing down that job, then looking for a small apartment near her.

He stopped cataloging the living room, closed his eyes, and slowly began to absorb the music. By the time the long piano cadenza, which Perry called "the first and greatest jazz solo in history," began, he was hearing the notes and feeling them. When it was over, they looked at each other and smiled.

"That was really something," Ray said.

"Yes, it was magnificent. I'm glad to see you smile again. Your smile is magnificent, too. I wonder if Bach was thinking of someone like you when he wrote it?"

Ray was about to say, I doubt it, or perhaps he did mumble those words, just as the phone rang.

"Ah!" Perry said, springing up from the sofa to answer it in his room.

Ray told himself that there was no reason to assume it was the call about the reviews, but after a minute he stood up from his chair, as if he needed to stand to protect himself. He looked at the photographs on the piano and on the walls— the continuation of the larger gallery of musical stars that filled Perry's room—but he couldn't identify any faces. Where he should have seen distinguishing features, he saw blurs. He thought, This is ridiculous, I'm not going to let a few words by someone who probably can't even read music destroy me. But he began to pace—he couldn't tell for how long—until looking up he saw Perry at the opposite end of the living room.

"Good news, darling! The reviews are very good. 'You are deft, you are poignant!' The *Eagle* loved you, too. Come here, listen. I told you you were in good hands."

# 13

B obby appeared at the door. It was as if he'd materialized on the spot. Perry was in the bathroom—there was nothing for Ray to do but go to the door. He had wanted to call Joy to share his jubilation about the reviews, but the more sober policeman inside his brain told him to talk to Bobby for a few minutes, that it would be a mistake not to be nice to him.

He carried one of the shopping bags into the kitchen and began unpacking it while Bobby, who obviously knew where everything should go, put things in their proper places. It was while Bobby was distributing and organizing the different things he'd bought that Ray realized Bobby thought of it as his house, too, and that he took a homeowner's pride in making sure everything was done correctly. At almost the same time, Ray became increasingly aware that there was a definite tension between them. He had not seen any of the varieties of Bobby's innocent smile, and although Bobby was making small talk, it was in an untypical tone of voice, with a faintly menacing edge to it.

When Bobby finally shut the last drawer and turned to face him, Ray felt strangely relieved. "Congratulations for the concert last night. It was really great," Bobby said, and for the first time Ray heard a note of insincerity in his voice.

"Thank you. That's very kind of you."

"I guess you and Perry have been celebrating this morning."

Ray looked for the smile, waiting for it the way he'd wait for a temporarily stalled car to start, but it didn't appear. Instead, Bobby's eyes stayed steady and deeply, incongruously serious. "I was too nervous to celebrate anything. Waiting for the reviews, you know, which finally came out and thankfully were good. Perry tried to calm me down and . . . "

"How did he do that?"

"Just talking to me. Then we listened to a record, and that helped, too."

"It must be fun for you to listen to music with Perry," Bobby said, a poignant expression in his eyes now that made Ray understand he meant something more enduring than "fun," something closer to "an honor" or "a privilege."

"Yes, it was."

"And, of course, to have him conduct your piece. I think I would just faint with joy if I were in your shoes."

"It was a great experience for me," Ray said.

"I guess you must feel pretty grateful to him."

"I do."

The steady, serious look was back in his eyes. "I saw you leave with Joy and your parents last night. That must have been really nice for you."

"Yes, we went to the Red Lion Inn."

"That's Perry's favorite place. I love it, too, of course. Have you known Joy for a long time?"

"We're old friends. I've written a couple of pieces for her."

"Oh, really. Your friendship grew out of music, then?"

Ray shrugged and said he guessed it did. He couldn't tell Bobby the truth about Joy and risk Perry's finding out, but he could say something about Bryna and clarify the ostensible issue of his sexuality that way. That was, finally, what Bobby was driving at, wasn't it?

"It was really good that she could come. Everything seemed to work last night beyond my expectations. My only regret is that Bryna couldn't come." He waited for Bobby to ask who she was, but Bobby stayed still like a focused bird, watching him with his steady-eye look.

"Bryna is a former girlfriend of mine who I am still close to as a friend." Ray looked at Bobby with hope, then noticed that Bobby's left hand was clenched tightly in a fist, as if it existed separately from his voice.

"I guess that's a good thing, but I've never been able to do that."

"I don't follow."

"Keep someone who was once a lover as a friend. I've always lost the person totally when I lost him as a lover. I didn't want it that way, but *c'est la vie.*"

"That's very painful."

"I don't think there's anything more painful. People say death is, but I don't think so. Do you? Certainly not for the person who dies. He just goes to sleep and feels nothing. It's like when a piece of music ends, the piece doesn't feel anything, it just ends. It stays in the minds of the people who heard it or saw it performed, but the piece itself is never resolved, it has nothing more to say and so it should end."

"What's this morbid talk I'm hearing?" Perry asked as he walked into the kitchen.

"Hi Perry," Bobby said, with a soft smile, the softness also returning to his voice. Ray noticed that Bobby's hand was no longer clenched.

"Any talk about anything that isn't simply glorious is strictly out-of-bounds this morning. Ray has gotten two wonderful reviews for his piece. One in the *Berkshire Eagle* and one in the *New York Times,* and I suggest we go immediately to the Red Lion Inn to celebrate. And don't worry, Ray, there's a stop right across the street where you can catch your bus to New York."

"Congratulations for the reviews," Bobby said, shaking hands with him vigorously. Apparently he hadn't heard Ray mention them earlier, or chose not to, or simply didn't accept the reviews as part of reality until Perry confirmed it. A minute later the three men left the house together. There was no time to call Joy.

HE WOULD remember that time mostly as a series of unusually bright pictures, no matter how many times he later tried to recover what was actually said. Perry did almost all the talking as he drove them into town—regaling them with improvised jokes and anecdotes about the early days of Tanglewood. Ray made sure he sat in the backseat so that Bobby could sit in his seat of honor beside Perry, as trees, cottages, and occasional glimmers of the lake flashed by, and the tension with Bobby already seemed like a few minutes of a separate world that had nothing to do with this day.

Just before they reached Stockbridge, Ray felt suffused with Joy's presence and with images of the morning and the night before when they made love. He was re-creating the sequence of gestures and positions they'd assumed in bed, and some of the words she'd said to him, as the car stopped beside the restaurant.

Despite Perry's wearing his darkest pair of sunglasses, three people approached him before they could sit down—one of them getting his autograph.

Ray didn't even remember ordering. His eye went automatically to the pharmacy across the street where they sold newspapers and where the *New York Times* delivery truck was now parked. A moment later he excused himself and returned with a *Times* and an *Eagle,* his hands shaking slightly as he looked for the review that Perry had already heard on the phone and that Perry now insisted he read out loud. Meanwhile, Perry had ordered a bottle of champagne, and he and Bobby each toasted Ray after he finished reading.

"To the new star of the Berkshires," Perry said as he raised his glass. "To the new star in the musical sky."

It was easier than he'd expected to leave after their brunch. He simply told Perry that he needed to be near his phone in case some calls came in, and Perry smiled and said he understood but wished Ray would consider staying a little longer. He really felt he just had to be there, Ray said, and he must have been convincing, or Perry must have understood, because there was little follow-up protest. Then—since the bus for New York left in front of the pharmacy across the street in seventeen minutes—everything was impeccably convenient. Perry hugged him and said, "Don't be a stranger." Then he stood next to Bobby, looking a little sad as he smiled, and they both waved good-bye in unison.

As soon as the bus left Stockbridge, he read the reviews again, then briefly worried that he might have offended Perry. It was that anxiety that started the parade of pictures in his mind, like slides in an art class occasionally identified with words, of the time he'd just spent with Perry and Bobby. Only after the parade had been reviewed and repeated was he finally able to think about his concert again and then his incredible night with Joy and all that might mean. It was shocking and almost frightening in a way (though also wonderful) to be suddenly attacked by happiness.

At home there were already a number of messages. Arnold called, told him his life would *really* change now, that he could get a record deal, that he thought the review was fantastic. Marty left a warm, congratulatory message; his parents left a message saying they were thrilled by the *Times* review; all but two of his students left messages; Bryna left a message, then called back before he could get to the last message on his tape.

"You must feel on top of the world."

"At least that I'm part of it."

"I bet you're flooded with phone calls. I should get off and let you take them."

"Why don't we have lunch in a couple of days?"

"Of course," she said. "I was hoping."

Finally he got to Joy's message. It was brief but heartfelt, but he'd hoped for something more romantic and immediately called her back. There was no answer and no machine on which to leave a message. He played the piano for fifteen minutes and tried again, but no one answered. He should have asserted himself and called her from Perry's. With a sudden bitterness, he wished that he hadn't been so careful, especially at that moment. He should have phoned her at the peak of his happiness, then worried about Perry's feelings later. Certainly he could have excused himself and called her from the Red Lion Inn. By not doing so he felt oddly deprived, that he'd cheated himself of sharing his proudest moment on earth with the person he most wanted to share it with, that he'd lost that forever.

He was becoming too sentimental, too obsessed with this, he thought. He was happy enough now, and when he'd tell her about the review, the feelings he'd had then would come back, and even if they didn't, why be so childish about it?

It was only during a short walk a few minutes later that he realized her absence was intolerable. He never should have left the Berkshires without calling her, especially after he'd not only said he loved her but mentioned moving to Philadelphia and marrying her. And she—candid as ever—talked about how hard it was to trust him, and already he was carrying out this deception, already he had lied to her about Perry. Maybe she sensed that. He'd sometimes felt certain people's insight was strengthened by love. When they had been lovers before, he often felt Joy could see right through him. But had she? In any event, these mental wanderings were beside the point. She was feeling vulnerable. She didn't want to get burned again, and he should have called her earlier and had to keep trying now.

He took a couple of swallows of beer before calling, and she answered on the fifth ring.

"Hi. What's going on?" he said.

"I was in the shower and didn't hear the phone at first."

"Should I call back?"

"Not unless you mind talking to me while I'm naked and dripping."

"Dry off first, I'll hold."

"It's OK. I've sort of worked a towel around myself. Listen, Ray, the reviews are incredible. Congratulations."

"I'm sorry I didn't call earlier. Actually I've been trying you for over an hour."

"I went swimming. After all the excitement I had to do something, right? But tell me what you're feeling about the *Times* piece and everything."

"I'm happy and excited. I'm mad at myself, though, that I couldn't speak with you before I went to New York. I miss you."

"Really?"

"Yes."

"I missed you, too. On the raft I kept wishing you were beside me or on top of me or whatever. You know how sexy it can be after swimming when the raft rocks you and the sun is out and a little breeze is blowing. Especially when you swim after sex."

"Stop it. You'll make me come again."

"Really? Do I really have that effect on you?"

"Don't you remember this morning?"

She laughed. "Oh yeah. I'm not likely to ever stop remembering this morning."

They were silent for a moment. He wondered if he should ask her again to marry him. He couldn't imagine wanting to be with someone more than he wanted to be with her now.

"How's the response been in New York? Your phone must be ringing off the hook."

"It's been good. All friends and family so far, though. No offers from the New York Philharmonic yet," he said, laughing.

"Your parents must be thrilled."

"They're very happy. I'm very happy. I'm thrilled . . . by you."

"Thank you."

"And I'm feeling weird about being so far away from you."

"Why don't you come back?"

"I was going to invite you to New York. I figure I need to be here for a few days to really test the reaction to the concert. But I'd have plenty of time, and if it got too hot, we could go to Westport or maybe to the Hamptons for the day."

"It's very tempting. But I have rehearsals, and I have students and a whole bunch of stuff I have to do up here, at least for the next week."

"That seems like a long time."

"If it's too long, you can come up and stay with me again."

"Won't it be crazy around concert time?"

"Yes, but if you can stand it, there's always a place for you."

He suddenly realized one reason he was being hesitant. Despite being an international tourist attraction, Tanglewood (which meant Lenox and Stockbridge) was small, and if Perry or Bobby saw him anywhere and he hadn't called to tell Perry he'd be in town, Perry could be hurt badly, and everything could be over just as it was beginning. He and Joy would have to stay in all the time, or he'd always have to be looking over his shoulder, and Joy would notice and get suspicious. How would he explain not going to the concert, for instance? But could he risk going and bumping into Perry, who might just go to see Joy and find out about his doings? It was all too depressingly byzantine, so he changed the subject.

"I've been thinking some more about the job in Philadelphia. That I'd really like to get it and leave New York—if you're still willing to put in a word for me."

"Sure. The principal's on vacation, but I'll call him as soon as he gets back. The timing couldn't be better. I'll read the review to him, just in case he missed it."

"Great. Thank you, Joy."

"This is news."

"Why? We talked about it before."

"I know. I guess I couldn't believe you were serious."

"Why not? You've got to realize that I'm serious about a lot of things, like you, for instance," he said, trying to soften his suddenly defiant tone. "And I'm willing to do a lot to prove it."

"I don't know. New York and Ray seem to go together."

"Maybe they did once, but they don't anymore."

"Let's see, in this corner, we have New York: Capital of Dreams, Ambition, and Artistic Talent. In the other corner, we have Ray: World-Class Dreamer, World-Class Ambition, World-Class Talent. Looks like a good match from where I sit."

"You didn't say anything about it being the Capital of Love. Philadelphia is the City of Brotherly Love, isn't it? Maybe I want to be near you."

She was silent.

"Is that so hard to believe?" he added a little nervously.

"Yes. No. God, Ray, things have certainly changed quickly. It's just a little difficult for me to suddenly adjust to serious, committed Ray, who even mentioned marriage, if I'm not mistaken."

"Yes, I did. Absolutely. Maybe getting the piece performed helped give me the courage. But while I only *acted* recently, I've been thinking about it, wanting it with you, a lot longer. You know that, you've always known that. That time I stayed at your place when I was visiting Perry and we had that argument, I didn't walk into your room to talk about Perry. That wasn't what I was really having insomnia about. I wanted you so badly."

"Wasn't that kind of just a lust-want, though?"

"No, Joy, it was a love-want. But love does create lust, you know, at least in me."

She laughed. "It's doing a pretty good job of creating some in me, too. But don't worry, it's only for you. And don't give up on me, OK? Like I said, it's still a little new for me to trust you like this and, I guess, to believe that things can be so good so quickly."

# 14

B ryna and he were eating lunch at Food, a self-service, cafeteria-style restaurant in SoHo. It was the kind of high-visibility place Bryna liked, where she was sure to see a number of gallery owners and dealers. He wasn't surprised that she was wearing one of her favorite dresses, a purple acrylic with a plunging neckline. Typically, she'd been candid about the networking opportunities of such lunches—"I need to do my shtick. Is Food OK with you? I've got to find a gallery to show my sheep."

There was no way he could object, certainly no precedent for it. Too much of their relationship was based on cheerfully using each other for sexual pleasure or for various kinds of career help—as long as the help didn't hurt the other person. And hadn't she loaned him some money to go to Tanglewood that first time he stayed at Joy's and visited Perry, not to mention sleeping with him after his experience with Perry? No, he couldn't object to lunch at Food, though he wished they were at some place more quiet or anonymous.

Ever since Perry called him last night, he'd been feeling a terrible pressure and sense of desperation about their relationship, compounded by the fact that no one else knew about it. Maybe now, at this lunch, he could confide in Bryna. With her eccentric past and genuine fondness for him, she might be uniquely equipped to understand him. But could he really tell her what happened and risk losing a certain amount of respect in her eyes forever?

He watched her closely while she ate her overstuffed tuna-fish sandwich, her own eyes moving restlessly to take in the full scope of activities in the increasingly crowded room.

"Ray, what's going on? You're not talking to me. Are you all right?"

"Sorry. I'm OK."

"You seem to be having this very serious line of thought, but maybe you don't want to tell me about it, I don't know. You know me. I don't like being a buttinsky."

"I got a call from Perry last night that upset me."

"Less than a week after your greatest triumph and you're upset already?"

"It isn't about the career per se."

"What? Is he falling big time for you, is that it?"

Ray looked away from her. The room was already filled to the brim with art-world types.

"Something like that."

"*Oy gevalt.* What are you gonna do?"

Ray shrugged his shoulders.

"Just stay away from him until he comes to his senses. You're under no obligation to sleep with him just because he conducted your piece."

"Can you be a little quieter, please?"

"Sorry. I didn't know I wasn't. As long as he hasn't physically forced himself on you and you never encouraged him, just keep keeping your distance. You know, be polite but just say no."

"I may move to Philadelphia."

"What, New York isn't big enough to avoid having sex with someone?"

"It would be easier with more miles between us."

"I thought he was in Tanglewood for the summer."

"He has an apartment in the city. He could come here any day he wants."

"I don't know, Ray, it all sounds pretty strange to me. You sure you're not overreacting to this? What's he actually saying to you on the phone, anyway?"

"You don't want to know."

"I do. I'm all ears."

"Well, I don't want to tell you. Just trust me—it's not subtle enough to be ambiguous. I know what he wants. And please, whatever you do, don't say anything about it to anyone, OK?"

"Of course not."

"Forgive me, but you have been known to speak a sentence or two of gossip in your time."

"Trust me, Ray, really," she said, putting her hand over her heart, her dark eyes fixed on him with a suddenly serious expression. "I can see that you're really upset about this. You don't have to be Sigmund Freud to see that. But moving to Philadelphia—isn't that a little extreme? I mean, he's in Tanglewood, for the next month anyway. Isn't he farther away from New York now than he'll be from Philadelphia when he returns? And who knows what will happen in a month? He may meet someone new. He may start fantasizing about someone else. Besides, what would you do in Philadelphia? What would happen to your students here?"

"There's a job I could take. A teaching job at a good school, a private school where I'm pretty sure I could teach."

"Oh. And is there anything else that you'd get in Philadelphia?"

Ray smiled guiltily. "Well yes, I was going to tell you. It seems that I've become seriously involved with someone, who I think I'm, you know, in love with."

Bryna blinked rapidly several times as if she were warding off an insect.

"And she still lives in Philadelphia?" she said, partially shielding her eyes from him with her right hand. He noticed that her nails were painted the same purple as her dress.

"Yes. She will be, in September."

"I assume that this is your former girlfriend you stayed with at Tanglewood? The tall blond I saw you walking around with once in SoHo?"

Ray nodded and smiled.

"So that really was a momentous trip you made to the Berkshires."

"I was going to tell you right away, but then I thought I'd wait until I saw you."

"Don't look so apologetic. I understand our arrangement. I remember the conditions. Who would understand them better than me? Didn't I make some conditions of my own a little bit ago about not wanting to sleep with you for a while?"

"That's true."

"Of course, I didn't know you were already seriously involved at the time. You might have spared me the pain of making that speech."

"I wasn't involved with her then. This all sort of solidified the night of my concert."

"Yes, you're a very good solidifier. . . . But you knew you wanted her the first time you stayed there."

"Wanting and getting have been two different things in my life. We didn't sleep together that weekend, or I would have told you."

"Oh, what does it matter? I always knew we had no future as lovers. I'm happy for you, Ray. I shouldn't feel sorry for myself. How can I be such a hypocrite when I just told you I didn't want to sleep with you for a while? I knew saying something like that could only speed up the process of losing you."

"You haven't lost me," Ray said. "I'm your friend as much as ever and I need you more than I can say," he said, extending his hands, which she quickly took in hers, across the table.

"Of course, if you want to, we'll be friends. I just don't understand why you're so upset. I would think with your concert and your new lover, the world would be yours."

He could see that Bryna was more hurt than she wanted to reveal. She said only the most cursory of hellos to two or three people before leaving Food with him. On the street she was quiet; her face looked gray. Knowing her pride, he felt the best thing was to follow her emotional direction and act like the silence between them was natural and didn't signify anything irregular. When they reached the outside of her loft, he asked if he could see her new work. "Not today, if that's all right. I need to digest my food and a few other things." She raised an eyebrow as if seeking his approval, and he said, "Of course." She told him she was happy for him again. Then they embraced lightly and she disappeared into her loft.

There was no way such arrangements ever went smoothly, he was thinking on the subway, heading home. Mixing sex and friendship always subtly tortured both people involved. How could you do that with a friend while your soul was always yearning for someone else? Although she had instigated the relationship, he felt guilty about it. He should have protected her. She was older, and in many ways that made it more difficult for her.

Walking the few blocks from the subway to his building, he felt a sense of dark premonition, similar to what he'd felt just moments before being mugged close to his building a few years ago. He got to his apartment safely this time, opened the door, and immediately noticed his answering machine was flashing green. He hoped the message was from Joy, of course—some midday need to hear his voice.

"Sorry you're not in, Ray," the message said in Perry's

resonant, precise voice that held just a suggestion of mischief. It was a voice, Ray concluded, that could speak almost as well as its owner could conduct.

"Maybe you can call me later tonight. I have a speaking engagement coming up in Santa Barbara along with a master class, and I spoke with the parties involved about getting your music played and maybe getting you to speak, too, and, of course, getting you some money for your trouble. But I do need to know quickly, so can you call me back soon?"

Ray paced across his studio trying to assess the message, which he eventually played two more times. The opportunity, sketchily described as it was, was fantastic. Any appearance with Perry was a major opportunity. But as far as getting his music performed, what did Perry mean? The Santa Barbara Symphony? Probably not. It was most likely a college-sponsored event, which meant chamber music but could (and probably would) still garner him some press. It would be minor compared with his Tanglewood concert, of course, but it would still be an impressive follow-up, as well as his first West Coast exposure. Soon he could start to build a case, especially if there were any similar events down the line, of being an emerging *national* figure. That would be excellent for getting grants and fellow-ships, of course, excellent for his resume, which he might soon be able to send to some colleges. Also to be considered was that he might start to be perceived as Perry's protégé—that in itself, once the image solidified, could land him a job or a fellowship or possibly a CD deal. Perry was certainly following through—more than Ray could have expected—and who understood about building a career better than Perry, who was an institution now, a rock-solid part of international classical-music consciousness?

And how delicate of him, how shrewd, not to mention anything but business on his machine. He was showing respect, and that was appreciated, too. But to travel with him (and to get, at best, an adjoining hotel room in Santa Barbara) was to place himself in obvious jeopardy. Perry would certainly expect some favors from him there, and what would Ray do then? The notion of sex with Perry somehow still seemed abstract, so that he was only now thinking of it, but he couldn't very well block it out indefinitely. Could he stand to have it happen again? No, of course not. That was unthinkable. And how would Joy feel about his trip? With her trust admittedly fragile, would she accept the idea of his going to California with Perry, just when he was supposed to be getting interviewed and moving to Philadelphia? Well, for a few days he guessed she could. She'd have no basis for suspecting anything was wrong, though she might *think* it because she *was* frighteningly intuitive. Still, it was too dark and potentially insulting a thing to bring up, and left alone as a mere thought, wouldn't it eventually recede, especially if he paid more attention to her than ever? He could call her every day from California and bring her back a present.

But the question remained: What did he want? He had wanted to talk about it for one thing; he'd wanted to talk about it with Bryna but found that he couldn't, not to her or to anybody. It was as if what he was doing were at once so preposterous yet so tawdry and typical that he couldn't tell anyone and so didn't know what to do, other than knowing that Perry couldn't be kept waiting indefinitely for an answer, especially when he was offering so much.

# 15

Ray, I'm so glad to hear from you. I thought my message might not have gotten through. Every time I leave one of those messages, I wonder, Do you suppose it really was recorded, do you suppose my message will really be heard? It's a bit like praying, isn't it? So thank you for answering my prayers, Ray," Perry said, laughing.

"It's me who should be thanking you. What you said sounds wonderful, though I'm not sure I completely understand it."

"Of course not. How could you? A while ago I thought it might be fun to spend a little time in Santa Barbara. Have you ever been there?"

"No, I haven't."

"And so when UCSB made their offer, I accepted. Basically they want me to give a kind of open-to-the-public lecture and then have their students play some of my chamber music. Lately I've been trying to give some exposure to younger composers at these college events, so naturally I thought of you, especially after your smash at Tanglewood."

"Thank you so much for that."

"Now don't worry about money. They'll pay for our tickets

and they'll give you two thousand dollars for your trouble, and we'll each get a room on campus. By the way, did you know their campus is right on the ocean—it's a fabulously wealthy school—but if you like, we can stay in town at a hotel instead. My treat. All you'd have to do is FedEx them one of your pieces, a shorter one, fifteen minutes or less would be ideal, and be prepared to talk about it for a few minutes after the performance. Then maybe sit on a panel with me for an hour or so later in the day."

"It doesn't give them much time to learn the piece."

"They're young and gifted and like to be challenged, and they've already undoubtedly overrehearsed my stuff by now. They'll be fine."

"It's an incredible opportunity."

"Yes, I think so."

"How much time do you think would be involved?"

"A day at the school. A day to get there and come back. Maybe you'll become as enchanted with Santa Barbara as I am and want to spend a couple of days afterward."

Though he said nothing about it, Ray couldn't stop thinking about the money he'd be paid, which he knew Perry had negotiated well above what they wanted to pay him, possibly as a condition of Perry's coming. Ray had never been paid for having his music performed; on the contrary, he often had to chip in a few hundred dollars or so to help finance some group concerts produced by other young composers in his situation. The money would be crucial just to pay off some debts and get a few things for his apartment, but it also suddenly seemed a real honor.

"I assume you need to know right away."

"That really would be best," Perry said in his even, infinitely civilized tone.

"I guess I'd be a fool not to go."

"I think so," Perry said, still without a trace of impatience or self-congratulation.

Ray thanked Perry again and said he'd better start preparing for the trip. Perry reminded him it was two weeks away and that they already had tickets. They'd be leaving from La Guardia. There was plenty of time to do everything.

Almost immediately after getting off the phone, he thought he would call Joy and tell her, but he couldn't. Eventually, of course, he would have to tell her (he couldn't simply not have any contact for four or five days or else call her from Santa Barbara and pretend he was in New York), and it would certainly be best to tell her as soon as possible. Still, he couldn't make the call no matter how many pep talks he gave himself. He'd waited so long for things to be this good with Joy, and he was afraid the news might upset her, that they would fight, and she might even sense the truth about Perry and confront him with it or end up giving him some kind of ultimatum about the trip.

He improvised on the piano for a few minutes but couldn't concentrate well enough to enjoy it. Then he turned his attention to what piece he'd select. This was something he really did have to do right away, along with a thank-you letter to the head of the UCSB music department, selecting and photocopying the score, and sending it FedEx.

When he eliminated his four orchestral works (the piece performed at Tanglewood was the only one he deemed of professional quality anyway), his fourteen piano pieces, which were among his favorite works, and those songs he wrote for piano and soprano (largely so Joy and he could rehearse and perform them), he was left with only a few contending chamber works that could fit Perry's time requirement. There was his string quartet, which ran about thirteen and a half minutes—his first post-Juilliard work. It was fresh, youthful, and fairly free of obvious influences but lacking in the power he felt some of his mature works had. There was also his piano trio with its little homages to Debussy and Bartók, a curious piece more tranquil than most of his work, a piece he'd always secretly liked more than he publicly admitted. But it was never anybody else's favorite piece—neither Joy nor Arnold nor Marty rated it among his best five, so how could he represent himself with it in his first West Coast performance? How could he feel confident enough about it, especially when he was representing himself to Perry as well? That left his violin and piano sonata, the piece he'd dedicated to Joy and often thought of as his "Joy Sonata," which he and his friends felt was definitely one of his strongest works. It was recent, too; he'd finished it less than two years ago. It did run slightly more than seventeen minutes, but he was sure Perry wouldn't object to two extra minutes. If necessary, he would gladly offer to speak less to make up for it. He didn't look forward to speaking and already realized that would require more work and worry than anything else. So it seemed definite, yet he still wanted to consult Joy. While Arnold knew more about contemporary music, she was the person he needed to check with because she cared the most about him, and he trusted her completely. Besides, he couldn't bear to keep something like this secret from her.

He called her then, but there was no answer and still no machine on which to leave a message. She was probably rehearsing or teaching, maybe even taking a swim. He found the idea of her swimming without him painful and tried again without success. Would the rest of his day now consist of these futile attempts to call her so he could ask her about which piece he should send to UCSB? He decided to do things differently this time. He wouldn't be the passive prisoner of his telephone, trying to play the piano while he waited for her to come home. He would photocopy the sonata and send it right now, then he would rent a car and go find her.

Just before he left his apartment, he did wonder if he should tell Perry about the length of the sonata, but decided not to. With Perry, appearing as independent as possible was crucial. Perry would take him more seriously as a composer, and, more important, when he'd have to make some decisions that Perry wouldn't like later on, there would be a better chance he'd believe him and not try to manipulate him as he had last time.

Outside, it was so hot he felt he was in a tropical world. His neighborhood passed by him in a kind of fog dotted with the homeless and a junkie or two wandering about that made him shiver slightly despite the heat. He just had to keep his eyes straight ahead—keep his New York soldier's face on tight and concentrate on his specific tasks: photocopy the piece, mail the piece with the letter he'd purposely kept short and simple, kept to three lines, in fact.

On the way to FedEx, two homeless men approached him within a block of each other: one a black man who was wearing shoes so thin they looked like strips of bacon; the other an elderly white man whose eyes were mere slits, as if their lids had decided to shut down out of weariness. He gave them each a dollar. Yes, the two thousand dollars would come in very handy, he thought as he rode the subway to Avis.

HE COULDN'T remember the last time he'd rented a car in New York. He knew he'd done it once with Joy when they first went out and then once with a woman he'd dated briefly before Joy, but that might have been it since he'd come to New York fourteen years ago. He never thought or was aware of cars in New York. Trucks and taxis, yes—but New York still seemed a carless city. No one he knew used one in daily life, and so it didn't occur to him that they were always available as a way to leave town. Instead, over the years he'd become a train rider or an airplane passenger or even a bus rider, but none of those would do for this situation. He felt an urgent need to see Joy as soon as possible. He knew there were speed traps all over the highway, but he still went ten to fifteen miles over the limit the whole way. The country scenes seemed curiously insubstantial as they flashed by. He thought if he really loved nature, as he used to think he did, especially when he identified with Mahler, who was famous for his love of nature, then he'd already be feeling better; he'd be getting some consolation. But he wasn't.

Nature was tormenting him, he was forced to conclude, not only because it was separating him from Joy, but because he kept picturing her in it—in scenes which always included cultured and attractive men. No matter how he rationalized it, he had to admit he was speeding in a car he had rented, with money he couldn't afford to spend, for fear that she was with someone, someone she'd kept secret from him, and that he had to get to Tanglewood either to learn the truth or to keep it from happening, because the thought of her sleeping with someone else was unbearable.

A few times, like a countermelody played by a flute or a piccolo barely emerging through the rest of the orchestra, he realized he had no reason to distrust her. She hadn't been unfaithful to him in their first relationship. Instead, when she felt things would never improve, she'd broken up with him. He'd always respected her for being the kind of woman who lets you know where things stand, rather than the kind he'd experienced more often, who gets back at you behind your back. That was Joy's code, wasn't it? If things got too bad, she'd simply leave. It was bizarre not to be able to produce a single example of deviance from this code (and he knew a good deal of Joy's history with other men) yet to get so little solace from it. He simply felt she was with another man right now. He wasn't sure if they were actually having sex, but they were swimming or playing tennis or taking a walk in the woods. It was not even inconceivable that she was with Perry, and that she'd somehow found out from him what had happened and was trying to seduce him right now. Hadn't she flirted with him all during dinner, and wasn't Perry at least a little angry at him for his obvious resistance? Could he even be certain that Perry would resist such a magnificently perverse experience? Did he even know for a fact that Perry had never slept with a woman? He'd never asked him. He'd simply assumed. Perry was a "homosexual"; therefore, he never slept with women; yet he, himself, was a "heterosexual" who had recently had a sexual experience with a man.

He felt a shiver again. Lenox was a mile ahead. He passed a golf course he used to play as a teenager during his brief flirtation with the sport, and suddenly, incredibly, remembering that Joy liked the game, could barely fight off the impulse to drive back to it and walk the course, thinking he might find her with some athletic musician she'd met at Tanglewood who'd convinced her to play with him on their day off as a lark.

I'm really starting to lose it, he said to himself as he turned left, heading for Main Street. He wished he'd taken his Ativan with him and wondered if he should stop to have a drink at one of the bars in town, or at least get some Tylenol at a drugstore, but he drove past a market without stopping. He turned left on the road to Tanglewood, and Lake Mahkeenac came into view. It was the lake where he was two-thirds sure she was swimming in her navy-blue suit. The road curved; the trees thickened; the lake darted in and out of view. The sun was out strong, making the lake sparkle and making it harder to pick up cars coming toward him around the curves. He heard them before he saw them, their engines blending with the sound of motorboats on the lake. When he arrived at Mahkeenac Heights, where Joy lived, and got out of the car, he was surprised for a moment to hear the air dominated by the sound of birds, the lake invisible behind a thick woods and network of hard dirt paths.

She wasn't there. He knocked on the door three times and called her name and even stood on his tiptoes and knocked on the windows, watching them carefully the whole time for a trace of her before finally sitting on the grass in her yard, not knowing what to do. For a while, he pulled up blades of grass from her yard, then ripped them into smaller pieces before scattering them in the air. Periodically he checked the cloud movements without knowing why, until he realized he was trying to determine when she might find it too cold or too cloudy to stay at the lake. Finally he decided he would go to the beach to find her himself. He felt like walking but thought, if they somehow missed each other, the sight of a strange car in her driveway might frighten her.

He parked first at Stockbridge Town Beach, where she usually swam because it was closest to her house, a beach halfway between Stockbridge and Lenox. Two young women and a man were playing Frisbee in their bathing suits in the grassy hills that led down to the sand, and a stray throw brushed against his knee.

"Sorry," they yelled in unison. He smiled and threw it back to them. A lot of people were on the beach. Some sat on their blankets talking animatedly or playing the radio, but lots of people were swimming, and both rafts in the lake were nearly full. He didn't see her on the beach, didn't think he saw her blanket either. He walked past the high white lifeguard chair toward the water, nearly bumping into a little girl clasping a beach ball to her tiny stomach. The first raft, where the water only came up to his waist, was filled with mostly little kids. It had a long yellow slide that he still liked to use. She wasn't there. Twenty yards behind it was the "adult raft," for sunbathing, discreet diving, and softer conversation. He looked carefully but didn't see her. He decided he'd walk around the beach to look for her blanket and had taken a few steps uphill when he heard his name called.

He heard it twice before he turned and saw Joy walking toward him in her long athletic stride, wearing her navy-blue bathing suit. He couldn't imagine where she had come from.

"I was just looking for you," he said, feeling relieved and for a few moments a little angry, as if she had somehow tricked him.

"I was at Beachwood," she said, pointing to the smaller private beach a quarter mile to the left. "Too many people here." He studied her face for traces of deceit, but what she said was obviously true. Finally, he smiled.

"Ray, what are you doing here?"

He moved toward her and kissed her lightly. "Are you OK?"

"Sure, of course, I'm glad to see you. I'm just flabbergasted is all. Is everything all right?"

"I tried to call you, but there was no answer, and I kept trying. . . . "

"I was at Tanglewood and then I came here for a swim."

"So, I just decided to see you."

"God, Ray, how did you get here?"

"I rented a car. It's parked at the top of the hill."

She was smiling at him, and he found himself studying the smile for authenticity, as if an inauthentic smile could send him back to his car and New York in an instant.

"Are you really glad to see me?"

"Of course I am," she said, putting an arm around his waist.

"Come on, let's go to the snack bar and I'll buy you a Popsicle," he said.

"There is no snack bar anymore. It's just an earth-toned, ecologically correct bathhouse. Didn't you notice?"

Ray looked and saw instantly that she was right and felt disappointed. The snack bar was one of the few things that hadn't changed in Tanglewood. There were always chips in the green painted wood and holes in the screened windows which several flies inevitably penetrated, always the same limited bill of fare. To shift weight while waiting for a Creamsicle on its swollen wooden floors smelling of mustard and damp bathing suits was to touch his youth again. He was feeling nostalgic for it as they walked slowly through the thicker grass, settling by a clump of birch trees at a recently deserted table. Her eyes were clear and blue. He felt it would be horrible if there was ever a time when he couldn't look at them.

"You seem nervous; is everything all right?"

"Do I?" he said.

"Yes, you do."

"I was having some jealous thoughts, crazy thoughts, on the way up here. I guess that's it."

"Silly Ray," she said, smiling and feeling flattered, he thought, in spite of herself. Then she looked at him more intently and said, "Is that all?"

She still had the talent for seeing through him, which made him nervous but also made him value her in a way that, if she ever somehow lost that gift, he would feel her to be somewhat diminished. "Well, yes, I do have to tell you something. It seems opportunity has knocked on my door again."

She raised her eyebrows, a potential smile waiting on her lips.

"Perry called with another invitation to have one of my pieces performed on a program with one of his."

"God, that's fantastic, Ray."

"It's more than a concert. It's at a university, and I have to be on a panel and maybe teach a class. I'm going to get paid for this, by the way, paid very well."

He looked at her, but the smile had disappeared and her eyes showed an equal mix of pleasure and anticipation. She seemed so beautifully transparent at times, so thrillingly honest, he wondered that he ever doubted her.

"The thing is this is all happening in two weeks, and it's going to take a few days. And it's in Santa Barbara, in California."

"Ray, this is wonderful news. You're going to become famous. You've become Perry Green's protégé. What could be better? You accepted, didn't you?"

"Yeah, I accepted. I'm just not crazy about going to California now."

"Everyone says Santa Barbara is beautiful."

"I'm sure it is. I just wish I didn't have to be so far away from you right now."

Her face became serious again. Then she looked at him almost quizzically. "Do you mean that?"

"Yes."

"Is this the same Ray who used to withdraw from me and who'd get angry because I wanted to see you more than just weekends? Who used to accuse me of micromanaging your life every time I expressed an opinion about anything to do with us?"

"That was a long time ago. People change."

"I'm beginning to believe it."

"The last time we were together at your house was so beautiful. It meant a lot to me. I don't want to lose that."

She lowered her head, looked at the ground for a few seconds, and said, "Me either."

"I guess I thought my going away might put a strain on us at just the wrong time. Remember how much we talked about trust."

"I think I overdid it a bit. Or maybe I'm beginning to believe you. I haven't panicked—much—since you've been in New York. I think I do trust you again."

"Really?"

"I think so. So your being in Santa Barbara for a few days, surrounded though you'll undoubtedly be by attractive, ambitious young female musicians hanging on your every word, won't be any different than your being in New York while I'm here in the Berkshires, will it?"

"No. I guess not."

"So let's celebrate. There's a lot to celebrate, don't you think? I think this calls for a drink." She took his hand.

"Let me do something first," he said, standing up with her. Still holding hands, they walked behind the birch trees.

She laughed for a second, then her face turned serious as she looked at him. He took her face in his hands and kissed her, prolonging the kiss while he caressed her hair and face.

"Can you stay tonight?"

"I'd like to."

"And after that?"

"I'd like to stay if I could maybe for a few days—if it's all right."

"God, you're really something. I love the way you surprised me like this. *Trés romantique*. This new Ray is really stealing my heart," she said, laughing. They were walking uphill, arms around each other's waist. It was only when they reached the road that he remembered his car.

"I better not leave my car here. Do you mind riding back?"

"Something make you forget about it?" she said, smiling at him.

"Yeah. Something. Something insanely compelling and addictive. The same thing that made me drive here in the first place."

THEY HAD never made love more spontaneously and happily, he thought, yet afterward, while he held her against him in bed, he felt oddly nervous. He had never wanted anyone so badly, and he wondered if he should try to need her less. How could he function otherwise? How could he go about his daily life being inundated by this feeling, knowing that she had it in her power to break off with him at any moment, as she had two years before? On the other hand, having felt this desire now, how could he live without it or even try to diminish it in any way?

Strange that just as his career suddenly had progressed dramatically, his love life should also develop in an equally sudden and surprising way. It was almost too much for him to comprehend. Of course he'd paid the price for his career break, but the woman lying against his chest with her eyes closed appeared to want nothing from him except what he wanted to give. This was the "private fame" Perry yearned for, and maybe it really was the most important thing in the world, maybe it was far more important than his career.

He must remember when he felt panicky that Joy was ultimately a reasonable person. She didn't just break up with him arbitrarily two years ago; she left because he was too afraid and immature to have a real relationship. She left because of the way he treated her, which resulted in too many fights. By any standard of objectivity, it was the right decision. Instead of frightening him, it should make him feel confident that she was strong and rational enough to generally make good decisions. It should help him believe all the more in her, and when he thought about it, it did. She seemed to treat him very much according to how he treated her. There was an elemental justice about that that pleased him—a living proof of the efficacy of the Golden Rule that was so rarely applied in personal relationships. He was not really then a passive object of fate but was to a large extent in control of the situation. He knew he needed to be vigilant about understanding what she was feeling, and, of course, he had to accept that he could never tell her about Perry, neither about the past nor about his fears for the future, specifically that inevitable moment in Santa Barbara when Perry would try to enact with him his own understanding of the Golden Rule.

He felt her move a little, thought he felt her eyelids flutter against his chest.

"Ray? Do you remember the beginning of our first time together?"

"The first time we slept together?"

"No, though the time I was thinking about was pretty near that. There was a two-week stretch when you started staying over a lot, and when we went out, New York seemed magical."

"It was magical."

"I remember I used to say a few times after we made love that this wouldn't be a bad time to die because the rest of life could never be anything but anticlimactic, or something like that."

"I said it, too, or I felt it."

"I just felt that way again now. For the first time since then, the first time in more than three years, I guess."

He put his arm around her and looked at the trees still partially visible through her window, and suddenly he, too, wished that they could always be where they were now, that time could be tricked, and nothing new would ever have to happen.

# 16

Ray had never flown first class before, but Perry had taken care of that through the college. They'd been flying for about an hour, and he hoped that with the wider seats he might be able to sleep or at least feign it. But each time he closed his eyes, Perry asked him a question, almost as if he sensed what he was doing and delighted in thwarting him.

"So what were your thoughts as the days before your trip dwindled?"

Ray opened his eyes and pretended to look out the window.

"Mostly I've thought about the work I had to do. And wondered how good the pianist and violinist will be. Will they have enough time to rehearse? I called both of them, and they made me feel a little better. We discussed a few passages, which reassured me a bit."

"Did you work on your speech?"

"A little, some. You told me to be spontaneous, so I'll be following your advice," he said with a short laugh.

"That's when people often make the most sense when it comes to talking."

Another brief silence, then "Have you had any chance to think about us?"

"What do you mean?"

"About what this trip might be like for us, might mean to us."

"I've been really focused on the work, the things I have to do. This is another great opportunity you've given me, and naturally I want to do well."

"And so you shall. I have no doubt of it," Perry said, turning toward Ray. "It's funny. When I have a lot of work to do, it often makes me more erotic, at least it did this time. I guess I'm incorrigible." He laughed and grabbed one of Ray's hands.

Ray let him hold it for a few seconds before withdrawing it.

"And with whom did you have erotic relations?" Ray asked, feigning a jealous tone.

"No one. I've told you that was my commitment. My increase in eros was all in my mind and heart and focused on you, as if you don't already know it," Perry said a little crossly.

"What did you tell Bobby about the trip?"

"The truth, of course."

"So he knows I'm going with you?"

"Of course he knows."

"What does he think of that?"

"He thinks it's good for me. He's glad I have company. I told you he's not the possessive type."

"And does he know about the erotic thoughts you just alluded to?"

"He doesn't ask and I don't tell."

"But doesn't he wonder why he isn't sleeping with you lately?"

"He's patient. He knows I have heart problems, that I'm an older man not getting any younger, and he doesn't ask. Sex has only been an occasional part of our relationship. I wish you would believe that and stop worrying about Bobby. Haven't you ever had a relationship with a woman that was at least somewhat similar?"

Immediately he thought of Bryna and conceded the point.

"I thought you did. It's not all that different on my side of the fence."

Forty-five minutes later, after eating lunch, Ray did fall asleep. He dreamed he was in a large room in a place that was familiar but that he couldn't identify. A long, oval pool with a number of Jacuzzis was in the center of the room. For some time he had been swimming alone. When he stopped, Perry was standing beside him, talking to him. While their conversation was going on, a warm thrust of water from the Jacuzzi kept hitting his upper legs, mesmerizing him and producing an enormous and obvious erection. After a while Perry pointed at it and then at his own erection that forced his navy-blue suit up at an angle.

"Look, we're twins," he said. They both laughed, but when Ray turned his head he saw Joy swimming toward him, an angry expression filling her piercing blue eyes.

Ray woke up with a start as the flight attendant was clearing away his tray, and he yearned for Joy more deeply than he had since his latest trip to the Berkshires, which again had ended with his staying for three days.

"I think you were dreaming," Perry said, too tenderly for Ray's taste. "Do I ever appear in your dreams?"

"I don't remember my dreams," Ray said, as Perry's smile of hope turned to a frown.

"It probably wasn't a pleasant one," Perry said, returning to the score he was studying. Ray got the message and made a mental note to be nicer to Perry. The goal of the trip was certainly not to alienate him. He shouldn't forget that Perry was his benefactor—his benefactor/rapist, Ray corrected himself bitterly. It was the first time on the trip that he'd thought of the incident at Perry's house, and he closed his eyes for a moment. Then he rang for the flight attendant and ordered a vodka and tonic.

162

"I didn't know you drank this early," Perry observed.

"Preconcert jitters," Ray said.

PERRY HAD made reservations at the El Prado Motor Inn, a moderately priced hotel just off the middle of State Street in the center of town. While he was parking the car he'd rented at LAX, Perry said, "I was tempted to take you to the Biltmore, where some of our presidents as well as foreign heads of state have stayed—it's quite a grand hotel, right on the water next to Montecito—but I think, if it's all right with you, that we'll be fine at our humble El Prado. It's clean, it's convenient—we're right next to a number of restaurants and other useful places, like the library and a twenty-four-hour market where they sell beer and wine, and we're only a few miles from the university."

"Sounds fine."

Perry locked up the car, and they left for the hotel lobby. It was a typical August day in Santa Barbara. The early morning fog had burned off around eleven-thirty, and the bright cloudless sky was drenched with sun, though the temperature was only in the low eighties. Perry put on his sunglasses, but Ray didn't wear his, not wanting in any way to look like Perry's "twin."

"I don't want you to think I was being chintzy in avoiding the expensive hotels. I just don't want to meet any people. Even in August there're apt to be celebrity followers in those hotels, a number of stars live in Santa Barbara, and then there's often press hanging around, so I thought if it's the same to you . . . "

"It's fine. I think you made a wise decision."

"Your room is next to mine, by the way. I hope that's OK?"

"Sure," Ray said, though he wasn't sure Perry even heard him, as he was picking up the keys from the desk clerk.

Perry tipped the porter and said, "I think I'm getting a little tired and should take a nap. Do you want to nap with me?"

The words bit into Ray, shocked him, and he turned his

head as if trying to find something that had been there a second before.

"I'm feeling kind of the reverse. Overstimulated, wired. I'd like to unpack and work on my speech a little, if that's all right."

"Of course. I didn't expect you to be in a sleepy mood just yet. Work well, Ray, work well." Perry smiled as he closed his door.

In his room, with his suitcase unpacked by his bed, Ray stood in front of a large window looking at a palm tree outside the hotel, directly in his line of sight like some hideous greenheaded spy. Whatever thoughts he might have comforted himself with (hopes, really, more than thoughts) that Perry wouldn't force the issue had evaporated like the morning fog. Perry had him isolated now; there was no place to hide in this sunlight, no excuse to use, not when Perry had created and paid for everything and was waiting in the next room.

It was not that it was such a sin, especially if he was careful. It was, objectively speaking, just a case of bringing some pleasure to a nice, aging man, in fact to an extraordinarily talented, aging man who had already made an enormous contribution to his life. If he felt so disgusted and terrorized, wasn't it in part simply because of the way he was socialized, that though he thought of himself as unscarred by any prejudice, he (like everyone else in the country) was far more homophobic than he realized? Suppose the sexual dynamics in his situation were altered. Suppose he were a young gay composer whom an influential older woman was helping and, in exchange, he was sleeping with her. People would think she was doing him a great service and would encourage him in his new heterosexual romance. Certainly there would be a minimal amount of fear or embarrassment in being in public together, and that alone would be an immense relief. No, he couldn't pretend that he wasn't aware of such ironies, such absurd hypocrisies, but neither could he deny that the real issue that made him sick at heart was his betrayal of himself. But wait. If he valued his work more than his pleasure, was "betrayal" the right word? It was shocking to realize that he was vulgar enough to be so ambitious, but if he was, and cared more about his career than his emotional happiness, he was actually being *true* to himself, wasn't he? He really wasn't betraying himself at all. He saw an image of Joy, then, her hair brushed back as she turned toward him in bed during their last morning together. He turned away from the window and the huge spying palm tree and left the room to go outside.

Turning left, he walked down State Street past a line of radiant restaurants and elegant shops as well as a plethora of imposing banks. The mountains of Montecito formed a backdrop, and from most points he could see the Channel Islands on the horizon with the sun shining white on the harbor. The people who passed by, an unusually large percentage of whom were blond, wore white or pastel pants and dresses, and in his New York black he felt something of an ogre. Perhaps he would start wearing the one pair of white pants he did bring and join in the spirit, for the people he saw all looked trim and vigorous, and many of them were smiling. Well, it was one of the richest towns in America; the people were living good lives; their smiles were understandable. They lived in a place filled with sunshine and flowers. There were no slums in Santa Barbara, and the few homeless people on the streets were almost discreetly polite. He walked past the courthouse surrounded by a large meticulously manicured lawn bathed in a lemon-colored light. Like many of the buildings on State Street, it was white with orange tiles and reflected the town's Spanish and Mexican past. On top of the courthouse was an observation tower that offered, besides the mountains themselves, the best view of the town. And just below the observation tower was a huge clock that lit up at night.

Why had he rationalized the way he had just a few minutes ago in his room, he wondered, as if there were nothing wrong with this Perry business, as if he really had no choice but to capitulate to what Perry wanted? Was all this sun making him dizzy? Did Perry himself count on this? First, intoxicate him with a cocktail of ocean and sunlight, then finish him off at the university with a main course of success. It made him shudder to recall his line of reasoning about helping a nice, aging man or of being true to himself. He realized that his walk was an act of self-protection, that he needed to be alone, specifically away from Perry, to think clearly and realize that when the confrontation happened, as it obviously soon would, he had to say no firmly, even if it meant the end of Perry's favors. It simply had to end now, and if the favors ended too, he could still walk away a small winner, more than he'd ever been up till now. The key was to do it in a way that preserved Perry's ego, to ensure that Perry wouldn't become his enemy, but that shouldn't be too difficult. Perry was essentially a reasonable man and old and successful enough to be forgiving. He tried out a couple of lines to himself as he walked toward the beach at the bottom of State Street. "If I were ever going to cross over, it would be with you, there wouldn't even be a possibility with someone else, but it isn't in me. It's just too confusing and threatening to my identity. I'm sorry." Or "I respect you so much as a musician and a man, but I know now that I can only fall in love with a woman and that I can't separate love from sex anymore. It's too painful."

*How do you know that now?*

"Because I have fallen in love with someone, someone I once loved years before who left me and who I always wanted back and who I now love much more deeply than I did then, because I've grown up and deepened."

He'd reached the end of State Street, and the beach, surrounded by thick rows of palm trees, lay in front of him. The water was mostly azure (turquoise in parts), and there was a pier extending a hundred yards or so into the water. To the right of the pier was a harbor with its bright white yachts. A group of bare-chested boys skateboarded on the last bits of cement before the sand began. Behind them he saw a pay phone. Should he call Joy now?

It would be a quarter of two and unlikely that she'd be in. She was probably at Tanglewood rehearsing or else taking a lesson and wouldn't be back for another three hours. Besides, wouldn't it seem odd for him to call her in the afternoon when it was understood that he'd call at night and when she'd gone out of her way to say she didn't really expect him to call until after the concert, that she understood how busy he'd be until then? Wouldn't it seem too panicky, and wouldn't she possibly detect some hidden but extraordinary pressure? He walked past the phone onto the sand. There weren't many people on the beach. Many more were on the pier shopping, but that was understandable. Swimming was almost year-round in Santa Barbara and so were the shining blue skies, and both were probably taken for granted.

He passed a young couple making out on their blanket, oblivious to the world. When had he last known a feeling of freedom and peace like that? Maybe in the first weeks with Joy, when they used to go to Westport on the weekends. The last few days with her were magnificent, but he worried about running into Perry every time they left her house. He walked closer to the water. In the distance he could see a volleyball net and the blur of a ball flying across it. Was Perry up by now? Had he already knocked on his door? Ray wished he could go swimming, though he hadn't taken his suit, and thought he could get by in his underpants. He'd noticed a couple of women sunbathing topless in the course of his walk. But he didn't have a towel and didn't think Perry would react well if he went swimming without him the first time. Perhaps he really should get back to the hotel.

Instead of walking along the beach toward Montecito, he

moved in an almost straight line toward the water. A hundred yards in front of him a sailboat with a large white sail was motionless. He couldn't see anybody on it and figured its owner might be swimming. Then he bent down and put his hands in the ocean. The water, lake-still, lapped up to the sand almost soundlessly. He put it on his face, thought of Whitman's phrase "The sea whispered me," wondered if anyone had written a song with that line in it. If not, maybe he should when this trip was all over. Write a new song for Joy, something she could really be proud to sing, something that could show off her expressive range, the power in her upper register. The line was from "Out of the Cradle Endlessly Rocking," wasn't it? Where were the Whitmans in today's world? Where were the Beethovens, the Tolstoys? The big spirits who had big things to say? His own output was so puny, though he felt he had succeeded in a few pieces in a limited way that showed sensitivity and skill and the beginnings of a kind of original voice, like someone sticking a toe in the water, afraid to jump in. He knew what was the matter. He'd spent too much time pursuing his career (that was typical of his whole generation) and not enough on his work. Now that he'd tasted some success, he'd spent all his time worrying about preserving it and plotting to get more. But meanwhile, off in a corner, the work waited like a neglected child. He could rationalize all he wanted about his generation—that as the always small opportunities for serious composers shrank to historic lows, more time had to be spent on one's career or all of them would become extinct. Still, he had only *his* life to worry about, and he *was* getting his opportunity now. The point was not to get too caught up in opportunity for its own sake while his own talent went unexplored, undeveloped. Once this concert ended, he'd begin composing again two hours a day no matter what. He wondered how Perry had handled this problem. There was probably a time when he was awkwardly transitioning into success. How had he done it? Or did he feel he'd squandered too much of his time, too? Perry could be intensely self-critical in a quiet way, but he also had a strange kind of self-confidence that transcended his career and allowed him to be self-possessed in everything he did. The bastard, Ray thought, laughing a little. He was a formidable man who could, if he wanted, become a formidable foe.

He turned away from the water. It was time to go back to the hotel.

# 17

They really did a good job, first rate under the circumstances . . . I mean, what did we have, two, really one and a half, rehearsals. So, yes, I was pleased."

"Did the audience like it?"

"They seemed to. Of course they have to applaud to be polite."

"Says who? God, Ray, only you have these audience-conspiracy theories."

"Well, the university people had to applaud."

"Were they the whole audience?" Joy said, with gentle sarcasm.

"No. It was a big crowd because of Perry. Five or six hundred people at least. The auditorium was filled. And they applauded warmly, I would say, and I took a bow, and it was very nice. So I guess they did like it, since they couldn't have all known each other and known who was coming in advance and all conspired to be polite for my benefit," he said, laughing along with her. "Thank you for making me feel better. You always make me feel better."

"You're welcome, sweetheart."

"Often *very* much better."

She laughed and told him she looked forward to their both feeling very much better as soon as he came back. Then she asked about the reception.

"It was pleasant, you know, California friendly. I met the critics from the Santa Barbara papers."

"They have two papers there?"

"The main one, the *News and Press,* and the alternative weekly. They each told me they liked it, which was nice."

"That's fabulous. You should be thrilled."

"It's nice; it's not the *Times,* but it's nice. Actually, I was told there was a critic from the *LA Times,* so I may call you tomorrow if he reviewed it and I can bear to talk about it."

"Call me anyway. I miss you. I love hearing from you."

"I miss you, too, horribly."

There was a silence, and he instinctively looked over his shoulder. He was glad he was calling from a phone booth instead of the hotel, where Perry was taking a nap.

"How was the panel? Did you talk much?"

"No, I pretty much kept that to a minimum."

"A minimalist talker, huh?"

"No, I spoke in reasonably long and fluent sentences. Sometimes I even got out a paragraph or two. Actually, I was asked about minimalism."

"What did you say?"

"I told the truth, or my truth. I said there's a certain poetry in Glass, for example, and a different kind in Reich. That shows it's a valid music because it can produce different kinds of poetry, but it's limited music, too. For myself, I might want to use it for a part of a movement, or for a whole movement, maybe even for a whole short piece. But I wouldn't want to submerge all my works in it. Then I would feel too constricted. Something like that is what I said."

"That's a pretty good answer. Were you really that articulate?"

"Yes. You sound surprised."

"Of course I'm not surprised. But weren't you nervous?"

"A little. It was right before the concert, so it was kind of hard to concentrate. Perry said I did all right."

"And how did Perry do?"

"Perry was Perry, master of every situation."

"You two getting along all right?"

"Sure. I don't see him much," Ray said, looking outside the phone booth again.

"Aren't you in the same hotel?"

"Yes, but he's tremendously busy. He knows so many people. We've had a couple of quick meals together, but that's it. . . . God, I miss you," he said. It had felt so good when she said that to him, and he wanted to make her feel good, too, and above all to stop asking about Perry.

The rest of the conversation went well, and they ended by saying they loved each other. He was glad he didn't have to tell her any direct lies, although he had led her to believe there were some things he had to do at the university tomorrow, when in reality his responsibilities had ended. He was staying the extra day because he'd promised Perry he would go to the beach with him.

"Give me a day with you in Santa Barbara," Perry had said. He could be surprisingly sentimental when he wanted, or was he just being manipulative, knowing that Ray had a sentimental core, too? Maybe both. At any rate, he couldn't say no to him, not after the gig had gone so well, turned out to be such a first-class experience, surpassed in his life only by the concert at Tanglewood. There were worse fates than being in the company of Perry Green for a day in Santa Barbara or anywhere else. If it weren't for the sex problem, he would consider himself blessed. The key remained making sure it didn't happen again, and he still felt he didn't know how to accomplish that.

He began walking briskly up State Street. He'd promised

to meet Perry at the hotel for dinner. How could he not have dinner with the man? Perhaps tonight he'd ask Perry about his life—or better about his career, maybe get him going on some of his anecdotes about Horowitz and Bernstein or Virgil. Or better still about his own music, since that was what Perry cared most about. Ray cursed himself for not knowing more of it, for not buying the scores or at least a few more CDs during all this time. He crossed the street almost in a run, then resumed his brisk walking pace under the giant lit marquee of the Arlington Street Theater. The hotel was two blocks away.

PERRY WAS sitting on the sofa wearing white pants, a pale blue silk shirt, and a cream-colored, unbuttoned sports jacket. His thin silver hair, dappled with strands of black, was carefully combed. He was sipping a Perrier—the picture of composure.

Ray felt unnerved, as he did whenever Perry made any kind of demonstrable effort with his appearance. When Perry took time to do things, he was doubly dangerous.

"Did your walk go well?"

"Yes. I just wanted to stretch my legs for a few minutes, and they got stretched," Ray said with a laugh.

"You should try to see some more of the town if you can. There are parts that are quite spectacular. I was thinking that, if you like, we might drive to the Biltmore and have a drink there before dinner."

"Sure. What's at the Biltmore?"

"It's a grand and glamorous hotel where old Reagan used to stay and entertain foreign heads of state, right on the borderline of Santa Barbara and Montecito. The view of the beach is magnificent. Then I thought you might enjoy it if I took you to El Encanto. It's a hotel with a fine restaurant in the mountains and a very beautiful view. It's a favorite retreat of some of the movie stars, so we're sure to be left alone."

"Don't they know you?"

"They know me the least of all American citizens. I've never been involved with Hollywood, though they've asked me to do film scores. They've asked a number of times, actually. Maybe I should have said yes, who knows? Schoenberg made some money that way and, of course, Prokofiev."

"Not to mention Stravinsky."

"Touché. But wasn't that a onetime thing for the circus? Anyway, let Phil Glass do all the arty film scores. That's fine. I no longer have the time to consider whether I should have done this or that."

Perry got up from the chair by the desk, paced a few steps, and stopped in front of the window that faced the hotel pool.

"The question is do you have the time and inclination to go to the Biltmore and then to our restaurant in the mountains?"

"Of course. Sounds like fun."

"Excellent. I was hoping it would appeal to you."

They took the longer scenic route, at Perry's suggestion, driving up a series of winding mountain roads that overlooked the ocean and Channel Islands. Ray said the scenery was beautiful, and Perry smiled. Then they drove downhill to the Biltmore, where Ray suggested they drink outside on the long lawn that ended only the width of a street away from a few feet of sand and the ocean.

They sat at a table lit by a glass-enclosed candle that reminded Ray of the table by Perry's pool in Tanglewood. For a few moments he felt nostalgic for that time before he'd crossed over with Perry.

"I think it's time for a toast," Perry said softly.

"Yes, of course." Ray looked directly at Perry for the first time since they'd sat down. Perry raised his glass in the air, and for a second it sparkled in the setting sun. Ray raised his glass as well.

"To your career, which took another dramatic and deserved turn forward today. I thought you were brilliant."

Perry and Ray's glasses clinked.

"And to us," Perry continued, "to wherever this improbable adventure leads us."

Again Ray had to clink glasses, but the smile left his face. What improbable adventure was he talking about? "Are you speaking about tonight?" he said as evenly as he could.

"Tonight is part of it. But I meant the adventure of our companionship."

Ray nodded. It was all he felt he could do. He concentrated on finishing his drink while pretending to stare at the ocean, then ordered another, and one more after that, claiming he still needed to unwind after the concert.

On the way to El Encanto, they passed the Spanish mission, a historical landmark whose pink walls and brightly painted statues made it appear somewhat surreal. Driving up in the mountains, they passed more scenic vistas, but neither said much about them. From the moment of the toast, Ray thought Perry had made his intentions for tonight unmistakably clear. He felt startled at first, although later he realized there was no reason he should have been. It was as if his whole being were put on alert to watch every word and gesture of Perry's with the kind of concentration that ultimately made him fall silent. Perry didn't struggle against the silence or even question it during the ride and spoke again only when they arrived at El Encanto. He said he wanted to take a picture of Ray standing in front of a pool in one of the lush formal gardens, and Ray said fine.

"We really ought to have a picture of both of us, don't you think? I'll ask someone."

Ray wanted to object, but how could he? On what grounds? The picture should be something to be proud of, something he could hang in his office (at some point, at some hypothetical university when he got an office)—a framed photograph of his mentor, one of the country's supreme musicians,

Perry Green. A middle-aged woman with blond hair and lots of makeup took the photograph of them standing in front of the pool. She smiled. She clearly thought it was sweet. Perry hadn't elaborated—he never seemed to need to elaborate to get his way with people—and the woman took the photograph. She probably thought Perry was his father.

They sat in the open-air dining room overlooking the forest and mountains. Perry commented on the view, and Ray merely said, "Yes," being in no mood to encourage him in any way.

"I imagine Mahler must have seen things like this when he wrote 'Das Lied von der Erde,'" Perry said, smiling benignly.

"The countryside he saw looked very different, I'm sure. He was a Bohemian, an Austrian, for Christ's sake. What would he know of California?"

"But trees and light are fairly universal. . . . "

Ray muttered a sarcastic remark.

"I'm sorry, I didn't hear what you said."

"Nothing." Ray pretended to study the menu. He had drunk too much and was vaguely aware that that was contributing to his irritation. He had to control himself; he was in no position yet to lose his temper with Perry.

"There are lots of choices," Perry said, "I think anything here will be very good. Have you found something that interests you? Remember to take whatever you want. You're my guest and money is no object, at least not tonight."

"I'll have the roast lamb," Ray said, closing the menu.

"Good choice. I'll have it, too. I want to eat the same thing you do tonight."

Ray looked at him sharply, then realized that Perry had had a couple of drinks himself.

"So it's settled. We'll have the roast lamb. And to drink?"

"I don't think we . . . I should have anything more to drink. I've had three already."

"Nonsense. You have to have wine when you're in California. If you sip it while you eat, you'll be fine. I'll order a Beaujolais."

Ray didn't say anything. Maybe it would be easier this way. To passively cooperate so that Perry could experience a sense of seduction, and power, might make him less angry when he was eventually turned away. And the alcohol that Perry was using to woo him might work against him. He was the much older man, and it could eventually tire him out.

Perry did almost all the talking at dinner, lobbing lines at him like soft volleyballs in the California sun. But the sun seemed to sap the strength from them, and they collapsed when Ray touched them, so that he could never hit them back. From time to time he looked at the mountains that were blurring as if they were composed of light green water. Then he thought he would listen to music in his mind. Music had rescued him before; he knew it was always there. He couldn't recall the opening song of "Das Lied von der Erde," although he knew the score well. Instead he heard a tune from Eno's "Another Green World," then tried to recall the tutti from his own trio. He thought vaguely that if he got drunk enough he might legitimately pass out, and problems could be averted that way.

HE'S ACTING like my chauffeur, but he's really like my tour guide or camp director, Ray thought as Perry drove him away from El Encanto. Everything is a mask between people, he thought, from the moment they see each other and their ears hear one another's first peeps of speech. It had been that way with Joy and him, too. There had been all this enthusiasm and intensity, especially on his part, four years ago, but really both of them were deeply afraid of being close. Though to be fair, that was more true of him. He thought the constant sex was making them closer, when really it was a way of distancing and even avoiding her. When Joy discovered this, she became bitter and suspicious. That's when her distrust of him began—not from a specific incident, but from the ongoing emotional game he didn't even know he'd been playing. Now, of course, he felt he'd outgrown those young man's fears, but now, of course, there was Perry.

They had been driving silently down State Street, the glass-enclosed street lamps casting soft light on the succession of chic eateries and dress shops, evening clubs, and banks. They all merged together, somehow connected by the lights and the flowers—hibiscus, birds-of-paradise, bougainvillea, and azaleas—and by the palm trees, magnolias, and evergreens. A bank was a kind of club, after all, a restaurant was a kind of bank, and the flowers made everything look and smell sweet.

"I thought you might like to see the harbor. This is Stern's Wharf. I didn't think there'd be many people on it, though."

The wharf extended about three hundred yards into the water. A steady stream of pedestrians paraded by its evenly placed lamps, and a fairly steady row of cars passed over the thick wooden blocks of the pier. There appeared to be three or four family-type restaurants still open, but of course that wasn't what interested Perry. He tipped the carhop at Moby Dick's and motioned Ray toward a dark corner on the wharf overlooking a deserted beach where yellow and white lights played on the soft lakelike ocean.

"We've had a full day, haven't we?" Perry said. "I thought it would do us good to be in a quiet spot for a while."

Ray looked out at the lights on the water's still surface.

"We've accomplished a lot, I think, though we haven't accomplished everything."

Ray stayed silent. He was not going to acknowledge any of Perry's double entendres. He was not going to play that type of straight man. Two lesbians walked by holding hands. Perry smiled and put his hand over Ray's.

"There's so much tolerance here. People let you be happy in whatever way you choose."

"I can't do this here."

"Even in the dark?"

"No, I can't."

"Let's go back to the hotel, then," Perry said. "Come with me, I'll get the car."

Ray didn't say anything. He had already said no to him, so he could wait and say no again in the hotel.

In the car he let Perry talk but barely answered him. He was thinking about time. How just as you begin to accept the fact of consciousness and its limitations, and the different species, and the way flowers pollinate and the stars are organized, your time is almost up; you are already too old to alter your fate and can only alter your perspective on it. He thought of talking about this to Perry but was afraid it would seem absurd, like the left-over ramblings of an acid trip. Certainly nothing Perry would want to discuss. Perry's attitude toward words was strictly utilitarian—though utilitarian to a heightened degree. He used words as weapons to give lectures and write books, to seduce people sexually and professionally. But he never showed an inclination to use them to explore the "eternal questions." If he did that kind of thinking at all, it was in his music, and even there he resisted it as if it were an inappropriate avenue for any art to explore. Perry's music was really about man as a social creature. It was not only civilized, but about civilization. It was social, witty, refined, elegant, but it didn't probe the riddle of the universe, and therefore, as far as Ray was concerned, it didn't probe the depth of man. That was something he yearned to tell him now as he was being so subtly smug, so controlling in getting him drunk like this and disbelieving in his freedom and will to refuse him.

They walked through the lobby to the pool. Everything

was neat there and in perfect Santa Barbara order. The frosted-glass-top tables with their white canvas umbrellas and white, hard plastic chairs, the equidistant banana-palm trees, the light blue chaise longues, each with a flowerpot beside it.

"Everytime I see a pool I think of our first swim in Tanglewood. I wish we could be alone here. I wish I could make everyone else disappear."

"Whom would you conduct for?" Ray said, half trying to make a joke.

But Perry continued to speak in his huskily soft, romantic voice. "For you. And you could compose for me. Can we go upstairs now?" he said, putting his hand briefly on Ray's shoulder.

Ray let it rest for a few seconds, then started up the winding green stairway. He was thinking that Joy was right years ago when she said he'd unconsciously sabotaged his relationships, including theirs, in part to please his parents—the better to remain an unattached child. That was also why he'd sabotaged his career for so long and done so many socially inept things for so many years—antagonizing or isolating himself from people who might have helped him. "I don't think you'll ever have children either," she'd told him. "That's the final way you'll think you've pleased your parents. You'll remain the ultimate child by never having one of your own." He'd dismissed what she said then as absurd armchair psychology, yet he remembered the words. But he was still a relatively young man. He had gone back and reclaimed his relationship with Joy, and he had asserted himself and even shown her off to his parents, who seemed strangely pleased. (Perhaps he'd exaggerated his mother's possessiveness. It mostly happened, now that he thought about it, when he was much younger and living at home.) And though he seemed the least likely person to benefit from knowing Perry, he had already capitalized in a major way with the promise of more rewards to come. Was it really so important then that the old man had had one miserable little orgasm from him, when he'd barely kissed or even touched him? Was his guilty, outraged reaction perhaps the last vestige of his destructive self, trying once more to sabotage things in the deceptive name of morality?

They were in the room and it was dark. Perry was breathing quickly. He heard him unzipping his pants.

"Like last time, OK?" Ray heard himself say. "I can't do more than that yet."

And then he lay down on the bed with Perry breathing over him.

# 18

H e was in the car again with Perry driving to Summerland, a beach town a few miles south of Santa Barbara. He had reluctantly agreed to stay longer and give Perry another "absolutely last day" in California.

"What's the matter?" Perry said, looking at him nervously. He'd been solicitous of him all morning and kept asking him how he felt, as if expecting him to bring up last night.

Ray looked out the window at the trees and flowers that lined 101 South and said he was thinking about the work he was missing in New York.

"You tell your pupils that you were in California becoming famous. Tell them that you were an East Coast representative of the composing establishment with Perry Green. For Christ's sake, Ray, you've got to stop worrying about your pupils so much and start thinking bigger thoughts, or you won't be ready for the bigger things when they come, and they will come."

"It's not just the pupils. I was supposed to be pursuing a teaching job in Philadelphia."

"Philadelphia? I didn't know that. Why would you want to leave New York, particularly now when things are going so well for you?"

Ray turned his head toward the window. Why had he told

Perry this, blurted it out like a guilty child? "It's a good opportunity at a school where I have a connection."

"And who is your connection there? Is it Joy?"

"Yes, it is. It is Joy. Is that a problem?"

"No, why should it be? You're lucky she's so devoted to you. Is this a university job?"

"No, it isn't. It's a secondary school. One of those good, enlightened ones."

"They'll work you to death there. They'll put you on committees and give you extracurricular work and you'll be cut off from New York and have even less time to compose than you do now."

"So you think it's a horrible mistake, obviously."

"No, no. I'm not saying that. You need to have a steady income; you shouldn't have to worry about money so much at your age."

"You don't seem very enthusiastic about it."

"It's simply that with these concerts under your belt, I thought you might have aspired for more."

"I don't know how to get more," Ray said, turning to Perry, who was half looking at him while he drove.

"I don't think getting out of New York is the answer. I should think you'd want to capitalize on what you've been building, that you'd want to be available to pick up engagements and offers that are sure to come your way."

"I couldn't get them in Philadelphia, an hour and a half away?"

"Not as easily. You need to make friends and build allies with people you'll meet at concerts and parties. You've been outside the loop for too long, and people need to get to know you, now that you've piqued their interest."

"From that one review in the *Times?*"

"I said piqued with a *q*. Interest in you has certainly not peaked," he said, spelling out the word with a smile.

"I guess I'm at a loss about what to do next. I mean, I

didn't win any competition or fellowship, which has a follow-up component built into it. My concerts were shots out of the blue, due, obviously, completely to you."

"But I'll still be on your side, Ray, and in New York I'll be even closer."

Ray stayed silent for the rest of the drive. Only when they reached Summerland and began walking along the beach did he feel angry about what Perry was doing. What was this objective advice about his career, after all, but a transparent power play to keep him in New York for his own purposes— mainly to make their meetings more convenient and to keep him as far away from Joy as possible?

The blue-gray water was calm as a lake. To the left, cliffs were covered with ice plants and, in the gardens that led to the few houses on the cliff's edge, extraordinarily bright flowers. It was cool and there were high clouds in the sky.

"Where are we going?"

"I'd like to get beyond these rocks," Perry said, pointing at them as if he were cuing the horn section of an orchestra. "The beach changes once we're past there."

Why couldn't he at least say that he wanted to be in Philadelphia to be near Joy? Perry should be able to hear and accept that, especially after last night, when he more than got his way again.

"It's a freer beach. You'll see. The spirit of the beach changes there."

The rocks extended a few feet into the water, but because it was low tide, they could walk around them in the sand. Ten feet from the rocks a tall young man with well-defined muscles was walking toward them naked. He smiled as he passed. Ray couldn't tell if Perry smiled back or not. Twenty feet farther they passed two naked, biker-type men with tattoos on their shoulders, arms around each other's waists. Ray decided not to comment. He was upset enough about other things. When he'd called Joy this morning, she'd told him that she'd run into Bobby in Stockbridge. She actually talked about him with enthusiasm and appeared to enjoy the meeting. Perry had said Bobby didn't know anything about them, had never asked, and wouldn't care if he knew, but how much could Perry be trusted on that issue? What else, after all, could he expect him to say about Bobby?

Another naked man, a blond riding a big brown horse with a flowing mane, saluted them as the horse trotted past. This time Perry smiled.

"Should we take off our trunks, too?"

"No."

"You don't like the feeling?"

"This is a gay beach and I'm not a gay man, OK?"

"Sorry."

"Can't we just go back to the other beach?"

"Of course," Perry said.

They walked back around the rocks and settled on the sand near the edge of the cliff covered with grass and ice plants. Perry, with minimal help from Ray, spread out a blanket composed of towels he'd taken from the hotel. Ray had never seen such a feminine gesture from Perry before. Was it possible that Perry would now allow more of his feminine self to emerge? Ray hadn't allowed himself to think of last night until then, but the image of Perry meticulously folding out towels and placing them so delicately in precise angles on the sand gave him a sharp pain, made him feel as if he were temporarily delirious. He could blame it on alcohol, but he hadn't drunk quite enough to reach that deliciously convenient obliviousness that could explain everything. So he was dismayed not so much by his capitulation as by the ease with which he capitulated. It even seemed that Perry hadn't been at all nervous, as if he never doubted the outcome of his evening's elaborate seduction. That Perry knew this about him when he didn't know it about himself made him feel curiously more insubstantial than a drop of dew, as if at any moment he might disappear.

What of his love for Joy? Was that all self-manufactured, a game he was playing with himself? No, it was real. He had felt a blinding hurt for her all morning. But he had felt a lesser form of that the whole time he had been in Santa Barbara. Maybe the strain of lying to her and covering up his lies had already made him feel that he no longer deserved her, that it was just a matter of time before he'd lose her, and yet he couldn't consider giving her up. Perhaps, then, he was punishing himself for his betraying Joy by submitting to Perry again, this time in a new and more dangerous way he'd sworn to himself he'd never let happen.

He looked up toward the sun, closed his eyes, and saw spots, felt himself reel for a few seconds before he opened his eyes again (Perry meanwhile obliviously lying down on the towel/blanket, a fragile smile on his face), this time not looking so directly at the sun. Was this his fate, then? Was he going to be Perry's lover indefinitely or at least until he'd become an established composer on his own, assuming that would happen, could happen? Right now he wasn't composing at all, but if he accepted this as his fate, he assumed he'd settle down and start writing again. And what about Joy? He couldn't leave her, nor could he ever tell her because he knew she'd never accept the situation. So his fate would include the continuance of his secret, his fear of its becoming known, and his ongoing need to deceive the woman he most wanted to be completely honest with.

Maybe she already sensed he was lying to her. He thought about their last conversation, playing it back in his mind. There was that not-so-subtle tension in it, a lack of warmth and a reserve that came from doubt. Though she couldn't know anything yet. If she did, she wouldn't bother acting coy about it; she wasn't capable of that. Joy was the opposite of an actress. When she knew something to be true, she said it directly without any kind of filter. She would yell and swear sooner than she'd pretend that something *didn't* affect her the way it did.

He closed his eyes again. The sun was too intense; in spite of his efforts he'd been looking too closely. When he opened his eyes he felt dizzy once more, and for a moment didn't know where he was nor who the older man with the thin silver hair was.

Perry was still lying down, but Ray leaned forward like a jockey in midrace, watching the water. A few minutes later Perry said, "Are you feeling better now?"

"Yes."

"I think we should go to Tanglewood after we get back."

"What do you mean?"

"There's a man coming the day after tomorrow from a record company, New West, I think it is. It's not a major label yet, but they're promising. They're doing some interesting work and they have pretty solid financing."

"I've seen their CDs."

"Yes. They get good distribution. They seem to have a sharp business sense. They put me on their board, and they listen to me. One of their producers wants to talk about a series he's preparing—an ongoing anthology of contemporary composers. If you're interested, I think it would help things if you met him."

"I'm not sure I understand."

"Do you want to be included on the CD?"

"Of course—that would be incredible."

"Then say hello to him. It will make things much easier if you're there when I tell him about you."

Ray stopped himself from asking why, stopped himself even from looking at him. The producer was probably gay, and Perry wanted to show him off to the producer; or the producer might be gay, and Perry wanted Ray to subtly flirt with the producer, to play him the way Ray had played Perry from the moment they'd first met. Getting on a CD would be a major advance, an important thing in itself, that could lead to many others. Perry was once again pushing him firmly forward in the land of opportunity, but why was he telling him about it at the last minute, when he would have to once more change his plans with Joy? Unless that was precisely the point—to cause trouble between them, as if he weren't already the main trouble they had. Or maybe there was another, less malicious reason. He had waited to see if Ray would have sex with him in California and, after sleeping with him last night, decided to reward him in this latest fashion, which in terms of his career could well be the most important reward to date. It could be that and just another chance to see him that Perry was really after.

"Can I go to New York first to catch my breath and get a few things in order? Then take the bus there the next day?"

"If you want to do things that way. It'll be a tight fit, though. He's coming at two-thirty, and I think you should be there when he arrives. I think it's important that he sees you as my ally, sees us as a team together, so he'll commit to you in my presence. Once he does that, he won't dare change his mind or let anyone talk him out of it later."

"I'll be sure to be there on time," Ray said, turning toward Perry. Was that all it was, then? Perry wanted him there in person to force a promise out of the producer in their presence. The producer undoubtedly worshiped Perry, probably bragged to anyone who'd listen about his audience with Perry Green at his Tanglewood home by the swimming pool and, under the spell of Perry's charisma and authority, could promise anything. So it was all relatively benign, and he could even feel it was one of the few times that he'd outsmarted Perry, since by staying in New York he'd avoid having to stay at Perry's house. But the next night? How long was Perry going to entertain the producer—till dinner and beyond? And what would he tell Joy about it, since he had no way of knowing when the meeting would be over? He felt he had to tell her he was in Tanglewood, and besides, he couldn't bear to be in Tanglewood and not see her. Nor could he take the chance of letting her think he was in New York when he wasn't. Joy still trusted him, but he sensed it was an increasingly fragile trust. One opening and the distrust that ultimately doomed them two years ago could come flooding through again. She would see things in a distorted way and panic. She was, like most people, at her absolute worst when she distrusted someone she loved. She panicked; she literally bumped into things or dropped them. It was as if her sense of reality became dyslexic. Thinking about it, he yearned to protect her, ached to be with her, but, of course, he was forced to realize that this fragile trust was in his hands, the hands that had held the genitals of Perry Green just the night before.

# 19

A gain the phone call had a subtle, unacknowledged tension to it, particularly when she said she was having lunch tomorrow with Bobby, whom she'd bumped into in Stockbridge the day before. For his part, he told Joy that he would drive to Tanglewood to see her sometime tomorrow as soon as he got things settled in New York. He was glad she didn't ask what things. He said he couldn't tell exactly when he'd leave, that he'd probably arrive in the late afternoon or early evening and would call if it was later. He decided not to say anything about the producer to Joy, thinking it would seem too suspicious to suddenly tell her about him right after his extra days in Santa Barbara, which in themselves had been hard to explain. An even more important factor in his decision was his not knowing how long the meeting would last—his not trusting Perry on that point either—and his realization that he would have to stay as long as it took. Still, he was far from convinced that he'd made the right decision.

HE THOUGHT about this decision and Joy virtually the whole trip to the Berkshires (Perry had given him the money to rent a car) and couldn't resist looking for signs of her as he drove through Lenox and Stockbridge. He reached Perry's house (by design) fifteen minutes before the meeting, not wanting to be alone with him in the house for any length of time.

Perry was wearing an atypically loud orange sport shirt and white chinos and had combed his hair back pompadour style. When he took off his glasses, his eyes looked as if he had slept well, and Ray couldn't help resenting his peace of mind.

"I was beginning to worry about you, but I should have remembered that you're always on time."

"I don't have the confidence to be late," Ray said with a little laugh.

"Nor I. I've been on time my whole life. You see how alike we are." He handed Ray a gin and tonic. Perry had already been drinking his own. "Of course, there's one obviously huge difference between us—you're smashingly good-looking, and I, well, I was never that. You can imagine how prompt I was on all my dates."

"I'm always on time for them, too. It's just something I believe in."

"Belief had nothing to do with it for me. When I finally got around to dating, that is. Of course, the world was so different then for so-called gay people."

"How so?"

"I was very surprised when I realized how I felt toward boys; I was ashamed and terribly afraid of my parents' finding out—or any one else for that matter. Then when I got older and started acting on it, I didn't get the kind of men I wanted in the way I wanted because I was so shy and prudish and unbeautiful."

"I'm sure you made up for it later."

"But I never wanted just sex, I was always the romantic. By the time I got money and a bit of a reputation, I distrusted my sudden popularity. I knew people were using me. . . . And now when I no longer care that much if they are, I'm really too old to be much of a player," he said, laughing.

Ray finished his drink and kept his eyes away from Perry. He was not going to let this be a tender moment of any consequence between them.

"Well, sorry to go on like that," Perry finally said.

"That's OK."

"You once asked me why I didn't think I'd get my private fame. You remember that conversation? Well, that's why. . . . Anyway, Glen is also prompt."

"Who's Glen?"

"The man from New West Records. He should be here any minute if he's true to form."

"So what should I do when he comes? Any particular way I should act?"

"Just the way you normally do will be fine."

"Is he gay?"

"Glen? I don't know. He's married to his work, I think."

"Like so many of us."

"I couldn't tell what his preference is beyond New West. But then I'm not as strong a presence as you in drawing someone out."

Ray smiled, but he was wondering about Joy's meeting with Bobby in town. He wanted to ask Perry about Bobby, to express his surprise that he was staying at Perry's house, but didn't. A few minutes later Glen Richmond arrived. He was an affable man in his late thirties, wearing a light blue sports jacket and cream-colored pants. He had receding close-cut sandy-brown hair, was perhaps ten to fifteen pounds overweight, but also had pleasant blue eyes and an appealing smile. Ray could see how he could charm people, that he was good at his work and that he was also somewhat in awe of Perry. The three of them had a drink in the living room and talked about the Berkshires in general and Perry's home in particular. Just before they decided to adopt Perry's suggestion and have their second drink by the pool, Glen excused himself to go to the bathroom.

"Watch your step, there," Perry said to Ray, who was walking up the stone steps carrying the glasses in one hand and the hors d'oeuvres in the other. Perry meanwhile set the bottle of wine on the white Formica table by the pool. The sky was flecked with only a few thin white clouds, but the umbrella shielded them from the strong sun.

"So what's your verdict on Glen?"

"I like him."

"And his preference?"

"Definitely gay."

"You really think so?"

"Just the way he cocks his head, I can tell which way his cock is headed."

Perry laughed for a moment, then said, "That's such a horribly sexist thing to say."

"I didn't know I had to worry about being PC with you. I didn't know you cared."

"Well, no, I don't, that's true. . . . Ah, here comes Glen. Glen, how do you like the pool today?"

"Beautiful and tempting," he said, smiling broadly.

"Well, give in. Give in to temptation and have a swim."

"I would, but I didn't bring my suit."

"That's no problem. I have a number of bathing trunks. Try one of mine."

Glen looked embarrassed. "No, no, I don't want to put you to the trouble."

Perry took a step toward Glen, who was near the top of the stone stairs.

"It's no trouble at all."

"Besides, I doubt your suit would fit me. You're so trim

and thin and I've gained some weight, Perry, especially in my stomach."

"Nonsense. You're looking fine to me, Glen. Really fine. And my suits are elastic. They stretch to practically infinity. It's a good thing, too, because just a few years ago I was a lot heavier. Did you notice that all the photographs of me on the albums then and even in the programs were head shots? That was no coincidence. But things changed and I began to lose weight. Sit down at the table and talk to Ray. He's one of the most brilliant young composers in America, Glen, and he admires New West enormously."

Glen's eyes looked animated. "Well, thank you, Ray," he said, sitting down opposite him.

"New West . . . it's one of the essential labels. One of the few essential ones. My apartment is filled with your CDs."

"Thank you. Perry speaks so highly of you that that means a lot. And of course he told me about your concert at Tanglewood, and I also read the nice review in the *Times*."

"Thank you."

"And you just came back from LA."

"Santa Barbara, actually."

"And you were a big hit out there, I understand. Perry just thinks the world of you."

"His support has meant a lot to me," Ray said, wishing that Perry, who had gone back to the house, were at the table now to help him structure this interview.

"Do you mind my asking if you have a deal with anyone?"

"A deal?"

"To record you."

"No. My options are open."

"You see, Ray, I wear two hats for New West. On the one hand, I'm on the business end of the company, but I'm also a talent scout. Could I get some tapes sometime from you to consider?"

"Sure. I'd be delighted."

"Glen, Glen," Perry said the name rapidly in succession, making it sound like "Glen-Glen." He was standing at the base of the stone stairs holding a black bathing suit above his shoulder. Glen rose from his chair, uncertain what to do. He seemed to wonder if he was supposed to walk down to get the suit, change, and start swimming in front of Perry and Ray. He walked toward the stairs, and Perry raised his other arm in one of his definitive conducting gestures.

"No, no. Stay where you are. We'll join you for a swim, too, but let's finish our drinks first."

"Sounds good," Glen said.

He stood until Perry finished climbing, walked to the table, and sat down. Perry poured everyone some wine and made a toast to Glen's health and happiness and to the prosperity of New West. They sipped their drinks, and then after a short silence, Perry said, "Did you two talk about business while I was gone?"

Ray felt embarrassed and wondered what Perry was doing.

"I asked Ray if he'd signed with anybody, and I was pleased to find out he hadn't, so I asked him to send me some tapes."

"But I've heard the tapes," Perry said with an ironic smile, "I've conducted his work, too. Ray Stoneson is one of the most brilliant composers in America, not just one of the most promising young ones. If you don't sign him now, at least for the anthology CD, I think New West would be making a grave mistake."

"Well," Glen said, "I'm certainly impressed by the depth of your commitment to Ray's work."

"I should have made you aware of my commitment earlier. That's my fault," Perry said. "I've been too involved performing it to wonderful responses on both coasts to explain it properly. And as a board member of New West, I should have explained it. That was my obligation to you."

"Well, Ray, if you'd be willing to send me a tape just so I can check out the sound, I'd be thrilled to include you on our *Anthology of Contemporary Masters* album. The CD is scheduled to be released around Christmas."

And that was all it took: in ten minutes Perry had managed to change his life again. He even got directly involved in the details of the deal this time, asking Glen to fax the contract to him to speed things up, since Ray didn't have a machine. A few minutes later, when the details were worked out, everyone shook hands with everyone else, and Perry made a toast to Ray's future with the company, which Ray was too embarrassed or afraid to listen to. He was thinking that no human being had ever done for him what Perry had just done. No one had come close, and he felt stunned, as if some kind of magician had invaded one of his deepest dreams and turned it around in broad daylight to end triumphantly. In less than a month he'd had a piece performed by Perry Green at Tanglewood that was well reviewed in the *Times,* lectured and performed at a major university in California, and made a deal to have one of his pieces included on a CD with a hot young company. Maybe he should have told Joy the truth about the meeting. She'd have understood if he had to stay a long time. She would've been thrilled for him. Why didn't he give her more credit for being understanding? Maybe he still could call her and tell her the truth, saying that he told her the other story because he didn't want to worry her about the meeting or jinx it by talking about it and have it ruin their reunion if the meeting turned out poorly. He could say any or all of these things, yet ultimately he couldn't risk her knowing now that he'd told her even a little lie, nor could he risk leaving early after what Perry had done for him. He would have to stay as long as Glen did; that was for sure.

After their drinks, they returned to the house and

changed, each in a different room. Then they walked uphill laughing and talking together. Perry told one of his anecdotes about Virgil, and Glen laughed loudly, helplessly. He loved these stories; Ray knew they would make Glen's trip and be something he would retell, though not as well, when he was back at his office in Denver.

And then they went in the water, still laughing. Ray closed his eyes and floated away from them. For a few seconds he let an image of Joy (a kind of idealized memory of her face during his last times with her) mesmerize him. Then he realized that they were all floating on their rafts, each on a separate course, until Perry steered toward him.

"How are you doing?"

Ray smiled. "I'm doing well. Thank you," he said, being sure Perry knew he was thanking him for more than the inquiry. Perry smiled as if to say that was all the reward he needed and discreetly floated off to chat softly with Glen. The issue of reward, of course, was something he couldn't afford to think about either. He tried to close his eyes, then, but they kept opening. He couldn't even stay in his prone position and instead sat up on his raft and looked around. For a moment he saw Bobby by the back of the house. His face looked unusually somber, almost ashen. Ray waved, but Bobby, who possibly didn't see him, disappeared into the house.

His raft drifted toward Perry, and he raised his head again. Perry's eyes appeared to be closed as if he were sleeping, but when Ray got a little closer, they opened and focused on him.

"Bobby's back. I just saw him."

"Marvelous. He can join us for supper."

Perry closed his eyes again, and Ray floated by, thinking, Doesn't he really mean Bobby is in time to serve dinner? Bobby's status, which shifted among lover, servant, and friend, continued to remain ambiguous. He saw again the bizarrely white color of his face that he'd seen in a flash minutes ago and cursed fate that Bobby had run into Joy in Stockbridge and wondered about his lunch with her. Could that mean they might conceivably develop a relationship independent of him—something that he'd be powerless to even know about while he was in New York? Now that Bobby had already seen him, he couldn't guarantee that Bobby wouldn't at some point speak to Joy about that or anything else he might learn from Perry. Clearly he had to call Joy and tell her where he was, explain that he got the call from Perry just before he left, tried to call her and couldn't reach her, and now was calling her at the first possible opportunity. Except that if she had been home all afternoon, as she might have been, preparing a dinner for him he'd fantasized about, then she'd know he was lying. Better to tell her that he got the call from Perry just as he was going out the door and decided to call her when he arrived. Then he could only be accused of making a bad decision, or a self-centered one. Her feelings would be hurt, but she could understand that he was temporarily overwhelmed by the news and wanted to rush to Perry's to close the deal. This was the one path to follow, the only reasonable thing to do. Why hadn't he thought of it earlier?

He paddled over toward Perry. "Can I use your phone?"

Perry's eyebrows rose as if he already comprehended the situation. "Of course. If you see Bobby, tell him to join us in the pool."

"Will do." Ray tried not to rush too visibly down the stone steps. Perry would have to be included in the new plan, he thought, Perry would have to agree to back him up about the last-minute phone call, and asking him wouldn't be pleasant either.

He let the phone ring a long time, hung up, and tried again, but there was no answer. She was probably doing some last-minute shopping or else swimming or running. She worried about her weight, generally, for no real reason. It was part of her perfectionism. He knew it had to do primarily with her image of herself and that, no matter how many compliments he heaped on her, the anxiety about her weight would stay with her. She would still run and exercise more than she needed to every day.

Ray heard a door close, looked around, took two steps farther into Perry's house, but saw no trace of Bobby or anyone else. It must have been Bobby shutting the outside door. He decided to wait a few minutes before going back to the pool. It was only four thirty-five; she wasn't expecting him for another half hour, so he'd try again then. Things would certainly be easier if she had an answering machine. How typical of Joy not to have one. He suddenly saw her not having a machine as tremendously revealing. She didn't think her life would change, at least not professionally. Though she was a professional music teacher and a professional singer, she didn't think enough of herself to expect any offers from outside the world of her everyday contact. Granted her everyday world was Tanglewood in the summer, but she was shutting out New York, Boston, Philadelphia, et cetera, where someone who had heard her sing or teach at Tanglewood might have a concert or job in mind for her and want to offer it on the phone.

But Joy didn't want the tension of a bigger career. She wanted a calm life of modest accomplishment and secure love. He knew that now. It was something he hadn't understood years ago. She was a modest person. She was not ambitious, as he was, and he wondered how she could love him. Except, of course, that they complemented each other; each acted out a part hidden inside the other. Actually, they'd discussed this several times. He knew that one of the reasons for his own intermittent depressions was that underneath his relentless striving was a deep skepticism about its value or meaning. Unlike any other form of life, human beings endlessly distracted themselves—whether through career pursuits or compulsive exercise hardly mattered, as long as one didn't focus for more than a few seconds on one's own extinction or on the passing into extinction of everything one loved. In his music, as in the music of so many composers he admired—for example, Mahler—lay that feeling or the realization of that feeling so powerful it could hardly be allowed to be felt. That was what he wanted to liberate in his music, the hidden realization of time. That psychological liberation was needed, he felt, if human beings were ever to experience even a modicum of psychic freedom or self-realization or any other of the concepts they loved to bandy about.

He heard the same door open and close again and then footsteps going upstairs and perhaps the sound of a second door closing. He stood up, deciding to return to the pool. He now wondered if Glen really was gay. In Perry's pool, everyone seemed a little gay. It was as if the water were a liquid orchestra under Perry's spell and so seemed more a homosexual place, say, than the gay part of Summerland Beach. When Perry came back to the pool it became still more gay, as if there were no straight people or places left in the discernible world.

"Did you reach the person you called?" Perry asked, surely knowing that it was Joy but not wanting to say her name.

"There was no answer. I'll have to try again in a little while, if it's all right."

"Of course."

"Did you see Bobby yet?"

"Bobby isn't feeling well, I'm afraid."

Ray looked at him closely and was surprised to see anxiety in Perry's eyes. "So he won't be joining us in the pool?"

"No. His stomach's upset. I hope he'll be able to have supper. Glen is fond of him, and he likes Glen, too."

Ray turned his head and swam a few strokes, then turned and said, "I think I'll take one more lap and then get out of the pool for a while, if that's all right? I'm feeling a little cold."

"Suit yourself, dear. You can rest or play the piano or watch TV and of course use the phone—whatever makes you comfortable. I try to run a home here, not a military school," he said with a little laugh.

Ten minutes later Ray went inside the house and changed into his clothes. Coming out of the bathroom, he thought he heard something. He looked to his left and right, then in the general direction of the upstairs, saw nothing, then heard a door close. Obviously it was Bobby. He looked outside at the pool. From his angle he could see only the empty table. Perry and Glen were still in the pool. He waited a little longer, giving Joy a chance to get home, stared at the silent hallway upstairs, hearing in his mind the opening bars of his piece that had been performed so surprisingly well in Santa Barbara. Then he called, letting the phone ring seven times before hanging up. She must still be running or shopping. Maybe picking out the right wine or else getting a good bottle of gin or vodka. He remembered the last time they drank, and began to get an erection. Better get rid of that before going to the pool, he thought, laughing to himself.

He walked to the piano, feeling the eyes of the photographed musicians watching him from the walls, and played a few Bill Evans melodies even more softly than Evans did. Every now and then he looked up where he thought Bobby had shut the door, wondering if his playing could draw him out the way Greta's violin had made Gregor leave his room in "The Metamorphosis." But when he thought about it, he realized that he didn't want to see Bobby. What would be gained by seeing him? Nothing, now that he determined he was going to tell Joy where he was and what he'd been doing.

He tried her number again without success. Perhaps he hadn't waited long enough since the last time, but he'd definitely stayed too long in the house. It was good that he'd played the piano, though. It was a way of showing Bobby that he wasn't afraid or trying to hide from him, a way actually of flaunting his own presence. But too much of that kind of thing was counter-productive, yet another lesson he'd learned from Perry.

Glen and Perry were toweling off at the table when he got to the pool, still talking animatedly and laughing.

"I've just made the sad discovery that Glen can't stay for dinner," Perry said as Ray joined them. "Isn't that a shame? First, Bobby conks out on us with a bum tummy, and now Glen tells us he's off to Pittsfield to catch one of those commuter planes to New York. My goodness, New West works hard."

"But my work pays off," he said, indicating Ray with his right hand. "I'm very excited that you'll be on the anthology CD."

"I'm really excited, too."

"I'll be sending you all the paperwork about it as soon as I get back."

"Do you have my address in New York?"

Glen looked temporarily perplexed, as if he'd assumed the way to reach Ray was at Perry's.

"No, I don't think so. Here," he said, handing Ray a pen and a business card. "Why don't you give it to me and it'll be in our computer forever as soon as I'm in Denver."

There was another round of compliments offered and swallowed like a round of drinks. More laughter, hugs, and a good-bye kiss on the cheek between Perry and Glen. And then the mysterious stranger from the West, the first person to prom-ise to preserve his work, vanished into his rented Camaro.

"Do you realize what you've accomplished today?" Perry said to him on the living room sofa.

"You accomplished it. I was just the innocent bystander."

"The point is you're going to be on a very chichi recording that will be in a lot of stores and will be reviewed in many places."

"Thank you again, Perry. It means a great deal."

"What piece do you think you should use?"

"I don't know. I was going to ask you."

Perry took off his glasses, rubbed his forehead as if trying to erase some of his wrinkles, then faced Ray, who was sitting on one of Perry's velvet chairs (the regal blue one) facing the sofa.

"Of course, you have to consider the time and budget limitations, especially since you're a last-minute inclusion. You don't want to seem like a prima donna when you're just starting out."

"Of course not."

"And I'm not really sure the players New West can get could learn your orchestral things in time; so all things considered, why not go with your sonata at UCSB?"

"I'd thought of that, too."

"I thought they did a very good job. Were you pleased?"

"Yes, generally."

"They played with a lot of color and they played in tune. You might see if the tape of that sounds all right. Have them FedEx it to you or to me. I can play it on my machine. Then we could send it to Glen, and he can have his engineer remaster it. The cost will be minimal, and they'll like you for being so prompt and economical."

"God, you're clever."

"I try to please you," he said, putting his glasses on and looking at him with what Ray had come to think of as his devoted expression. "I had Bobby get all your favorite hors d'oeuvres in town this morning and, of course, lamb, your favorite meat."

That meant Bobby had known he was coming for dinner all day long. He suddenly looked around for a phone, forgetting for a moment where it was.

"What's the matter?"

"It's just that I have to make a call. The person still isn't in."

"By all means, go ahead," Perry said, gesturing definitively with his hands.

This time when Joy didn't answer it was more of a battle to believe she was still shopping. It was six-fifteen, a little past the time he said he'd be arriving. He had to get away, to at least leave a note on her door telling her where he was, saying he'd explain later.

"Still not in?" Perry said, raising his eyebrows significantly.

"I really should be going soon."

"What? You're going to leave me to eat dinner by myself on this historic occasion?"

"I'm afraid I have to. I . . . "

"Well, at least have a drink with me, won't you?"

"Sure," Ray said, startled by Perry's tone.

"Sit down on the sofa so I can be next to you during your final minutes and I'll fix you a celebratory vodka."

Ray began to relax. There would be no absurd demands that he stay for dinner, no seduction attempts either, apparently. (Perry wasn't that greedy, or perhaps he was sated since Ray had slept with him once more on the last day in Santa Barbara.) And a tremendous thing had happened with the CD deal with relative ease, giving him at least a statistical chance of developing further without Perry's help. If he got the right reviews and someone else got interested in promoting him in a company other than the Perry-dominated New West, he might no longer really need Perry's help at all. At least that hope could exist, for compact discs, Ray thought, were the contemporary composers' only real prayer. "Buy Me, Play Me, Love Me, Tell Your Friends, Make Mine a Cult Piece," went the prayer. One had only to remember what recordings had done for Phil Glass, Arvo Pärt, or Goreki. In each case the public knew them directly through CDs that made them famous and, in effect, critic-proof. The consumer was becoming the new critic, especially in today's crumbling economy, which he knew would stay crumbled for quite a while; he was sure of that. Now money not only talked, it created reputations as it never had before.

So he would have this drink with Perry, and he wouldn't gulp it down either. He owed the man that much, didn't he?

Perry was saying sweet nothings to him, letting his hand rest on Ray's knee, but Ray was unconcerned. These were the kinds of romantic moments Perry cherished, and as long as they didn't lead to more, he felt he could tolerate them, so he finished his drink slowly and let Perry continue his rhapsodies. At least Perry never begged. Like his music, he reached a certain point of passion, then pulled back and kept control. . . .

By the time they were having their second drink, the touching had stopped, and they talked quietly. Ray was vaguely aware that it was getting darker, though in Berkshire houses it was often dark, and one could be fooled quite easily about time. He wished he hadn't forgotten his watch. He hated to keep asking Perry what time it was, especially since he'd clearly established that he was leaving soon. For the same reason, he hated to keep asking to use his phone. It felt as if he'd tried so many times and certainly he'd tried within the last half hour. Still, he'd almost asked again in between the first and second drinks, thinking it wouldn't upset Perry too much if he asked once more or simply left the room and tried on his own. But it was embarrassing to return each time without reaching her. He didn't like Perry knowing there might be some problem with Joy. He hated the thought of the pleasure and sense of hope it might bring him. It was also making him a little angry that she wasn't at home. Where was she? Was she playing some kind of game with him? He would definitely try her again as soon as he finished his drink, and if she wasn't in, he would simply tell Perry that he had to leave. He could even create an imaginary phone call for Perry's benefit if he had to, anything to get out.

He heard a sound. They both did. His first thought was Bobby, but this sound was downstairs. Someone was knocking.

"Oh, Christ, I forgot to lock the gate," Perry said. "Will you see who it is? Someone came around back."

Ray carried his drink with him, glad to leave the room, thinking he'd make his phone call on the way back.

He asked who it was but heard only more firm, persistent knocking. Then he stared through the peephole, but the image was ambiguous. Yellow hair, black kerchief. He opened the door, stepped back, and saw Joy.

Her face was white and drawn, its severity heightened by her hair that was piled up on top of her head and by the kerchief that framed it.

"I've been calling you all afternoon," Ray said.

"Well, here I am. What did you want to say?"

"Are you upset? Why are you looking at me that way? Why are you acting this way?"

"You have no idea?"

"Because I couldn't reach you on the phone earlier?"

She cut him off with a sarcastic laugh. "Stop it, Ray. You don't have to lie anymore. I spent the afternoon talking with Bobby. I learned a lot about you while you were away."

"What do you mean?"

"I know what's been going on now."

"What are you talking about? Will you let me explain to you? I got a call from Perry just before I left this morning about a record deal taking place here. I've been trying to reach you and was just about to leave."

"Is that a good drink?"

Ray looked at his drink reflexively.

"Can't I come in and join the party?"

"There's no party."

She walked ahead of him into the living room where Perry was still seated on the sofa holding his drink. He looked up, uncertain for a moment who she was.

"Oh. I see it's a private party."

"Perry, you remember Joy."

"Of course I do. I was swept off my feet by her."

"Really?" she said in an oddly toneless voice. For a moment the one-word unanswered question hung in the room, and Perry's look of puzzlement slowly changed to alarm.

"You look puzzled. I meant, is that so, or is it just a line you automatically produce without thinking about whether it's true or not?"

"I assure you I was devastated by your charm."

"And I assure you I know you're a great man. But are you an honest one?"

"Is she teasing me in some way, Ray, or is there something the matter?"

Ray said nothing. He was awed by the intensity in Joy's eyes, which were focused on Perry.

"It was Ray who really swept you off your feet, wasn't it?"

"Both of you did."

"But you felt something for him very different than what you're pretending and different from what you told Bobby. But Bobby found out because you couldn't resist writing about it, and now we both know what you were doing with Ray. A little repressed honesty broke out in your journal, and now we all know."

Perry looked stricken. "I've heard all of this I care to," he said as he began walking upstairs.

"Are you denying that you're in love with Ray? That you've been sleeping with him?"

"I'm not denying anything. I don't need to deny anything. I'm removing myself from the room," he said weakly as he continued his climb up the stairs.

"Yes, you better talk to Bobby, if he'll still talk to you," Joy said; then turning, she left the room, and Ray followed her down the hallway to the door.

"What are you doing? Will you let me talk to you?"

"I'm leaving," she said as she opened the back door. "I'm leaving you and this whole fucked-up house." Ray caught up to her outside the door and grabbed her arm. There was a large yellow light above the door, and he could see she'd been crying. Behind her he saw the steps that led to the pool.

"Let go of me, Ray," she said, fiercely.

"Just give me a chance to talk."

She laughed bitterly. "Look, I know *everything* about you and Perry—don't you get it?"

"Know what?" he said, trying to sound more angry than scared.

"I know that you've been having sex with him. OK?"

"Because of what Bobby said, that jealous, twisted little asshole, and you believed him?"

"Don't lie and don't put him down. He saw Perry's diary, and it's made him sick, so leave him alone."

"But Joy, if—"

"But nothing. Do you deny it? Can you look at me, and deny that you slept with Perry?"

She was staring at him as intently as she ever had.

"I didn't sleep with him," he said softly.

She looked at him for another moment, then swung her head back and forth quickly like a metronome. "Liar!" She ran to the car.

"Joy, stop. Listen to me."

"You're lying. It's all been a lie and you're still lying to me."

"It's not a lie that I love you—more than anyone in the world."

She slammed the car door, turned on the ignition, and backed out. Ray turned for a second and thought he saw Bobby watching from the upstairs window. Then he ran after the car, pleading with her as she drove away from him. He ran back to his car. He was not even aware that he was shaking as he started his car and drove after her. But where? He assumed she'd drive back to her house, but if she wanted to avoid a confrontation, she might go anywhere. In the dark, in her state of mind, he worried about her driving.

And if he did catch up with her, if she let him talk to her at her house, what would he say? She already knew he was lying. He could deny it with all the fury of his being, and she would still know he was lying. Lying to her was as pointless as lying to himself. It was even more pointless.

He couldn't see her car. Sometimes he thought he did, but then one of the rare street lamps would show him he was mistaken, that he was merely projecting an image onto the black curving road the way a dreamer projects an image onto his dream.

He went faster, trying to remember to beep his horn and turn his lights on high before the blind turns that came one after another.

At Stockbridge Beach he caught up with her. She had to stop to let a car pass that was going downhill before turning right and climbing the hill that led to her house. Sometimes when he was near her he could feel her feelings, but now he couldn't tell if the panic was hers or his own. But if she was feeling it, it was because she wanted to get away from him, and nothing terrified him more than that. He pulled next to her as they went up the hill, undoing his seat belt as he parked, to get out faster. He was in her yard a split second before her, but she no longer tried to run away from him, merely walked in a straight line toward her door and did not acknowledge him. He continued to run until he stood in front of her on the small porch. "Please talk to me. I can't stand this."

"What the fuck is there to say? Are you still going to deny it?"

"No," he said, "it only happened two or three times. It never meant . . . "

"Please," she said, closing her eyes as she shook her head this time and waving her right hand as if to shoo away a fly.

"Believe me, nothing happened that could possibly endanger me or you. I'll take a test and prove it to you."

"You're willfully missing the point. You lied to me, you betrayed me about something that meant a lot to me. I was very clear about that. We were even talking about marriage, for Christ's sake. You can't dishonor me, dishonor us, like that and *marry* me. I meant the things I said to you. I lived them. We can't play games anymore like we did in our twenties. I wasn't even playing *then*."

"Of course he—it—meant nothing to me. It disgusted me."

"Please don't. I don't want to hear about your humiliation. I have my own to live with. I know why you did it. I've always known what comes first with you. And I accepted that, but not this kind of betrayal, not this. You don't deserve me anymore, don't you understand that?"

"I love you more than anyone in the world, doesn't that mean anything to you?"

She turned her head away, and one of her large shoulders seemed to shake. Then he heard a single sob from her that was almost indistinguishable from the wind, it was so soft. He realized he was close to crying, too, and he struggled against it because he felt he needed all the powers that he had to keep her from shutting him out of her house.

"Joy, please," he said, putting a hand on her shoulder. She let it rest for a second before moving free of him toward her door. She had her key out now, like a little gun that would simultaneously shoot open the door to her house and shoot out his life.

"Can we talk about this in your house? Just for a minute?"

"No, Ray. I can't let you in my house anymore. You'd better go back to Perry's."

"Joy."

"Ray, I mean it. Why are you pretending you don't understand? It took too much from me to trust you again, and that's all destroyed now."

"What happened with Perry meant nothing and will never happen again. I just did it . . . "

"I know. You just did it because you couldn't help doing it. Because your career is so important to you that you'd do anything."

"That's not true. What did that little freak Bobby tell you?"

"Don't insult him and don't try to hurt him either. He was betrayed, like I was. He didn't even know about our relationship. He told me this because it overwhelmed him, it was *his* tragedy he was describing. He didn't understand how it affected me."

"That's a lie. He knew about us."

"No, he didn't. The only time he saw us together was when you introduced me as a friend. You've got to promise not to hurt him."

"Of course. I promise. But you've got to let me talk to you inside for a few minutes."

"No, Ray. I really can't. I can't do that."

"You act like I murdered someone."

"You murdered us, Ray. We're really dead now," she said, opening the lock at last and shutting the door on him.

He stood still for a moment, then stepped off the porch and stood in the yard waiting to see which light she'd turn on. A light wind moved through the thick trees. He couldn't hear any cars, just the wind and the crickets.

He shifted his position and walked to where he'd sat down once and waited for her the day he eventually met her at the town beach, then returned to her cottage and made love. A pain passed through him that nearly doubled him over. He felt extraordinarily weak, like a stalk of grass instead of a man.

He thought the house grew lighter, and he moved closer

to it to peer through one of the living room windows where the drapes had already been drawn. The light probably came from there. A little table light, just enough so she could see as she fixed herself a drink or a series of drinks strong enough to allow her to sleep. He knew what she was doing, and it filled him with pity for her and terror for his life, terror for how he could even get through this night. Should he go back to Perry's? Should he call him from the road? If he went back to New York, he feared he'd lose her forever. But how long could he stay here when he had so little money, and how could he fight for her if he stayed at Perry's? He felt himself getting dizzy and sat down on the grass for a moment. Perhaps he should bang on her window, but he remembered how determined she'd sounded, and thought that would be disrespectful of the first wave of pain that was just hitting her. One of Joy's persistent themes was that of not being listened to, or not being taken seriously enough. It had surfaced as a complaint during their first relationship, and he had tried to be aware of it ever since. But the thought of just driving away and leaving her alone was too atrocious to bear. Maybe there was some middle course. Perhaps he could leave her a note telling her how much he loved her, begging her forgiveness, pleading with her to contact him at any time if only she would give him a chance to talk with her. But where would she call him? To leave Perry's number might infuriate her anew. Did he have enough money for even one night in a motel, say the Card Lake, which was the cheapest one he remembered? Did they even have phones in the rooms now? It had been at least ten years since he'd stayed there, and the whole place might have been upscaled by now, like the Upper West Side.

Still, she must know that he wouldn't desert her. It was reasonable, it was to be expected, that she'd lock him out, but he couldn't desert her tonight. Going to Perry's would be the worst thing he could do. At most, he should call Perry to thank him again and to give him some kind of explanation. Perry was probably nervous, too, and who knew what kind of situation he was having now with Bobby? Maybe he could drive down to the town beach and call Perry on the pay phone, then return to Joy's and keep vigil in her yard during the night. That's exactly what he should do. He should spend the night in his car so she would see him there as soon as she woke up in the morning.

But if he drove to the beach, she would hear him, and even though he could be back in less than ten minutes, she would know what he was doing. She'd figure out that, in effect, if only for those ten minutes, he was putting Perry first again. He thought of the way Joy confronted Perry just a half hour ago—how fearless she was! No, he couldn't take the risk of leaving. He wouldn't leave her yard until she told him to, not even for a minute.

He stayed in her front yard, seated on the grass, or sometimes when the scenes of their past were too vivid, he paced to the maple tree at the end of her small backyard. It was as if, completely on its own, part of his mind was intent on torturing him with these images, to make sure he realized the magnitude of what he was losing.

He didn't remember a sunset, though the sun had been out all day, and in what seemed years ago, he had actually gone swimming with Perry Green and the man who was producing his first CD. But as he thought about it briefly in the car now, he hadn't looked for the sunset; and the trees, being so tall and thick, could have blocked out a good part of it even if he had.

Inside, the car was cramped and cold. He would not even try to sleep; he wouldn't even go into the backseat, where it was slightly more comfortable, because he wanted to stay alert in case she suddenly left the house and went somewhere in her car or on foot. In this darkness a late start could be fatal, and who knew what she was thinking or what would happen if she couldn't sleep? She might kill herself or even him in a moment of rage. He would stop the former, of course, but if she came at him with a gun, he didn't think he would resist. She would know something deeply true about him, at last, and he would die knowing that she knew it.

He felt himself on the verge of tears and with no one around let himself cry for nearly a minute. When he was through he realized that he didn't want to die, of course, that even alone with himself he could imagine things he didn't mean.

He closed his eyes. It was possible that he'd slept for a few minutes. When he opened his eyes he felt a pressure building inside him—a welling up of energy he often felt before he improvised on the piano. But he couldn't leave the car, much less play the piano. Instead, he tried to look at his situation objectively, tried to *think* about it, and soon was having an intense, if paradox-filled, line of thought.

The point was to live, to experience a bit of the world, with someone you could be yourself with. It seemed easy enough and reasonable enough, yet nearly the whole world was incapable of it. Were intense love and intense ambition really impossible to reconcile? It would seem that they were intrinsically at odds, if for no other reason than to give time to your career took away time from your love and vice versa. And to follow ambition, the way he and his colleagues at Juilliard had, took more than time—it diminished one's self in many ways. There was no denying it. Why was it that so many people's deepest commitment was to success, even though it was conferred by a society those same people expressed contempt for? Did these people secretly love authority figures—critics, the audience? Was it all just about the frantic search for so-called fame? Didn't anyone else notice this bizarre schizophrenia of artists heaping scorn on the status quo, the public, the critics, while yearning to be revered by them? If so, why wasn't everyone (anyone) shouting about it? No one was, which proved to him that this dirty little secret of the artist's soul was true. But what was at the root of it? Nietzsche's will to power, a striving for displaced parental approval, the illusion of some kind of immortality? Yet love provided its own immortality. He had rarely discussed having children with Joy, but once during the happy part of their first relationship, she'd smiled at him quietly when he mentioned it. He never forgot that smile, what it meant to him was an opening, a sign that, of course, someday they would have children together; of course they would create life. Maybe that was why Joy was so relatively unambitious professionally. She had other things in mind. That's what her Mona Lisa smile had been about—not such a mystery, after all. But he'd been too stupid to pursue that opening, too. He'd been addicted to the other way. And now he was locked out of her house in the total darkness of his car.

# 20

He didn't sleep more than a half hour. When he woke up, he kept his eyes closed for a while, but his mind was filled with a grotesquely dissonant theme, like a march from Tchaikovsky gone awry. He opened his eyes, and the music started to fade. The sky was dark gray with streaks of purple, and he felt the cold again. He'd been shivering intermittently throughout the night but had grown to look forward to it, as it distracted him for short bursts of time. All night there'd been only the images of Joy and the excruciating pain that accompanied them—and then the repetition of that distorted march. He'd been tempted to turn on the radio but worried (irrationally, he knew) that somehow she might hear or know that he was listening, or that suddenly she might appear and catch him having his private concert on her lawn. It would be a violation of his vigil. He would be once more aestheticizing grief, and at the worst possible time.

The radio remained a constant temptation, but he didn't give in to it, and now that it was getting lighter, and he knew that Joy might appear in a few hours or even in a matter of minutes (that she'd at any rate notice his car), he knew that he'd continue to resist it. In a similar way he'd been tempted to call

Perry, who was probably anxious or angry, though as it got impossibly late that temptation diminished.

And so he waited with his eyes open and the radio off as the sky passed from deep gray and purple to a lighter gray and then a thinner fog-textured gray that typically began a Berkshire summer morning. It got to be seven-thirty, seven forty-five, two minutes past eight. He began regularly checking the clock in his car, as if upon reaching a certain time it could guarantee her appearance.

Joy was not typically a late sleeper, but he was sure she'd drunk a lot to get to sleep, and who knew how much more if she woke up in the middle of the night? She liked beginning her day early, having immediate access to her energy, often without a cup of coffee. She liked to work early and scheduled her students or her classes first thing in the morning whenever possible. That way she could have the latter part of the afternoon free to run or swim. He'd often imagined the kind of routine they would live. He would compose in the mornings because he, too, liked to work early. He'd eat lunch, then teach. His day would probably end later than hers, so she would already have gotten the run out of her system (he, himself, never ran). At night, she dressed up a little. She liked to transform herself from working musician to athlete to glamorous woman, and she did it seamlessly, modestly. At night he'd take her to eat at a good restaurant, or else she'd make one of her exquisite creations. (Her energy really was incredible, all the more so because it rarely veered out of control. In that sense, she had something in common with Perry.) After dinner they would walk, maybe play a little light music together, he'd accompany her on the piano as she sang the songs he wrote for her or else any number of songs from Schubert to jazz to Broadway tunes. Then they would make love, or if the day had been too full and they were too tired, they'd fall asleep in each other's arms. It was a routine they could follow in any city, and in the summer they could do it in

Tanglewood. It would have the sweetness and richness of a real life. Eventually, there would be children.

This was a vision that made deep sense to him now. It had nothing to do with being famous, but somehow he had gotten on the other track. He couldn't blame it on Columbia or Juilliard or New York. He knew he had already been that way when he arrived. In New York he simply learned how many thousands of people were like him and the extent to which they would go to satisfy their drive. Though little attention was really paid to it in the media or elsewhere, he realized that for millions of people (especially in the arts) the pursuit of fame had not only replaced the American Dream of family but religion itself. Like most religions, fame offered a grand prize of personal immortality, if only you were good or, much more important, famous enough. Because in this religion, he thought, it hardly mattered if you were good if the world didn't know about you, appreciate you, and preserve your work, thus granting you a secular version of immortality that was to its followers far more important than the oblique immortality one got through having children, and far more believable than the immortality you were merely *promised* from heaven. Instead of a monotheistic God, there were many gods—Shakespeare and Beethoven and Joyce and Picasso. There were no churches to pray in, but there were concert halls in which one could listen to Mozart and Stravinsky in hushed reverence in one's best clothes and then, when the concert (or service) was over, burst into rapturous applause and shouts. There were no temples or shrines, but there were museums where one could gaze directly upon the works of the gods Rembrandt and da Vinci, Kandinsky and Matisse, and there were libraries where one could read the words of the gods Tolstoy or Dickens or Proust. Instead of paintings or statues of Jesus and Buddha, one could wear a Hemingway T-shirt or own a Wagner poster. This was the religion, supported with countless millions of dollars from Madison Avenue, that he had unwittingly followed with all his heart and soul for as long as he could remember.

Why didn't America, despite all its surface protestations, glamorize the family dream more? Why did the intellectual world so often treat it as an object of derision or tragedy or at best as a symbol of all that was ordinary and trite? "Family values" were bad, stifling, ridiculous, antiart values. But beyond all that, why was *his* biggest fear that of being an ordinary person? Had he, too, simply fallen to Madison Avenue and peer pressure? Yet his parents were ordinary in many ways, and he'd loved and respected them his whole life. To be ordinary meant to have a family, and how could that be derided? To what end?

An hour or so passed. He no longer thought about being anywhere else—as if his car had become his coffin. The sky was still gray, the fog intense, though it had gotten a little warmer, and the fog might lift in a few hours. His eyes were half closed and he was still in the driver's seat when she came toward him, so that when he saw her she was only a few feet from the car, like a sudden large shape in a dream. She knocked on his window, and he rolled it down.

"What are you doing here?"

"Waiting for you. Hoping you'll talk to me."

"There's nothing to say." Her face looked pale but for the dark circles under her eyes.

"I wish you'd give me a chance."

"I did, Ray. I really did."

"I meant . . ."

"Don't you understand this is unbearable? Please go." She turned around, her wide shoulders authoritative, seeming to power her across her yard and up to her door—along with her stern unwavering voice—as she disappeared into her house without his moving.

He stayed frozen a couple of minutes more in his seat, then noticed he was sweating, that his shirt was almost soaked through. He backed out into the fog, began driving down a road. He didn't know where he was going. There was no reason to go anywhere; there was no place that offered relief. If he went to New York, he could sleep at his apartment, but he'd be too far away from Joy to see her. If he went to Perry's to explain or apologize, he'd reduce *that* anxiety (so minor now that he barely felt it), but he'd also assume the additional anxiety of being in Perry's company.

It was as if space had flattened out, and no place was physically different from any other. When they had broken up the first time, he immediately started drinking and within a few days sought out other women. He couldn't consider either possibility now, knowing neither would make a difference, would only make him feel worse. But why hadn't he had such realizations before he gave in to Perry, or at least after the first time? Such doubts might have saved him, yet somehow he'd kept them at bay—rationalized or denied everything he was actually doing and focused on other things. It was too torturous to think about, especially since the parade of images of Joy that had been so relentlessly vivid last night was starting to recur.

He didn't remember making a decision or even turning off the road that wound past the lake and Beachwood, but somehow he was driving in Interlaken, where the fog was less intense, since it was farther from the lake, and then he found himself parking directly in front of Perry's house.

It was twenty past eight as he walked to the gate, which was closed. He pressed the buzzer and heard Perry's anxious voice over the newly installed intercom.

"It's Ray."

There was a click, and the gate opened. Perry, wearing a bathrobe, met him at the front door, opening the door before he knocked.

"I was worried about you."

"I'm sorry. I couldn't call."

"Come in," Perry said. It reminded Ray of the way his father used to speak to him when he'd go out in the yard to tell him it was time to come to dinner. "Bobby is very angry and upset about us."

Ray sat down on a chair beside the piano bench, his back to the piano, while Perry stood like some kind of slender tropical tree, hovering. When he took off his glasses, Ray saw that his eyes were slightly bloodshot.

"I'm sorry."

Perry looked profoundly touched. "And I'm sorry for you, too. You look like you haven't slept. I'm so sorry this has happened."

"I don't know if Bobby knew Joy and I were lovers or why they even . . ."

"I didn't tell him." Ray saw Perry staring directly at him, a hint of anguish in his eyes, his hand over his heart like an old Boy Scout.

"No, I know that. She told me how she found out. She said Bobby told her—they'd become friendly while we were in California. She said he'd read your diary and was confiding in her about his own pain and didn't know about my relationship with her when he told her."

"I don't keep a diary. He must have seen some letters I wrote but never sent you when you were in New York, the silly snoop. I'm afraid Bobby left here in a royal snit."

"I thought you said if he knew he'd accept it."

"I thought he would. I assumed he would and that he might know anyway. I plead guilty to being vague with him and to misjudging him, and now he's hurt and angry at both of us, I'm afraid."

"He's angry at me?" Ray said, clenching his fist. "Are you sure you didn't tell him I was Joy's lover?"

"I don't know why I would."

"So he wouldn't suspect us."

"I don't think I did. But you're making me nervous and it's becoming awfully hard to remember anything. What difference does it make anyway? Everyone knows everything now."

"You're right," Ray said. "It doesn't matter. The only thing that matters is to get her back."

Perry winced slightly, then quickly regaining his composure said, "I hope it happens soon. I hate to see you suffer like this. I feel so guilty." He almost swallowed the last word.

Ray looked at him closely, but said nothing.

"I stole you from her, in a way. I did."

"That's not true. It was my decision, ultimately. The first time I was with you, Joy and I were still platonic friends. You didn't even know we'd been lovers."

"But in California I knew. I made you stay those extra days. I owed the world of love a little more consideration. I owed it more kindness and justice."

"To you, she was just a singer who came to your house once for dinner."

"Oh no, I was touched by her and by you two together."

The sudden softness in his voice made him think Perry might try to hug him soon. If he touches me, Ray thought, I might hit him or throw him against the wall into one of his photographs. But Perry stayed still, was pointedly studying him now.

"Can I get you something to eat? I could make you some eggs."

"No thanks."

"Or something to drink. Coffee or whiskey?"

"I have to drive back to New York, so I don't think so."

"Well, coffee then. You said you hadn't slept."

"But I'm completely awake. I don't need coffee; to add to the mix would just make things worse."

Perry stroked his chin contemplatively for a few seconds.

"Are you sure you should drive now, in the frame of mind you're in?"

"I'll be all right."

"You could stay here in the guest room and have a couple of good meals and get some sleep and then go."

"No, I have to go now. I just wanted to explain what happened and apologize."

"No need. I feel so badly for you. If you ever need me, for anything, if your suffering gets too bad, just pick up a phone," he said, his lips trembling for a moment.

"I will."

"'All my pretty ones, did you say all?'" Perry said with a sad smile. "Be careful driving then. And be careful about Bobby. He's not himself now."

"Why would I need to be careful? I'm not going to see him."

"In case he plans to see you, darling Ray. Do be careful in everything you do."

# 21

He didn't notice New York, passing through it like a fish in an aquarium, eating each meal at the same restaurant, the nearest, cheapest one, two blocks away. In his apartment he didn't compose and rarely played the piano or listened to music. Nor did he respond to the messages Arnold, Bryna, and Perry left on his answering machine. After two days he began calling Joy, but she'd finally installed an answering machine (probably to avoid him), and after four separate messages of his were ignored, he stopped leaving them and hung up as her brief, almost toneless message ended. It was as if she wanted the voice on the tape to have as little impact on him as possible, as if she didn't even want to sound like herself. The next morning, instead of calling her, he wrote her a two-page letter and sent it FedEx.

He had a series of dreams about Joy. In the last dream they were living together. She'd been sleeping a long time, but when he went to their room to check on her, he saw only a formation in the sheets meant to look like her. She'd tricked him and was missing. When he woke up, his shirt was wet. He sat for a moment before taking a shower. It occurred to him that he'd forgotten to take one the day before, and it suddenly seemed like an oppressively difficult task. He associated water with

Joy—the lakes and oceans they'd swum in and, of course, the showers they'd taken together. Though their showers and the ocean visits were mostly during their first relationship, they were all part of the same vivid landscape, where images from years ago were now just as immediate as those from two and three weeks ago.

Just before his shower ended, he masturbated quickly, the sperm leaving him almost instantly, like water emptied from a glass. He uttered a short single cry, then forgot about it, standing still in the shower while he immersed himself in an image of Joy swimming at Stockbridge Beach by one of the docks. When he finally left the shower, the green light on his answering machine was flashing—apparently he'd gotten a call that he hadn't heard while he was in the bathroom. It was Perry.

"I haven't heard from you and I'm starting to worry. Please give me a call or just leave a message telling me you're all right."

Instinctively, he shook his head. He was beginning to feel that she would never call him again, never respond to any of his messages. He turned away from the phone and paced, forgetting about Perry and his call almost immediately, as if he couldn't retain impressions from the outside world, or the world outside of Joy. As far as that went, he was an amnesiac. He was merely passing through his apartment with the image of Joy in her blue bathing suit rising from the lake up the ladder where she would sunbathe on the second dock.

He stopped only when he began to get dizzy. It wasn't an entirely unpleasant sensation, and he stood still as he had in the shower to see if it might be a kind of diversion, however transitory, that could give him some relief. But his "normal consciousness" returned in less than a minute, and the thought of the pacing, the waiting to see how the dizziness felt, the answering machine filled with messages he hadn't answered, the cramped, small, airless apartment where he still couldn't compose or play the piano, blew through him like a noxious cloud.

He put some clean clothes on. He had no idea what the temperature was; he knew only that he needed to go outside. The phone rang as he opened the door. He picked it up just after the second ring, but the caller hung up. Immediately, he pressed *69, hoping that the operator would say the call was from a different area code so that he could at least imagine it was from Joy. Instead, he got a busy signal. He decided to stay in his apartment for a few minutes to see if the call would come again. Two minutes later, the phone rang.

"Is this Ray?" The voice sounded nervous and distant, as if it were muffling itself.

"Yes."

"This is Bobby Martin. I'd like to talk to you."

"Sure. What is it?"

"I'm calling you from just outside your building. Can I see you?"

"I'll be right down," Ray said. He was glad that he hadn't invited him in. Bobby didn't sound right. It was definitely better to meet outside. But when he got to the lobby and saw that the invisible doorman was absent from the lobby again, he wondered why he'd agreed to meet him at all. He could have handled this on the phone. It was early afternoon—he could have said he was giving a piano lesson.

He opened the door, stood at the stoop, and looked across the street where he thought the phone booth was that Bobby had called from.

"I'm here," said a disembodied voice. At the foot of the stairs he saw Bobby. Ray walked down two steps, then stopped.

"What's up?"

"I want to know what you have to say for yourself."

"What are you talking about?"

"What am I talking about?" Bobby asked, his voice rising, jabbing his index finger twice into Ray's chest. "What the fuck do you think I'm talking about?"

"Calm down, will you, if you want to talk."

"I'm furious with you. You stole Perry, you took him away from me."

"That's not true. It was Perry who went after me."

"You said yes, didn't you? Why did you do that? You're not even gay, are you?"

"No, I'm not."

"So why?"

Ray looked around, but no one was watching them. People were passing by, but no one was watching, which surprised him because he thought they were speaking more loudly than they were, thought, actually, that Bobby was yelling.

"I asked him about you. He said that he thought you knew or at any rate that you wouldn't care. He said that you two had an understanding."

"Would you care if the person you loved slept with someone else?"

"Look, I've lost the person I loved because of this, because you told her. That ought to be enough for you, isn't it?"

"Joy. . . ." For a moment, Bobby's expression changed, as if he were considering something. "I didn't know about that. I wouldn't have hurt her that way if I'd known. But why did you hurt me? I thought you were a friend. I drove you to his house."

"I'm sorry."

"It doesn't make any sense. If you loved Joy, then why would you sleep with Perry?"

Again Ray felt as if he were being watched.

"Do you want to have a drink and talk about this a little more calmly?"

"I'd be afraid to have a drink with you. I'd be afraid of what I might do."

"How about a cup of coffee then? Or could we at least go somewhere else to talk, instead of the front steps of my building?"

"There's a bench across the street." Bobby pointed to Riverside Park.

"OK, fine."

They crossed the street in silence. Ray followed Bobby for a block and a half, eyes fixed on his bright green shirt, the color of the pepper-tree leaves in Santa Barbara. They sat down on a bench just off the park, a few feet apart, Bobby staring at him as if to remind him that it was his turn to speak.

"The point is I didn't believe I was betraying you, or that Perry was. That's the main point, and also, of course, I'm very sorry that it happened. I've paid dearly for it, too."

"It wasn't for the sex. I trusted him about that," Bobby said, with his face partially averted. "That would have hurt, but only a little, I think. A world-famous man like Perry gets temptations all the time. I would have to be really naive to think that I'd be enough for him. That anyone like me would. But you weren't after sex anyway, were you? It was only your career that you cared about, isn't that basically it?" He stared at Ray suddenly with a strange expression in his eyes. It was as if someone he was playing chamber music with had caught him in a terrible mistake.

"But the point is it's all over. I'll never do it again."

"But it isn't over for him."

"What do you mean?"

"He's in love with you. You're all he thinks about."

"He knows my mind is completely on Joy. He must know whatever happened with me is over. I'm sure he knows. But if he should ever ask, I'll spell it out for him . . . I'll just say it, anyway, the next time we speak."

Bobby looked hopeful for a moment, and Ray began to quickly reconstruct his last conversation with Perry, after his vigil on Joy's lawn. Hadn't he said it then? Could Perry still believe it could happen again?

"I'll call him myself. I'll make sure he knows within twenty-four hours," Ray said.

Bobby's head was lowered slightly, and he was pressing his hands tightly to his temples.

"Are you OK?"

"My head hurts, that's all. . . . He's everything to me, I don't have anyone else."

"Why don't you go back to the Berkshires? I'm sure he wants to see you. Needs to see you."

"I have to work tonight."

"Can't you call in sick one time?"

"Maybe."

"It would be worth it, believe me. If you drive back today, you could have tonight and tomorrow."

Bobby's mouth curled into a little smile, as if to say, You think . . . ? It was pitiful and heartbreaking about Bobby, Ray thought while he sat on the bench. He would certainly call Perry tonight and tell him clearly where things stood. The way Bobby had walked away—head bowed, eyes inflamed, as if their purpose were merely to hold his tears. A person so hurt he no longer recognized or cared about his own humiliation.

Could Bobby's perceptions be trusted? Was Perry in love with him? He had felt it was true as soon as Bobby said it, though he hadn't allowed himself to think about it. It was easier, and certainly threatening enough, to focus on Perry's lust, but a part of him had known from the Tanglewood dinner on (when Perry gave him that long look) that love was involved. So Bobby's statement was more of a confirmation than a shock. It was entirely possible then that Perry might not have accepted or even sensed that everything was over between them, even though he'd witnessed Ray's grief over Joy. Ray had often felt that unless love is equally reciprocated, it impairs the perceptions of the one who is loved less (and sometimes also the one who is loved more). For the deprived one, suspicions and jealousies are magnified, but so are hopes, and bad news is often blocked out. He had to make it crystal clear to Perry, but was the phone the best way to do this? As he started home, he thought not. The way to say exactly what he wanted, not to be diverted from his point, and, more important, not to lose his temper and hurt Perry more than was necessary was to write him. A one-page letter would do. He would not spend a great deal of time on it either. (That would be a betrayal of Joy, in a way; that would be a travesty.) Besides he already correctly sensed that he would lose interest in the letter thirty minutes after composing it, at about the time he would have written a page. After all, how many ways could he say, It's all over?

# 22

The next morning he went to the bank. He had two hundred twenty-seven dollars in his savings account, and after paying his rent, Con Ed and phone bills, substantially less than that in his checking account. There was not enough to stay in the Berkshires more than a few days, now that he'd have to stay in a hotel. Reluctantly, he called Bryna.

"I thought you got lost somewhere and fell off the earth," she said.

"That's not a bad description."

"So, come over, let me see you before you change your mind. I never thought a summer would go by where I'd see you so little."

He put on a long-sleeve shirt and a pair of jeans and grabbed two tokens. On the train he wondered if Joy had gotten his letter yet. He went through different scenarios about how she might react. In his favorite one, he pictured her rising from the kitchen table, leaving her tea and marmalade toast to call him.

Bryna met him as he got out of the elevator that led to her loft. She looked smaller somehow in her brown skirt and yellow top and also older around her eyes, which weren't made-up as much as usual.

They embraced, and she kissed him lightly on the cheek.

"Not much oomph to your hug, Ray. You must be in a bad way."

He smiled thinly and apologized.

"Come on in," she said, walking into the loft. He followed her, immediately noticing the profusion of sheep sculptures. Apparently they hadn't sold well, and he decided not to ask her about them. They sat next to each other on the long couch where he had smoked pot with her shortly after Perry first seduced him. As if reading his mind, Bryna said, "This is the couch where you usually tell me what's bothering you and where I try to help you if I can."

He glanced at the floor a moment to compose himself.

"Joy broke up with me."

"I figured you must be pretty serious about her. That that was why you hadn't called."

"I wanted to marry her."

An angry look shone in Bryna's eyes for a moment but was quickly replaced by the blend of sorrow and compassion he'd hoped to find there.

"So you're devastated, you feel like dying."

"Something like that."

"I'm really sorry," she said, her eyes glistening now.

"Thank you. But I haven't given up yet."

"So what happened? What went wrong?"

"I don't want to get into that now. I can't. The point is I still hope to convince her otherwise, but she's in the Berkshires for at least two more weeks."

"So you need some money to stay there for a while and plead your case. Am I right?" she said, a strange smile on her lips. Ray nodded.

"I did pay you back most of what you gave me last time."

"True. So, you're pretty much tapped out of your savings account?"

"Yup. If I hadn't just gotten the check from the California

concert I told you about, I would've had trouble making the rent." He explained that the private school in the city where he received a part-time salary only paid him from September till June. At the college where he was merely an adjunct, he was paid less than two thousand dollars for his one course.

"You ought to see if you can get paid with twelve checks a year instead of nine."

"I will. I could've done it that way, but then the checks would be so small I could barely stand to look at them."

Bryna smiled. "But then you'd have some money to spend on a regular basis. I think when you get something, regardless of the size, you tend to spend it."

"That's true," Ray admitted. It stung him, but he appreciated that she was reproaching him gently.

But the next time she caught his eye, there was a serious expression on her face. She got up and paced off a semicircle in front of the couch, stopping a few feet before him. "I can give you a thousand. Would that help?"

"That would help a lot."

"But I'm going to ask you to give it back to me as soon as you can, or at least some of it. My economic situation hasn't been too hot either. You know how much I sunk into my sheep sculptures? I'd be embarrassed to tell you how few of them have sold."

"I'm sorry."

"Sorry isn't the half of it. . . . I think the world is trying to tell me I made a mistake."

"But if you believe in it . . . "

"I don't know what I believe about it at this point. Guess I'm having a midlife art crisis," she said, and they both laughed.

"The thing is," he said, "with art, if you've made a mistake, all you've got to do is recognize it—admittedly not always easy—and start in a new direction. With love, if you've made a mistake, you need the forgiveness of another person, or it's hopeless."

"True, but it's only hopeless with that person, isn't it? Can't you start in a new direction in love, too, with other people?"

He saw then that she still didn't understand what he felt for Joy, and perhaps it was better that way. So he merely nodded and a minute later they left the loft. The check was too large for him to cash at his bank, so they walked to a MAC machine and she gave him the cash on the street. It was the first time he'd walked around SoHo in weeks, and the stores looked surprisingly bright and cheerful. He wasn't offended by the rampant commercialism (as he sometimes was), the gentrification of what had once been a solemn territory for the arts. He felt pretty good for a few moments, laughing and talking with Bryna before they said good-bye. Of course, the new money in his pocket helped. He felt he had a plan now, and it was merely a question of whether he should leave late this afternoon, assuming there was still time to rent a car, or tomorrow morning. Just before he entered his building, he noticed it was a quarter past five, and he wondered how he had ridden the subway during rush hour and been oblivious to it.

The phone was ringing as he opened his door.

"Hello, Ray. It's Perry."

He mouthed a silent, Fuck! and said hello.

"I'm in New York. I'm calling you from my apartment."

"What happened?" he said dumbly. His heart beat faster in spite of himself.

"I got your letter for one thing, and it made me want to see you, but I thought I'd better call you first. . . . It was naturally quite a blow to read all about how you don't want me," Perry said, laughing ironically for a moment.

"I'm sorry."

"I've missed you terribly, darling Ray. When can I see you again?"

"Anytime, more or less. I just wanted to be clear about what our relationship had to be."

"I don't understand why you're being so final about things. Why the rush to judgment? You're very upset now, don't you see?"

"I *am* very upset, but I've thought about this. I've thought about this for some time."

"It's all over between Bobby and me, you know. It was always all over the moment I saw you, but now I've made it clear to him. He came back to the Berkshires last night and I told him."

"How did he react?"

"It wasn't a very pleasant experience. We had a fight. I've never had a fight with Bobby before."

"Again, I'm sorry."

"And I'm sorry about Joy. Really I am. If there's anything I can do to help you with her I will. If you'd like me to speak with her, for instance, I'll do that."

"It's me who has to do something. That's why I wrote you the letter."

"But I don't understand why you feel the need to punish . . . us. That's not going to help."

"I'm not trying to punish anybody. And I'd be more than glad, as I wrote, to be your friend."

"Then I don't see . . ."

"What? Don't you understand that I lost Joy because I betrayed her with you? I'm just not going to betray anyone anymore—not even myself."

"I see. Well, this is a disappointment, a great disappointment. I thought I had done some things to make your life better. I thought you . . . well, never mind what I thought. I'm not going to compromise my dignity and start insulting you or begging. I think I'd better hang up now and lick my wounds in private. Good-bye, Ray. I hope you feel better, and please call me if you ever need to."

Ray paced off a circle, then halfway through the second

circle stopped. His heart was no longer pounding. He sensed that in ten or fifteen minutes he would not even be thinking about it but would instead have sunk again into the pool where Joy was everywhere, like water. Now he could tell her truthfully, definitively, that he had ended it with Perry. On the phone, in one minute, he'd thrown away the career break of a lifetime and in that minute accepted the total obscurity that undoubtedly would again become his daily life. And even if she wouldn't listen or didn't believe him, or even if it didn't change anything, he was glad he'd done it and wondered why he hadn't long ago. And he'd done it so succinctly, so without fear and trembling. He hadn't even mentioned the meeting with Bobby, which might have been a mistake. No, it was better this way. Perry knew about Bobby; they'd already had a fight. In a day or two, they'd probably be back together again. But could he even be sure he could get through another two days?

He thought again about leaving to see Joy as soon as he could, which would still mean arriving late at night. What he had to do, he realized, was to focus on the effect things would have on her. She would be skeptical, probably extremely skeptical, about anything he'd say or do while she was so hurt and angry, so how would she react to a late-night visit? She would feel threatened; she would probably feel he was being selfish, possibly out of control, in any event, disrespectful of her emotions, of her need to grieve in private and, of course, to sleep. If he waited for the right time, on the other hand, his visit might accomplish much more. He remembered during their first relationship she once became exasperated and wanted to break up, and simply because he left her alone for a few days she calmed down and ended up taking him back and even praising him for letting her think things out. The key was to resist his need to see her immediately and try to do only what was most likely to help mend the relationship. He had to demonstrate maturity in his decisions, though waiting too long could be equally disastrous.

He lay down and closed his eyes, and a few minutes later fell asleep. When he woke up it was dark. He was surprised to discover he'd slept nearly four hours. He thought he'd call Joy one more time but decided to play the piano before the call. He began with a few minutes from Bartók's "Mikrocosmos," then without stopping (as if he had planned to play an intricately linked medley) segued with a few chords in a related key to the opening movement of his own piano sonata. He played expressively with very few mistakes until the last measures of the coda, when he felt his first sharp awareness of what he had given up with Perry. But he was still relieved he had done it. It was probably why, in spite of his pain over Joy, he was able to play so well now.

He started playing a series of Cecil Taylor–like tone clusters and arpeggios and improvising, first in Taylor's frenetic style (until the thought of Perry disappeared), then in a somewhat more coolly cerebral but still propulsive mode à la Lennie Tristano. When he improvised, he didn't worry about playing wrong notes (one of the joys of improvising was turning those wrong notes into new areas of exploration), but he also generally inhibited his playing to a degree by wanting to make sure everything made sense—could be justified in some formal way. It was as if he were editing, often overediting, while he was creating, which could defeat the very purpose of improvisation. But tonight he put the editorial part of his musical self on hold and simply played—using a range of dynamics and a dramatic shifting of keys and styles and playing as one can only when in that fabled zone that athletes sometimes reach when they shed the last vestiges of fear or self-consciousness, and their concentration makes the game seem unusually large, slow, and fated to work for them.

After this explosion of free playing, he felt flooded again by Joy's presence. It wasn't a particular image or series of images that invaded him but a kind of total emotional recognition of her. For a few moments he felt he would probably have to stop, but as his fingers kept moving, playing softly and mostly slowly in a minor key, he realized that instead of paralyzing him, the presence urged him to continue, as if his playing were necessary to sustain its life inside him. He'd heard and admired to a degree Virgil Thomson's musical portraits without thinking much about the premise. Now he understood it as he realized he was improvising a kind of sonata which tried to somehow capture the secret emotional life and qualities of Joy. He had, of course, dedicated a number of pieces to Joy, the violin and piano sonata that would be on the New West CD, one for soprano a cappella, and two others, with her voice in mind, for soprano and piano, which they had performed years ago at small concerts in New York. But those were entirely different matters. He hadn't attempted then, as he was now, to express in musical terms the essence of her self. It would never occur to him to do that. This was a unique moment in his musical life inspired by a presence that he felt rather than saw, as if for the first time he didn't need a visual image of her to feel her completely but instead had become a totally auditory person.

He never knew exactly how long he played—it was somewhere between twenty minutes and an hour—nor could he ever reconstruct anything from his playing but a few motifs and the memory of the shifting tempos, from slow to medium, mostly in minor keys, those and the presence that flickered inside him like a candle until he heard someone knocking fairly loudly on his door.

He didn't swear as he might have for being interrupted at such a time. He was so amazed at his experience that he simply played a few chords to give what he had played some sense of closure and then got up to answer the door. But who would visit him, and why didn't they use the buzzer?

He took a step toward the door and said, "Who is it?" thinking for an awful second that it might be Bobby.

"Ray, is that you? It's Perry."

He stared at the door, and at that same instant the presence inside him vanished. For a moment, Ray hoped Perry had heard some of his playing, that perhaps he had even listened to a few minutes of it before he knocked, so that there would at least be one witness to his extraordinary experience that was gone now as completely as Joy's "presence."

He opened the door and saw a bizarre expression on Perry's face, a mix of fear and hope—a vulnerable, worried old man's face he'd never seen before. Perry was wearing gray pants and a black silk shirt. Another romantic outfit.

"I hope I haven't startled you too badly."

"No, not at all," Ray said, instinctively walking backward as he realized there was no sofa or equivalent piece of furniture where they could sit, just the minimalist wooden chair from Ikea at his desk and his bed. When he wanted to eat, he pulled the desk chair over to the bed table. But it was Perry who was asking him to sit down. Ray sat on the chair and asked Perry if he wanted to sit on his bed.

"I'm too upset to sit down. I'd rather stand when I'm upset, it's a carryover from being a conductor." Perry smiled ironically. "I guess you know what I'm upset about."

Ray nodded, unable to think of anything to say.

"I think the speed with which things happened is upsetting. When things happen so quickly, it's hard to make good decisions, don't you think? People weren't meant to be bombarded by events; we're too fragile for that, and yet life demands that we keep making choices. As if enduring shocks and tragedies isn't enough, we have to decide things while they are going on."

Ray thought of the constant decisions he had to make about when to call or try to see Joy. "I understand," he said.

"Of course you do," Perry said, gesturing with his right hand toward Ray when he said "you," as if he were cuing a violin section. "What I'm saying is very obvious, but it needs to be acknowledged. It's a bit like the mystery of the universe. No one really has anything to say about it because nobody knows anything about it, but every now and then we have to acknowledge it, don't we?"

"Absolutely." Ray felt strangely ineffectual, as if invisible in his own room, and dreading the inevitable moment when Perry's philosophical preamble would end.

"As far as you and I are concerned, I *do* feel stunned, I guess, not only with disappointment and hurt, but by my own decisions and behavior. I knew Bobby much longer and you for such a little time, I sometimes think I dreamed you. Yet I chose you, just because I couldn't help myself. Just like I couldn't help myself from coming to see you now even after what you said on the phone. You see, I've come to you even though I know it's a mistake."

"It's not a mistake."

"From the point of view of my goal, it's a mistake. Or most people would say so. To make oneself so vulnerable, to throw oneself at someone. I never would have done that when I was younger. I almost did once, years ago, but then I stopped myself. It was a point of pride; it was my code. But now, pride seems such a useless emotion—useless compared to love, useless against it. Like the little boy trying to stop a flooded dam with his finger. It's funny, isn't it, that only when your life is mostly over do you discover what your maximum capacity for happiness is. That's why it's taken me my whole life to appreciate you, because you never happened before. So I'm here before you in spite of what you said, hoping against hope that you'll reconsider. It's why I came to New York, as you probably knew anyway. Because I've missed you, Ray. I've missed you horribly. It's as if I'm dressed wrong and can't speak right when you're away. The words may come out correctly in a technical sense, but there's no feeling or awareness behind them. Something is always wrong when you're gone. Incomplete. It's peculiar that this should happen to me now in this way, isn't it, but I sensed it even the first time we spoke in New York. And I found myself thinking as early as our first lunch by the pool, Let me just have him for a year. Let my life know him for one out of all its years. And then to discover that I was not only so attracted to you but also admired you so much as a musician, a composer, and then could feel so natural with you as I did in California. . . . I wonder if you ever feel a wisp of that for me?"

"I think that's the way Bobby feels about you."

"And you don't?" Perry said, arching his eyebrows.

"No, I'm sorry. I don't."

"And you can't?"

Ray stared for a moment at the perspiration above Perry's upper lip, out the same way it was in his home in the Berkshires, like an orgasm of defeat, the first time he'd said, "I'm not going to get you the way I want, am I?"

"No, I can't."

Perry's hand wiped the perspiration away just before he spoke. "And our little agreement about helping each other? Do you have any interest in continuing that?"

"No. I can't do that anymore."

"I see." Perry looked down at the bed and patted the bedsheet a couple of times as if he were considering sitting down. But he remained standing, and his eyes locked with Ray's when he spoke again. "And those days in California? Those extra days when I felt so natural, when we made love so many times? What was going through your mind then?"

"It wasn't natural for me. I was trying to carry out the agreement."

"When you finally let me give to you, and you finally let yourself come in my mouth?"

For a moment Ray saw the bed in the motor lodge, how he'd kept his eyes closed as he tried to imagine it was Joy. "I shouldn't have done those things."

"Why?"

"Because I love Joy. It was a sin against her, and myself, and you, too."

"Your sin was my pleasure, my deepest ecstasy in so many years."

"Perry, please. That can't be. Ever. I mean it."

"So nothing can be."

Ray looked down at the floor. "We could be friends. That could be. That would mean a lot to me."

"It would be difficult for me, I'm afraid. I'd always be hoping. My feelings for you are too intense."

Ray raised his head and saw a serenity he hadn't expected to find in Perry's eyes.

"I'm sorry," Ray said.

"Perhaps I'm the one who should say I'm sorry. It appears I've made another mistake in coming here like this." He started to move toward the door, and Ray rose from his chair. "I must have been imagining things that weren't there simply because I wanted them to be. Well, no fool like an old one," he said as he walked toward the door. "Good-bye, Ray. You can always change your mind, but for now, I'll see myself out."

Ray stood frozen in front of the chair, thinking that Perry had never left without a hug or a handshake, thinking that he must be furious as well as sad, that those two emotions would increase and persist, especially in a man as proud as Perry, so he would never see or hear from him again. And that made Ray sad and frightened, but he'd had no choice; that was the way the script was written.

# 23

The Card Lake or some other hotel would have been cheaper, but when he discovered there was a vacancy at the Douglas House, he decided to stay there. With its unfashionable wine-red-painted wood (a color from a pre-ecologically correct era), it had been there as long as he could remember—two cottages away from the town beach and about seven New York City blocks from Joy's home in Mahkeenac Heights. Ultimately, the location was too good to pass up.

By the time he'd checked in, unpacked, sat outside for a few minutes, then taken a shower, it was ten-thirty. He wanted to go straight to Joy's, but thought that he should call first. He reminded himself that he had to demonstrate stability and consideration. She didn't answer his call, but this time when her answering tape ended, he told her where he was staying, that he wanted to see her and would try again. She was probably at Tanglewood rehearsing or having a lesson. If he left now, he could find out where she was and possibly even have lunch with her at Tanglewood.

When he saw the red Mazda he had rented waiting for him, he laughed, thinking how it clashed with the Douglas House. He was feeling suddenly giddy with hope as he drove to

Tanglewood, the lake darting in and out of view through the trees, already sparkling from the strong sun. He turned on an AM station just for the incongruous fun of hearing rock and roll. He remembered driving a rented convertible once with Joy on the way to the Hamptons. How delicious it felt to have the wind rush through their hair. He stuck his head out the window and inhaled the blue country air. "Can't Buy Me Love" was playing on the radio, and he sang along as he passed the Lion's Gate and then the Red Cottage, where Hawthorne had once lived. The lake came into view again.

In his mind's eye, he saw Perry's face stiffening before he said good-bye in his studio. He doubted he would ever see him again. Perry could never forgive him for the rejection, but he'd said the only thing he could. Besides, he knew he could live without Perry; it was Joy who was irreplaceable. There were always two schools of thought on how much you should love people. The one currently in vogue said that you should diversify your love (much as you should diversify your investments) between lover, family, and friends, never losing sight of the fact that at the center of your life was you, yourself. Losing one person could never destroy you, then. That was the central idea, and who could argue against it? Except he also knew that people were not stocks and bonds, that in each life certain people truly were irreplaceable, and not to realize that and to treat them accordingly was a tragedy, *his* tragedy.

His head was back inside the car now, and he turned off the radio. The main gate of Tanglewood was straight ahead. He was surprised that the parking lot was more than two-thirds full, then remembered that open rehearsals were always held on Saturday mornings. He paid at the gate, took a program from one of the guides, and walked toward the Shed. What an ingenious idea Tanglewood was! People simply couldn't resist the culture/nature package where one could celebrate the arts and the environment at the same time and thus achieve a kind of simultaneous orgasm of political correctness. Tanglewood, as always, was quick to capitalize, though it had to do so in an appropriately understated way. He noticed, for example, that his program was crammed with ads for restaurants, banks, record stores, health spas, schools, realty companies, hotels, boutiques, art galleries, and even a nursing home. But all the ads were done in muted, quasi-arty graphics and soft-sell language. It reminded Ray of the way the snack bar at Stockbridge Beach had been recast in earth tones.

The Boston Symphony was rehearsing Verdi's *Requiem* for tomorrow's concert. Joy would be rehearsing, then, with the Tanglewood Festival Chorus, and if he were able to get close enough to the stage, he would probably see her. He walked quietly over the grass just to the left of the gravel path, where he had walked with her and his parents after his concert on the happiest night of his life. As he maneuvered inside the Shed, he found himself longing for a pair of binoculars. How much pleasure he would feel to see the features of her face—her eyes as they concentrated on the conductor, her mouth as it opened to sing. And now he was reduced to spotting her on a stage filled with perhaps two hundred people—like finding a dot in a painting. Even so, after this amount of time scanning the chorus face by face, he should have seen her, shouldn't he? Could she be sick and at home? Maybe the breakup had affected her more than he realized.

He was about to get up from his seat when he suddenly realized that Joy was not even *in* the Tanglewood Festival Chorus. That was a Boston-based organization of amateur singers that she had once belonged to years ago, but that had nothing to do with her musical life now. How could he have made such a stupid mistake! Still, she had friends in the chorus, he knew that, so she might well be in the audience out of curiosity. After all, the *Requiem* was one of her favorite pieces.

There were at least three thousand people seated in the

Shed. He twisted his head and rotated it owl-like left to right and then more slowly right to left to try to find her among the people seated behind and on either side of him (he was seated close to the middle of the Shed, just behind the box seats). He looked in front of him, where he saw only heads of hair and a sea of necks. Then turning right, ten or fifteen rows in front of him, he saw her, her blond hair falling down to her strong shoulders. He kept his eyes fixed on her while the music swelled around him. He was actually the ideal distance behind her, in terms of keeping an eye on her while remaining out of her sight.

Instantly, he remembered images of their past life together, in New York, at beaches, their one week in Paris, their weekends in the Berkshires. It was an odd sensation to see her in the present and to feel their past life so vividly—odd and overpowering, too much for him right now. The next time Ozawa stopped the orchestra to make a point, he got up from his seat and left the Shed. He was not ready to see her just yet. He walked across the lawn toward the formal gardens. Of course, the music reached him anyway. There was no place in the old Tanglewood where you couldn't hear the orchestra when it was playing, but he needed to keep moving. The gardens were always his favorite part of the Tanglewood estate. Even now, when he read or heard the word "garden," he would often think of them, because he had loved them so much as a child. Their quiet elegance and labyrinthine quality had fascinated him so that whenever he encountered the word "labyrinth" he often thought of these gardens as well. When Joy and he had walked through the spectacular gardens at Versailles, he had actually gotten nostalgic for the little garden of Tanglewood, its marble pool, its trellis and clipped shrubs and view of the lake. He had told her so, and she had laughed and hugged him. Now he walked around the analemmatic sundial set in the center of one of the gardens, his cream-colored shirt wet with perspiration before he stopped walking, and briefly considered sitting on the stone seat that marked the street-side end of the estate, bordered by an even row of hedges, eight feet high. But he decided not to. He didn't want to stop moving, so he left the gardens, walking past the Chamber Music Hall, then in the opposite direction by the wooden Theatre Concert Hall, the café, the music store, and the Glass House, which sold gifts. He thought of going inside each of the two stores to kill time while he waited for the rehearsal to end, but Perry's CDs, records, and scores would be everywhere in the music stores. And in the gift shop there'd be postcards of Perry and T-shirts, too. He thought of Perry's offer to speak to Joy on his behalf. Perhaps he'd dismissed it too quickly. A properly motivated Perry could be as persuasive as anyone he knew—he'd had firsthand experience of that. And surely Joy would not refuse to meet with Perry . . . or would she?

He walked away from the store, suddenly afraid lest the rehearsal abruptly end and he miss her. He returned a few minutes before the piece ended with its dark thrilling hush, his eyes on her every second. There was the loud applause of the audience followed by Ozawa saying something boyish and charming to the orchestra that some of the audience nearest the stage heard and acknowledged with laughter. From the moment the piece ended, Ray began moving toward the stage, keeping his eyes fixed on her. For ten vertiginous seconds or so he lost her, then saw her again just before she passed through the backstage entrance. He went in front of the first row and across the width of the Shed until he was facing the stage door about twenty feet in front of him. There was no way of knowing what she was doing backstage or even if, somehow, she had seen him and was actively avoiding him or planning an escape by the rear door. More likely, she was talking to people in the chorus. Laughing and talking, or perhaps someone in the chorus or orchestra was flirting with her while he waited.

The two possible exits where she could leave the Shed

were about a hundred yards apart, and now that he forced himself to think about it more clearly, he thought there was also a backstage exit that led to the box parking lot. Why hadn't he gotten a pass from Perry when he offered so he could go backstage as well? In the situation he was in now, it would be physically impossible to monitor all three exits, but he could watch the two on either side of the front of the stage and, if at a certain point she didn't appear, deduce that she'd used the exit behind the Shed. Then if he ran he could possibly catch up with her before she reached her car. (He wondered also why he hadn't looked for her car when he was in the parking lot and simply stayed by it, knowing she would eventually have to return to it.) Of course, he didn't know her schedule, and she might have to stay at Tanglewood to take a class or teach a student for the rest of the afternoon. It wouldn't be reasonable, then, to imagine standing by her car until she returned when he knew she was somewhere on the grounds. It wouldn't be psychologically bearable. Still, there would be something magical about finding her car, knowing that she would eventually have to be there. It was so tempting that he nearly left the Shed.

Ten minutes went by, fifteen. The door kept opening, and musicians carrying their instruments streamed past him, but no Joy. The longer he waited, the more sure he became that she *had* seen him and had left by the rear exit to avoid him or else simply left there by chance because it was nearer to her car or the car of the person she was talking to. He felt the awful pull of the parking lot again, and took a few steps in that direction, when the door opened, and he saw her in a pale blue summer dress. For a few seconds she didn't see him. Then her eyes met his while she was walking toward him, and her face became white.

He moved forward, thought he said her name, and she stopped for a second, shook her head back and forth, and kept walking.

"Joy," he said, out loud this time. He didn't say it loudly, but urgently enough so that she stopped. Musicians were still walking past them; he knew she didn't want to have any kind of scene.

"Please let me talk to you." He turned toward her now that he was beside her. She kept her face slightly to the left, avoiding his eyes, and kept walking, though at a slower, even pace.

"There's nothing to talk about."

"There's everything to talk about, if you'll give me a chance."

"What is it that you think there is to say?"

"Just let me walk you to your car, OK?"

"I'm not going to feel very good about driving you anywhere."

"I have a car. I rented it."

They walked in silence for another minute until they passed out of the Shed into the bright sunshine.

"Joy, please look at me."

Again she shook her head, back and forth.

"I love you totally. Life without you is unbearable. . . . Can't we please talk about this?"

"I can't," she said softly, not much louder than a whisper, he thought, but with unmistakable determination.

"Needless to say, I've ended my relationship with Perry. . . . I'll have no more contact with him."

She turned halfway toward him, perhaps enough to get a quick look at his face.

"I regret what I did, of course, more than anything in my life. And if there were any way I could undo it, I would. Joy, I can only beg for your forgiveness because I want to marry you and dedicate my life—"

"Ray, please." She turned to him with tears in her eyes. "I can't have this conversation with you. I can't bear to listen to this anymore."

He said nothing and walked silently beside her out the

main gate into the parking lot. When she was a few yards from her car he said, "I've taken a room at the Douglas House. I'm not going to go away this time. I won't give up with you like I did last time. I know we can get beyond this. It's only one point in our lives. It doesn't need to rule us and keep us from being together and doing whatever we want forever. Can you tell me why it should? Why this has to happen? Why you won't even talk to me?"

"All right, Ray. Let's review a little history together. I spent two years of my life with you, remember?"

"It was the most beautiful time of my life."

"But it ended very badly, and there was a lot of anger, and not just at the end. There was anger and fighting and distrust at different times from the beginning."

"There was love all through it, too. I never, never stopped loving you from the moment I began."

"That isn't really the issue anymore, unfortunately."

"What is then?"

"The way people treat each other, the way you treated me. Trust is the issue, Ray. You did this to me once before, remember? Only then it was a woman, and it was because I hurt your ego one way or another. But that's where I drew the line—you knew that about me. You knew that about me, yet you went ahead two years later."

"I regretted what I did every day for two years. That's why I didn't make any sustained play for you all that time, because I was working and waiting to regain your trust."

"And so you did."

"But this disgusting little thing with Perry happened before we slept together, before we tried again."

"It happened in California, too. Don't try to say it didn't."

"It wasn't even sex."

"Prostitution is a form of sex."

"OK. Granted it was despicable, it was revoltingly weak

of me, it was a horrendous mistake, but it had nothing to do with us, it didn't affect *us* at all."

"It made you stay longer in California. It made you lie to me over and over. It even made you distrust me, and it's made me unable to trust you again. I can't help it. I'm a simple person, Ray. I don't have a very worldly response to things, but I do know my own feelings. I do know when I feel dishonored and when I just can't trust someone anymore, no matter how much I may want to."

He stared at her and knew she not only meant what she said but had used all her vast reservoir of honesty in answering him and so left nothing out, as he so often had. He felt not only humbled, but silenced, although he said something he would never exactly remember about how he was going to stay, wanted to talk to her again in a day or two (a request she said nothing to), as he moved away from her car and let her enter, close the door, and then drive away from him.

# 24

He'd realized yesterday, within an hour of returning to it, that his room would not provide any relief. There was a documentary on TV about the O. J. Simpson case, which he'd once followed intermittently. It only made him think more about Joy and Perry—for what else was the case really about except the awful power that love holds, how it is even stronger than the fame and the fortune that Simpson had amassed, and he hardly needed to be reminded of that. Moreover, his room, the inn itself with its dark hallways and well-shaded but smallish lobby, made him feel claustrophobic, as if it were closing over him, coffinlike.

He went outside, as he had yesterday, to walk around the yard and look at the lake through the openings in the thick tangle of trees. There was a clump of birch trees he could see below the inn that he especially liked, that made him think of Robert Frost, and made him hear again a theme he'd created just before the summer for a piece he was planning to call "Frost." It would be a musical portrait like the one he'd improvised on the piano about Joy—but scored for six trumpets playing high and soft, eventually joined by double basses. He'd jotted down the opening theme and harmonized it, but hadn't done any more with it than that.

The Douglas House yard, bisected by a partially torn-up tar driveway, sloped uphill dramatically. Across the street were two small yellow houses with pea-green shutters, one belonging to a family named Koss, the other to a family named Kohl. They were perhaps the homeliest houses he'd seen in the Berkshires, and he wondered which family copied the other, or if the houses, which were similar in size though not identical (like the names of their owners), were painted at the same time.

A wooden picnic table was about thirty feet from the inn where he had sat yesterday thinking he could hear the phone in case Joy called. Instead, he heard not only the phone at the front desk but a series of phones from other rooms, so that seemingly every five minutes he got up from the table and moved toward the house (a couple of times walking into the lobby itself) to see if the calls were for him. It would be even worse to sit there today and hear what amounted to a symphony of phones.

He decided to go to the beach. A fog was over the lake, and he couldn't see the Seranak mansion or Tanglewood Beach or even the little island a few hundred yards away that he used to row to as a kid. It was as if it were not really Lake Mahkeenac, he thought, as he walked down the lawn toward the beach, but an anonymous lake, Lake Anywhere.

He walked past the seesaw and swings, thought briefly about sitting at one of the green picnic tables, then continued down the lawn until he reached the small beach. He could see the first raft that the little kids used, that once had a long yellow slide (though even this raft was half obscured by fog), but the raft twenty yards behind it, where he had lain next to Joy in the sun (and imagined her next to other men), was now invisible. It only existed in his memory, not in this moment, although he was staring at it.

He thought of going to Beachwood, to the beach Joy had used the time he'd driven from New York and looked for her in vain at the town beach, only to have her surprise him by emerging from the trail of sand that led to Beachwood.

It had been twenty-four hours since Joy had driven away from him in the Tanglewood parking lot. He had long ago regretted that he said he'd call her in a couple of days. The prospect of waiting another twenty-four hours seemed unendurable, yet he wanted her to think he was under control, dependable, capable of keeping his word. He sat down on the damp sand. He could hear the water curling just before it reached the beach ten feet away. It occurred to him that he'd sat in this same position—legs out in front of him, hands pressed flat to the sand to help anchor him—twenty years ago. It seemed that certain images recurred as if one's life were a kind of time-delayed fugue, where years might pass before invisibly, but on cue, the image returned. It was probably part of the cosmic plan, or the human part of it, to include these repetitions, Ray thought. Without them, *being* really would be unbearably "light." That was why he could never love atonal music as much as tonal music, precisely because of the absence of repetition, the very factor that gave reality what little but touching solidity it had. When he yearned for Joy, it was not ultimately to experience anything new (except perhaps to have children, though even that involved genetic repetition) but to see those same smiles, whether mischievous or ironic, hear that same enthusiasm or self-deprecating sarcasm in her voice he'd known for years, because without them, his sense of the world would be as diminished and obscure as Lake Mahkeenac in its morning fog.

Well, good to know there was a sound philosophical basis for his feeling for Joy, he thought sarcastically, and laughed for a moment. He stayed seated. It was comforting to stay in this position. He closed his eyes and listened to the water, then to the birds and to the slight stirring of leaves in the small breeze.

He wondered where she was. With his eyes closed, he tried to imagine what her morning had consisted of. Had she perhaps unplugged her answering machine so he couldn't leave a message on it, or perhaps unplugged her phone to not even be bothered by its ring? He could sympathize with that. There had been many afternoons or nights when he'd done the same thing in his studio simply because he couldn't bear to talk to a human being. It sometimes seemed the last act of freedom to withdraw, to literally lock your door and disconnect from the world. Who was he to challenge that freedom, to threaten her dignity with his persistence? He opened his eyes for a second, stared at the fog that was lifting slightly but still shrouded almost all of the second raft. He felt stunned by this thought, then closed his eyes again and concentrated. He decided his persistence was justified simply because he knew that he loved her, knew it beyond thought, in his bones. And he was not convinced that her love for him was dead. Even she had not said that, so he could not stop yet, couldn't even think about no longer trying. He would wait a day, because he said he would, and call her tomorrow morning. He could take advantage of the car to help divert himself (though once inside, it would be hard to resist the temptation to look for her). He could go to Lenox, spend some time at the library that he'd always loved, perhaps drive to Williamstown and visit the Clark Museum, which had a fine collection of Impressionist paintings. At night, if the concert was too painful to go to, he could drive to Pittsfield and go to a movie. Or he could just drive in a random direction and find someplace new. Maybe head toward Mount Greylock and try to climb it. He laughed as he realized he was still sitting in the sand like the proverbial old woman who couldn't get up from her fall, as if quicksand had embraced him.

He felt slightly dizzy when he stood up and wondered if he'd sat there longer than he realized. He hadn't worn his watch today, couldn't remember seeing a clock, or a newspaper, as if the fact that he wasn't even going to attempt to speak to Joy today made chronological time irrelevant. Looking behind him, he saw the high white lifeguard seat—something strangely solid in the ghostlike landscape—and thought about climbing up the steps and sitting in it. That was something he always liked to do as a kid, though there were few chances to do it. There was the feeling of power, the thrill of perspective, of heightened vision. But today he wouldn't see much, just this half-imaginary, half-visible lake and the damp, still beach with no one on it but himself.

He didn't take a step toward the chair, but he didn't want to go back to Douglas House either. He was little better than a rat in a maze at the inn—no relief outside, no relief inside, no place where he could, as it were, stop twitching.

He thought about Beachwood again. There was a grove there behind the beach, where he used to play Wiffle ball, and a wooden love seat between two massive evergreens. He'd had his first kiss there, and years later, during their first relationship, he'd kissed Joy on it as well.

He started walking uphill, thinking that this might be the time to go for a drive in a new direction just to look at things that weren't so thick with the past. If only the fog would lift more quickly so that he could see things more clearly.

When he reached Mahkeenac Road, a boy on a bike whizzed past him, a dog (impossible to tell if it was friendly or hostile) following close behind. He wanted to warn the boy not to ride on such a foggy morning or at least to wear brighter clothing, but he didn't think of it in time. He only gave a per-functory yell of "Hey, kid!" but the kid didn't stop; either he didn't hear him, or was afraid, or didn't want to bother. He couldn't blame him. He didn't think he'd have stopped at that age for an anonymous man yelling at him out of the fog.

He walked past the Koss and Kohl houses across the street, mosslike in the fog. He would have to remember to keep his headlights on and to make liberal use of his horn. Maybe he should even lie down in his bed for ten or fifteen minutes and let the fog lift a little more. He went inside Douglas House. A TV was on in the lobby. He walked down the narrow ill-lit hallway (like something in a cheap fun house) that led to his room. There was a message taped to his door. He was so surprised when he read it that he took it inside and turned the ceiling light on to be sure he'd read it correctly. Joy had called and asked *him* to call her!

He stared at the piece of paper, read it again, and then called her, still holding the paper in his hand.

"I got the message that you called."

"Are you going to be there for a while?" Her voice sounded nervous and hollow.

"I don't have any plans."

"I need to speak with you. I'll be right over, OK?"

"Of course."

There was time only to check his appearance, urinate, brush his teeth, rub on a little cologne. Then it occurred to him that she didn't know what room he was in, that it was the landlady, Mrs. Douglas herself, who had in all likelihood taped the note to his door, and that even if Joy did know his room number, she might feel uncomfortable coming to his room.

He walked into the hallway. A woman was moving toward him. He felt himself tilt slightly as if he were walking on a ship in rough weather. For a moment, before he nearly collided with her, he thought it was Joy, and he felt a rush of giddy pleasure, but it turned out to be a middle-aged woman who was staying in a room at the end of the hall. He excused himself, passed through the lobby in a daze, walked out onto the porch, and saw Joy coming down the driveway. They waved at each other at the same time. She looked sad, shaken. He stopped a few feet short of her and said, "We can talk over there," pointing toward the picnic table thirty feet away on the lawn.

"OK," she said. She looked as if she'd been crying, and even in that one word, her voice had an empty quality to it he didn't remember hearing before. He studied her face carefully across the table as she spoke.

"Did you read the paper today?"

He shook his head no.

"Something terrible happened," she said, and her head made the same metronome-like motion from side to side as it had the day before at Tanglewood. "There was a car accident, and Bobby was killed."

"Oh my God!"

"Yes, it's horrible. He was only twenty-five. I didn't know he was so young."

"Christ!"

"It was a head-on collision last night. The other driver is all right, fortunately; he just had minor bruises."

"I don't believe this. How did it happen?" He saw Bobby's face with its enigmatic smile.

Joy took a deep breath. "Bobby had been drinking, he wasn't wearing his seat belt. . . . There was a blind turn."

Ray got up from the table, staggering a few feet toward the lake. When he turned around, she was beside him.

"I didn't know if you knew. . . . I didn't think you should be alone."

He reached out and they hugged each other. He felt a moment of relief, so profound it was almost ecstatic, and then he felt her body resisting him, and he released her, and he was back in time, and Bobby was dead. He saw Bobby again, sitting next to Perry by the pool.

"When did you find out?"

"I knew last night, late. I was listening to the radio."

"I'm sorry for you. He was your friend."

"He was starting to be. He was starting everything in his life. . . . When you're that young, you're always starting something."

"It will be horrible for Perry. I wonder if he knows."

She nodded. "He probably does. Maybe when you feel a little better, you should go see him."

"You think so?"

"Yes," she said, tears falling down her face, and he suddenly realized how difficult it was for her to be here, to ask him to see Perry, to even utter Perry's name. He should tell her to go home and care for her own wounds, but he couldn't. He felt dazed. A feeling of guilt spread over him, had entered him the moment she said Bobby had been drinking. He watched her and sensed she knew what he was feeling.

"I feel like it's my fault. That it would never have happened. . . ."

"It was an accident," she said, putting her hand to her lips to stop him from talking. "Don't talk that way."

"But he was drinking, and he was a recovering alcoholic, and he didn't wear a seat belt. It seems like a suicide to me. Why not face up to it?"

"You don't know that. It's not true. Don't start thinking those kinds of thoughts; they don't accomplish anything. Remember, he died from a head-on collision around a blind turn."

"Was it right away?"

"The paper said he died on the way to the hospital."

Ray winced, felt light-headed, and sat down at the table again.

"So just drive those thoughts out of your head."

"But he *was* drinking, Joy."

"Drinking out of depression and forgetting to put on a seat belt aren't the same thing as suicide, or I would have been dead dozens of times myself."

"OK, so he was playing Russian roulette with his life. So it may not technically have been."

"Think how Perry feels," she blurted in a louder voice that momentarily stunned him.

"I can't believe this happened." He felt tears welling up in his eyes.

"But it did," she said.

He was afraid to look at her. He could hear the delicate wind moving through the leaves. "When do you think I should call him?"

"As soon as you're able to I think you should offer to see him, don't you?"

He turned toward the water. He could feel how difficult calling Perry would be but knew that he had to. He wondered briefly if he would know he should call if Joy hadn't told him.

"I can't say I relish that, but of course I'll call him and see him if he wants me to. I'm sure you didn't relish coming here to see me."

"I didn't think you should find out alone, or be alone after you found out."

"Thank you. That means a lot." I won't read anything into it, he almost said, but stopped himself. It was clear that that was all it meant—a humanitarian mission, and not an easy one at all under the circumstances. He'd best not say anything or hope for anything either. He'd best curb his feelings and focus on mourning Bobby.

She wasn't that way. She had a proper sense of tragedy, a kind of spiritual decorum or perspective. She was not as central to her own sense of the universe as he was to his, he thought. That was what limited her professionally, but made her infinitely admirable. If he couldn't be that way, at least he could admire and learn from her and act like her in a situation like this. Even now, she was asking him if he would be all right, and he hesitated, in spite of his resolve, and said he thought he would be. Even now she was asking him if wanted a Valium, and he said no, he had brought his Ativan along. They laughed together for a few seconds, and he felt again, in those seconds, that sense of safety that was a kind of ecstasy before it vanished.

He couldn't move. He knew how hard it was for her to be there with him, yet he couldn't bear to let her leave. And he knew she knew this, too, just as she knew that as soon as he heard about Bobby's death, a part of him would always see it as one of the consequences of what he'd done with Perry. He imagined then, as he would imagine after she left, how despite the anger, the outrage, that she felt toward him, her mercy was stronger. She didn't want him to suffer more than he needed to. She wanted at least to be sure he wouldn't do something irredeemably self-destructive. So she still felt a concern about him that was a kind of love in itself, and perhaps that should be enough for now. When the shock over Bobby began to wear off, who knew how she would react, what effect it might have on his chances of getting her back? He couldn't bear to think of it; it was obscene to think of it, of something involving his own pleasure, and so finally he didn't. He had to let her go and tell her that he would be OK and ask if she would be, too. And when she said he could call her if things got too difficult, he made the same offer to her.

They were standing by her car, and he looked at her eyes deeply, and opened his arms. They hugged again for a few more seconds, and then he had to release her to her car and the fog and the forces that had seemingly conspired to take her away from him.

# 25

I t was five o'clock when he decided to call. He hadn't thought
that Perry would be home, or even if he were, he didn't think
Perry would necessarily answer the phone. But he answered
on the second ring, his voice barely recognizable—almost toneless—making Ray feel as if he were talking to an impostor.
Perry asked Ray how he was, and Ray said, "Do you want me to
come over?"

"Could you?" Perry said in a voice that sounded infinitely
vulnerable. Ray suddenly felt ashamed for postponing the call
and drove directly to Perry's house. He thought, because of that
voice, that Perry might be standing in front of the gate to meet
him, but no one was there. When he went to ring the buzzer, he
noticed that the gate was open. He walked in and closed it behind him, feeling vaguely as he had the last time Joy had
dropped him off at the gate and he'd stood before the house
alone, not knowing where Perry was or what would happen
when he found him. He began climbing the stone steps that led
to the house. It was only at the top step that he remembered
he'd seen Bobby that day in his T-shirt and madras shorts on his
way to go shopping in Stockbridge. It was Bobby who'd told him
Perry was in his room and had given him directions—then

walked away whistling—an image of innocence so extreme it was comical. How could Bobby's life have been ultimately poisoned by what went on between two men so decidedly unlike him, whose relationship took a fateful turn that day while he went to fetch food for the man he adored?

Ray inhaled a few times to steady himself as he knocked on the door lightly, waited, as if counting the beats in a measure, knocked more loudly, then waited again, and heard nothing. He looked in the window, saw the shape of the piano and behind it the magic walls where the photographs hung. But he didn't see Perry. He began to get scared and half ran around the house past the tiger-lily gardens and up another tier of steps until he saw Perry standing by the pool, facing away from him. It was an image so private he didn't want to violate it and waited until Perry turned before taking another step toward him. Perry was wearing a wrinkled pair of pants and a black sweatshirt. His hair was uncombed, his face ashen, while his eyes looked slightly startled.

"Hello, Ray, thank you for coming." He extended his hand. Their eyes met. Ray ignored his hand and embraced him for a few seconds. He thought he could feel Perry trembling against him and, when they broke apart, saw tears resting almost peacefully in his eyes.

"I'm so sorry, Perry. I'm terribly sorry."

"Thank you, dear heart."

"Are you managing OK?"

"I've been busy all day. I had to speak to his parents. He didn't leave a will, although he once told me he wanted to be buried next to me, and I know he meant in the Berkshires. But I spoke to his parents and acceded to their wishes. They want the body and the funeral in Iowa, and I had to manage that. They don't have the money to have the body shipped, you see."

"I thought they were more or less middle class."

"It doesn't matter. It's just something I should do. I have

much more than they have, and it's the least I can do, so I insisted. It's just a damn complicated thing to arrange, that's all. But it kept me busy. The funeral's on Thursday."

"Are you going?"

"Yes, of course I'm going. My plane leaves Wednesday afternoon. Bobby was the dearest person in the world. I wish you could have known him better. Of course I'm going to his funeral, how could I not?"

"I thought it might be too painful." Ray said. He realized then that they were both standing, that Perry hadn't thought to ask him to sit.

"What's too painful is the thought of his wasted life. The time he should have had to live and won't. What's painful is to realize how blind I was to him, how something kept me focused on other things. Or maybe I was just too damn used to getting people to behave the way I wanted to think something like this could happen."

"You can't blame yourself for what happened."

Perry blinked a few times, as if his eyes had just taken a succession of photographs. "Maybe I should tell you what happened if you feel up to listening."

"Of course."

"You know Bobby and I had a fight before I went to New York. He'd asked me why I was going, and I said to see you. He asked why, and I said because I was in love with you, just like that. But I thought I was only saying the obvious. How could he not know? I thought he knew it all along and saw no need to rub his nose in it. We did have our agreement, that we could sleep with other people. And then after that evening when Joy broke up with you and came over here—well, it was because of what Bobby told her after reading my letter, the one I was half planning to send you and never did."

Perry looked away at the half-visible hills. "I don't know what he was thinking. They say hope is the last thing to die.

Maybe he was hoping that I was just infatuated with you. . . . He could have been hoping that the same way I was hoping you would get over Joy, or the same way I was hoping that he understood and accepted something he couldn't. I was surprised that he ran out of the house that way, with a little yelp at first like a wounded puppy. I was flabbergasted, really. We'd never had a fight or at least not a fight like that before. But I didn't go after him or call him. I went to see you instead. I thought I knew him so well, but I was blind to him. Blind and deaf. Something in me, or something about my life, made me criminally oblivious, just when I should have been alert—don't you see? Otherwise I would have called him and at least been sure he was all right before I left. Instead, I was angry at him; that was one of the last things I felt, I'm afraid, besides my desire to see you and plead my case to you one more time."

"That was the last time you saw him?"

"No, I went back to the Berkshires the morning after I saw you, apparently around the same time you did. Perhaps our cars were moving side by side along the highway. It wouldn't surprise me. I was feeling vaguely concerned about Bobby, but mainly I was feeling sad about you and the things you said to me in your apartment. When I got here, there were no messages— just a call from Glen saying that he liked your piece and that things were going swimmingly on the CD. But you knew that already, I'm sure. So I started to worry a little more about Bobby and decided that I'd call him in an hour or so and ask him to come up for the rest of the weekend. I was thinking of going to Tanglewood Beach—I didn't feel ready to work yet—but at the last minute I grew afraid of seeing people who might know me there, and I wound up going to the pool. That's where I saw Bobby lying on his stomach on a blanket by the diving board, staring at the water."

"How did he get in?"

"He has a key to the house and pool—but naturally I

asked him what he was doing and he said, 'Looking at the water,' still without turning to me. I asked, 'How long have you been there?' and he said, 'Since last night.'"

"'Why didn't you stay in the house?' I said.

"'I don't feel like I belong in there,' he said. 'I don't feel that I have any place there.'

"'That's silly,' I said.

"'So did you fuck Ray?' he said, still in this strange voice, head down looking at the water.

"'No I didn't, and I've just discovered that I never will,' I said, full of self-pity.

"So 'He's finally feeling guilty?' Bobby said.

"I told him not to talk that way. Then I think I said he must have frozen last night. He shrugged and said it didn't matter. 'Your keys are over there,' he said, pointing to the very end of the diving board. 'I just wanted to say good-bye.'

"I asked him where he was going and moved next to him. 'What do you care?' he said.

"'I care very much,' I said. I'm sure I said something like that, though I was feeling a little exasperated and also, suddenly, very tired. I remember I asked him to get up and touched his shoulder and he turned and looked at me, trembling with emotion or maybe just from being cold, and said, 'I don't belong in your life. I'm throwing away my life on you.'

"I told him there was a time when he said I'd helped his life. 'I made a mistake. You don't want me,' he said, suddenly springing to his feet. 'You want him. You left me alone to go to him, and whether he wants you or not, you still don't want me. If you can't get him again, you'll start wanting someone else in a few weeks, and you'll throw me out again.'

"I told him that I'd never thrown him out of my life, and he stared at me and said, 'You did yesterday.' I said that I might have said the words in anger, but he knew that I didn't mean them. 'No. I didn't know,' he said in the same strange voice.

"'I'm asking you to stay now,' I said. He said, 'I can't stay. I can't go on like this, worrying about every person you meet, knowing you don't really want me, that I'm just there to cook for you and keep you company and once in a while fuck until you can find somebody better.'

"Bobby said all this with conviction, but in a low, almost mild voice you couldn't even say was angry. It was as if he were giving an unanimated reading of the news. That should have scared me, but I still felt angry and maybe guilty, too. I might have been realizing that he only pretended to accept our terms because he'd been afraid to protest, because he felt powerless to do otherwise for fear of losing me."

"I remember looking at his face closely, at the circles under his bloodshot eyes. 'Have you been drinking?' I asked him.

"'Don't talk to me like that,' he said, more defiant than petulant all of a sudden.

"'I asked you a question, an important question. At least, it's important to me.'

"'You can't talk that way to me anymore.'

"'Like what?' I asked.

"'Like you're my father or something. You're not my father anymore, and I'm not your little boy.'

"I told him I hoped he hadn't been drinking, that it would be very sad if he had.

"'You're not the police either. You can't check my breath. Can I check you for signs of penetration, or is he just your catcher?'

"'Shut up!' I said. 'Stop talking that way. Stop being so absurdly brutal.'

"He looked at me. For a second or two, our eyes met, and I thought we could make up. Then his mood changed again, 'I'm sorry,' he said softly, 'I don't have the right.'"

"He said that sincerely?" Ray asked.

"He was heartbreakingly sincere. He didn't know sarcasm. And then I held out my arms to him, or I began to, but he ran past me down the lawn wildly. 'Bobby!' I called out after him. I ran to the fence and said his name again, but he was gone. An old man can never catch a young man, anyway, certainly not one in flight.

"A few minutes later, I wondered why I hadn't noticed his car when I drove in. I thought for a moment that maybe he didn't have it with him for some reason. But when I went to investigate I saw his tire marks twenty feet or so up the road. Apparently, he really did feel like he was a burglar invading my grounds, that he didn't belong otherwise.

"I felt completely helpless. What could I do? I could get into my car and drive toward New York on the assumption that that was where he was going, but I didn't even think he *was* going back for the weekend. It turned out I was right. It wasn't as if I could call him on his car phone, because, of course, he didn't have one. I was the only one who had that useless gadget. The only thing I could do was wait. I tried to work on the Stravinsky book, but I could only do three sentences in an hour. My mind was racing, and I couldn't concentrate on anything. I was so desperate I even thought of going to the concert, just to try and distract myself from the hellish waiting and worrying, but I needed to be in the house in case he came by or called.

"It was odd, but sitting at the piano, unable to do much of anything, I suddenly looked around the living room at all the photographs and whatnot on the walls of all the so-called great men, and I was surprised and sad that there was no picture of Bobby there, nor in my bedroom either. I felt terribly guilty, too, and I wondered how that made him feel, or if he even had a strong enough ego to be hurt by that. He certainly never said a word about it to me.

"I got up from the piano bench to get myself a drink, and that's when I made another discovery of a different kind. He'd taken some of my liquor, 'stolen' it, if you will, and left me a short note saying he was sorry and promising to reimburse me for the scotch and whiskey. On the note was his first install-ment—thirteen dollars and seventy-five cents."

"Christ," Ray said.

"Yes, Christ indeed. After that, I didn't know what to do. There was nothing to do. I had a couple of drinks myself and waited. I felt like a ghost in my own house, or maybe more like a vampire in his cave. I had a fantasy of burning down the house, I suddenly hated it so much. My mind was racing again. I couldn't tell if the alcohol was slowing it down or increasing its speed to the point where what was going through my mind was a kind of antithinking. I know that I thought a lot about Bobby and, God forgive me, even more about you. I don't remember any specific thoughts except that there were two kinds of people who were more sinned against than sinning. Everybody in gen-eral, and then those special ones like Bobby, where the tally wasn't even close, where he was an astonishingly pure victim, and such a cruelty-virgin that his idea of revenge was taking a couple of bottles of my liquor, then writing an apology note, and leaving me some money. What chance did he have in this world, filled up with people like me?" Perry said, raising his eyebrows.

"And me," Ray said, softly.

Perry looked down at the pool—the water gray and still like ice.

"At some point, a little after ten, I got the call from the police. In Bobby's wallet, on the back of his license, he had a note saying to call me in the event of an emergency. I asked him to do that in case there was ever any trouble," Perry said, lips trem-bling slightly. "I went down there. The poor boy had died on the way to the hospital. He never had a chance. I went down there. I saw his body stiff and stonelike, like something permanently twisted in stone. And I never told him I loved him before he ran away from me. I never got the words out." Perry cried openly now.

"He knew that," Ray said, as he held Perry again in his arms. "You'd told him before."

# 26

They ate TV dinners and Campbell's chicken noodle soup for supper. There was no other food in the house, and neither felt like shopping or going to a restaurant. Without saying anything about it, they stopped talking about Bobby while they ate. But they didn't try to talk about anything else, settling into a mutually understood silence. While he helped Perry clear the food away, Ray thought that his mission of charity had turned into something else. He didn't want to be alone tonight either.

They moved into the living room—Ray sat on the sofa, Perry on the piano bench, leaning forward. Only the muted light by the piano was on; the gallery was half shrouded in darkness.

"I have the feeling there's something on your mind. Maybe it would do you good to tell me about it," Perry said.

"I'm just feeling a lot of guilt is all. I'll just have to deal with it."

"You shouldn't. Not for Bobby. He wasn't your lover or friend. I always told you he'd accept you and me. I made the great mistake in understanding. It was my blindness you adopted secondhand."

"I could have done more, said more. I saw him in New York, you know."

"No, I didn't know."

"He called me and we spoke for a few minutes in the park. It was just before you came. He was upset, very upset. He wanted to know why I stole you away from him. I told him I was out of the picture, that I was sorry and wrong and that I was in love with Joy. I told him to go back to the Berkshires and see you. That I knew you wanted to see him."

"What else could you have said?"

"I don't know."

"You are innocent in this."

"It's not that easy. I don't feel that way."

"Nevertheless, you are."

THEY CONTINUED sitting, saying very little, as it grew darker. Ray was thinking that at every turn of Perry's monologue about Bobby, he'd wanted him to stop, yet Perry had persisted in confronting it and telling it (just as Joy had done when she came to deliver the news to him, when she so easily could have done otherwise). It seemed his instinct was always to protect himself from pain, that everyone else was more equipped to deal with it than he. Even now, when Perry was more than sixty and protected, one would think, by fame and wealth, he faced the pain of Bobby unblinkingly and accepted more blame for it than he needed to. Ray could only *imagine* himself doing that. He could only hope at some point that he would, but he felt now only dread at what the days that followed would bring when he was alone and would think about his role in things, the words he might have said, the actions he might or should have taken. It would not leave him alone—his mind—yet he would seek to flee from it, at least he always had, through pills or alcohol or television, even through music, though he feared listening to music now, knew that instead of being a palliative, it would accentuate his pain.

"Are you drifting into dangerous water?"

Ray felt himself shrug in the dark, a slight reflexive gesture that Perry might not have even noticed.

"Yes," he said.

"Do you want a drink or a pill of some kind?"

He laughed for a second. "I was just thinking that I've taken too many pills in this kind of situation."

"When has there ever been this kind of situation in your life? You mustn't be too hard on yourself. There's no point in doing that."

Ray nodded. "I'll be all right. Are you OK?"

"It's Bobby who drifted into the really dangerous water. I try to think about him. My troubles always start when I think too much about myself."

"You shouldn't be too hard on yourself either. I mean . . . it was an accident."

"His leaving my house and drinking and not wearing a seat belt were not accidents."

"But there was another car involved. You don't think he'd jeopardize another person just to do himself in?"

"No."

"If that's what he wanted to do, he could have driven off a mountain."

"Perhaps he was on his way to do that."

"Or just turned on the gas and shut the windows."

"He might have been going someplace to do that, as well."

"But he didn't. He hit another car."

"He went through the windshield, the poor son of a bitch. It doesn't matter how he died. That only matters to the rationalizing survivors. It's another form of my thinking about myself, don't you see? Even now, though I'm ashamed to say it,

I'm feeling drawn to you and wishing I could be with you one more time in some way . . . "

Ray stared at him for a moment—saw the old face in the half dark with the eyes still young and unnaturally alert.

"Though I know it can never be. And I've been quietly hating myself for thinking it, and now even that quietness is gone."

"It's supposed to be common for people to feel that after someone they love dies."

"Yes. After my father died, I turned into an erotic monster for about a week, though there was no one I was in love with then. I guess it's a way of proving to ourselves that we're still alive, of resisting the pull of the other side."

"Is your mother still alive?"

"Yes, God bless her. She's eighty-eight. A young mother and a long life."

"Where does she live?"

"In Florida, in a town called . . . "

But Ray's mind drifted. He was thinking how he'd always liked Joy's mother and father, and her brother and sister, too. Bright, good-looking, cheerful people who liked to tease one another, who actually enjoyed doing things together. The incarnation of the mythical happy family that lived in the heart of the country, in Athens, Ohio. A family that played touch football together while he visited them, that ate two-hour-long meals during which they talked and listened to each other and reacted to what was said with feeling, not neurosis. A family with a brother and two sisters, which he, who had grown up as an only child, had always longed to have.

He wanted to be with Joy then so strongly he stood up from the couch, and having to say something said, "I'll be right back. I'm going to the bathroom." When he returned, Perry was standing and facing him about as far away as he had during the afternoon by the pool.

"Do you want to go home now? You must be exhausted."

"I can stay a little longer. Are you going to be all right?"

"I'll be all right. It's gotten late while we've been talking. Time kept passing, anyway, so cruel of it."

"I could stay on the couch if you like."

Perry laughed ironically. "That would be like a mosquito whirring around my head, knowing you were sleeping in my house a few feet away. It would keep me awake. You see, Ray, I'm still in love with you. And now, I must learn to let you go—just as I must learn to let Bobby go—my darling mosquito."

"I still hope one day we might be friends."

"For me, that day is a long time away—my feelings are too strong for you. You look surprised, but I think you understand. Could you be friends with Joy now? In any case, would that stop the riot in your heart?"

# 27

When he was seven years old, he was playing the outfield in a softball game one evening in the Berkshires. The game was in the large front yard of one of the kids he'd made friends with that summer in Mahkeenac Heights. Someone hit a ball well past him into the ferns and wooded area between their field and the start of the neighbor's yard. For a while kids were screaming at him to get the ball, but after the hitter crossed home plate, the screaming stopped, though the obligation remained. It was his job to find the ball so they could all keep playing, but the ferns were so thick and the wooded area so dark that it was difficult to find. He was about to plead for help, when he saw the half-gray softball between a clump of ferns and some wildflowers. It was while he knelt down to pick up the ball that a bee stung him. He closed his eyes as the pain surged through him and for a few seconds saw nothing but an intense orange light. The light was so bright and pervasive that he thought of it as an orange world. Now, in his thirties, in his hot, airless studio in New York in late September, the orange world had found him again, and his eyes closed as he lay back in his bed as if he were built backward and was blinded by the sun whenever he closed his eyes.

The letter from her was at the foot of the bed. Its absence of anger, the very fact that she had answered him so promptly, merely confirmed that she meant it when she said they "could never happen again." But he had known that anyway. As the days passed without a word from her, he realized that Bobby's death had sealed the situation that was probably already irreversible, that his death had taken their relationship with it as well. Still, after he read the letter, while he'd entered the orange world for a moment, he could not think or know if it was day or night; memory itself almost disappeared. There was only the bee-sting feeling of pain and the orange light, and since there was no time, the relatively few seconds that it lasted never precisely ended, but persisted in him, like an insidious drug, for hours.

His chief weapon against it was his routine, and he followed it assiduously and then, finally, automatically. He'd wake up within a few minutes of six o'clock. As soon as the first wave of images of Joy or Bobby hit him full force (usually before six-fifteen) he'd take half an Ativan, then a long shower at six-thirty. He ate a cheese omelette from the breakfast place on the corner and made sure he sent out two resumes before lunch, except on Thursday, when he taught his one class at the college. In any event, he had lunch (pork and vegetables) at the same Chinese restaurant on Broadway and in the afternoons taught his other New York piano students (except on Tuesdays, when he had to go to New Jersey again to teach). For dinner he went to a nearby delicatessen and ordered apricot chicken salad (sometimes substituting carved turkey breast) and pasta primavera to go, then took it back to his studio and ate it while he watched the news. Nights were a carefully orchestrated mix of TV and doing bills and paperwork. At ten o'clock, he'd take his second Ativan and begin a long walk on Broadway, usually uptown toward Columbia but sometimes downtown toward Lincoln Center. When he returned from his walk, he went back to television.

On one of his night walks he called Bryna from a pay phone. He thought he was going to tell her everything about himself and Perry, but only told her that Perry's lover, Bobby, had died in a car accident. When she asked him about Joy, he said he'd gotten a letter from her and now knew it was all over. Bryna asked if he was all right, and he said he was and that he would call her again in a few days. He hung up, faced the street, and discovered he was shaking.

THERE WAS an otherworldly quiet to his apartment that intensified at night. Sometimes it seemed as if it were part of the surface of the moon. A moon with a piano he was now unable to play. But as long as he followed his routine, the moon was inhabitable, and the orange world was kept at bay. For days at a stretch the routine worked. Then on a Tuesday, he was returning from Ken May's home in Fort Lee, a student he'd begun teaching just two weeks ago. Ken was an earnest high school math teacher who had his heart set on learning a Chopin nocturne. He seemed totally devoid of musical talent, yet had a genuine love for Chopin. It was ironic.

On the bus back to the city, he couldn't help narrating the lesson in his mind to Joy, imagining her laughter, which he'd heard so many times before when he described some of his pupils and which was always the perfect reward for his comic exaggerations. Through the window he saw the darkening sky. It was early October—the busiest and best time of the year in New York and in Philadelphia, too, where he could be working now, teaching at Joy's school, if he'd gone after the job instead of going to California. He'd be living in an apartment near her, or perhaps he'd have moved in with her, merely keeping a small studio to teach in. He'd be composing and teaching. They would have dinners where they'd joke about the faculty; they'd go hear the Philadelphia Symphony on Friday nights. They'd walk through Fairmount Park and picnic at Valley Green on Saturday and Sunday. In the summer, they'd go swimming at the Jersey Shore, come back, and make love. They'd get married perhaps at Tanglewood and go to Paris or maybe Greece on their honeymoon.

He heard a screaming sound in his head, then the sense that it was filling with an intensely orange liquidlike light, rising steadily, as if filling the once-empty pool inside him. It was like a heart attack in his mind, and had it lasted another second, he would have gotten up from his seat and demanded to be let off the bus.

He checked but had forgotten to bring any pills. If only he could walk on the street where he'd have to pay attention to other people, he could get some relief, but the bus was winding in its inexorable way to the Port Authority like a fat, slow-moving snake. He was locked in it, and no one was sitting next to him. It was unfortunate that he was at the back of the bus, or he'd have more faces to look at. Instead, from his vantage point, he was staring at the back of people's heads. He wondered if he could leave the bus as soon as it got off the highway and stopped at a red light. He could tell the driver it was a health emergency, and he could perhaps get him to let him off now on the highway, though that would do him little good. There was no subway on the highway, no way to get home any faster. There was nothing to do now but wait it out. Apply self-discipline, apply whatever techniques of self-control he could, perhaps try to distract himself by listening to music in his head. If he could hear passages from his own compositions, he could remind himself of his identity as a composer, but he couldn't hear the music—just a kind of buzzing.

As soon as the bus stopped, he went to the first phone booth he could find and called Joy in Philadelphia. He called literally just to hear her voice and was glad she wasn't in, in a way, because there was more of her voice to listen to on her answering machine than if she simply said hello before he hung up. It worked. He felt relief. So much so that instead of heading home, he decided to keep walking. Why hurry back to the moon?

To walk, if he did it the right way, by becoming a perception receptacle for the sensations in front of him, was to stop thinking for a while. Certainly he needed that kind of reprieve, though it could sometimes be disconcerting to pass from one economic stratum to another so quickly as he moved up Broadway. What was New York if not a noisy museum of the most outrageous contradictions? The key was to make no judgments, to become instead a kind of ambulatory recording device, merely seeing the shapes in front of him as if he were a tourist on a different planet, where his occupation was simply to observe without comment and above all to keep moving.

He walked up Eighth Avenue past the sex shops, the restaurants, the weave of people at whom one was warned not to stare but at whom he did stare now. They seemed like people made of stone or petrified wood—suddenly given the power to walk.

He crossed over to Broadway at Fifty-sixth Street. In front of Carnegie Hall a white-and-black flag proclaimed THERE'S ONLY ONE CARNEGIE HALL! Wasn't there a time when this was obvious, when they would, at any rate, have been too refined to advertise it à la McDonald's? Across the street from the back of the hall was Patelson's Music House, or "composer's hell," as Arnold used to refer to it. It was the only place in New York (and possibly America) that housed a large number of contemporary scores, and Ray was never sure if Arnold called it hell because he was envious of the composers whose scores were on sale or because, once there, the scores were buried in their binders and remained unbought and unread.

In the window was an exhibit of John Cage books, scores,

and memorabilia in commemoration of his recent death. For a moment he wondered how many composers were secretly glad Cage had died because there was one less "great man" on the scene. He went inside. The bland green walls were decorated with two-foot-high photographs of Verdi and paintings of Bach and Haydn—the people it was safe to love now that they, like Cage, were dead and not as much of a threat to the store's composer clientele. He scanned the titles in the Cage exhibit, then moved on to other books. *Mahler: His Life, Work, and World* and *Alma Mahler or the Art of Being Loved.* A sign at the counter said PLEASE DO NOT ATTEMPT TO RESHELVE MUSIC. LEAVE THEM ON THE COUNTER. THANK YOU. He bent down and saw the George Crumb section, the scores pressed as close to each other as keys on a piano. A paranoid quiet filled the room. He looked at the other men in the room as they checked the sales of their scores or their rivals as solemnly as men in a peep-show booth. Then he left.

The light was more black than blue as he approached Lincoln Center. He saw the smooth white planes that connected the Center like a Florida condominium complex. A few feet to his right a glass-enclosed, ten-foot ad said:

> Meet the Artist at Lincoln Center.
> Meet, speak, and dine with a world-class artist followed by a special Lincoln Center performance.
>> Meredith Monk, singer, composer, choreographer, multimedia wizard
>> Wynton Marsalis, triple-threat artist: trumpet prodigy, jazz composer, artistic director of jazz at Lincoln Center
>> Perry Green, internationally celebrated conductor and . . .

He didn't need to read the rest. Maybe Perry would meet someone new through the program. That might have been his main motivation for doing it, though of course it was great publicity, too. Ray walked up the stairs that led to Juilliard, suddenly feeling a desire to visit his old practice room. Inside, a black security man stood in front of a table by the doorway and asked to see his ID card.

"I used to go here, ten years ago."

"Do you have an active ID card?"

"No."

"I'm sorry, sir. I can't let you in then."

"OK. Thanks anyway," Ray said.

He lingered in the lobby for a few minutes (where his own ad was thumbtacked to the bulletin board), reading some of the other ads.

Steinway for sale. Mint condition.

Cello for sale. Beautiful, modern cello by Italian maker, performance quality, Seifert bow included. Asking $5,000.

Next to that was the longest, most imploring ad on the board:

Classical guitar lessons, Jan Goldberg, guitarist. Juilliard grad. Finalist in 3 Nations Competition. Teachers include Sharon Isbin, Eliot Fisk. Unlock the musician in you. Unlock the music in your instrument. Learn the basics or refine your technique. Improve your playing in any style. Broaden your musical knowledge. I am an experienced and patient teacher. Lessons are tailored to suit your stylistic and career goals as a player. My rates are very reasonable. I teach all levels (including children). House calls possible.

Out of the corner of his eye he saw his ad. He didn't want to read it. He remembered that Joy had helped him write it, that he had once used it as a pretext to call her during their friendship stage.

Outside, it was getting dark. He walked downstairs to

the Lincoln Center subway stop and waited. The subway was halfway between the hells of the bus and the street. On the subway it always felt like night. There would be plenty of people frozen in their seats, there would be another forest of necks, but it was also a semiambulatory world where people constantly got off and on or else moved from one car to another. After a short stay in his seat, he spent the rest of the trip switching cars out of the sheer need to keep moving.

Pictures of Joy passed in and out of him as he walked out of the station. The street lamps were on. Joy would be in her apartment now in Philadelphia, taking a shower after her run, or maybe eating dinner.

A man appeared in front of him asking for money. He was black, around forty-five, and was wearing a pathetic collage of rags. Ray gave him all the change he had—less than a dollar—and walked on: Why was he so startled? Didn't this happen two or three times a day? This was New York, after all, where he had once seen a woman defecate on the street, where he had seen a man stabbed on the sidewalk and had then held him while the man bled and trembled until the police arrived. The city was just another undeclared American war. Races were at war with one another, workers were at war with their bosses, and artists were among the most furious warriors of all, plotting for themselves and against each other. With AIDS, the war had spread to the act of love itself. And there was no protection—even the AIDS test was illusory. Like the sun, it didn't really reveal the present, merely what was once there, in the past.

How could America be anything else but a nation of paranoids, and how could paranoids keep from making war even as they tried to make love? It was no longer a question of cheating or lying; it was a question of killing. Othello, who such a short time ago seemed a man from another era, was more relevant than ever. Othellos were everywhere now. Perhaps he had just given his money to Othello. How could he ever hope that Joy could trust him again, make love to him again? Someone had already died because of all this business, he thought, as he saw an image of Bobby smiling by Perry's pool and shuddered.

He walked past his Glenn Gould doorman, bent over a newspaper again on his desk in the dim lobby. As he got off the elevator, he realized that Joy had never seen his studio. During the friendship phase of their relationship, which coincided roughly with the two years he'd lived in the studio, he always visited her in Philadelphia or met her at a restaurant, museum, or bookstore in New York. Once or twice he did meet her in the lobby, but he'd been ashamed to have her see his studio—so small and hot and piano dominated that there was barely room for two people. Now that he was inside it—back on the moon, as it were—he wished he'd let her see it so he'd have a memory or two of her in the studio that could only have helped sweeten it a little. Almost no one besides himself had spent any time in it. There was Perry's short, dreamlike visit, Bryna once or twice, and a couple of other women he'd tried to have sex with. When he remembered those nights, he shuddered again.

On the subway back home and on the bus ride, he'd anticipated taking his Ativan, but now he hesitated. He was afraid to fall asleep an hour or so from now when it would kick in. It was too early. If he did, he'd be wide awake at three in the morning, the time Fitzgerald had aptly identified as the dark night of the soul. He looked at the piano keys—a forbidding white lake, silent and frozen—then at the TV on his windowsill. He felt a slight spinning sensation as he usually did before the orange world closed over him, and he reached for the phone and called Bryna.

"Hi, it's Ray."

"Finally, I hear from you. How are you? Never mind, dumb question. Is there anything at all I can do for you? I've been worried about you, but took you at your word, that you needed to be alone."

He felt touched and moved his head away from the receiver for a few seconds, staring at a slit of sky.

"Really, Ray. What can I do? Spit it out, please."

"You're being so kind. You always have been. I don't deserve it."

"It's your fate you don't deserve."

"I'm feeling that I do."

"No, nobody does. Nobody deserves their fate, but fate is tricky, you know. It stays hidden until the bitter end. Listen, Ray darling, you must be going out of your mind. Who's helping you? Are you staying with anyone?"

"No. Right now I'm in my studio by myself."

"You really sound terrible. Would you like some company? Would you like to come over and be with me for a while? Stay over if you want to. Eat some decent meals."

"You sure?"

"Yes, I'm sure. I've got kind of a boyfriend now. Remember Ed, the guy I started going out with the last time you called? But he'll understand. He's not the jealous type like me. Besides, I'll go to his place when we do that stuff—it's no problem. I think you should pack some things and take a cab here right away, on me. I just sold a piece so I'm feeling rich again. Will you do that? Will you promise me you won't talk yourself out of it and just come see me?"

# 28

He certainly hadn't planned to stay at Bryna's more than the night, but she urged him to stay longer, and since he'd felt better at her loft, he decided he'd stay for a few days. He could get his phone messages at Bryna's, and he had no reason to expect any important letters, certainly nothing from Joy, who in her last letter had not only told him a relationship between them was impossible, but had also asked him not to write her anymore.

From the morning after the first night at Bryna's, Ray wondered if he should tell her about Perry. She had gone to do some errands and then to meet her boyfriend, Ed, for lunch, and he found himself thinking about, then actually visualizing, his confession. He wondered why he wanted to tell her. What would he get out of it? Who would benefit from it? Certainly not Bryna, who was deeply involved with Ed and was clearly acting out of friendship and concern alone in inviting him to stay while she was in the middle of her romance. So if her chief concern for him was simply his welfare, the question remained: Why did he want to tell her? Was it merely a question of guilt? That was substantial enough, especially since Bobby's death. And whom else could he tell besides her now that the only people who knew what had happened—Joy and Perry—were for different reasons people whom he could no longer talk to? Guilt, then, was a large factor, but how exactly would it be diminished by telling Bryna? Wasn't it precisely because he knew it wouldn't be diminished that he wanted to tell her at all? And was that worth the risk of jeopardizing their friendship or at least the degree of trust or respect she felt for him?

He didn't tell her when she returned from lunch. He realized later that he might have, but she'd come back with Ed, and there was no real opportunity then or during the next two days when Ed was with her in the loft so much. It was odd to see her with Ed, a carpenter who co-owned a small shop in SoHo. He was a heavyset man somewhere between forty-five and fifty with smiling blue eyes, and he seemed direct, unaffected, and very fond of Bryna, no doubt the most exotic woman he'd ever been involved with. Ray didn't feel jealous, merely strangely removed, like a spectator in a play, as he watched them speaking in hushed, intimate tones. Clearly they made a point of keeping their relationship muted while in his presence, but they still were unable to hide their pleasure, which kept breaking through in smiles, whispered words, and vivid gestures. He wanted to tell them it was all right to be happy in front of him. A couple of times, he told Bryna that Ed was great and should stay over, but true to her word, she went to his place to make love, returning each night to stay in the loft with him.

She'd offered Ray her bedroom, but he felt too heavily in her debt already and slept on the futon at night in the living room area, surrounded by her sculptured sheep. He'd slightly decreased his dosage of Ativan and was generally successful in sleeping five or six hours—enough time so that he didn't have to wait too long for Bryna to wake up. Mornings, he discovered, were the most brutal times. On the morning of his last day there (he had told her he would leave before lunch), he woke up much earlier than he wanted, hit with a pain that staggered him. It was another heart attack in his mind, and he tried to walk it off between the sheep in her dark, gigantic loft. Just before he reached the kitchen, he bumped into a table and swore under his breath, worrying for a moment that he might have toppled one of the sculptures—but there were none around. He didn't think he'd made that much noise, but the light went on in Bryna's room and soon she was walking toward him.

"Ray, is that you?"

"Yes."

She was next to him now in the dark, the light in her room shining faintly in the distance.

"Do you want some food? I could fix you something."

"No. I'm sorry I woke you up. I was just walking."

"I couldn't sleep either. Do you want to talk?"

He shrugged. "Maybe."

She turned a floor lamp on low, and they sat at the dining table just off the kitchen. He looked down at the table, and Bryna asked him if he wanted a drink. "That's a good idea. Do you have vodka?"

"Of course. I think I'll have a scotch myself."

He sensed that she was nervous and thought he noticed her twitch as she returned to the table and handed him his drink. Taking two good-sized swallows, he looked up at her.

"There's something I need to tell you, that I've been afraid to tell you till now."

"Why would you be afraid?"

"Because of what it would make you think of me."

"My God, it can't be that you cheated on me, given our understanding."

"More like I cheated on myself. No, this has to do with Joy . . ."

"Of course."

"And what I promised her."

"You slept with another woman while you were with her?"

287

He looked away from her for a moment. "It's a little more unusual than that. I slept with a man."

She put her hand to her heart and inhaled more deeply than usual. "But why would that make you afraid to tell *me* of all people, though I admit it's rather startling news. Didn't I tell you that I had sex with a woman once or twice during my commune days?"

"You don't understand. This wasn't because I was attracted to someone or wanted to experiment. This was with Perry Green, and I hated everything about it. This was something I did out of sheer ambition for my stupid career."

"And it worked."

"And the worst part is, it worked. It did help my career, so I had to do it again, and then Bobby found out and told Joy, which is why she broke up with me, and then Bobby . . ."

"Bobby is Perry's lover who died in the car accident?"

"Yes."

"But you can't blame yourself for that."

"He was a recovering alcoholic and he was drinking after having had a fight with Perry about me."

"You're not responsible for that."

"He was drinking to escape the pain Perry had caused him because of me, don't you see? He'd been sober for nearly two years."

"But if Perry betrayed him, that's not your fault. That's between them. You barely knew Bobby, am I right?"

"I can't pretend I didn't know him, but I didn't know him well."

"Ray, what I'm trying to say is that what happened is horrible enough; you don't have to try to add to it by blaming yourself. You didn't do what you did with Perry to hurt Bobby. And you didn't do it to hurt Joy either. That was the last thing you wanted. How did she find out, anyway?"

"Bobby told her. He'd read a love letter Perry had written to me but unfortunately never mailed."

"But she knew why you did it, obviously. She knew you didn't care about Perry. She might have forgiven you."

"She couldn't. Trust is everything to her. I promised I'd be faithful and she trusted me."

"I'm just saying some women would have forgiven you, wouldn't have been so absolutist. You told her how you felt about her, didn't you?"

"I told her I wanted to marry her, that Perry was meaningless and would never happen again. And I told Perry I would never do it again also, but how could she believe anything I said, after she found out about Perry? How could she believe I loved anyone but myself?"

"I don't think that's it. I don't think you're being fair to yourself."

Ray got up from his chair, walked a few steps toward the center of the loft, then turned and faced her.

"Look, I know what you're trying to do, and I appreciate it. And I know we're all cynical liberals, and that we're all very permissive and understanding about careers and sex, but still, *still,* there have to be some things that are objectively horrible, and what I did *was* horrible. There's simply no rationalization for it, and it's important to me that you acknowledge that and . . . what's the matter?"

He saw that her lip was trembling.

"You're starting to yell," she said.

"I'm sorry. I thought I was just speaking with emphasis. I certainly don't mean to yell at you."

She took a swallow of her drink before talking, while he sat down at the table again.

"It's just that it's horrible for me to see you in this kind of pain and not know what to do. I mean, you seem to want me to condemn you, and I can't."

"So you're saying I did nothing wrong? Someone died because of this."

"You did something to help yourself, not to hurt her or

Bobby. And it started before you got her back. If I remember the sequence of events right, you were already involved with Perry before you got reinvolved with Joy. And then you got your concert so quickly, your reward. I guess you started to get addicted to it. But who wouldn't? You'd tried so hard and waited so long and weren't getting anywhere. And then you got your concert, and the thing is you deserved it. You are a good composer."

"So you're saying I should just let myself off the hook?"

"I'm saying you made an unwise decision, but you don't have to make yourself meshuga. You've already paid the price big time and would have paid for it for the rest of your life whether there was an accident with Bobby or not. I'm also saying that you're a worthwhile human being, one I'm very fond of, and I think you don't need to add to your punishment, which is substantial enough as it is, believe me."

"OK. Thank you, thanks. You're being very kind. I shouldn't have expected anything else from you, of course."

"But you say that like you're disappointed, which makes me feel that I've failed you somehow, but maybe that's my karma, to always fail you in some subtle way."

"No, why do you . . . "

"No, Ray, really, it's true. You're always so careful with my ego, maybe because of our arrangement or because I'm older, but you don't have to be. Certainly not now. I'm very happy with Ed."

"I know. I'm glad for you."

"So I'm feeling a lot stronger and more confident now. I've got my chutzpah back, or some of it. Which means you can be a lot more direct with me without worrying about it as you may have in the past. So if I ask you what it is that you want from me that I'm not giving, or what is it that you want me to say that I'm not saying, you shouldn't mince words with me. You should be completely direct and spontaneous. I think that's important."

"OK, OK, I hear you."

"Well, what is it?"

Ray looked at her for a second but said nothing.

"Is it that you want me to condemn you, to call you a sinner who deserves everything he got, who deserves to suffer as you are? I can't do that. I don't believe it."

"You've never done anything like I did, and you're ambitious."

"Please, I've done hundreds of things I'm ashamed of, believe me."

"Not like this. You can't really say that and mean it."

"I don't carry around a scale of justice on my back. Otherwise I'd look even more like a camel than I already do. But I've definitely had sex with people for all kinds of questionable reasons. Did I ever do it to help my career? Maybe not, but sometimes the reasons we really do things are blurry, or sometimes we fib to ourselves about why we do them. So I can't even be sure about that in a couple of cases."

Ray felt oddly nervous. "What are you saying? That there was some other reason why I slept with him besides my career?"

"Ray, darling, I'm talking about myself, not you. You asked me about myself, and I'm answering or trying to answer you about myself and myself only. I'm not an expert on you and never will be. I'm not even an expert on myself all the time, like I'm saying."

"But what you're saying is applicable to my case, too, isn't it?"

"I'm speaking only about myself. When it comes to your life, I'm inclined to believe whatever you say. I will say this. I have one obvious advantage you don't have, without which I would've done even worse things than I did. I had money—you haven't ever. For that alone, I can't judge."

"It wasn't money. I was in rough shape, but I was getting by. It was for a worse motive than money. To be famous in a stupid world I no longer care about. How's that for a grand irony?" he said, forcing a laugh.

Bryna looked at him sadly. "So, Ray, do you want to try to sleep again?"

"I don't think so. I don't think I'll be able to."

"I could give you a sleeping pill."

"No, it's not a question of that. I'm too awake now."

"You wouldn't want to join me in my morning jog around SoHo before you go? We could laugh at all the bad art in the gallery windows."

"So that's what you've been doing every morning. I thought you were shopping or something, but then I never saw the food."

Bryna laughed. "Food is what I'm trying to stay away from. Food *is* the reason for the running."

"But you look better than ever, Bryna."

" 'Than ever' I don't know about. But thank you. I have dropped a few pounds. I've gotta keep in shape for Ed, you know; it's getting a little frightening. I'm beginning to think it might actually work out."

"I think so. I think he's right for you."

"God, I hope. You know, I'm going to miss you. I'm going to feel your absence and worry about you. Please stay in touch and come back if you start to feel bad again."

"Thank you. I will."

"Maybe Ed and I can find the right kind of woman for you."

"Oh no, Bryna, I can't even think about that. I'm really just trying to get through each day."

"Of course. I didn't mean to make light. . . . But some-where in your mind you can still think of *some*day, can't you?"

"The truth is, though I try telling myself otherwise, I still haven't given up on Joy."

# 29

He felt separated from his normal sense of time. It was not that time passed more quickly or slowly for him, rather that so often each day seemed like the same one, a feeling that the routines that governed his daily life naturally enhanced. He continued to wake up at six o'clock (no matter what time he fell asleep), when his memories of Joy were most intense, especially while he was taking a shower or eating breakfast. After a quick perusal of the newspaper, he'd start his house calls. He'd accepted more students than ever—and liked scheduling them in the morning or early afternoon while his energy was at its height. In addition to providing him with income, his students gave him the necessary amount of human contact he needed to get through the day. For the first time in his life, he felt regret when he closed the door on the last one, for by the time he reached the subway or the bus stop he was feeling the loss of Joy acutely again. Sometimes he reviewed his last conversation with her, sometimes what he could have done differently while he waited in his car in her yard. Other times he'd simply feel a sense of her personality as it expressed itself in a phrase like "Now I can die. I've dined with a great man," which she'd said to him after meeting Perry, or perhaps simply the way she smiled as she first walked into a lake or the ocean.

When he got home from teaching, he continued to go to the same restaurants (the nearest Chinese restaurant and the local deli), where he generally ordered takeout. He turned on his TV while he ate and returned to it later in the night, after his walk, until its repetitive voices and laugh tracks eventually helped him fall asleep. Perhaps once a week he ate lunch with Bryna (who was now engaged to Ed) and less often had a drink with Arnold or Frank Trigona. Except for one postcard, he heard nothing from Perry during these months, which didn't surprise him. He couldn't help feeling some regret that Perry had disappeared from his life, but in the main he felt relieved, as if a kind of tumor that had attached itself to his soul had finally been removed.

At night his dreams seemed to willfully clash with the dull routines of his waking life. They were vivid, unpredictably erotic, and bizarre. He had one repetitive dream about Joy which occurred at least three times a week. They were making constant, rapturous love in the bedroom of her Berkshire cottage, where the yard had suddenly expanded to include a lake and raft. Other nights his dreams involved sex with women he had never seen before. In some of those dreams, Perry was in the room with a wistful expression, watching Ray perform. One night after an especially intense installment of his dream with Joy, he woke up, heart pounding, body soaked in sweat. That afternoon when he called her, expecting again to hear just her answering machine, she answered on the second ring. He began by saying he was sorry, that he knew she didn't want to hear from him. Then he started asking her questions about her school in Philadelphia, and if she had any good students this term. He didn't expect to talk to her for more than a few minutes, and after he had started, wondered how he was going to manage to make it last that long. He continued asking her questions about her daily life, neutral questions—certainly nothing overly personal or threatening—and she answered him about her apartment and her boss, and her private students, then about a recital she might be giving in the spring. They were not exactly dutiful answers, not exactly impersonal, or tense, but muted, somewhat unanimated, and ultimately hollow. What he felt she was really saying to him was, It is painful for me to talk to you, every second hurts. I meant what I wrote in the letter. I do not want to hear from you; it is the only way I can manage this. I feel sorry for you, too. I do not wish you to suffer more than you have, more than you will, but there can be no more chances for us. I had to decide that, I have to live with that, or I will not be able to live at all.

When the conversation ended, he felt that he shouldn't call her again, not even just to hear her voice on the machine.

IN JANUARY the anthology of contemporary music CD that Glen produced came out with his piece on it. When he saw it in Tower Records just a day before his own copy arrived in the mail, he immediately bought it. He thought the performance of his violin and piano sonata surprisingly good, and the sound quality excellent. He was also pleased that the five other composers on the album all had reputations that far exceeded his. Their pieces were interesting, too, for the most part, and for several days he found himself listening to the whole CD. It was the first album he'd listened to in months, and having broken the barrier, he began listening to and occasionally buying more contemporary music. A few days later Arnold called to tell him there'd been a good review of the CD in *Gramophone* and in *Ear* magazine, and that each had made a nice reference to his piece.

"Ray, think for a minute," Arnold said. "You've had a piece performed at Tanglewood by Perry Green that got really good reviews, another one performed in Santa Barbara, and now you've got a piece on a CD by a respectable commercial label that's gotten some very nice notices already. Don't you think you should redo your resume and go after some kind of teaching job? You know, strike while the iron's hot."

Ray followed Arnold's advice and sent a new resume out to almost all the private schools in the city, as well as to those colleges where he'd heard there were openings or where his Juilliard or Columbia connections might be of some value. It was in part through a piano and harmony teacher at Columbia with whom he had a reasonably good rapport that he got an adjunct position as an introductory composition instructor at City College in New York. It didn't pay enough for him to cut down on his private teaching, but he definitely had his foot in the door. A month later, when a tenure decision went against one of the younger composers who decided to forsake his lame-duck year to teach in Oregon, the department head offered Ray a one-year contract at the instructor level (which saved the school more than twenty thousand dollars annually), renewable up to three years (which saved the work of conducting a search for a tenured replacement). Ray was excited and took advantage of his option to start teaching full-time in the summer term.

Now he could eliminate some of his pupils, the beginners and those who lived outside the city, but now, also, he felt an added pressure to compose. Probably he could get away with not producing anything new and still be rehired for a second year if he simply taught well and didn't make any enemies. But he doubted the grace period would be extended for a third year—not for a job in New York that hundreds of productive composers across the country lusted for, low paying though it was. And if he had any fantasies of the job's being extended beyond three years or possibly becoming tenure track, it was absolutely essential that he get more works performed, published, or recorded. Not only did this seem almost impossibly daunting now that Perry was absent from his life and he had no network of any kind to get help from, but he no longer knew if he could compose, if musically he had anything left to say.

He decided to try something simple, almost as an exercise, to prove to himself that he could at least still put notes that made sense down on paper. He called it "Five Sketches for Piano" and modeled it slightly on Prokofiev's "Five Melodies for Violin and Piano." But after a week of working several hours a day on it, he had thrown away all but the opening bars of the first sketch. Still, the mere fact that he was composing, getting ideas down on paper again, made him hopeful.

A few days later he turned thirty-three. The Tanglewood season had already started—it had been almost a year since Joy had left him, almost a year since Bobby died. Christmas and New Year's had been difficult to get through, but he knew the summer would be harder still. He stuck, essentially, to the promise he made. He didn't write her and only called twice, just to hear her answering machine, when he was fairly sure (correctly, as it turned out) that she wouldn't be home.

He had no plans to go to Tanglewood. He wouldn't do that to himself. Sometimes he wondered if Perry would come back, or if he had rented or sold his house. Ultimately, he couldn't resist checking the schedule in the newspaper where he discovered that Perry would be conducting Beethoven's Ninth in late August. That meant he'd have to be in Tanglewood for at least a week.

Though Ray was working every day on his "Five Sketches" and already teaching at City College, it was difficult not to think of each day in relation to Tanglewood. One day marked the anniversary of his first visit to Joy's house, another their dinner at Perry's. One day was the anniversary of his ride to Tanglewood with Bobby, another the anniversary of his concert, of making love with Joy again after having waited so long. He began to wonder if Joy had returned to Tanglewood. It was not inconceivable that she would rent her cottage and go somewhere else for the summer or part of the summer. Perhaps the Jersey Shore or somewhere in Europe. He went through a series of scenarios for about two weeks, until somewhere near the end of the summer he called her in the Berkshires, heard her answer the phone in person, and quickly hung up. He shouldn't have been surprised. She was not the kind of person to try to escape by traveling. She always met things straight on. She was not like him that way. It was something else he loved about her.

Those two seconds (he had hung up after only one hello) proved more enduring than he could have imagined. Like a tune he couldn't get out of his mind, it persisted for the next two weeks—an inextinguishable sound that could not be described or explained by language, that seemingly could not be diminished by time.

WHEN HE was on the train to Philadelphia a week into the fall term, he told himself that the telephone call had made him decide to go. It was paradoxical. His trip appeared to be an impulsive decision—technically he'd only decided to do it the day before—but really it was the last exposure to her voice and his inability to rid himself of it that had sealed his fate.

The train took an hour and a half to reach Philadelphia, but the time seemed a single extended moment. The newspaper that he had brought to read remained unopened. He did not remember looking out the window either, or whether or not he sat next to anyone.

First, he wondered where they would meet. He hoped it would be in her school just as she was leaving so he could walk her home. He didn't want to have to call her first, to give her the chance to refuse to meet him, which he knew was certainly possible, just as it was possible, for one reason or another, that she might not even be in Philadelphia on this particular day. Still, having had his hypothetical meeting with her somewhere in or near her school, he thought next about what he would say to her, specifically the things he should say first that would set the tone and, more important, give him the time to say more later. He realized that he mustn't frighten her or appear in any way out of control. It would be frightening enough to her that he had come without calling, without having spoken to her in six months, nor written in three. She would be shocked to a degree, no matter what her other reactions might be, so he had to be gentle and careful in the first things he said to her.

He tried imagining her responses to him. He wasn't seeking a fantasy response; that wouldn't satisfy him because he couldn't believe in it. Instead, he tried to imagine how she really would answer various remarks of his, and the more verisimilitude he was able to give the hypothetical dialogue between them, the more fully engrossed he became. Then like a dessert he had saved for himself, he pictured the clothes she'd be wearing. He had met her a few times at school or after she'd taught a private pupil during the friendship phase of their relationship and had some idea of how she dressed for work. There was a blue dress (almost the color of lapis lazuli) that he remembered fondly that came just below her knees. He also recalled a beige business suit that she wore either with a pale yellow or white ruffled shirt and sometimes with a black brooch he'd given her for her birthday. If he missed her at school, if she got off early that day, for example, and had gone home and changed before he met her, she could be wearing anything, of course, from a short black skirt to her Levi's and running shoes.

He, himself, had been uncertain what to wear. Part of the problem was that she knew him and his limited wardrobe so well that anything special, like a sports jacket or tie, would be instantly spotted and might send the wrong message. He was hardly in a position to dress like a suitor or to come bearing flowers. He'd finally decided to wear a pair of newly pressed black pants and a green shirt she'd once told him she liked. In the briefcase that he carried was a copy of his anthology CD that he wanted to give her, although, if he did that too quickly, it could convey the wrong kind of message as well. It was important to wait for the right moment, and if that moment didn't come, it might be better not to give it to her at all.

The train reached Thirtieth Street Station at two-thirty. Her school was at Seventeenth and Cherry, a fifteen-minute walk—which would get him there before she left. He felt strangely calm, destiny driven, as he walked down Market Street looking at the Schuylkill River moving brightly under the mostly blue sky. September was the best month in Philadelphia, Joy once told him when she used to paint word pictures of the city for him. September and October. It had been a year and a half since he'd been in Philadelphia. He'd invented a job interview at the time and used it as an excuse to explain his visit so that he could have dinner with her. Except for their hello and good-bye embraces, there had been no physical contact between them, but they were wonderful embraces. They had kissed each other on the cheek both times. It seemed to him he could still recall the exact sensation of her lips on his cheek. He remembered also that they each had duck at Friday/Saturday/Sunday, a good neighborhood restaurant in Center City. It was an easy conversation, punctuated with lots of laughter. They talked about their families, their jobs and apartments. They swapped stories about musicians they knew and talked about their plans for the summer that was just a few months away. The restaurant was filled with mirrors and candlelight that reflected their images to infinity. Only a few times during the dinner did he wonder, as he had many times before, if the obvious warmth between them meant that a breakthrough was possible, whether he should make some kind of move. But he hadn't wanted to spoil the evening. He had spoiled a few others when he'd suggested they try resuming their relationship. It was only after his triumph at Tanglewood that he'd felt the confidence (and desperation) to try to win Joy back, although, as he thought of it now, she seemed peculiarly receptive that night to having her mind changed.

Friends Select, where Joy taught, was just off the Parkway, a tree- and flag-lined boulevard modeled after the Champs-Elysées that extended from the museum to the William Penn Building. Above its reddish gray brick loomed the white phallic-shaped Wyndham Hotel. There was a black gate, already opened, in front of the glass doors, like the gate to Perry's house. On the doors was a painted notice that IDs were required and that all visitors had to immediately see the receptionist. Twenty feet from the door, behind what looked to be bulletproof glass, was the receptionist's office. She was a cheerful enough black woman who wore bright red lipstick and thick-rimmed glasses. She told him Joy was teaching her last class, which would end at three o'clock, and that he could certainly wait in the lobby if he wanted. That would be fine, he said as he turned to sit on a bench.

Students passed by him holding notebooks or schoolbooks, a few with as much of the grunge look as the dress code permitted. He wondered vaguely if some of her students had crushes on her and then wondered why he was wondering. Was there really any doubt about it? If he had ever had a teacher as good-looking as Joy, he would certainly have fantasized about her relentlessly. And she was getting these kids just as they were starting to masturbate, too. He could remember sitting in his high school biology class watching the clock, imagining what time it would be when he could get home and see the new magazine he had bought and jerk off again. It was a question of how many hours he could wait then, and it took a lot of willpower to make twenty-four.

He stood up from the bench and met the gaze of a uniformed security officer who stood by the stairway wearing a gun. Ray sat down again. The calm he had felt as he walked by the river was gone. He looked at his watch—seven minutes till three.

It was probably an awful idea, but he couldn't help himself. He could not go on without seeing her again, and she would have to understand and forgive him. It had been more than a year.

WHEN SHE saw him, she was at the foot of the stairway in the center of the lobby. He saw her first, talking with a student, and then a few seconds later she saw him. There was a startled look on her face, of course, but there was also another expression he hadn't seen before that surprised him. She turned toward the student, and for a moment he wondered if she'd decided to ignore him, to act as if what she saw was a hallucination or else that she simply didn't see him at all. Then the student, a girl with straggly blond hair and a green school bag slung over her shoulder, walked toward the door, and Joy, who was perhaps thirty feet away, walked toward him. He had stood up as soon as he saw her and moved a few feet forward. She was wearing a flower-print dress, reminiscent of the sixties, that he didn't recognize.

"Hello, Ray," she said, making no move either to embrace him or shake his hand. There was a different expression on her face now, but he couldn't decipher it.

"I came to see you, obviously. I wanted to talk to you for a few minutes. Is that OK?"

She nodded and looked down at the floor for a moment. It was such a subtly lovely gesture that he nearly tried to touch her face.

"Let's go outside," she said.

They walked through the entranceway toward the sidewalk. Kids raced by them, and the flags on the Parkway streamed in the breeze, which seemed much more vigorous than it had been half an hour ago. He saw the red and white flag of Austria, the blue, yellow, and black flag of the Bahamas, waving by the traffic light.

"You look great," he said. "You look beautiful."

"Thank you," she said in a neutral voice. She avoided his eyes.

"Were you going somewhere?" he said.

"Just home."

"Can I walk you?"

"We can walk for a while."

They crossed the street, walked past the white circular Embassy Suites, then headed toward Market Street, where he saw a sudden proliferation of brown and gray high-rises.

"I know it's unfair to suddenly appear like this. I know it violates our agreement, and you certainly have every right to be angry at me . . . "

"It's all right. I'm not angry. I am startled but . . . "

"I had to do this; I couldn't just call you, you know what I mean?"

"I think so."

"Could we possibly sit down somewhere? It's hard to talk like this while we're walking."

"Rittenhouse Square will probably have some free benches. Do you remember it?"

"The park near your apartment that we walked through, in the center of town?"

"Yeah. It's just a couple blocks away."

"It had that beautiful fountain and all those flowers."

"There won't be many flowers now, and they've shut off the fountain. But they do have benches."

"I always thought it was a beautiful park with all those elegant buildings surrounding it. Next to Valley Green, it's probably my favorite place in Philadelphia."

He looked at her face, but she had no particular expression except that of a person concentrating on where she was walking. He didn't know what to think, and so kept quiet until they saw the park at Eighteenth and Walnut. The park was less than half full, and several benches were available.

"Sun or shade?" he said, pointing to two different wooden benches.

"Sun," she said.

They walked to the bench and sat down facing each other. She looked right at him with her steady blue eyes.

"Like I said, I came because I felt I had to see you. It was disturbing me that I hadn't seen you in so long, really disturbing me to think that you were disappearing from my life. Not that I would ever forget you, of course, there's no chance of that ever happening, but you were becoming too much a product of my mind. I was thinking about you too much, to the point where I couldn't be sure what I was inventing or dreaming and what was, is, really you."

"Ray, please don't—"

"No, let me finish, OK? It's just that I still love you, am still in love with you, and know that I always will be. There hasn't been anyone else since you, of course, and I'm wondering if there's been any change in you or how you feel."

There was a shift in her face, an unmistakable look of sadness in her suddenly moist eyes.

"There's been a change. I've met someone."

"Met someone?"

"I love someone. I'm sorry to tell you like this. I know this must hurt," she said softly.

"When did this happen?"

"I met this person nine months ago, a few months after we ended."

"Why do you say 'person'? Is it a woman?"

"No, it's a man."

"And you fell in love right away?"

"No, I wasn't ready to love anyone then. I was still grieving over you. You know that. We were friends for quite a while before we got involved."

"Aren't you going to tell me his name?"

"Do you really want to know this?"

He asked her question silently to himself, then moved his hand, which had been clutching his shirt. "Any friend of yours . . ." He smiled weakly.

She looked away. She wouldn't play this game with him.

"I'm sorry. I do want to know his name. Is that OK?"

"His name is Stephen."

"Is he a musician?"

"No. He likes music, but no, he's not a musician; he's an architect."

"Really? Successful?"

Joy looked simultaneously puzzled and irritated. "He's not rich if that's what you mean."

"That wasn't what I meant."

"He's not well known by the general public."

"That wasn't what I meant either."

"He's a successful *person*."

"I didn't mean anything. I don't know what to say. I'll try to be happy for you if it lasts."

"That's the thing that I guess I ought to tell you. We're going to be married."

He stared at her deeply. "Why so soon?"

"I know it's kind of soon, but I'm sure it's right. A few weeks ago, I found out that I'm pregnant. Can you believe it? I'm going to be a mother."

Ray stood up and turned away from her toward the fountain that wasn't working in the center of the park, then stared up at the glass high-rises that towered above the trees in the horizon. He drew in a few breaths, kept his eyes open, and sat down again, facing her.

"Let me try to assimilate all this. You met someone, someone you love, you're getting married, you're pregnant. That's a lot to assimilate. That's why I stood up. I was afraid I might faint from overassimilation."

"It's a lot for me to assimilate, too," she said, choosing to ignore his sarcasm. "But remember, all that began over nine months ago. It's just the way I told you, in installments, which I regret, which was stupid of me. I should have told you all at once."

"One big bomb instead of four separate ones."

She looked away. He couldn't tell if she was more sad or angry.

"Ray, I'm sorry," she said, tears in her eyes now.

He stared at them, fascinated. It was as if they were some kind of fragile life raft that connected them. "I came. I asked for it. Like I say, I will try to be happy for you. Part of me already is, although it's not exactly the part that's being expressed right now."

"Ray, for the first thirty-two years of my life, you were the only person I loved besides my family."

"And now you're thirty-three."

"It wasn't easy for me," she said, "not at all."

"You know if people realize, really realize, that they're going to die, it actually can be liberating," he said. "It can free a lot of things. I mean, there's a tremendous forgiveness potential out there. It must be the biggest untapped source of energy in the world if people would just realize there's no reason to hold back because we're all going to be extinct in a very short time, and nothing that we can do can make up for that cruelty."

"Ray, this isn't about forgiveness. I have forgiven you. I don't think I could have loved anyone again if I hadn't forgiven you."

She took his hand and pressed it for a moment. It was the last thing that he would remember clearly from their meeting, which ended five or ten minutes later. The expression in her eyes, the utter absence of theatricality or malice as she pressed his hand and he heard her words again like a bittersweet death sentence.

FOR THE first week, he told himself that it was much better that she be happy than not be. That the worst outcome would have been if she'd never found anyone and never had taken him back either. It was shameful and completely selfish from any objective point of view to feel anything but gratitude and relief for the outcome, even for the finality it offered, which gave him the chance (slight though it seemed to him) to meet someone himself. But he felt anguish and jealousy too for the invisible Stephen and his invisible child. They haunted him like ghosts that inhabited his apartment, already overcrowded with the ghosts of Perry and Bobby. For he discovered that in those moments when he was not thinking of Joy, he wondered about Perry, and to think about Perry would always mean remembering Bobby, whose death also meant the death of his relationship with Joy and the death of the person he had been when he was with her. He was not only haunted by Bobby, Perry, and Joy, then, but also by the ghost of himself, and against this quartet of ghosts, he had only his work as a weapon. For a month or so, his concentration was not as good as it had been before his trip to see Joy, and there were days when he only worked an hour, but when the fall term ended, he was able to truthfully tell those few City College professors who inquired that he'd finished the first draft of his "Five Sketches" and was making plans to write a string quartet. The quartet, in fact, soon absorbed him so much that he abandoned the sketches, which remained in their first-draft form. Now he was composing three to four hours a day—as intense and consistent a pace as he'd ever worked on any piece.

It was not programmatic music, of which he was generally wary, but sometimes he couldn't help thinking of the different instruments of the quartet as expressing the souls of Joy,

Perry, Bobby, and himself and the dark drama he had played with them two summers ago. Sometimes this made working on it difficult, but for the first time in a year he didn't shrink from something that was bound to make him think of Joy more intensely than he normally did.

By mid-February he'd finished the first movement and worked out some structural and thematic ideas for the rest of the piece. He felt he'd done almost nothing else with his free time but write or think about the quartet since he'd begun it and that he needed a break. A few weeks earlier, he'd seen an advertisement at Lincoln Center announcing that Perry was conducting the Philharmonic at Avery Fisher Hall in early March. He'd bought a ticket and since then wondered if he should go. Had he really sufficiently distanced himself from Perry that he could experience his concert as an *aesthetic* event? And now that he was in a good working rhythm, was it worth the risk that he couldn't, that he'd instead be disrupted in some way? Even if such a disruption were only for a day or two, it seemed a high risk to take. He'd thought of buying a ticket for Bryna, but now that she was engaged to Ed, the truth was she hated to be away from him for a night. He called Arnold and told him a few tickets were still left and asked him if he wanted to go. But Arnold was more fiercely wedded to his avant-garde coterie than ever. He said that watching Perry Green conducting Mahler was not the kind of thing he wanted to spend money on. Why the bitterness, Ray wondered. Then Arnold told him that he'd seen Perry the night before holding hands with a young dark-haired man in the Village, laughing and talking animatedly as they passed by him on the street. Arnold had been miffed that Perry hadn't recognized him.

So Perry had a new young man in his life. So he was a tough old bird, after all, who had found himself some new private fame already. As far as his own career was concerned, he was quite sure Perry would neither help nor hinder it. It was better this way. Perry had already made his contribution. And it was better, Ray decided, not to go with anyone else to the concert. This was something that he needed to do alone; how else could he really discover or prove anything to himself?

It was a cold, clear night, and he wore his overcoat over his navy-blue sports jacket. There was a subway exit at the Lincoln Center stop that led directly to Avery Fisher, but he decided to walk out on the street. He liked the delicate, triangular Lincoln Square Park and liked as well (though they were far from his favorite works of art) the sight of the Chagall murals in the illuminated windows of the Met. He walked into the courtyard where the fountain was always working and where soon, when the weather got warmer, the Panevino Café would be roaring with business. With its white tables and chairs and large white canvas umbrellas, it reminded him of the outdoor cafés in Santa Barbara. He had walked through the courtyard hundreds of times when he was at Juilliard but realized he hadn't been to Avery Fisher in almost two years or to the Met in much longer than that. Perhaps that was the real reason he'd come earlier than he needed to tonight, he thought as he walked into the hall.

Inside, the building was buzzing with intersecting businesses. There was the Espresso Bar, a cocktail restaurant (with a trail of posters outside it advertising Mostly Mozart concerts), a gift shop that sold T-shirts, including, of course, a prominently displayed Perry Green T-shirt to capitalize on tonight's performance. Next to Perry was the Yo Yo Ma T-shirt. His concert was a month ago, but he'd been a big hit on a recent *David Letterman Show,* and his new CD was a best-seller. Ray looked at a huge glass-enclosed ad that said PROGRAMMING 101: ASK KURT MASUR, MUSIC DIRECTOR OF THE NEW YORK PHILHARMONIC, and decided to go downstairs. At the bottom level, near the parking lot, he stopped in front of the Performing Arts Shop. In the windows was a major display of white plastic figurines of performing musicians and of white busts of the great composers that made him think of Bryna's sheep for a moment. Next to the Arts Shop, in the gallery exhibition, was a show devoted to "Great Tenors Past and Present"—another excuse to hawk merchandise for the ubiquitous "Three Tenors," Carveras, Domingo, and Pavarotti. He decided he'd forgo a visit to the Met and go upstairs to his seat. Tonight would be a classic Perry Green program—a short, elegantly witty Haydn symphony (the G Major) before intermission—the composer Ray felt most mirrored the best qualities in Perry's own music—and then Mahler's Fourth, the most refined of Mahler's works. Whenever he programmed a concert, Perry, like all the best conductors, always painted an aesthetic portrait of himself.

He was going to go directly to his seat, but stopped outside the entrance to the hall at the Bruno Walter Gallery. There were photographs of Leonard Bernstein with Jackie Kennedy at the opening of what was then called Philharmonic Hall. There was a reproduction of Aaron Copland's "Connotations for Orchestra" that was performed that night and a photograph of a much younger, very serious looking Perry Green. People were streaming past Ray now. Having eaten and drunk, having bought their posters and figurines and T-shirts, they had a concert to go to, too. Ray went to his seat on the first floor near the back of the hall. Already the balconies around him were filling up. He tried to empty his mind of enough to concentrate on the music and, just before Perry walked onstage, felt he'd succeeded. He had been wondering if he should see Perry backstage after the concert, but had decided not to. It felt more natural, now that Perry was onstage, to be part of the audience applauding him, for Perry had earned the applause, after all.

The Haydn symphony was as fine and crisp as he remembered, and Perry and the orchestra performed it superbly. He'd forgotten how much he enjoyed hearing live music, and he stayed in his seat during intermission thinking about the piece and how good he was feeling. But a few bars after the bell-filled opening of the Mahler's Fourth, Ray remembered that this was Joy's favorite Mahler symphony and how much he'd enjoyed hearing her practice the vocal solo in the last movement. It was amazing and frightening to him that he'd blocked this out of his mind until now, that while he was conducting his internal debate about whether or not he should attend the concert he'd never considered how this symphony was linked to Joy and how that was bound to affect him. He was all right the first couple of movements, but during the slow movement he saw her face again in his mind's eye—now smiling in a mischievous way, now reserved and introspective, now expressing the love she'd given to him and trusted him with. It was not merely these visual memories he saw but a compelling sense of her spirit that was inseparable from them as well, in much the way he'd internalized her face *and* spirit when he was improvising that long musical portrait of her in his apartment, which only ended when Perry knocked on the door. Tears fell down his face. He didn't struggle against them. Instead, he bowed his head as if he were about to fall into a pool where he'd be spending an indefinite amount of time.

With the onset of the more serene last movement, his anguish ceased. He became aware of the magnificent job Perry had done, the exquisite balance and quality of sound he was able to get from the orchestra. As the audience rose to its feet applauding, Ray found himself standing and applauding, too. But after the applause ended, as he turned to leave, he saw a man several rows to his left pointing at him. It was Bobby, his face constricted in rage, mouthing a silent curse and keeping his arm and accusatory finger rigid as it singled him out. Ray turned his head away and, when he looked again, realized he'd been the victim of a hallucination. There was a man, but he was pointing at the stage, and while he slightly resembled Bobby, he was at least ten years older.

Ray walked briskly down the aisle, then downstairs even more rapidly, until he was out of Lincoln Center. He shivered for a second, then began walking uptown. There was a light purple suffusing the otherwise black night sky and a curious yellow ring around the moon. For a while the city seemed oddly muted, as if he were walking on a country road. He decided to keep walking and to take the subway at Seventy-second Street. After three more blocks he remembered the contorted face of his hallucination and realized that the words it had silently uttered were, You're dead. Ray shook himself to dispel the image, but after walking another block stopped and said to himself, No I'm not.